THE COLD LINE CROSSES

THE COLD LINE CROSSES

A NOVEL BY

JAMES DOUGLAS McCOMB

James W. McComb

UNPROOFED

Paperback
ISBN-13 978-0-9896284-0-2 | ISBN-10 0-9896284-0-X

Kindle
ISBN-13 978-0-9896284-1-9 | ISBN-10 0-9896284-1-8

Printed in the U.S.A.
All paper is acid free and meets all ANSI standards for archival quality paper.

3 5 7 9 10 8 6 4 2

For Brynn...

I've known the scent of her passing before sunrise and her unwashed evening kisses, and now all language is flat without her — a foreigner's gnawing tongue adrift on the icy sea

Voice of a sinking ferry, somewhere in the San Juan Islands
November 16, 1986

CHAPTER ONE

THERE WAS A TIME when these island waters could nurse a child's idea of heaven over all that lived with us as earth and sea under a dome of sunlight and turquoise skies. A time when my family could hold back the rising tide, call back the setting sun, and sift the impending weight of obligations down to the seductive tug of a folded sail, resurrect the spirit of that breathless canvas by afternoon and have it waltzing with the scuffling reflection of a turtle-back island come evening.

A calligrapher's brush once passed thru *Jimmy's Campground* and left behind a linen postcard that captured this same feeling. It lies hidden behind a twig frame which houses the business license for our bar and café — ask the barkeeper to see it sometime. On the surface of the linen cloth there is a single black line of fluctuating dimensions, a disembodiment of something that was once whole. The line hovers above another which portrays a series of coiling red circles, seemingly, of indeterminable origin or ending. The brush strokes are simple and effortless in design, really. But when you *see* it, when you see that the beauty of a sunrise born from the bleakness of the darkest horizons offers no refuge, no union, you understand that it is not the payment we would make to Caesar but to God that would break us.

Now, as I allow my tired eyes to trace all that we have buried over the years in these icy island waters, it is with a bittersweet commandment that I call back a time when the scent of that linen card could corral my spirit completely. A time when I believed in the promise of this young calligrapher's life, her father's life, and my wife's too. Once, when the four of us had sailed our summers thru the inlets of these pastured islands, a covenant of the heart had tied us to the sea and each of us thought of the other as family.

The floors of *Jimmy's Campground* are burnished with ancient dog stains which run dark and gouging around the benched corners of the room's moon-faced sandpit — more ashtray these days than the art Salvador and his driftwood gladiators had intended — but otherwise, the pine flooring mostly carries the warm beetled scarring of something ancient all the way to the room's fireplace of stone and stainless steel and into both wings of the bar's dining room. Along the bar's cedar-planked backyard wall, stacks of faded newspapers and racks of magazines mop the faded etchings of a madrona-inlay shuffleboard, the stories within their pages decades old but still able to paint frowns of puzzlement on the faces of tourists caught looking thru them for the first time. Chairs and tables the size of tablets crowd both sides of the paned windows overlooking the bar's covered porch, the legs of most every chair hobbled with the rust of wire and the soldering of Salvador's crazy twisted welds. The timbered rafters, which support the *Campground's* vaulted ceiling high above the sandpit, are roped and sagging with toboggans and sleds and snowshoes. Over Salvador's mantelpiece, where a checkered arrangement of photographs anchors the scale and form of the large fireplace, a bit of our public history as friends and family is posted within each of those stick frames. And that picture-less black frame which hangs in the center of all the others? That is our most private history, the secrets we have kept from one another, all that is missing or unknown of the others anguish.

My wife and I are half owners of *Jimmy's Campground*, but almost nothing which hangs within these walls reveals our deeply personal history with the man who has poured his good name and blood into this temple. No, the *Campground's* genius is all Jimmy's. His island of sand and shuffle, his self-monitored doctrines, his journal of heartaches, abandoned dreams, and rekindled addictions, the indisputable truth of what effort and attitude could accomplish. For Jimmy, above all else, the bar offers refuge from an old promise never kept always forgiven. But that is not why I am here — forgiveness is not something I seek or would trust if I found it.

"Mark!"

In the bar's mirror, I saw myself nodding back at the man behind the cathedral window. He wasn't finished with it, wasn't ready to lay down his chisels of fire and ice from all that was still missing, all that had yet to be taken back from the window's promises.

The resonating coarseness of Jimmy's voice struck me again, this time, causing my body to flinch and making the wooden legs of my barstool scrape over a slab of uneven stone before the slap-a-tap-tap of the *Campground's* screen door had settled.

"God lord, old man!" Jimmy's broad smile became a friendly laugh as he walked by me, his shoulders squared and his bare back ripe with the juice of fresh strawberries he'd been picking all afternoon, his long ponytail flopping like an empty knapsack over his perfect tan. "No need to panic. Just me calling out your name, not juicy fruit Joe over there calling you out for some exercise. Though our friend could use a little road work, couldn't he Joe?"

Joe had followed Jimmy in thru the *Campground's* front door, his bicycle by his side like a blind man's cane, and now man and machine were both looking to take up their usual residence near the room's fireplace.

"Eh, Jimmy. Caught me daydreaming."

"Bullshit. You been on the island almost a week now. None of it's been about day dreaming."

At the far end of the bar, Jimmy stopped to place his three flats of strawberries on a cutting board covering one of the bar's sinks. Pasty red streaks of strawberry juice and the dried smudges of island soil patched his chest and legs, the same combination of disjointed colors I knew would accompany his voice, and a serious prodding, about to work its way towards my end of the bar. While he rolled the tip of his tongue over his lips, the golden crown of his head beginning to dance to some solitary tune only he could compose, his sandals tapping and shuffling against the bar's foot rail, and his eyes about to close in feigned thought, I watched him become a practitioner of street-side theatre about to stage a preacher's scripted, over-the-top sermon.

"No god of Joey's ever gonna show up under these old rafters on a Friday afternoon. Not Saturday, Sunday, nor Monday neither."

From his comfortable seat on the stem of his bicycle, Joey grumbled and tapped his fingers against his step-brother's mantle.

"Ain't that right, Joe-eey? No god to be found on the roof of this old church up on the hill."

"I think God may have dumped Jimmy in our paths, Joe, just to test our faith."

"I don't think so, boys. Either of you seen Jackie or Jill come in yet?"

Our waitress, Jill, I knew. *Jackie* was a name new to my ears.

"You talking to me or you talking at me, Jimmy?"

"Joe? How 'bout you do your little sermon on the dismount and give these strawberries a proper baptism. Ferry traffic's gonna hit us like a rogue wave tonight."

Joe was wearing his favorite yellow racing jersey, and from his perch on the seat of his bike he looked like a giant parakeet about to squawk.

"Jimmy don't bu-bu-believe in God."

"No son, I don't. All doctrines, they all read just about the same when you get right down to the fine print."

"No sir, not mine." Joe's feet pumped the pedals on his bike back and forth. "And my name's not Joey. It's Joe or Joseph."

A hyperbolic dismount — executed more steadily than the flow of his words — landed Joe on his feet and addressed the shadow of Jimmy's challenge.

"And yu-yu-you shouldn't use our Lord's name in vain so much."

"Quite right, Joey. And you shouldn't play with your prophet peter so much."

I tapped the bar with my fingers. "Jimmy, another shot of Jack before I go. If you're done preaching."

"Where you off to? You're on tonight, you know."

"Gotta get my sorry ass down to *Red's*."

Jimmy freshened my drink. Joey moved in behind the bar and began running warm tap water into both the bar's rinsing sinks, filling one while preparing to wash his hands and face in the other. Jimmy shuffled in alongside the boy, humming to himself and mumbling something colorful as he filled his glass with water from the faucet. I sipped my drink and watched both men splash their faces with water, wondering if the time would come when Joey might, mistakenly, abandon his silent prayers to restrain from violence and take a swing at his belittling boss.

Physically, Joe's body framed twenty-two years of productive cell growth, so far, cursing the island only with the exceedingly large side-effect of having left his deductive reasoning capabilities thoroughly discovered and extinguished during the first fourteen of those twenty-two years. Or, as Jimmy would often recite to patrons while working his side of the bar: 'two good dog years of usefulness left in that boy...if only we had known then what we know now, we might have tossed his old man out to sea the second the boy's step-brother was born.' Salvador, Joey's step-brother, could just as quickly pounce on his younger brother's Christian intolerances: 'Bigoted little brat busted out of his playpen one day and built himself a six-foot, eight inch pulpit...did it without changing his last name, too... Fuck.' And, though Joey had yet to show any sign of a consumptive craving for public office, beyond the unsolicited salvation of the souls of islanders and lost tourists, the scary possibility sometimes reared its ugly head in his heated conversations with Red; Red's voice sometimes growing exasperated at the bar by Joe's refusal to listen to reason, and often, abruptly ending all conversation with Joe by telling the boy: 'Joe, you may well be the most sought after and wretchedly ineffective weapon the island's Christian Right has ever impounded.'

"This your dinner, old man?" Jimmy waved his hand over the empty glasses in front of me. "On us today, is it?"

"How's business?" I asked, rapping the mahogany bar with my knuckles and cocking my head in the direction of the new hole in the *Campground's* back wall. "Busier than the fellow who ain't got around to closing up that hole in the wall, I hope."

"Oh, all business are we now?" The shoots of another toothy smile crossed his post-card face. "Your day is at hand, Mister. You're gonna know busy tonight, that I know. But me, I'm gonna be rolling myself a pair of sevens. And smiling, knowing you're on this side of the bar standing dog-tired.

"Maybe I will, maybe I won't." I taunted.

He blew the first plumes of smoke from his freshly fired cigar into my face, squinted and let his playfully eyes wander the bar. With the wave of a hand he fanned away another blue plume of smoke settling over the bar.

"This bar is the best thing that ever happened to you on this island. You, my friend, need this place. Speaking of which," he'd remembered something he wanted to show me and quickly slipped around Joey to lift the bar-gate. Another step or two and he'd pushed open the double doors to Hazel's kitchen with his shoulder, shouting some sniff of sarcasm back at Joe and me which we were still pondering when he'd returned to the bar with a paper wand of rubber-banded, legal-sized documents in his hand.

"Accountant, he says he needs both our signatures on these financial statements."

"Quit your grinning and give me the pen."

I signed the first and last couple of pages of the document and initialed a couple of others without reading any of it.

"Christ Mark, you don't even look at the numbers anymore."

What did it matter? Reading the Campground's math was like looking at a black-and-white diagram of something already out of the box and wrongfully assembled. Do you really want to pull the thing apart, at this midnight hour, and put it back together again?

"I know Depot Island takes you hard. If I thought I could call you home I would. But you wouldn't come. Not yet, anyways."

"What else you got?"

"Hey, look here." Jimmy took the papers from my hand and stabbed one of the circled numbers with his index-finger.

"Three or four more quarters like this one, maybe four more years like the one we had last season, and this castle is yours, mine, and hers. Free and clear."

"You've done well, Jimmy."

He put the papers aside to fuss with a few of the strawberries Joey had trimmed and carefully placed in a colander.

"Been at this a long time haven't we Mark, the three of us. Tough year for all of us."

"Especially, Dianna."

"Yeah. Hey, can you watch the bar a minute? I gotta step out back and shower." Jimmy let his chin roll across his chest and looked down at the rippling of muscle strapping his stomach. "Look at me — my fans will be after me berries tonight I show up at the tables like this. Big crowd for you in here tonight, I think. But you'll be fine. Jackie's a rock in any kind of weather."

When Jimmy reached the framed opening in the *Campground's* north wall, he ducked under the rails of a tapered ladder hanging sideways across the opening, his ponytail swishing more outdoors than indoors by the time he'd twisted 'round to grab hold of two of the ladder's wooden rungs.

"Soon, very soon, this doorway will open up onto a new deck and patio. What do you think — we plant a bit of your geometry out back to frame the yard in and the church folk out? A water wheel is going up over there where my shower stem is now. Sally's idea, of course."

Jimmy suddenly let go of the ladder rungs as if he might let his body free-fall just for laughs, but quickly enough slapped a new handhold over the rails of the ladder and stuck his head thru two of its rungs to become a man pretending to be hopelessly imprisoned. His chin now hanging over one of the rails, his eyes targeting Joey, he tried, rather recklessly, to wiggle the spindly ladder free of its hooks.

"Joey, for the love of Christ, save me!" Pleased with his

antics, Jimmy turned his back on us and dropped thru the hole in the wall.

Joe and I waited for the sounds of painful cursing, but instead, heard only a kind of feline screaming, scratched with a bit of laughter, rise up from the clutter in the Campground's back yard. Joe looked annoyed, but managed to throw me a frown while holding his tree-trunk stance over his baptism pool which was now full up with ripe red strawberries.

"Joe, I think I'm in need of a nap. See you 'round about closing time, eh?" I'd already made my way to the bar's front entrance and was about to kick open the screen door to the porch.

"Mr. Jacobs, you promised Jimmy you'd watch the bar."

"You watch it."

"Excuse me, sir, but it's not my job to manage the bar."

"God's will, Joe. Gotta go."

I turned and backed my way out onto the porch and, as quietly as a church mouse, closed the screen door on Joe's frustration — three of my fingers now pointing to the heavens while I stared back at the boy.

"Strong possibility *He's* offering you a career move here, Joe. Maybe moving you up the ladder tonight from baptizing strawberries to *money-changer*."

From the *Campground's* covered porch, my eyes travel across the cold chop of the channel to run the bluffs of Depot Island, where its shoreline waters no longer trace the outline of a swimmer's stroke. I remember everything about our lives on Depot Island. Everything. But the memories hold little more for me, these days, than to color my thoughts with a brackish tint of disbelief. Memories which have served only to break my back and swallow me whole whenever I visit that island, memories that would have me bury every good moment, good hour, good day that once lived, with innocence, on that island's grassy bluffs;

heart-lines of words come and gone and so easily capable of carrying back in time, to *her* time, take hold of me whenever I am with the sickness of that island. *Depot Island* — one little corner in my world of what is missing from that picture-less black frame over Salvador's mantle. So much more than what we've become lived in these islands before Jessie's death, so much more music played in our heads, music that drew its color from the people and places we once loved here. Music that danced in the leaning lofts of standing-room only taverns and funneled its snaring spine over pine-needled trails and stone-stumped lawns, where it stretched its reach to storm the buxom dormers of shingled cottages now sagging wet with the laurels of lament. Once, an evening romp with Jimmy in the island bars could magically reappear before our eyes on the crackling grate of a Saturday morning campground fire, where lightening-blue smoke could sleeve its way thru the pines to settle over the cattail edges of Jessie's favorite lake. Countless summer afternoons at *Red's Marina* all but frozen now in a cube of time which once lived and breathed, so weightlessly, so touchable, before so much of our faith in so many possibilities went missing — time spent doing little else other than watching yellow-leafed hatch-covers and hopscotch planking twirl the summer hours timeless. Guiltless, too, we were once upon a time; tireless days which pinned us to the sails of a boat. Days which could gather up a week in the slip of an untied noose, weeks which could corral summer's chant and deliver it back to us by October hardly a day older. Once, no hopeless thought ever erupted from the cast of a breaking shoreline wave beneath the bluffs of Depot Island. And now? Now, even the evening skies sleep wide-eyed from the taste of all we've tried to leave behind us. And we've left so much of everything behind us. No, no one swims the shoreline waters of Depot Island, anymore. No one calls out our names from the chop of the channel's brilliantly cold waters, no one any of us would recognize.

At the foot of the *Campground's* landscaped hillside, the street greets the gate to Jessie's courtyard garden with the humming sounds of anxious golf-carts, their motoring song lingering in the street long enough to search the town's back alleys and footpaths for old acquaintances. It is an idling tune which the last of these turf cabbies is playing me with today as it passes by, a harmless offer that I skip my scheduled ferry ride to Depot Island and join them on their parade towards Main Street.

Only a few days earlier, I'd been surrounded by the muteness of Seattle's concrete towers, walked the city's university campus where I've worked for years in the math department, walked for hours considering how disturbingly close my wife and I were to ending all things familiar between us. *Wasn't that what we'd come back to the islands to accomplish, each of us in our own silent way.* In Seattle, I'd locked the doors to our house, looked out one last time at the city I loved, said goodbye to the neighbor's Brittany spaniel but to no other. Left town. And now, now I was here. Here for the *derivative duration* of summer, as Jimmy liked to put it in my face, in the thick of all things real and imagined.

I walk with a kind of insular numbness to my thoughts which keeps the movements and moods of island pedestrians around me at bay. Main-street is an easier, less triggering, form for me to face today — I engage well with an empty street — and I'm content to watch how it weaves its way between fruit and vegetable wagons on its round-about-way to the ferry docks. Postage-stamp parking-lots hidden behind coffee shacks potted with more baskets of hanging geraniums than varieties of "bean and bun" posted on chalkboard windows. A leafy alley of pastel specialty shops that seem always to weather another shoddy tourist season by scraping away last year's mask and replacing it with fresh paint and new-found emotion.

After its hilly sweep thru the commerce of town, Main Street gives up its sidewalks, favoring the border of clump grasses and thistle along its roadside route to the ferry terminals and the graveled, potholed service road to the town's only marina.

Red's Marina is a cocoon of calmness; all who come here have the chance to capture the change in attitude it promises to eventually unfurl. It is a common and reliable sedative, a marina, and one's worries are lessened the moment the feet sway the cracked planks of its pier. Under its spell, obligations willfully recede here and the wind respectfully dims to a breeze. Sunlight brightens and drizzles with texture over the decks of boats and empty slips to dress the prance of an incoming tide. Toxins slip from your pores to melt away much of what has grown unpleasant to the mind, casting into the out-going tide whatever beastly burden is swelling or decaying beneath your skin. Pockets are emptied here. Entire lives spread out onto galley tables. All flavors of napkin poetry are intended here, each sentiment cupping the lure of some *other's* intended life wishing to be tied or mended or simply pushed aside under the pillow of another lost afternoon.

"Mr. Jacobs. Look!" The boy is crouching over a spread-eagle shirt on the pier, both boy and his sacrificial shirt smeared with the smell of caught fish. The boy's button-less vest and T-shirt stained with fish guts and gathering flies. Pure pride written all over the kid's face, a single mindedness gripping the hand that holds the task at hand.

"Nice looking shirt, Danny. Makes for a real nice cutting board, don't it?"

The boy straightened his row of three ripening fish spread out from armpit to armpit.

"Nice?" The boy took hold of a broken hacksaw blade and began sawing the head off an undersized salmon. "Way better than nice. These here are awesome fish!"

"Jesus, don't cut your drum fingers off." The way the boy was sawing the cockeyed hacksaw blade thru the fish looked like an accident waiting to happen.

"Red know you're cleaning your fish on the dock?"

"Red don't care." Juan, the boy who had caught the fish spoke up from the end of the dock. He sat with a bamboo rod switching in his hand. Eyes glued to a baseball-sized red and white bobber twitching a ways out into the channel, the tip of his fishing rod heavily weighted with a glob of duct tape securing an eyelet the size of a basketball rim. "So long as we blackjack 'em before we cut their heads off, Red don't care what we do. Hey Danny, show this man how we show mercy."

"They're all dead now, Juan. You gotta catch me a live one first."

"Show him on a dead one." The tips of Juan's boots dipping in and out of the slurping water.

"No way. That's too weird."

"Well damn it, Danny, I can't catch one on command."

"That's quite all right, guys. Catch you later."

"You might, 'cause we ain't going no where fast. Are we Juan?" Danny put the saw blade aside and ran his thumb inside the stomach of the opened fish.

"Juan?"

"Yeah."

"You and Danny looking for some extra money this summer?"

"Yeah, don't everyone."

"Stop by the *Campground* next week and we'll talk. Wear a clean shirt."

"How much?" Juan asked.

"Wear a clean shirt."

Walking in the sunshine with *Sound Bound*, *No Name Discernable*, a pair of slimy kayaks, two empty slips, and a trawler named *Wise Guy*, I felt more at ease about facing Red.

"Mark! Welcome back."

"Hello Red. How are you?"

"Fine. And yourself?"

"Good, now that I'm back."

"That's the spirit." Red brought his clenched fist to his chest and softly pounded his heart. "And your better half? Any change in her outlook on life, today?"

"Haven't mustered the will yet to face the ferry crowd."

"Understood. Well, perhaps this will be the season that changes everything for the both of you." Red reached for my shoulder. "You know this, of course, but Anna sends her usual prayers. Just on the phone with her. She was telling me all over again about those pearls your wife brought her all the way back from Japan. You be sure and remind Dianna what a nice thing that was for her to do. Will you do that?"

"I'll do that. And you thank Anna for thinking about us."

"I'd like to but she's in Seattle again. Six weeks this time. We've got ourselves a granddaughter. Boy, oh boy." Red can't talk about anything dear to him without rubbing the back of his ear. "Yes sir, how Anna loves to spend her summers with those grand-children. Eight pounds, nine ounces the last one. Can you believe it? Well, come along and let's see if I can't find that spare key of yours. Moon's gonna bite us both in the ass if I don't. Where's yours, anyhow? Throw it overboard in a fit of clarity, did-jah?"

We walked a bit, Red's bad hip leading the way to the marina's store. His hip has needed replacing for some time but he hates the idea of being hospitalized, so much so that he tolerates the deep swings his body makes whenever he pushes the pace of his footsteps. On the docks, I always gave him plenty of room to place his steps.

Danny's panicky voice stopped us at the storefront — *I'm trying to Juan but sometimes you know they flip around right when you're about to knock 'em out. Yeah, well bite me. I'm not perfect you know* — the sound of the boy's blackjack thumping at another missed target flopping over the dock.

"A couple of nuts and bolts, those two." A bit of tobacco juice trailed Red's words. "Ah, nothing changes 'round here but a boy's name, eh Mark?"

"You trust the black-haired boy?"

"Oh, they're both good kids. Your eyes have seen that in them, I've watched you watching. Though, I admit, the two of them skewered together never been half the workers you and Jimmy were that one summer."

The door to the marina store is one of a kind, an antique from a century old captain's quarters. Years of scratches and gouges left to bleed for another hundred years around the door's pitted brass handle and latch. Inside the store, the space between its shelved walls is as cramped as a closet-sized pantry, and remains open more as a tax deduction beneath his loft apartment than as a serious business venture. If you head down the *Fishing Gear* aisle and meet someone even slightly overweight, one of you must either skittle backwards or you both uncomfortably learn what undergarments the other is wearing. And in the *Hardware* aisle...

A gawking foursome walked in and took Red's attention.

My favorite aisle in the store is *Photographs*, a product-barren corridor squished between *books, beans,* and *dangerous things.* It is an aisle where the shelf-life of store dust lives to a ripe old age. It serves the town well as a stage to present hundreds of scuffed-up photographs. Most of the photographs have been pricked by pigmy darts and the smudge of fingering browsers, so that whatever printed glory the pictures once possessed has long since come and gone.

"— Mark, hold your water. I'll be right back with your key."

"Help your customers, Red. I can wait."

"— Ice is out back," Red says to a sunburned, guppy-faced man, "around the corner and to your right. Gentlemen, everything I have in the way of new anchors and oars is this way."

The walled aisle which houses *Photographs* is full up with pasted and pegged squares of life; contained moments revealing frozen faces and dated clothing. In one block of prints, Jimmy's daughter is in grade school. She's wearing culottes, a baseball shirt, and an oversized black and white plaid hunter's cap — although, in the color of real life, I'm certain I remember Jessie's cap being red and green. Dianna and I are pictured on the pine shelf below her. We look to be in our twenties, piggybacking, and about to jump from the pier. Next to us, behind scratched glass, Red's sixth grade class — all fifteen of them — sitting bareback on Mr. Crawford's work horses; Red is the only kid wearing leather chaps with his white shirt and necktie. In another picture Red is pushing a metal wheelbarrow across the dock with Jimmy's little girl inside. Loving the wheelbarrow ride, Jessie is waving her dad's plaid hunter's cap at the camera's eye.

There is so much more on these shelves for my eyes to track; high-school graduates from '55 and every graduating class thereafter, the dock beneath them noticeably submerging a little deeper into the harbor in each succeeding photo of *the graduating class of ___*; Christmas carolers huddling under the pier's red and green light bulbs; a matted St. Bernard puppy receiving mouth-to-mouth from a crew member of the U.S. Coast Guard, the dog surviving and reaching its full growth in the next two photos; the bizarre blizzard of 19___ which banded its ice on the masts of skeletal-looking boats. Higher up the shelved wall, a boat with a broken mast folded over its bow and across part of Red's damaged dock. On the white border of this particular photograph a scribbled heading reads: "African lightning did this." *African Lightning* was the name we'd given to a powerful cube of hashish smuggled in from Canada that summer. Moving on, my eyes roll over their solitary review of a film crew and two well known actors; Red is in this picture, too, and Jimmy and Salvador, Paul, Perez, Becky, Trish, and Dianna all squeezing in around the famous faces. Finally, my eyes jump to the aisle's top shelf where my thoughts rest for a time on one of my favorites. This picture holds a bonfire in the center of its picture frame and a circle of performing musicians sitting around the fire's cove of light. Jimmy, me, Dianna, and five-year old Jessie — asleep in Dianna's lap — make up another half-circle around the musicians. In the same photograph Jimmy's chin is on my shoulder and we are both staring at Dianna's cradling arms. Friendships peaked that night, Jimmy whispering "isn't it grand that Jessie has three parents," followed by a chorus of sighs from the musicians. The following day our African friends offered to play at our bar's opening. The musicians stayed on for three more weeks, playing in exchange for room and board and who knows what else Jimmy provided. To this day I don't know what happened on their days at sea with Jimmy, but that's definitely one of them hiding under the broken mast across the bow of my boat. The penciled heading on the photograph is still legible: *Jimmy sailed us in, Mark bailed us out!*

Red found me my key to my hatch cover. As I was leaving the happy isles of his general store, the last picture my mind took was of one of his customers stepping outdoors to place a chunk of ice on the back of her neck, under a giant fin of driftwood inscribed with the words: *Showers and Lockers: no cursing, cussing, camping, or cuddling!*

The treatment facility's residential cottages are in full view to most all ferry passengers long before our sluggish inter-island ferry docks at Depot Island. The cottages are squatty-looking, many of their cedar-shake rooflines sprawling along the island's grassy bluff to look out over a utilitarian ferry landing. Unobtrusive enough in their detachment from the more modern main compound, the view-cottages sit quite noticeably aloof on the ridge of this otherwise flat, farmland island.

Next to me, the arms of a passenger have found a space on the ferry's railing. The man winces when he attempts to stretch his back. His face is as narrow as a blade and just a shade darker than old ivory. He's especially pasty in the swales of his cheeks. He raises one of his hands to palm back a fresh haircut and rub the perfume of his musky aftershave. The man's fleece-lined denim vest tightly buttoned over a long sleeve Pendleton. The island air is warm and so is the breeze, but some illness is making this man's body cold inside. On my other side, pressed low against the ship's railing, the web of a child's matted hair. Hovering annoyingly over the child is the puttied scowl of her loud-mouthed mother. A flannel scarf wraps the woman's neck. In stature, she is a silo of a woman. Her fatty face almost fecal in form. The child is timidly asking her mother a question — I see the child's words before she speaks them, hear the mother's hoarse response before the child's second syllable will fall into the sea. *Shut-up! You eat after I meet your father at the casino. Quiet! You want another smack like the one I gave you this morning? Do you? Stop being a little shit.*

The voice of our ship's captain drops from the sky. *Arriving Depot Island. All foot-passengers please prepare to unload at this time.* I smile half-heartedly at the child standing beside me. She smiles back at me, a dismal loss of expression returning to disfigure the girl's face when the arms of her mother yank her from the ship's railing.

Last December I made several visits to Depot Island, each time intending to visit my wife, but had often remained aboard this same ferry for the entire day — choosing, instead, to ride the ship back and forth between both islands, never stepping foot on Depot Island, never visiting my wife, never meeting with her therapist, never calling to say I wasn't coming, mostly, the entire day spent trying to drink my way back to the dream of Jessie's life. January's return to the islands was no different, the waters of Depot Island always pulling my heart towards its cold brailed whitecaps and my hands towards nothing else but the ferry's icy railings. February was little more than a binding month of disparagement and denial from island to island.

The ship's engines howled and eased into reverse, and caused the upper decks of the ferry to vibrate almost as much as the churning ocean waters racing to surround the ship's hull. I leaned out over the railings to watch more of the engine's mushroom-shaped eddies chase and circle the ferry's slowing approach to the dock.

In a matter of minutes, I am scheduled to meet with Dianna, ask and answer a few loaded questions, think *yes* but say *no* to the invitation of an over-night guest pass, pretend too many frayed smiles, and generally, be reminded that the once glistening quality of conversation with my wife is now morosely absent. It is a menacing dialogue inside my head that I've brought aboard, this day, and it brings back images of winter, sickness, and most of all, a relentless guilt. Brings back images of staff members positioning white wicker furniture into small circular clusters on the facility's communal patio, where visitors and patients were encouraged to settle during summer evenings like the one unfolding, where Dianna sometimes sat and focused every drop of her attention on the rhythm of the swirling ponds and tried to rid herself of all thoughts of my presence.

A line of automobiles, their ignitions scratching the air, are preparing to leave the ferry's lower deck. I watch the first few cars bounce across the ferry's corrugated steel ramp and motor up the short incline of the island's gutted gravel road.

What more would I say to her, how would I say it?

The last vehicle to depart from the ferry's openmouthed cavern speeds across the steel ramp and into the road's rising amber dust, its driver eager to keep up with the caravan of bike racks and roof-top carriers disappearing over the bluff. But I remain onboard, on the ferry's empty upper deck, feeling far worse about opening a two-week old pack of cigarettes and smoking again than about missing another scheduled visit with my wife.

Inside my boat, I found the edge of my bed and sat there for a time. Let the run of my eyes fall upon the lace of the window's curtain. Sometimes, it is too much to think about my relationship with both women. Sometimes, I think I must let the memory of one of them go and start living, or dying, for the other. It is so easy to give way to the loneliness of this caging hour. The last pleasant thing I remember feeling, before my past took hold of my thoughts, was the hollowness of the incoming tide slurping at the marina's pier.

Somewhere between midnight and the damp morning hours of dawn, I awoke to the prodigious stench of regret. I've been here before, wasted too many winter days and nights waiting for divine intervention to come while watching more friendships abandon ship. I am alone, clinging motionless to the ladder in my boat's galley. The boat is rocking slightly, and there is the thin rattle of aluminum cans coming from the cockpit floor. My head hurts badly, and my earlier defense that *the world pushes me first and I simply push back harder* is as far away now as the boy in my high-school pictures. I'm so cold. The wind has come up and looks as though it has been skating circles in the galley all night. She is sneaky, this island wind, always she tries to mask her true intentions. Pretends there is time for her coiling tears to heal me before my mind becomes hardened and gray with doubt.

My chest lifts from the crush of the ladder rungs and I face the night sky, my mind echoing a fragment of thought. *Was I, this night, the mast of some other's measured forgiveness?*

I managed to climb the galley's ladder. In the cockpit, my eyes try to focus on the fluorescent sign of *Red's Grocery*. But everywhere I look it is more of the same, more neon arches of streaking color playing in the night sky. *Daylight soon*, I think I hear myself say aloud before passing out.

Awake again. The shell of *Red's Grocery* still shifting. My stomach aches. So strange and lonely how Jimmy's doctrine left some people out in the cold, left some of us wide awake in the desperate hours, left us wondering where our spouse, our lover, our daughter had gone — the bleakness of its pen falling back upon us a little more hysterically with each passing day, daring us to remember a little more about our mistaken identities. *What food feeds the beast of our grief? Emptiness? Is there a soul in that emptiness, gasping?*

My fingers and hands smell, and this is not me. My clothing is soaked and stained with vomit and cold to the touch. I try to take hold of my boat's tiller arm, but my body is generating such an enormous trembling that I must give up the effort. A bedroom light comes on in the window over Red's store and I watch how his hunched form slouches and quickly disappears behind the blinds of his loft window. I have fallen into the muck of my boat's cockpit, and the next words I will hear will be Red's.

"Now don't go getting mad or embarrassed, Mark. I'm just going to help you find your bearings."

Red comes aboard. He's squatting over me like I was a fishing-lure entangled in grass and mud and decaying bark.

"It's a little before three in the morning, but still a tad-bit early to be waking the neighbors. So the two of us are going to have to keep it down. Okay? Okay?"

"Sure, sure." I think I mouthed my understanding without shouting.

"I can see that you're colder than a witch's tit but don't move anymore than you have to. Alright? 'Case something's broken."

"Alright."

"Here," his arm reaches under me, "first thing we do is drain this cockpit of a bathtub. Don't move. Don't move, I said!"

Embarrassed as I feel, it was a comfort to feel the hardness of Red's forearm under my backside. He'd found what was plugging the drain hole. A gurgling sound erupted.

"There, that ought to get us started."

"What's plugging it?"

"Chunk of your small intestines, I would imagine."

"Probably right," I said, "no one else came to the party."

"Know I'm right. Had Jimmy's blue-plate special yesterday and it don't look near this good."

I didn't mean to, but when I felt Red touching my face I reacted quite loudly.

"What the hell you doing, Red?" With a single sweep of his open fingers Red had parted my oil-streaked hair.

"Keep it down, man." Red scolded in a strong whisper.

"I'm just checking your head and face to see where the blood's coming form. There, there's the cut. Must have been that nose of a swordfish you had on your line."

"How big?"

"Oh, not bad. Been dried up and caked on for three, maybe four hours I'd say."

"You sure the cut is closed?"

"Sure as you're a royal pain in the ass." His voice is tiring.

"I think I'm feeling alright now," I said. "Sorry about all the trouble. Go on back to bed."

"I'm up now. Let's drive up to the fire station and have that cut looked after?'"

"No. I'm fine now. Got it all out of my system."

"Come on. We'll get you cleaned up before we drive up to the station and have that cut looked at."

"Red, you're not listening to me." I lifted myself up and onto a tear in one of the boat cushions. Next to me, the silver handle of a butter knife was sticking out of a blue slice of marine vinyl. Red took notice of it. There was a moment of absolutely no wind in the marina, a few uncomfortable seconds dropping around us as we both considered the violence which had repeatedly thrust the knife into the cushion, and then the sound of running water breaking from the wrinkles of my raincoat.

"Has it been raining," I wondered the words, and then heard myself asking the same question.

"Come on, you need to go to the station. No one will ask any questions if I go with you. I promise."

"Red, listen to me. I was feeling sorry for myself last night. But I'm over it now. You want to do something more to help, you unlock the shower-room for me on your way back to the house and don't say another word." I patted his kneecap, "Got it all out of my system."

"Come on," his hand clamped my elbow. "You need to go to the station."

"I know what I fucking need, old man." I pulled my arm back. "I need you off my boat."

The look on his face. I shouldn't have said it, shouldn't have even thought it.

Red was on the wharf, my boat rocking and already missing the weight of his friendship, by the time I looked up at the hurt in his eyes.

"You know, Mark, I heard stories about you last summer, about behavior like this. Didn't believe any of it. None of it. Hell, man, I even defended you."

I wanted my old marina back. I wanted its powdery-white glow returned to my galley table. Wanted my nose and my throat and the moon to be full again with yesterday's anticipation. So I thought nothing more of my offence, letting Red shuffle back into the night without saying another word, morosely certain that before daylight could address my behavior I would somehow be gone.

CHAPTER TWO

FROM MY HOLLOW OF beach stone and sand, I drifted out from beneath a cold and wet and scratchy haze to watch her naked form find life again on a surfer's wave. The sea beyond her black but for a ship's rusty hull which had peeled back the blistering skin of her father's candle-eyed waters, where each of us lived and hid beneath the sureness of all that was precious and all that was missing from our constructions of Jessie's death.

All thru the night Jessie had come and gone from my hours of sleeplessness. Once more, I closed my eyes to try and call her back and to take her with me into the world of sleepless dreams, my bloodied elbows and stomach worming the rest of my body back into my earthen hollow as cautiously as the crease of fog before me would melt the stony shoreline.

I awoke to the thinness of sunlight passing thru a rolling fog. My tarp tent had collapsed and taken on my body's trenched form, which was not so unlike a broken bale of hay left to rot in the brambles and gullies and rain of some hard to reach triangle of island pasture, but had at least folded back some of my pitted arrogance that I could not have fallen this hard again. In the minutes that would pass like needles to my skin, I wanted only to will myself back into the dream where *she* would live again and to leave the thought of last night's blackout scattered among the beach stones around me. But the smell of engine oil and spilled fuel on my blanket pooled so strongly with my own metallic body odors, and so sickened me whenever one of my coughing spells stirred the miserable odors beneath the blanket, that sleep was pushed aside for a time. When the coldness of the ocean air won out, and I finally pulled the woolen blanket over my head, and wrapped what I could of the blanket's sourness within the folds of the plastic tarp, my chained arm and shoulder shifted deeper into the stony pit and some of the sea's soundless screeching quieted.

Sleep finally shadowed my body, and beneath its frayed cover, farther back even than the infancy of any cast of God who may have left elemental traces of his love within me, in the beginning, I found the colorless emptiness of the Word — watched it spin orange spikes of flame from the charred understanding of regret, felt its heat boil within me as its fire engulfed the channel to Depot Island, all history of my presence there consumed and allowed to drizzle into the greater currents of the greater Sound.

When I awakened, I became sick to my stomach and vomited. After the nausea left me I began to peer out from under my blue tarp more often. The fog was heavier now and battered with less color, but I could at least see a band of shoreline edge. Somewhat comforted, I closed my eyes and wished for sleep.

In the dream that followed, I found Jessie. Her hair was oiled and glistening and floating on an icy pallet of seawater.

I knew she was drowning by the way her guillotined smile was no longer part of her body. Some paralyzing force was orbiting within me, or about me, and would not let my body do more than swim circles around her struggle. A white terry-cloth robe and belt entangled her like some butchered and useless life-vest. I pleaded with her to remove the robe but her eyes only fixated on some horizon beyond my scope of understanding. The robe released her and she began to sing the most beautiful song. Her eyes becoming the music and commanding me to listen. I became so infused by the haunting burst within the song's voice that I wanted nothing more from the world than to be completely and forever a part of Jessie's being. She sang of the great monarch of beauty that erupts in the great pairing with formless Death, with the endless One, of a great orbiting ring of consciousness that lives, thereafter, in each of us. I began to weep for the story her song told of a great ring of dusk which, formless and gasping, star-punches an endless breath into the great ache of all death, perilous in its great draw of all that was ever part of the Nameless One, would be again if ever we drew one common breath.

When the dream ended a cold rain had sliced and tilled the shoreline sand and stone and, for a moment, I thought it possible that I might be just up the beach from Salvador's cottage studio and not far from the wooded stream where his dogs dipped their muzzles on warm summer days. But it was only a pleasant dream of a wish, an appendage to my night dream, nothing more. My clothing had twisted and bunched so tightly about my legs, the coldness and bruising along my shins and knees so buckling and muddied with pain, that I hesitated to try to stand and stretch for fear of worsening the crimping aches gathering my body into a ball. Along one of my shoulder blades, a painful muscle spasm had begun to ripple down to my wrist, the pain sometimes branching into my neck and tunneling thru my chest before concentrating its burn in the bones of my wrist, pain which I could no longer deny or ignore. The thought actually crossed my mind, and briefly brought me to the edge of panic, that I might have mangled my arm or shoulder in the propeller of my boat's engine, hours earlier, while trying to escape either Jimmy's or Red's hold on me in the marina. This thought led to another fractured memory that during the previous night one of my wrists had been trapped and tied with something I was now certain had possessed very sharp teeth. And then all the fragments of this memory came home to roost, and I could feel what the blue tarp had hidden from my eyes — that my left wrist had been handcuffed to a block of concrete the size of a small nightstand.

In that pounding hour of sleeplessness which was to follow my disbelief and anger over the previous night's events, an anger which was to hold my eyes to the jawing circle of metal caging my hand and its steel link frozen in stone, some grated state of sedation must have found me and taken hold of my manic despair. It must have protected me somehow from myself, from the shame of last night's blackout, until sleep could take me back once more.

I awakened to the pouncing thought of how *almost no one swims in these waters anymore,* and to *another's* vision of seeing the blood in Jessie's lips turn blue with hypothermia, and to the memory of how far she could swim these shoreline waters as a child whose eyes mirrored our indigo skies. Her arms like spears in the water and her neckline polished with gem-laced shells and a whistle as piercing as a candle's flame in the night. How brilliant the sunlit air once blanketed these mystic islands. How heated the unfolding of our blanket once shared. How is it such colors as these live only once?

In the warmth of a sunlit afternoon, I climbed out from under my cover of dampness. Off shore, a light chop crested silver along the edges of the ocean's cold line currents. Sunlight slashing my beach and warming the stones near my hollow of a bed.

I rubbed the crust from my eyelids, and in the shakiness of my hangover thought I could make out the spray of a small boat crystallizing on the surface of the channel. When my vision cleared somewhat, the arrowhead bow of the small rickety boat I'd seen was in the midst of changing course and about to cut a sloppy arch against the out-going tide so as to make its way closer to my section of beach. In tow, a craft resembling the split shell of a giant summer squash bulleted from side to side behind the small boat like a knife buttering toast. In the bow of the small boat, a boy frantically waved in my direction. Seated behind the animation of this boy, his black-haired companion steered their boat steadily closer to my position.

I bunched my blue tarp up plenty thick around my wrist and handcuffs and the block of concrete, and waited. I did not have to wait long, mere minutes passed before the grinding of sand and stone ground the boat's hull and the young boys ashore.

"What the heck happened, Mr. Jacobs? Did your pup-tent collapse in the night or something?"

Except for his unbuttoned leather vest, which sagged from Danny's scrawny shoulders like wet clothes on the line, the boy had ridden ashore bareback and swung down from the boat's tipsy bow while excitedly waving at me and displaying a toothy smile, all this before falling flat on his face trying too quickly to run towards me.

"Slow down, Danny!" Juan admonished.

"Don't worry yourself about me, chief. I'm okay, just resting a little."

Juan stood in the boat and stared down at the backside of Danny's purple vest.

"Call me that again, Danny, and you're gonna pay."

Danny waved off his friend and continued to talk to me from the shoreline while brushing the sand from his hair.

"Mr. Jacobs, you up? You awake? Look at all the stuff we brung you."

Bumping a bemoaning elbow on a protruding oar, the boy reached under the bow of the boat and pulled out a barbecue grate. Some clothing had gotten caught up in the grate, and now a white t-shirt was hanging from the grillwork which the boy was lifting over his head for my inspection.

"Check this out, Mr. Jacobs. Whoops, I guess we brought you clean underwear and a Salvador-dolly clothesline to boot. Get it?" Danny set the barbecue grate on the beach. "Yup, we've been packing this mule train for you all morning but now we're here."

"Danny!" Juan stopped working the canvas hood over the boat's little egg-shaped engine long enough to shout and stare at his friend. "First things first. Tie the boat up. Over there, that big ass stump will do. Well then do it why don't you."

"Consider it undone, captain." Danny flashed me another toothy smile and then turned his back on me. "Be right up to see you, Mr. J. Got something big to tell you. Something special."

In the painfully bright sunlight, Danny's high-octane voice is another annoyance to contend with, though a voice I admit fits well with his ring-tossed silver and turquoise bracelets catching the sunlight whenever the kid waves his twig of a forearm at me.

Danny's feet perform spittlebug gyrations in the rocky sand when he runs the beach to pass a rope thru the gnarly roots of an overturned and half-buried stump turned gray by the wash of the sea. By the time he has returned to the boat, he's caught me studying him and seems to have calculated the odds of ever finding another audience quite like the one he's got trapped on the beach. He faces me and jams a black derby hat over his long stringy hair.

"Damn it all, Juan, this fuggin' hat's too big. You want it?" Danny flings the rimless hat like a Frisbee at his friend. The hat strikes Juan square in the chest and topples into the boy's hands.

"Piss on it, it ain't me." Juan throws the black hat back to his friend. "Best you boil it with tonight's dinner. Might shrink up some by morning."

Dan picked up the hat and made it gingerly dance on the fingers of his hands like it was one of Hazel's hot-buttered buns.

"Whoa, I feel a fine fit coming on come sunup —"

"Get over here and help unload."

"It's a fulltime job for you, isn't it chief, keeping me in line?"

"We gotta get this gear unloaded and up over that hill before dark. That sound alright with you, Mr. Jacobs? We'll be out of the wind that way. That, and no one will take the liberty of stepping in on one of Danny's famous campfires."

"Good idea," I answer.

It hurts to speak. But the thought of getting up and over a steep hill overwhelms me more. Last thing I want to do is to climb or to explain. My body is still sweating out yesterday's alcohol, and my throat is raw from so much coughing. My head begins to swirl something viciously at thought of so much activity taking place along the shoreline. And then I vomit.

"Jesus," I hear Danny moan at what he's just seen me do, "he's puking all over himself like some old Seattle bumdrunk fisherman."

"Shut it."

For a few pressing moments no sound finds my ears. None. Another bout of vomiting has brought my face to the sand, after which, I hear every crushing word the boys speak.

"You think he knows he just puked on himself?"

"I swear, Danny."

"We should of brought Red with us."

"Fuck Red. We ain't at his marina right now."

"Shove it. I like that old fart."

"Bullshit."

Danny is peering in my direction.

"You think he's made himself sick for losing his wife or something?"

"Maybe."

"That all you got to offer me?"

"How's this — don't neither of us have no dad around and you don't see me puking about it."

"Geese, you're a hard ass today."

"Well, we ain't exactly being paid to clean him up and take him to church now are we?"

"You stole that from Red."

"So."

My insides are coiling like a ring of barbed wire but I manage to sit up and face the boys. Rocking my body in my pit seems to help ease some of the stomach cramps, so does focusing on the work the boys are doing. Juan is standing on the beach. He's carrying the rattling of a steel cooler towards a growing pile of supplies spread out over a large slab of ledge stone. Danny's in seawater up to his knees working the back of the boat, untying the twisted webbing of rope and a tangled chain of dog leashes that crisscrosses a stack of wood in the boat's tag-along-turned-firewood barge.

"You want help pulling that raft ashore?" I hear Juan ask.

"You got your way, I got mine," Danny puffed. "Don't

you worry about nothing, Mr. J. We're everything you're going to need this weekend. I mean, we've *got* everything you're going to need this weekend. Hazel sent food. All kinds of food that Jimmy don't know about neither."

"Danny!"

"And shampoo and shit-rag too."

"Dan! Mr. Jacobs don't need you talking at him right now. Hang up and pull that raft ashore."

"Who tied this mess up anyhow, Juan? Me? Geese, I tied this thing up good."

"We should try and get that firewood up that monster of a hill first."

I was too far back from the shoreline to be certain of the tally. But with all of his talking, I don't believe Danny had loosened a single knot or link in the rope harness securing the firewood in the rubber raft.

Juan walked back to the boat and reached in under the seat for something. A pistol, the older boy was now holding a pistol, holding the gun in his left hand and aiming it at Danny's backside.

Danny let out a long high-pitched yelp and grabbed at whatever it was that had bitten him in the butt. His knees lifted high out of the water, and when his legs came back to earth his feet danced in uneven circles. Only when the boy had finished stomping and kicking at stones did the shore-line waters begin to calm.

"You're a complete shit-head, Cochise!" Danny was vigorously rubbing his cut-offs. "Jesus, you didn't have to put a b-b in my ass."

"Sorry to plug you one but you know how wound up you can get sometimes. We agreed on this, remember." Juan studied his friend while shifting the pistol he was holding back and forth from one hand to the other. "You okay, son?"

Danny rubbed his butt ferociously. But there was also a grin inching its way across the boy's face.

"You should be proud of yourself, Dan. I think that's the closest you've ever taken one in the ass."

"God, it's still stinging. I ain't got no ass as it is, you know."

"Here," Juan prepared to toss Danny the pistol, "take your best shot and plug me one if it'll make your bony ass feel any better."

"Forget it, maybe later."

"Let me see that b-b gun. Bring it over here. Now!"

Juan walked the pistol over to me.

"That the only weapon you brought with you?"

"It's not a weapon. It's a b-b gun."

"Give it to me." I took the gun by the barrel, and after shoving my tarp aside, smashed its plastic handle, its false chamber, and the pistol's trigger mechanism against my block of concrete.

"Why'd you go and do that? You could of just asked me not to use it."

"Go help your friend." I snapped. "He is your friend, isn't he?"

The glare in Juan's eyes shifted from my face to the exposed handcuffs. The boy did not speak a word, choosing instead to step away from my stone pit and walked back to the boat as I had asked.

The pile of supplies on the beach continued to grow; a mounding of clattering tent-poles, dropped pots, pop cans, two coolers, and a heaping of firewood and blankets. Danny would wave to me after each roundtrip from the boat to the beached stump, and occasionally, give me the thumbs-up sign. I waved back to the boy but once, my free arm flopping to my side after the effort as if it belonged to a stroke victim.

It was work even to rest my chin on my chest and to watch

the boys traipse from the shoreline pile of firewood to the daunting edge of the hillside woods behind us. A motionless rabbit watched with me from the shady half of the sunlit shore before skittishly scrambling deeper into the advancing shade, its white tail and its broken lines of tawny washed-out fur disappearing into a wide ravine of salal growing near a tall grove of pine.

I fought off sleep as long as I could, watching the wind trimming the bottlebrush branches of scraggy pines climbing the mountain on the uninhabited island and seeing the rabbit once more bolt from safe cover to run the beach wild and unattached.

It was late when I opened my eyes. My stomach churned with hunger and with the last consumptive stains of my heavy drinking. The bruising ache in my shoulder still persisted but the intense white pain which had accompanied it earlier was gone now. The evening sky painting a few broken stars against a ribbon of cool gray clouds which still lingered over the western horizon. Near my shallow depression in the damp sand, a toothbrush, toothpaste, and a fresh bar of soap rested on a dry beach towel. Other than the precious sight of these items, I saw no sign of the boys. No trace of their boat, the raft, or the pile of supplies and firewood I remembered having fallen asleep to.

I waited until nightfall had erased its seam from the edgeless ocean before removing my clothing. My shirt is already so badly torn that one more tear along its chained cuff finishes the job. Not so difficult, either, to lift my lump of concrete from my beached depression and to drag it over sand and stone to the shoreline.

The ocean's first bite is the coldest and produces a welt of breathlessness in my lungs whenever any line of dry skin on my body sinks deeper into its burning ice. I tell myself to use the sea's baptism to let go of *her heart* and *her hand* in this secret I am willing to take to my grave, and too quickly my prayer is answered. Too easily my anchor of stone feels at home under water, its lopsided weight sliding so fast into the natural bowl of a submerged ledge that my feet slip and my back is wrenched by the effort it takes to slow its slide. My face and then my head are suddenly under water, which gives me a terrifying moment of panic when I realize that the block of concrete is still rolling and that I may not be able to prevent it from slipping off the ledge and into the bottomless sea. The shorelines of so many of these islands are riddled with deadly drop-offs and hidden currents, currents which have pulled divers to their deaths and trapped their bodies for days beneath ledges of basalt like the one I'm struggling to hold my body to. My panic vanishes once I am able to stop the skipping momentum of the submerged concrete and move the block closer to shore, where its weight becomes no more, no less, than a fitting punishment for all the pain I've brought back to these islands. Oddly enough, the chill of this scare is at once replaced with the funny thought that *I cannot swim*, and my only concern becomes not dropping or losing the bar of soap the boys were kind enough to leave me.

I scrub my face and head and chest, squatting several times to rinse before washing my legs and butt and my gritty backside, and plunging my body in and out of the ocean's blue-black veining, more slowly now, so as to enjoy its wash of a thousand stings. Pleasant, also, to hold my breath and to keep my head under water for a minute or two, a spellbinding experience which I repeat several more times and which seems to keep some of the mania in my head at bay. Under water, the ocean's cold gives a most unexpected emotional lift to my spirit. With each successively longer dip I take, I seem to come closer to an understanding of how dizzying and addictive the promise of a weightless life might become to someone in a desperate state of mind, how dimly an obsession might shine only for itself knowing that voiceless death lay just beyond a stone shelf beneath the sea.

A muffling of tongues speaks from the shoreline darkness. Voices of children sent to overpower the dreary memory of Jimmy's parting prophecy the night before he brought me here to dry out. The ghost of Jimmy's voice with them, too — *the deeper you sink the greater the pressure, remember that. Remember this night.*

"I think his hand is stuck somehow. We gotta do something. He can't lift it, he can't!"

"Leave him be a minute." I hear Juan's voice countering Danny's concern.

"Something's wrong, I'm telling you. We gotta do something."

"Mr. Jacobs, you okay?" Juan's question is like a concussion entering my head thru my teeth. "'Cause if you ain't okay, I think Danny and me can help pull you out."

My head lifts from the sea and my lungs choke out water and air.

"Satisfied, Danny? If he's choking he's living, ain't he?"

"We didn't mean to bother you, Mr. Jacobs. 'Cept we forgot to leave you clean clothes and had to go back to camp."

Juan stepped back from his friend's stance and from the wet band of shoreline which separated us, apparently uninterested in my condition or Danny's explanation for their absence.

"You want to go with us now up the mountain? After you dress, I mean? We got a good fire going just over the hill. We saved you some dinner."

"Get out of here. Go on. Go back to your puppy-ass camp. Go on."

"Come on, Danny. Leave him be."

"You too, you filthy dirty little fucking scab. Get. I don't need your punk help. Go on, I said!"

Danny didn't budge. He'd buried his sneakers up to his ankles in the water. His body in reach of my free arm.

"Danny!" Juan commanded. "We have to go. Move back. He don't want any part of us right now."

"That's the first smart thing come out of your mouth since I tripped over you last summer. Little spic of a prick."

"Come on, Dan. Best we let him dry off or dry out. Whichever it is he can manage."

A burrowing despair took hold of Danny and held him in place. He began to cry a little.

I cursed when the brutality of my sobering nakedness broke from the ocean's coldness. The boy's sobbing pulling more fear and more tears from his eyes when he saw the handcuffs. I was more on land than on sea now, shivering and stumbling to find some cornering hole in the sand, beaten down by the scales of a long day's night and by a belief in something which once crawled from the sea to shed its skin and walk this same shore — seeing for itself in the wavering of the ocean's mirror the serpent it had become.

"This what you want to see? Now you've seen it. Now go. Go!"

Danny stepped back from the water's edge. The fear that had slashed its lines across the boy's thin face gone now and replaced with a child's trawling resentment.

"Go on!" My free arm flailed one last time at the lumpish backside of the retreating boys. Juan had taken his friend by the shoulder and was gently coaxing him towards the island's veil of woods. Exhausted, I fell to my knees.

After the boys are out of sight, my arms and legs begin their pulling drag over the beach stones and a wide vein of rooted basalt which, at its crest, tables a folded blanket and a small pile of fresh clothing.

I dressed half wet. The frost in the night air penetrating each awkward movement of my limbs which struggle to find an opening in my clean clothes. My fingers unable to shake off the deepest of the ocean's cold until they have made several attempts at lacing my boots. If I want food I've no choice but to make the daunting climb thru the dense underbrush and steep grove of pine leading up to Juan and Danny's camp, a climb which promises to be more mountain than hill.

In the woods, many of the pines have branched low enough and green enough to withstand the weight of my strenuous pull. But the terrain on which the trees stand is so steep, so wedded with the sinewy stems of salal, that falling or slipping backwards becomes a constant concern. Already the handcuffs are donning a slippery bowtie of sword fern and lemon leaf. Maybe rest a minute in that clearing up ahead, the one Jimmy and Jessie used to favor, the one which overlooks the hillside's marshy bog of skunk cabbage. Pretend this ball and chain is not what it is. Make believe it's one of Jessie's beach balls and not the weight of her father's cross. Shrink the weight of this tomb I'm in and *think* my way up to the boys, the food, and the campfire.

Our father's sins of omission to spur us up each new mountain. But they were not the sins we were guilty of — not mine, not Jimmy's — ours would come and go with tomorrow's tides, hide behind our public faces, busy our hands, and flail for forgiveness beneath our divided memories of Jessie's kisses.

It is a fabulous site, Danny's fire. An earthen canoe quartered by dugout stone, and soil, and red coals breathing a flaming light into a halo of a clearing beneath the looming pine.

I'm warm enough from my uphill struggle. Wish to stand,

but take a seat on the ground without being asked, near the fire's smallest of flames. Three tents, arranged in a triangular configuration, block what little view there might be of the beach below us. Two of the tents are not much more than canvas tarps held up by sagging ropes tied to trees whose trunks are twenty, maybe thirty feet apart. No floors in these makeshift pup-tents. A radio dangles from the tilted awning of the third tent; a large cabin tent pitched under the brown curls of some scorched lodge-pole pines.

Juan is seated on the other side of the fire pit, opposite me, poking a stick into the coals the fire has chiseled from the log. Danny steps from the cabin tent and into the camp's smokeless ring of light. Understandably, neither boy will speak to me or look my way.

"We, we don't know one another very well, but that's —" the flaring pain in the bone of my shoulder about takes my breath away, "but that's no excuse for my behavior or my words. I owe both you boys an apology. I was wrong to say those things. I knew it was wrong when I was speaking them. And I know it more so now."

"Juan and me, we was only trying to help." Danny anxiously puffed on a cigarette. He'd positioned his rat-hole sneakers close enough to the fire's coals to make the shoe's rubber soles steam. "That's all we was trying to do for you."

"I'm sorry I yelled at you Danny. Wouldn't blame either of you if you packed up and left without me in the morning."

Juan twisted more of his fire-stick into the bed of flickering coals. More steam from Danny's pedaling sneakers too close to the fire rose with the blue smoke of his cigarette.

"This isn't me," I carefully jiggled my chain, "this isn't what I am. This thing — this is a knife that's fallen off the kitchen counter. A knife I haven't yet reached for and put back in the drawer where it belongs. But I will. Soon as I get some food in me. Soon as I get some sleep and my sorry ass back to the marina."

"Cold beans and eggs sound okay to you?" Juan spoke up. A slight smile crept over his face as he tossed his stick alongside the long fire log.

"Juan's a nut ain't he Mr. J? We got stuff way better than eggs. Want your dessert first? No, I guess not. Guess you probably want to eat real food first."

The pasta was lumpy and spotted with too much burnt cheese. The baked beans were cold and crusted over like two scoops of fried ice cream. Hazel's famous gingerbread sliced too thin to satisfy my hunger for more. And every spoonful of food that Danny placed on my paper plate was unbelievably delicious.

"What you thinking about this time, Mr. J?"

Danny had pulled a pocketknife from his vest and begun to hatchet frozen chips from a block of ice clunking wildly against the walls of an ice chest. When he was finished he blew the pine needles out of a paper cup he'd grabbed off a winter's supply of firewood, filled the cup with chips of ice, and squeezed a plastic bottle of berry-flavored syrup over the ice until the liquid had filled the paper cup to the rim and drizzled onto his fingers.

"How to get these handcuffs off me without bothering Jimmy for the key."

"That's easy. Me and Juan will head back to the marina in the morning and get you Red's bolt cutters. I seen him use them all the time to cut the locks off hatch covers and all kinds of other stuff shouldn't have been locked up. Hey, you want one of these? You want a snow cone?"

"No thanks, I'm saving room for those bolt cutters."

"Me and Juan are going to try and get on at the shelter this summer."

'You are. I'm not." Juan eyeballed his friend.

"The shelter?" I asked.

"The animal shelter. You got a favorite breed, Mr. J?"

"I'm fond of Sally's Springer Spaniels."

"Oh yeah, they're fine dogs. I still like mongrels the best though. My mom says that's because I think like one. 'All over the board' as my shop teacher likes to say to me when I'm in school."

"Who sent you boys out here?"

"We volunteered. Yeah, we did. It was a no brainer after Red told us we ought to make a whole camping trip out of your ordeal. But Hazel and Ms. Jackie, they was the ones worried most about you."

"Your folks know you're here?"

"Our moms know where to find us. That's good enough for them on a Saturday night."

"What about your fathers?"

"Neither of us have no dads in the picture. That's a sore spot with our moms. But I don't mind. Grown-ups think we should care about junk like that but I don't. One's enough to keep my bed made and my ass in line. Get it, Mr. J?"

"Neither of you were wearing lifejackets when you motored in. How come?"

"We got 'em in the boat — one for you, too — we just don't like wearing them. Juan's a great swimmer anyhow."

"And you?"

"I don't even float. On account of I only weigh eighty-five pounds. That's what some physics teacher told Juan anyways."

"*Displacement.* You've not got enough of it."

"Can I ask you something personal?"

"Who's stopping you?"

"Why'd Jimmy put you in those handcuffs?"

"I broke a promise."

"Oh, you did? What's it like having them on you?"

"Like a scared dog in a steel cage thrown from a moving truck."

"That don't look pretty in my head." Danny frowned and fidgeted. "At least you knew probably someone was coming to get you out. Can I ask you what your wife is like? If you don't mind me asking, I mean?"

"I do. I do mind you asking, son."

"Sorry Mr. Jacobs."

From the same side of the firing line, Juan addressed me.

"There's aspirin and some stomach medicine on your sleeping bag."

"Which tent do you want me in?"

"Suit yourself." Juan answered, and with two fingers pointed at the two sagging pup-tents. "Only *that* one is Dan's. And *that* other one is mine."

"That's just Juan trying to be funny. He's just begrudging you like he does me sometimes. If you ever saw the humor in him you'd see it's just his way of saying you don't have to make like a snow-ball and roll back down to the beach."

In the morning the boys are gone. And they do not return to the island — their boat motoring out from behind a curtain of marine air to bounce with the chop of the channel's shimmering waters, Red's yellow-handled bolt cutters cheering high over the head of one boy — until the midday breeze had begun to stir the beach.

By late afternoon, the sun had folded its silk into the changing tide and the boys have had enough of fishing. It is a fine day, our bodies full and the islands free of some of yesterday's hammering encounters. The boys seem okay to have reeled in nothing more than their empty hooks and the channel's priceless lure which they will carry into another day.

That evening the boys talked about their summer interests; fishing from the *tourist docks,* making money in the back yard hole of *Jimmy's Campground*, riding in the back seat if Juan could ever get his driver's license, *crashing* one of the state campgrounds *'round midnight…We'd go to Seattle and watch the Mariners if we could, but Juan says to get that one out of my head.*

While the sky was darkening to an orange bruise, I gave my thanks to Juan and Danny in their temple of a camp. I left them alone with their promising summer beliefs and my amputated block of stone, and made my way down the mountain to the shoreline.

Nature is a scrambling force, sometimes well intended, sometimes a bullying accident. Skip a stone across these island waters when you're a boy and it may come back to haunt you, years later, with a rabid bounce towards something that has learned to live its most desired life in secrecy. Makes me wonder how much is mapped out before we are born, or born again and again.

In the swaying tug of my yellow raft, I rowed closer to the scaffolding piers of the ferry landings. The harbor resort wide awake and blistered with people, her hillside cottages peering sleepily down at me. Hugging the high banks of the harbor, the rooftops of houses lean out over their neighbor's basement windows, and higher still, along a curved cliff of basalt, rows of amber porch lights slash the night sky.

I drifted for a time in the yellow raft. The faint splashing of bundled creosol poles sometimes cushioning me from the communal blaze of noise along the harbor's benches and cradling tables, sometimes jig-sawing a welcoming wave at one of my oar strokes. Emptied of all passenger vehicles, the public docks and its surrounding asphalt canvas now pulsated with the quilted colors of a human chain-dance moving to the wine-laden hollering of cheering onlookers. A communal seizure had taken hold of the town's waterfront, beneath a tube of chimney-blue smoke which funneled over the dancing heads of the crowd.

I rowed on, true to my jellyfish course of staying just beyond the water's frosting of harbor light. The raft's oars dipping their fallen obelisk wave at the crowd's laughter. In the final frame of an oar stroke, which took away my last sight-line to the ferry docks, the assemblage of dancers took on the image of a giant porcelain mask with a hundred latex eyes.

I rowed on, inching closer to the hilly spit of land which separated the town's waterfront from Red's marina. I could see the mast of the sailboat that anchored my solitary summer room, and in my mind, hear Jessie's father saying for the hundredth time —*people come to these islands for one of two reasons, to die or to exercise.* Her father's cocky voice retreating to a shredded corner of my memory before I could challenge the silliness of his doctrine, before I could remind the tailing wind of its apparition that there were, at the very least, a couple of other reasons why some of us came back to these islands.

CHAPTER THREE

THE LAST OF THE moon's fullness disappeared behind the longest of three visible creases in the swooping roof covering the work stage of Salvador's outdoor studio. *Salvador's Sail, the Circus Tent* — two of the nicknames the locals used to describe the great sheet of white canvas which protected the steel floor of Sally's work stage from the elements. Designed with a mechanical efficiency both fascinating and ingenious, the studio roof's three piece pyramidal sail could be raised or lowered by means of a masterful combination of cable and rope and pulleys according to weather and willful inspiration.

Resting on my side, on one of Sally's patio cots, the final flake of the moon's departure encouraged me to shift my sights to the work taking place on the studio's stage, where Sally was wearing his welder's apron and busy tying off some extended piece of his spirit to a two-story metal pole that was anchored center stage. There were other players on the stage with him, an interesting collection of recycled misfits ready to upstage his solitary performance; a tall stack of pallets, a scattering of several wood and metal saw-horses, some see-thru cages which housed varying lengths of channel iron and brass rods, a fence row of shiny metal boxes filled with welding rod. Green and orange oxygen and acetylene hoses snaking circles over the floor of Sally's massive stage, before being neatly coiled near some dangling, lacrosse-like metal spot lights welder's depend on.

A howling in my head has reduced my vision of the studio's surrounding gardens to a keyhole view of what Salvador would more accurately describe as *a swaying of shadow and sunlight which hides just how cash-strapped I really am*. And while I've slept, a cape of mist and grainy sunlight has snuck into Sally's compound to feed on the lushness of so much greenery. At last, the movements of my ghostly dancer is all too much for my head to handle and all light and color slips from my one open eye.

I slept thru most all of Sally's workday. *'Hardly any motion out of you all day,'* Sally would say to me later, *'not so much as a tug on my apron to ask which way to the privy.'* While I'd slept, Sally had cajoled my cot out from under his patio's breezeway and rolled the bed and its capitulating human flounder into a garden room of tall ornamental grasses and zebra-striped bamboo. *'Thought the stronger sunlight in the African garden might make you perspire more, and rid you of some of those Seattle toxins you always manage to smuggle into our islands. Truth is, though, I was having a customer and her companion over for lunch, and half-a-cadaver on the patio was not what they were expecting on their plates.'* After his business luncheon, Sally had then carted my unconscious body into a patch of shade on the lawn by the pond *'with great fuggin' difficulty and no help at all from you.'*

By late afternoon, I was fully awake and Sally took the rarity of my clear-headedness as an opportunity to share more of his colorful remarks about the great spawning my unconscious body had endured in his compound. It was easy listening to Sally have so much fun at my expense, so much simpler to laugh with him than if it had been Jimmy's voice telling the story. I hadn't felt this good, this clean of tomorrow's worries for the longest time, and though my elation of spirit was probably the by-product of my body's out-going toxic tide it made the medicine of Salvador's obvious counseling that much easier to swallow.

Sally pointed and I followed him down the garden path which led to his outdoor shower. The water from the shower head was as cold as the sea, but the dance I performed under the water's icy bite delivered none of the fear that had shaken my soul an island ago.

"Almost nine minutes," Salvador chided, tossing me a towel over the copper crown of the shower stall, "this year's record so far."

Pulling the shower's canvas curtain aside, I joked with him that having no choice but to shower with cold water must keep consumption down.

"That's the idea. Well water's cheap but there's not much of it around here."

"I see you've taken on a few more projects since I was here last. Your lawns look beautiful. I remember that far side of the pond being nothing but blackberries last year."

"Physical labor is a remarkable drug. Keeps the demons at bay, know what I mean?"

"For sure."

The runoff from the stone floor of the shower trickles under my feet and over a swale of river rock which separates two long rows of budding lettuce leaves. At rows end, today's chopped and fallen weeds lay to the side of a hoe blade. The grounds which separate Sally's irrigation pond from the compound's largest cottage, where Sally lives, slope away from his home's patio and have been well trampled by the run of dogs and a maze of stony footpaths which cut thru the taller field grasses and wild flowers before dead-ending near two dilapidated cottages. On a small rocky knoll, which hugs his patio and serves as a foot bridge to the backsides of the two smaller cottages, another kind of garden grows; a garden of sprigs of squash and pumpkin plants which, by summer's end, will spread their vines over the knoll's egg-shaped boulders and descend upon the broken windows of the two run-down cottages. A potter's sagging clay cylinders have been randomly tucked into the steepest side of the knoll. The cylinders to be used as steps which lead up to a thicket of raspberry canes now standing at attention near a steel trellis that Sally has fashioned to look like a giant spider web encroaching on his kitchen door.

"Get dressed, you're staying for dinner." Sally shouted from the patio while kneeling by the fire-pit to light its cube of kindling, a welding rod in his hand readying to poke at the tumbling flames.

You forget some things when you're hungry — your promises and ideals, the closeness of accidents avoided — and concentrate on eating. The sight of big yellow bowls full of pasta and bread, beaded tumblers of tea, and a blackberry pie cooling near a pot of fresh brewed coffee brought Jenny and Brynnie, Sally's English Springer Spaniels, out of nowhere to lounge on a cushioned futon a few feet away from the patio table. The attended canine lady and her guarding gentleman watchfully studying us all through our dinner.

"We cleaned up your boat. Jackie helped."

"I wish you hadn't."

"There was quite a lot of your clothing in the cockpit. Some of it we heaved. The rest of it Jackie washed and folded and put on the galley table. Your wife's robe, at least, I assumed it was hers, was torn up pretty badly. I put what was left of it in a paper bag on your bed. Hope that was all right."

"I thought maybe it was Red that had come aboard and cleaned up the mess."

"No, he was still too pissed off at you to lend a hand."

"Wants to hang me by my nuts, does he?"

"You said it, not me."

"I owe you, Sally," I said rather meekly. "Thank you."

"Stop it. Friends don't owe friends anything. Besides, if I'd left all your shit where I found it one of your neighbors would have called the sheriff before you had a chance to explain yourself."

"Thank you."

"You're welcome. Now, we've a bit of business to take care of."

Sally brought up the matter of the unfinished ornamental gate Dianna had commissioned him to build for our Seattle garden.

"I'm afraid each half of the gate is going to weigh out at about one hundred and eighty pounds. Thing is, each gate support will require that its seven-foot-high axle has its own dead-man post at the base. And you'll want that dead-man to be made of steel and buried three feet below grade. Use plenty of rebar and Portland cement. Don't use fencepost mix. Don't use any of that pancake batter of river rock and mortar mix the way you did on last year's piece. Promise me."

"Can I see it?"

"No."

"Rusted shut already is it, Jenny?"

I looked down at the smaller of Sally's two bird dogs. The dog lifted her head from the arm of the lounge to look at me, a sad ambivalence in her eyes at the notion of any gate being allowed to rust shut.

"Be nice, or we'll see to it that your gate never closes." Sally winked at the dog. "Won't we, Jenny-girl? Actually Mark, I was wondering how you would feel about, about bringing Dianna by to be the first to see it. Would she come?"

I watched Sally adjust the black frames of his steel-speck-led eye-glasses and run his long fingers thru the thick brown waves of his long hair, a model's forehead wrinkling his light tan darker.

"That may take some doing, Sal."

"Would next week work for both of you?"

My brain was scrambling how best to elaborate on Di-anna's despondency, how much detail it wanted to dissect and hide from him before sharing what would still amount to false excuses.

"It's difficult for her, for us to — it's been difficult this year for me to find the Dianna you remember."

"Everyone's different, huh? Some people keep hurting long after the rest of us have exhausted ourselves."

I could feel the real truth coming on in the back of my throat. Feel its quivering ugliness about to strap the facial muscles around my lips and take away all interest in what's living and breathing outside of my shell. Feel the edges of a memory much older than that of Jessie's death begin to tighten, feel the dryness of its ageless life about to crack a tear or two from my eyes. But, as quickly as the anxious feeling had rushed me, its ugliness teetered back under my control, a friend of so many years gone by.

"We lost a child once. A beautiful baby girl. She died four days after we brought her home."

Sally let go of a deep and distressing breath.

"I never knew that, Mark. I never knew that you and your wife had lost a child."

"It was an awful time, Sal. Awful hardly tells the whole of it. After the baby died, Dianna found a way to love Jessie all the more. Some years, it was only Jessie she loved. That's how she coped with the loss of our child. Found another life to love all the more. And now that she's lost Jessie. Well, I guess you know how she feels."

"And you?"

"Me?"

"How have you been dealing with the loss of Jessie?"

"I think about it all the time. I always will."

Sally fussed with the blackberry pie, turning the glazed pie plate back and forth in half circles on the table. And there was a breeze to pass over the patio to seal the stillness within our shared glances.

"Well, shit." Sally spoke softly. "I sure put my foot in it, didn't I? No offense, but I think this may be the last god-damn garden gate I ever make for anyone."

"Don't say that," I said. "Don't say that."

But what I wanted most to do right then and there was to open his unfinished gate and run. Find a rock in some other's garden where nothing was known of me and crawl under it. Drink and shrink and take down whatever groveling thing inside me would never be completely quieted, return to a place where no explanation, no waning pilgrimage, or promised allegiance to anyone existed.

"Let's eat that pie now, Sally." I extended my hand to Sally's arm, and the day began a second time. He did not comment or stare at my injured wrist.

"Okay Mark. Okay. Good idea."

When the table was cleared Sally and I walked around the pond to its hill of trees and turf, the pocket view to the channel below us a waxing of the ocean's blue heart and the sky's silver tongue and each of us doing our best to tailor our conversation to a pearl-sized point of understanding of the other's life.

We finished our walk under the drip line of the studio's great canvas sail, where Sally patted me on the back before jumping onto the stage. He whistled and displayed a hand signal for the dogs to join him. Jenny and Brynn quickly jumped on stage and the three of them, dogs and man, curled their upper lips in anticipation of some exciting thing about to take place. Sally smiled at me, pointing at the sniffing dogs and mouthing the word *biscuits* while he straddled a weight bench.

"Spot me, will you?"

Sally had already begun bench-pressing what looked like a shortened car axle; a crooked crowbar with motorcycle wheels welded to each end, tires still mounted and the tread splitting in spots where canoe-shaped cuts and sidewall print understated the true weight of each tire's concrete tubing. After several repetitions he invited me to take the bench. I pressed the weight six times. His turn. Mine. Again, until he was up to twelve repetitions on his fourth set and I was down to four and massaging my sore shoulder.

"I feel like an automobile mechanic." I said, nearly out of breath. I couldn't imagine the lifting of a small car — even the front end of a Volkswagen bug, which Jimmy used to do in high-school while I frantically worked to change the car's tire — being any more difficult than the engineless remnants of the motorcycle I'd felt I'd just violently hoisted over my head.

"You're welcome to use the *garage* anytime." Sally pointed to a roped off corner of the stage. "Chin-up bar over there, Jimmy's jump ropes, Joey's old bike, pond, shower facilities, fruit and vegetable bars all over the campus." He waved for me to follow him. "Come on, the dogs and me are going for a walk. We want you with us. Take all of an hour. Have a guy like you back here in two."

We closed the compound's backyard gate behind us. Sally signed another hand written message in the air and the dogs bolted up the road. Gravel and dust and the wings of all the dogs gone by flying right behind them, and with them, the dirt road ahead of us becoming an air-strip in the midst of some sputtering getaway gone bad gone roaring good again.

A cloud of dust to follow, which would flank the road with ingots of gold and the taste of chalk. The dogs running free and safe and with purpose along the slurry edges of their canopied tunnel of light and smoke.

"Now that's a pretty sight."

"They love to run, especially Brynnie. That asinine circus they came from kept them kenneled day and night. For a while I was fearful it had squeezed the spirit out of Brynn. But by the looks of this dust storm I guess I was wrong, huh?"

"Guess you were. Guess you are."

We walked comfortably up the center of the deserted road. The dogs slowing some to bark a squirrel up a tree before resuming their spirited run towards the creek. When we caught up to them at the bridge, both dogs were up to their brown eyes in the rushing water. Sally and I took up positions on opposite sides of the one-lane wooden bridge, content to watch and listen to Brynn and Jenny fish for crab-sized rocks on the bottom of the mountain creek. Their heads dripping and snorting and dipping again to paw at rocks too big even for Brynn to move.

Within minutes of leaving the bridge, we were hiking up the perpetually shady side of the island's highest mountain. The trail up the mountain was well maintained, highway wide and pine-needled at the base of the mountain, brazen switchbacks of loose stone to maneuver nearer the top where the trail unfolded its last mile along the ridge of a basalt cliff.

We reached the top of the mountain in well under an hour. Sally pointed to an overgrown foot-path which would take us to a small parking lot and a stone tower. At a picnic table at the base of the parking lot's observation tower, Brynn and Jenny settled by our feet. The view was spectacular. To the east and southeast, a noble assemblage of islands lumbering in the water like a majestic herd of African elephants wetted and mud-creamed and sloshing in the evening light. At least, it was pleasant to think such a view existed.

The hike back was fast and strenuous, an easy jog at times, and we arrived at Sally's backyard gate with plenty of daylight left. Before I said goodnight, Sally and the dogs thanked me again for the use of my boat last winter. Seems the three of them had slept there like kings and queen on my boat whenever the island had lost power. It didn't take much imagination to see the family of three standing before me jostling for more space under my bed's down comforter. I scratched and rubbed Brynn and Jenny, but stood uncomfortably rigid against the musculature of Sally's body when he gave me a long and powerful hug.

I made my way back to the marina, showered and dressed, and prepared to take the ferry over to Depot Island. I did not encounter Red, nor did I go out of my way to look for him.

The cottage door to my wife's furnished room was partially open, but I knocked anyways before stepping into the room's dim light. A thin black frame awaiting the arrival of a photograph, any photograph, could not have portrayed Dianna's bleakness more justly than the skeletal sway which greeted me from a corner of the room, on the other side of her single bed. The small bed was unmade, and though it might have seemed more deeply set into a corner than the rest of the furnishings, only because my mind pushed it to that spot so often, it was not. She stood in her white linen summer dress in her white wallpapered room, and when her gaze passed thru me I felt certain that she knew more of Jessie's life and death than she would ever speak of. Her linen dress covered her to a point of pressure just above her ankles and bare feet, where it trembled ever so slightly from the nervous touch of her fingers on the cloth's waist line.

The cottage room is a bedroom, only it's not really, it's not a bedroom. A child's antique wicker rocker in one corner of the room, in a motionless corner where memories are placed to bear witness to another's stillness. A stuffed toy rabbit alone in the rocker, tall as a child, its carrot stick of orange tweed the only vibrant color in the room. A rabbit which is made to tremble behind the antique wicker rocker in a corner of the room, did I say that? One wall in the square room is salamander in color. The woodwork along the walls of the floor some sort of shade of putty. The oak floors, less than autumn's color, narrow the room. The door to this quiet space a picture frame like all the other doors in all the other places my wife and I have walked thru.

"You don't want to be here."

"No."

"With me?"

"With anyone."

"For Jimmy?"

"Why do you run me down with the same dialogue every time, Dianna? Why do you do that?"

"I'm sorry."

The softness of her crying. The insurmountable guilt it would know.

"Why do you come back here, Dianna? Why did you choose this month?"

"I don't know. I don't know — I don't know." Her face is as pale as her scream withheld behind her softly spoken hysteria.

"How much misery did you pay for this time?"

She sat on the edge of the bed, her limp wrists burying her fingers into the folds of her lap.

"Do you ever think about *us*, Mark?" A new gentleness about her helping to mend her voice.

I looked at the spindly black rocker and a painting of an old barn in another corner of the room. Outside the window by her bed, in a window box, red zinnias stiffened in the shade of a passing shadow. Inside, on the window sill, a tray of stubby candles had melted cold.

"Of course I do," I answered.

"Is it Jessie's death that still reminds you of — of our own loss?"

There were no trains on any of the islands but I know I heard one coming, felt it tunneling beneath this room's very foundation, heard its ear-piercing whistle inside these walls. And I saw a solitary soul cringing inside its single carriage. I saw Jessie crouching, I did not see *us*.

"Oh Mark, please say something."

"I feel like everything around us is dying and the right thing to do is to hurry it along."

"You believe that? You honestly believe that?"

Something pockmarked and deformed bellowed inside me after she had confronted me. But it was not a sickening face, it was the face of truth and I could not stop its anger from coupling with what must have been the savagery of Jessie's last swim.

"When I was a boy, God was promised to me. And when I grew up I found only this — this shit life."

There was a depression in the air in the room, a depravity which set more of my belief in motion.

"I mean it, Dianna, that's what pounds my head mad every time I think about her — your merciful god's broken promises. And you and everyone like you would bow down to such a savage. Shame on you. Shame on anyone who would bow down to such deceit."

"And you think you are the first soul on this earth to feel

that way? This is the life we have, Mark. It's not a perfect thing. It's not about waiting for happiness to come and go. It's all wrapped up and picking its way apart. It's just life, a chance to love."

"I'm not like everyone else. I'm not like you."

"That is trite of you to say such a thing. Anyone can say it."

There was no television in the room, no radio, no doorway greetings from unarmed callers to carry me away.

"You only deepen the rut for all of us. You've become like the rat that is given a little arsenic each day until it can eventually tolerate a great poisoning."

"No, that's what you and Jimmy have become!"

But she was right in another way. I was like an unwanted rat in her cottage room, a creature searching for a way out and fearing the door at the same time.

"And you would make her into an angel — to punish us — to punish yourself. Beautiful, innocent Jessie. Far from it."

"How dare you. Jessie never brought an ounce of darkness into anyone's life. But you did."

I looked into Dianna's eyes and saw the trembling of a winter sparrow, saw the greatness of an unstoppable receding.

"I'm losing you, aren't I?"

Her eyes ominous and blackened and wishing to filter out the part of me they'd just seen. Eyes whose retreat extended far beyond the limits of her insomnia, and whose sunken stare was begging me not to remind her who she was or where she was or the place we were moving towards. Enormous, fearful eyes. My own cruelty imagining her dress slipping from her shoulders and dropping to the floor, where I might watch the nestling flesh of her stomach and thighs creep towards me on her hands and knees, believing completely that I had reduced this woman to the very seed of everything repulsive and self-destructive in our marriage.

I could not help her. I could not say to my wife *of all the molds available for mortal consumption, choose this one.* I managed only to sit with her on the unmade bed so that I might separate myself from her drooling stare, thoughtlessly mentioning Salvador's gate and talking of the hay barn we'd known in our youth and which was now someone's island home. She wept. And I held her. And her body became more rigid, her eyes continuing to hold me in their catatonic stare of the distant harbor lights locked outside the room's window frame. And for both of us the darkest time existed for the longest hour inside the quiet bedroom.

CHAPTER FOUR

"Loosen that line and lock the motor's tiller arm, will you." Jimmy hummed.

I shifted the boat's engine into reverse and stood to take hold of the long wooden tiller arm in the center of the cockpit.

"Alright, push off." I said.

Jimmy's body danced from the dock to the bow of my boat, his wide grin showing off his gleaming white teeth and leading the way. Onboard, his well oiled arms casually found the boat's boom and folded sail, his stage at sea to show off his bust of copper-tone conceit and bottled anticipation. I had to admit, even without the gifts of a model's face or fairy-tale hair, his forty-six year old body often drew second looks from younger men and could pin back the irises of women caught staring at his body.

"Watch your starboard side, Mark." Jimmy pointed. "Hell of a gnarly stump just beneath the surface. There, by your shoulder. See it?"

I nodded.

"Cigar?"

He threw me the cigar's plastic tube before I could tell him that I knew about the submerged stump. It really hadn't grown much since last year's lesson. I clicked the engine back into neutral. The motor moaned and then quieted to a wilted grumble.

"Thanks," I said. "This your smoking apology?"

"That's the spirit," his voice prancing across the bow.

I shifted the outboard motor into forward gear, twisted the throttle, and we made our usual wide swing around Red's store to meet the channel's current.

"Take us to higher ground, Mr. J." Jimmy spewed, throwing me his gold-plated lighter with its battered palm tree shadings of emerald and ivory. "But first I've got to go over to Depot Island and bury another piece of her. What else would she have us do?"

Jimmy's remarks regarding Jessie's death had been delivered in a cold, almost dismissive tone, and produced a chill of anger in me that a father should find it an inconvenience to visit the site of his daughter's death. But I kept my mouth shut, watching him step back from the bow to slide back the boat's hatch cover. Down he went and up hopped the trapeze sounds of jazz into our pulpit. Music, the leash of our obedient promise not to talk too much, too long, or too honestly of all that was missing on our boat.

Jimmy fiddled with the cover on the mainsail, while I did little more than listen to the water slapping at the hull. A bit of a hall monitor at times, his presence onboard at least restrained some of my bodily indulgences, and always there was a discipline about him which injected a serious element of confidence to my limited sailing skills.

Across the channel, some distance away from the treatment cottages on the bluff, the morning sun was beginning to paint the corners of a fenced off pasture; that same sort of invigorating light that could cause my students in Seattle to flirt with sleeveless Friday afternoons in June and September.

"Keep the pulpit buttoned on Jackie's barn. Straight ahead

until you reach that buoy near her raft. Then hard to starboard and shut her down. See that ferry? She's about ready to leave the dock. So make allowances in your throttle speed as we motor closer. You know the drill."

After last summer's near crash with a floating green and white acre of ferry, Jimmy was always captain on my boat irregardless of which one of us was at the helm. As a boy, for one year I had sailed the shorelines of these islands in my centerboard and had come to know the confidence that a small boat can generate in a beginner sailor. But aboard this thirty-two foot slice of heaven, I had quickly regressed to loving the image of sailing more than the attentive skill and planning these cold waters required of all sailors.

"What kind of *bounce* you got brewing in the kitchen today?" Jimmy asked, his red tank-top and yellow visor jump-roping the question he'd asked.

"My what?"

"The *bounce,* that Seattle coffee bean you're so fond of."

"Here, take the tiller, and I'll go get you a cup."

"No, no, no. You stay right where you are. I'm gonna make half a sailor out of you yet." He pointed across the channel at four stories of ferryboat. "Better open your throttle a bit if you're going to get across before she sets her course. Your sail's not up, remember? So don't assume you have the right of way."

I did as he instructed, and at once felt a stronger current slapping at the hull.

"Feel that? A smaller boat would be slapped sideways silly in this tide change. I'm going below."

"No you're not. You're going to remain on deck and help me out."

"Christ, you've enough booze down here to carry us clear thru to Australia, even if we go by way of Cape Cod." From below deck he let out another soft guttural moan. "Jesus, where was he hiding it all?"

"Knock it off and come up here. We're closing in on the buoy and that raft."

"Ah, Seattle mud. So this is why you stay in the city."

From the galley stairs, he sipped his coffee and mumbled something more about how uncluttered the cabin looks when I was not lying face down on its floor. More stalling tactics meant to toy with my anxiety.

"Relax, will you. It's the state's motor pool I'm worried about you crashing us into. Here," he threw me one of the life-jackets he'd brought up from the fore cabin and cast the other aside, "better put one on."

"You're not helping things. Get over here."

"Think of me as a stress test."

Without putting any real thought into the consequences I turned the boat hard to starboard, and at the same time used my free hand to take hold of the motor's throttle grip and power down the engine fast as I could. The sharpness of the boat's turn, combined with the sudden loss of engine power, knocked Jimmy backwards to the galley floor and sloshed the boat hard against Jackie's raft of metal drums and rotting wood. From beneath the raft's wooden deck, the metal drums thumped and banged their surprise at our early arrival.

"What the hell were you thinking?" Jimmy was struggling to right himself on the galley floor.

"Oh, only that evidently things on water appear much closer than they do from land."

"Jesus Christ, you can't just cut back on the throttle when you're in the middle of turning a boat this size."

"What do you mean, I can't. I just did."

"If I didn't know what a shitty sailor you are, I might think you'd done it on purpose."

"You think?"

On his feet again, Jimmy tried taking hold of a teaching moment.

"There's no wind to deal with this morning. But if there was, you might have bit that rocky shoreline but good. And the tide's coming in strong. Something you seem to always pay absolutely no attention to."

Jimmy took the helm.

"Always think current and wind, Mark. Remember? Don't think one without thinking the other up. Maneuver with those two killers in mind. Here, get your ass over here and take the tiller."

He had me slowly circle the buoy a half dozen times until I got a better feel for the tide's influence on the boat.

"Let's see you anchor this beast. Just remember that your boat's anchor will have a longer scope than a mooring line. Pretend Jackie's raft is another boat when calculating your swing circle. Go on, get to it."

I repeated last year's course on anchoring in "twelve-and-a-half too fucking long minutes," as Jimmy so mildly put it. While I was pulling up the folding grapnel he asked what he inevitably always got around to asking me on the boat — why I had bought the boat in the first place.

"— that, and because I like being transported to places unknown in the middle of the night."

"You could have done that with any boat. Why a sailboat?"

"I don't like engine noise." It was part of the truth.

"But why did you buy such a big boat?"

"I need more elbow room than most people."

"But you sleep alone," he persisted. "And anyhow, how much elbow room do you need when you're flat out not moving on the galley floor?"

"We had a plan. Remember?"

"I let go of it. Why can't you?"

"That's good, a good comeback. That, I'll remember."

"Why not build yourself another. Why not build yourself a small A-frame over on Depot Island. You know, kind of a sailboat on its ass. Suits your general posture these days."

"I don't know, Jimmy, it's a mystery to me."

I looked to the shoreline hoping to find a reprieve from his antagonism. A small aluminum boat napped on dry ground under the canopy of a nearly leafless apple tree. A thin chain collared the boat to the tree's tremendous cankerous trunk, and nearby, a slip of a beach was about to be swallowed by the tide. Healthier looking fruit trees had been planted on the grassy slope upside the older shoreline tree, enough of them so that one might reasonably call the collection of trees an orchard, and some of the young saplings still bearing white blossoms. Bordering the property's line of fruit trees, several thickets of heavy blackberry canes had been pruned back to give the drip-line of the new orchard room to breathe and find sunlight. A lush, sloping green field dominated the property and cut its way up to a mid-century house barn.

I felt the boat lift and then settle back into the water, her port side giving the gentlest of hugs to the raft's almost breathless welcome. Jimmy shut the engine off.

"Now what? Jumping jacks and push-ups?"

"Tie us off, old man."

I wrapped a line over a jingling cleat and ran a second line thru a couple of the raft's rotting floorboards.

"All this now belongs to a woman you just hired to work in the bar?"

"*Jackie*. She bought the place last fall. Not all of it. Just the five acres from the barn to the beach. I told you that last winter. Wants to raise children or chickens, I can't remember which. There she is, up on the roof again."

Jackie's backside faced the water, her brown canvas overalls and her wide-brimmed straw hat steadily moving her slim body across the barn's green corrugated metal roof. A climber's harness and rope linked her to some unseen crampon on the other side of the barn's steeply pitched roof.

"Jackie and I thought a meeting at her place would be a nice way to coax you out of your cave and go over a few things that have changed at the *Campground*."

"Today? Now?"

"A couple of hours, that's all. Then we'll sail. Make our way over to Timberlee Harbor this afternoon. Hey, easy. You'll like her. She's a teacher herself. Trust me, she won't preach. Okay, you alright with this?"

"Doesn't look like I have a choice."

"Wait here, I'll get you a cab." Jimmy stepped off the boat and onto the raft, and seconds later dove into the ocean's ice.

I watched Jackie's foot fish for the ladder at the barn roof's copper gutter line while Jimmy swam to shore. When her feet were on the ground Jackie unsnapped the rope from her harness, gave a wheelbarrow a polite push to the side of a stack of boards, and walked under the cover of a grape arbor that shadowed the rubble foundation of what had once been the farm's milk room.

The old cow barn breathed new colors. A half-painted, tangerine-colored cupola christened the roofline. And many of the barn's original wide planked boards had been replaced with sun-bleached lumber about to receive their first coat of mahogany stain. A new split rail fence marched alongside the barn's five-foot high fieldstone foundation, the climbing rosebushes planted at each of the six cedar posts beginning to paint the rails with green leaves, and the rise and fall of Jackie's yellow rubber boots in the tall field grass to frame the perfect postcard. The hopscotch movements of her legs hurrying her long stride towards the shore. The wishful, precious imprint of seeing Dianna's linen dress flutter loosely over Jackie's suspenders, her hips, the other's bare feet. And the sight of Jimmy, on shore, squeezing the saltwater from his ponytail and waving Jessie to hurry along.

"Where are your manners, Jimmy?" Jackie playfully warned him from the edge of the field. Jimmy sticking his tongue out at her as she brushed by him on her way to her little boat.

"Hi Mark, I'm Jacquelyn. Please don't feel you have to swim to shore like this old show-off. I do have a boat for my guests."

With Jimmy's help Jackie nudged the small boat into the water and rowed out to the raft.

"It's a pleasure to meet you."

"It's nice to finally meet you, Jacquelyn."

"I hope you don't mind a dirty seat?"

"Not at all. Beats swimming."

"Definitely."

In her rocking boat I shook hands with Jackie and took my seat in the bow.

"You've done wonders with the place."

"I've had a lot of help. Sally has been an inspiration."

"Do you have family out here, Jackie?"

"No. All my family lives in New England. Connecticut, mostly."

"So you're the maverick in the family?"

"I wouldn't say that. It took me more than ten years to work up my goodbyes. Sometimes, I feel like I'm still saying them."

"Oh?"

"Yeah, my dad and I are real close."

"Well, by the looks of your new home you seem to have found work that suits you."

"That's exactly what my dad said when I sent him pictures. And he's right, the work really does suit me. I'm discovering a passion for renovation I didn't know was in me."

The little boat scraped the shore.

"He's old, Jackie," Jimmy patted me on the back when I was on solid ground, "but he remembers everything. It's a kind of birth defect with this guy. So guard your family secrets if you've got any."

"Don't you have a marathon or two to run this morning, Mr. Jim?"

"I'm going, I'm going." Jimmy seized the little boat and pushed off.

"Something I said, Jimmy?" Jackie asked sarcastically, watching him row back to the raft.

"Left my running shoes on the boat, smarty pants."

"You don't run barefoot?"

"I will if you will."

"Are you really going for a run?" I called out to him.

"One of us got to keep the faith. You two run along to the office. I'll be back in under an hour."

"Take your time." Jackie said. "Change a tire for someone. Plow a field."

"See you, Jimmy."

"Yup."

"Shall we walk up to the house, Mark? I need water and some lemonade."

We walked thru the lower field to the grassy service road hidden behind the property's blackberry hedge, Jackie telling me how much she was enjoying working at the *Campground* and asking how much the tourist season would change the complexion of the islands.

"If not for the long ferry lines you'd hardly know the tourists were here. So tell me, where did you teach?"

"I taught American literature at a small New England prep school for nine years."

"What made you leave it all behind?"

"Would you believe the poor pay and a —" she stopped walking long enough to punctuate the airborne syllables of her next word with her forefinger — "*ex-tin-guish-ing* career as coach of their lacrosse team?"

"Yes ma'am, that I would."

"Actually, my grandmother. I was eight years old the first time I visited these islands with her. Gram used to proclaim that the very best vacations in life were the ones where you behaved like rabbits on the way out of town and turtles on the way back. It took Gram and me just four days to drive from the east coast to Seattle. But it took us seventeen nights and eighteen days to get back to Hartford. Before Gram died she left me a little something and asked that I spend a little of it out west remembering our trip. Guess what, Gram? I spent it *all* out west."

"Good for her. Good on you."

"What about you? You teach mathematics is that correct?"

"Yes."

"Oh, say. I left a message for you and your wife —"

"Yes, I got it. Sorry I didn't get back to you." My words rushed out from behind my tight-lipped smile. *How to explain, how much to explain, how many bandaging words this time to squelch a stranger's interest in my personal affairs.*

"It was probably terribly insensitive of me to leave a house-warming invitation for you and your wife with Red. It's only that, at the time, Jimmy thought it would be the surest way to reach you. And I did so want you and your wife to know that you are welcome here. Always."

At the top of the hill a rusty chain linked two massive stumps on either side of the service road. Mossy and needled, the tree stumps rested like fallen kings in an otherwise uneventful after-life. I stopped and pressed my handprint against the shaded side of one of the spongy stumps.

"Don't apologize," I said. "She's been — my wife's been dealing with depression for a couple of years." I released my handprint on the stump and watched its mossy coat spring back like a sponge in water. "I don't suppose Jimmy's spoken much about his daughter's death. You know about it though, of course."

"Yes, some part of it."

A tiny bulb of earlobe peeked out from under Jackie's tasseled hair and made me think of holidays and holiday ornaments.

"Jessie drowned a year ago. Almost a year ago. Everyone that knew her has had a rough time with it. Understanding it."

"My heart goes out to both of you."

"Do you know that my wife and I haven't been asked out as a couple for over a year? So you see, Jackie, your invitation was really very thoughtful and kind."

"Good, then it's a standing invitation. And in the meantime, please know that you are both always welcome here. Even if I'm not here, Mark, please tell your wife she is most welcome to come here anytime she wants."

"Thank you. It's not likely she'll visit anytime soon. But if you haven't already put a cross and skull bones next to my name, I would love to come to your house-warming."

"Absolutely, please do." She brushed her hair away from a bothersome bee and I saw the sleek folds and the thinly carved lines of the whole ornament; her ear perfectly pitched, as delicate as a finely cut porcelain but with an Irish pulse. "And don't loose faith. It is such a rare commodity these days but so often it is powerful enough to help us heal."

We walked to the barn's old fieldstone steps which led

to a coarsely laid stone and mortar floor of a milk house long since demolished and removed. The milk house floor now spotted with granite and field stone and presently functioning as the home's showpiece patio.

From the patio we entered Jackie's kitchen. Yellow pine flooring beautifully knotted and square-nailed. Two of the barn's original carrying beams spanning the width of the barn and helping to define the air space above the open kitchen; the tremendous beams carrying evidence of an ancient fire and the fresh markings of a carpenter's chisel, most of the checkered briquettes left behind by the fire's surface burn having been meticulously chipped away to reveal each beam's structurally sound wood.

"My chapel. You like it?"

"Gorgeous. You must take on the day's work with the appetite of a sea otter."

Jackie poured lemonade into tall orange tumblers. Made of salvaged hatch-covers, the kitchen countertops looked colossal in weight and dimension and bore a deep ebony coloring between straps of galvanized metal. Under the countertop, plank shelving had been installed inside Salvador's open ended steel cabinetry, a design which evidently intended no door fronts ever be attached. Overall the design was pleasantly industrial, something along the lines of a stilted boardwalk attempting to bridge the usual gaps which follow most any architectural coup.

"No telephone yet. But the electrical work is nearly complete. And the entire barn has plumbing for the first time in its life. I'm thinking of naming the place The Hot Water in a Hay Barn Farm. Rather Ver-mon-tish, don't you think?"

"Maybe you should apply for a bed and breakfast license while you're at it."

"That would mean company every morning, wouldn't it?"
I laughed.

While Jackie placed pickles and yellow peppers over the opaque images of locust fired in clay, I gazed out of one of the barn's great window openings at my rafted boat and across the channel to the empty ferry docks.

"Would you be interested in an early lunch? I'm famished. Fresh croissants and homemade chicken salad. My grandmother's recipe. It's fabulous, I swear. We could make a mint serving it up at the *Campground*."

"Absolutely." I nodded in the direction of leafy rows glowing at the far end of the patio. "Could we eat outside?"

"Yes, of course. It really is too nice a day to waste another minute indoors, isn't it? I'll give you the Yankee tour thru the vegetable garden after lunch, if you like. Historically of no significance, not yet anyways," she skipped by me to the refrigerator, "but the pilgrim in me has got some grand ideas."

"How 'bout you put me to work weeding for an hour? You can fill me in on the bar business while I get my hands dirty. No, no, I want to. I've been cornered in classrooms all year. Besides, I feel like I need to work off some of the baggage I've dumped at your barn door."

"Stop it."

After lunch a careful walk down a slanting row of stringy seedlings, the soil dry and chalky and supporting inch high bean plants all but disappearing into the encroaching field grass by rows end. Up the next row, careful not to step on the tender shoots of squash plants, and me thinking that Jackie's grandmother must have sung the most beautiful nursery rhymes to her granddaughter all the way from Connecticut to Washington because of the way a jump-roper's spring is lifting Jackie's legs over the garden ground.

"This is my real passion," Jackie told me, shielding her eyes from the sun. In the center of the garden a large circle had been cut out, raised, and heavily top-dressed with cocoa-colored soil amendments to feed the tiny sprigs beginning to parade their oddly shaped fins over the mound. "Chinese herbs for sale someday, I hope."

Where the garden began to slope upwards towards a dirt road and her neighbor's rusty barbed-wire fence that had been strung with faded *No Trespassing* signs, Jackie stopped and pointed, informing me that she planned to plant a long hedge row of corn to keep back the dust of passing sightseers.

"I think corn is king in any garden. It'll make a splendid autumn hedge here, don't you think?"

"Has anyone mentioned the deer in the neighborhood?"

"Everyone."

"They'll take this garden down in a day if they find it."

"I thought I might try using some sort of netting."

"That's thoughtful, but they don't eat fish. Ask Sally to borrow his trailer and go over to Anacortes. They've got a decent farm supply store there. Metal lattice works best. Buy the panels, not the flimsy stuff that comes in a roll. If it's in your budget, fence in the entire garden. If not, at least buy enough to protect your herb garden. It's the only way to keep the deer out."

"Well you're a bowl of cherries after you've had your lunch, aren't you?"

I laughed.

We walked back to Jackie's moon shaped herb garden. Jackie grabbed a worn down hoe handle from a nearby clothesline displaying a few shoddy looking hand tools; dull and pitted hoe blades attached to varying handle lengths, the tapered wood handle of one hoe stubby as a ruler, another sized for a giant, two rakes and two weaved bushel baskets, each of the tools hanging from its own hook on the clothesline.

"Your efficiency reminds me of some people I once knew. Only you're doing it so much better."

"What, now you tell a happy story to take away my fear of a deer stampede?"

In far fewer words, I told her of a couple who had cashed out, dropped out, left the city of Seattle and two very promising teaching careers so that they might squat on a scab of an island. How they'd lived out of two canvas cabins for the better part of three years, living like monks the first year — reading, exercising, scrubbing something clean again each morning and evening — and how, by year three, a disabling despondency of spirit had curtailed their experiment.

"Whatever happened to them?" There was genuine interest and at the same time a touch of sadness in Jackie's voice.

"They vanished."

"Vanished?" Nothing ever really vanishes, does it?"

"Precisely."

"Anyone I might come to know?"

"Not even I would recognize either of them, anymore."

It was easy for me not to tell Jackie the whole truth and at the same time not lie to her. It was one of the things Jessie's death had changed about me. What I hadn't told Jackie was that what had started out as wishful thinking, on a ferryboat carrying all of our belongings away from Seattle, had later mutated to become the single parent of my wife's silent prayers and that, together, my wife and I had gone on to experience the mirrored fruitlessness of every one of those prayers when the real nightmare started. It had been so much worse than any shared words could hope to capture, worse than any word I'd dumped in Sally's lap to describe the ordeal. The journey had ended horribly for the couple — had left them heartbroken inside a crumpled and damp cubicle of neighbor-less lighting which had stood watch over their dank comings and goings — had reduced them to mere notes of their former selves which sobbed inside an empty bottle at the bottom of a fire pit each night, this, the only corporal evidence that the couple had ever set up camp on the island's mountain of a hill. No, I did not share everything with Jackie, the details I kept to myself. From the crib to the grave, the details I will always remember to keep to myself, because in that third year of closing her eyes each night, under the pressing weight and madness of grief, before sleep would take her back to a place where no word could speak its power, I watched my wife think of nothing else but the death of our baby.

Jackie had turned away from me to kneel and pull at a velvety clump of weed.

"I've made you uncomfortable."

"It's alright."

"No, it isn't. This is your home. I've no right to advise you or to make trite comparisons."

"Here," she poked me in the arm with the hoe handle, "you can work off an apology."

"Alright, enough said."

I took hold of the short-handled hoe and grabbed a blood-stained bushel basket from the clothesline, the kind of basket New Englanders use when they're picking Macintosh apples on a golden autumn afternoon.

"Are all these plants going to produce gourds?" I asked, noticing the seed envelope that had been slipped over a twig stake.

"I don't know as I've planted enough, really. It's funny, but long after the garden is nothing more than straw and mud these gourds will bring summer back to me. So I like that about them. I like a little of that around me when it's dark at four in the afternoon."

Maybe an hour grows bigger than a day in a garden. In the dry, shade-printed trenches along the lines of green seedlings, along the crumbling slopes of their elfin levees, Jackie and I buried any weed petiole poking its beak thru the soil. We chopped and pulled at the crowns of any plant not part of an orderly soup line. We worked fast and in a determined way, the dull clink of a hoe hitting egg-sized stones, the wire rim of the apple basket creaking and stretching a little more each time we tossed another languid wig of crabgrass into the full basket. More than once I divided a number of bean plants from the streets of their community. *Chop-chop, chop-chop, chop, chop, chop* — there, now the innocent bystanders were small enough to hide from Jackie's evening inspection. I hoed and dug and discovered that Jackie's interests gathered, more often than not, around the good intentions of people than with our blemished causes and failures, in the health of her neighbor's spotted cows and crusty llamas, in the alcoves of their hand-dipped candlelight and smoky cabin laughter which side-saddled their kitchen card games. And, in the talk that fell down upon us like a warm mist, I concluded that not much had changed at *Jimmy's Campground* except the sizable varieties of French-press coffee drinks, and the educational requirements of our waitresses, both of which had gone up considerably.

> *I met an angel along a garden path*
> *We worked and walked and sang sweet songs*
> *And when I stood to thank her*
> *My sweet angel was gone*

When Jimmy returned from his run, I thanked Jackie for lunch and for the expediency with which she had moved me thru the *Campground's* blistering new routines. When I asked if she had been compensated for today's time with me, she planed some of the saltiness off her brow with the tips of her fingers, looked at Jimmy and told me that today was a *done deal,* that the time she had spent with me was repayment for Jimmy's fine job of tilling her garden last month.

At the water's edge it was an uncomfortable arrangement

the way we parted company with Jackie, me climbing into her boat and rowing out to the raft while Jimmy swam alongside. After he rowed the boat back to shore, Jimmy swam back to the raft. I paid his stunts no attention, taking my time loosening the boat lines from the raft's jiggling cleats and pulling a quarter from my pocket to stick deep into a mushy crack of one of the raft's old wooden planks — no particular reason, it just felt like something Juan and Danny might have done to preserve a good memory. I waved once more to Jackie and pushed off.

We found wind a hundred yards off shore. The boat's sail gulped it, worshipped its touch as if the wind had the power to protract a day's sail into a week's passage thru the islands. She enveloped us, this wind, on the fare side of Depot Island, cuffing the Strait's great canvas of water with incandescent shadows, at last, unleashing us from all landlocked smothering routines.

"You ready to raise the spinnaker and let this lady sing?"

Jimmy's back was to me and the spinnaker already noisily slashing in the crease of wind off the bow when I shouted, "Jessie loved to sail, didn't she? Fearless like yourself."

If he heard me he gave no acknowledgment.

We rode the wind around Constitution Point, the boat cutting gracefully thru a sea of slashing blades, our wake eventually brushing the hull of an idling trawler and its spool of pooping crab rings and the spat of flying gulls off the trawler's blue sky stern. The boat's spinnaker soon swallowing whole the sight of two cargo ships in the Strait's shipping lanes. Paddle greetings from a knot of shoreline kayakers and the drab necktie stare of a *cable-crossing* marker on a shoreline ledge of basalt. The icy, marooned peaks of the Olympics unhindered by human sight and sound and thought.

CHAPTER FIVE

WHO'S TO SAY WHAT clues and premonitions have been offered up to us in the playing decks of each and every day gone by; gifts from an unfolding God spewed out upon the islands of the earth in diluted wisps of passing insight.

Slumped on one of the couches by the lounge's sandpit, the bulbous eyes of the strange woman I'd met earlier in the day watched me studying her. The woman was wearing the same outrageous outfit she'd constantly picked at while trying to cool off on Jessie's bench before the bar had opened. Only now, the tapered columns of the woman's wildly striped bell-bottoms were spread out wide as flying saucers over ankle bracelets large as necklaces and a pair of glittering high-heels teetering on the edge of the sandpit, the soles of the woman's child-sized red shoes tapping the air and badgering me whenever this morbidly obese woman caught me studying her from behind the bar. A black leather vest wrapped the woman's yellow halter-top as tightly as any ill-fitting horse harness and pulled at her tremendous jutting chest whenever she laughed with her newfound, mud-spattered, yellow-jacketed bicycle guppies positioning their walnut-sized butts on the bench seating surrounding the pit. Adam, a frail short man twice the woman's age, who I'd come to believe was her husband or lover, sat stiff as a board by the fat woman's side.

I'd met this woman in the afternoon, in the quiet of the courtyard before the *Campground* had opened. From a stone seat, positioned on a diagonal line opposite the teak bench whose commemorative plaque read *In Memory of Jessie Young,* I'd been looking at the delicate black stems of a deer fern growing thru the open rails of the wooden bench. I had not sat alone in the courtyard for quite some time and the sight of the neglected ferns growing from a smudge of bunch-berry, along a rill which no longer spilled water into the cobblestone basin set at the feet of the bench, had triggered a bit of sadness. But my sadness had been pushed aside by the stupefying appearance of this woman, Ottava, opening the courtyard gate and plopping her mushroomed shaped body down on Jessie's bench. For that's when the woman had looked over at me with her sea lion eyes, feigned a smile, and blown me a kiss. The experience had been un-settling, this kiss from a stranger, because the last time I saw Jimmy's daughter alive Jessie had done the same thing to me while sitting on this very bench. Ottava's great size had practically filled the bench from arm rail to arm rail, obliterating the sight of Jessie's plaque in a most annoying manner, and leaving but a shoebox of space available for the old man shuffling towards her. *"I'm Adam, her younger brother,"* the old man had said to me after he'd squeezed in next to Ottava. Adam had then tucked his thumb inside the collar of his polo-shirt and repeatedly tapped his in-dex finger against the shirt before pointing it at the woman about to swallow him. *"My big sister, Ottava."* Considering his wrinkled face and the woman's youth Adam's statement had seemed preposterous to me and I'd almost chuckled, except that at the very moment he had pointed Ottava's fingers had begun to rub at Jessie's plaque in a most insensitive way and she'd asked: *"Who do you suppose Jessie Young was, Adam?"* Adam had solemnly lowered his head before asking: *"Was she someone's sweet child, someone's good friend?"* Ottava answering: *"Oh Adam, all of that and a lot more to someone sitting with us."* At once, Adam had offered an explanation for his companion's smugness, an explanation which he seemed to have memorized and spoken aloud many times: *"She was born with a gift, my wife. Sometimes it is a great gift. Sometimes it is a speck under the footprint of a ladybug. But it has never come with much restraint. And sometimes her need to show it off can be as big as her belly."* Lifting his palms to the sky, he'd added, *"I guess that's where I come in — born into this wicked world to play stage coach driver whenever she's about to get us run out of town."* The fingers on Ottava's hands were like short chubby breadsticks, and she had been in the process of stacking the left four over the right four in a prayerful, herring-bone formation when Adam repeated himself. *"My wife has a gift, she does. She relives events that have happened to other people — fragments of it. Sometimes she sees things that are about to happen, but mostly she relives things."* Annoyed with these two strange penguins, I'd been flippant — *"Hell, I do that every day."* Ottava had scoffed at my response, promptly dropped her hands to her lap and sat up straight as a potato to recite: *"Jessie Young was in love with you. She told you so while she sat on this very bench. In Seattle. When this bench was in Seattle, that's when she told you — in Seattle— in the summer — in a flower garden where a gate is missing. Bet you, bet you not two friends in your whole world know that. Bet you more that no one knows you told her the same things. Pshew! Glad that's done, Adam. Those words were like salt on the roof of my mouth when I thought they might taste like sugar this time. We can walk some more now, darling. Slow as you like, my lovely little man."*

All evening Ottava had done most of the buying for her new fans, voraciously sucking on lemons between sips of straight vodka. When she would laugh her star-fish hands had a habit of playing with the sun-dial jewelry on her wrists, and her body would convulse like a giant sunfish trying to breathe out of water. I could find fault with almost every inch of the woman's scalloped body. But the revelations which Ottava had made earlier, while seated in the courtyard, had been flawless on every count; no one in my world knew what Ottava had somehow plucked from my thoughts, not my wife, not Jessie's father. Somehow, this woman had found wind on a sea that could not possibly have existed outside the confines of my mind.

I wiped away the water circles from the bar in front of Red and Joey, and the memory of Jessie's wishful fingers sleepily parted the drapes from a balcony window — a papery sun drizzling its light thru the blue fog in the bay to dry some of her tears before she came back to my bed, her colorless lips trembling like the fallen wings of a dying bird at sea.

Red and Joey had been comfortably seated at the bar for the better part of Joey's dinner break. Both men taking turns digging into each other's views on religious scripture and the likelihood that the islands would be overrun with condominiums and jet skis one day. Even with all the chatter coming from the lounge, and the scraping of chairs in the *Campground's* dining room, I've still been able to hear Red's algae-laced rubber boots regularly squishing against the bar's foot rail; something Red always does when he's fed up with Joe's refusal to allow logic a seat at the bar. For the moment, religion is getting top billing over each man's beliefs about regulating urban growth boundaries. But apparently, Joey has just swallowed some sort of verbal bait I'd not heard Red cast out, because Red is now dressing his lines with his take on the story of Adam and Eve — the incestuous interpretation — which, understandably, Joey wants no part of. It's no town secret that Joey's never happy when Red stoops to the brother-sister argument to explain Genesis. So when I notice Joe's dinner fork has begun to strum like a drum stick against one of Hazel's untouched dinner rolls, I pretty much know what's going to spill out onto my bar. Joey huffs, and for a second the glare in his eyes looks like a flare gun about to fire a warning shot over Red's frizzy hair.

"That's blasphemy, Red."

With his wolfish hairline, blemished forehead, and his shrunken white T-shirt all lurching over his dinner plate, Joey looks like an angry inmate seated in a prison cafeteria.

"I-I, I suppose you agree with Red, Mr. Jacobs? You not being a regular at bible study and all."

"Been in and out of strip-mall kingdoms my whole life, Joe. But I appreciate you taking notice that I wasn't in class last week."

"Seriously Red," Joey's already turned away from my remarks to pick up where he left off with Red, "what kind of Christian would question Genesis?"

"I carry my own pew, Joe." Red answered, winking at me before spitting tobacco juice over the lip of his empty coffee mug.

A bizarre, bottle-neck bruising of human heads erupts on the porch steps and puts a premature end to tonight's church services at the bar. Giggling scraps of laughter come with the commotion going on outside. Stomping feet and bumping backpacks and the hammering of porch boards hoofing something less than music, something more than the usual turbulence of approaching customers. School children! A whole herd of them within inches of molesting the *Campground's* screen door.

The moment took me. My hand took hold of Joey's forearm and held it tightly to the bar. I stared expressionless at the pudgy faces smothering the outside, bottom half of the bar's screen door and began to recite, from memory, something wicked from psalms.

"'And He will send down fire upon the sinful. Fire and sulfur and burning wind will be the cup they drink. For the Lord is right and good.' Come in, children."

The school children quieted and stared up at me wide-eyed and laughing.

"Blasphemy?" I smiled and looked into Joey's startled eyes. "Yes, guilty as charged."

Joey scowled, picked up his dinner plate, and got up from his barstool.

On the porch, first in line behind the screen door, is Claire, Hazel's daughter.

"Hi Joe!" Claire says, pressing her nose against the screen. "We're all here because there's a bomb on our ferry. But they brought two German Shepherds on board. So the bomb probably won't go off."

"Claire, quiet in line please." One of the teachers instructed from the top of the porch stairs.

"Children, form a line please." A second teacher has approached the screen door to girdle the ruckus Claire has sparked in her classmates. "Quietly please. Once inside I would like everyone to form an orderly line against the wall. There is to be no talking until we have been seated. Best behavior, girls. Understood? Clair, would you be kind enough to show us the way?"

Once half the island's schoolyard was inside, Jackie wasted no time walking the children single-file around the fireplace and seating the group in the farthest corners of the dining room. When she walked back to the bar, she did so at a sprinter's pace.

"You heard the news?" Joey asked her.

"The entire bar heard."

Red backed off his bar stool. "I better get back to the marina and see what this is all about."

"Send up word if you hear anything about another ferry coming in to take people home, would you Red?"

"Will do, Jackie."

"Well, there's nothing we can do for the time being but prepare for a crowd, is there?" Jackie dusted the edge of the bar with her penciled fingertips. "We'll probably know as much about it as anyone by the end of the night."

"I better get to helping Hazel." Joe said, and headed towards the kitchen door with his dishes.

"You ready, mister?"

"They all gonna want something different, aren't they?"

"A bartender's nightmare. You ready?"

"Go ahead, girl."

"Twenty-five Shirley Temples. And two cappuccinos for our over worked class-mates."

"Oh, that's funny."

I started in on the drinks, one punch-bowl at a time.

Jackie grabbed her tray and headed for the kitchen. A volcanic hiss from Hazel's grill and the thundering clamor of Joey's dishwashing billowed out from the kitchen and into the bar, as Jackie reached the kitchen doors. Another prism of cooking and cleaning noise erupted, which Jackie patiently waited to settle before entering Hazel's kitchen. One more rally of hissing and sizzling sounds, and something in Hazel's motherly voice that suggested she was trying to calm something in Joe, before I could hear Jackie placing her dinner orders.

"Hazel, are you ready for the single largest order of the day?"

"Go ahead, sweetie."

"Fourteen cheeseburgers, eleven macaroni-and-cheese dinners, and ten baskets of French fries. Oh, and Hazel, two nice dinner salads for the teachers. Please."

"Got it. Joe says my Claire's out there?"

"Yes, she's here. She's organizing an anti-terrorist, soccer squad team to track down all *weird-wacko-ferryboat-bombers*."

"That sounds like my Claire alright." Before the kitchen door floated shut Hazel called out — "that's my boy, Mr. Joe. Slice and dice and dish it up fast. No cookie cutter shapes necessary. These are local kids, not tourists."

The *Campground's* screen door opened and a family of five entered the bar, the parents and grandparents posturing to take up as little space as possible along the windowed wall, the boy with them eagerly stepping out of the line his family had formed, his shoulders held back by the hands of his grandfather. When Jill walked by the family, a basket of Hazel's braided rolls in her hand, the boy's face posted a wishing well smile and his head tilted back to search for his grandfather's approving eyes. The women in the family smiled warmly at the boy, striking-looking women, white-haired herons in blue denim blazers, black jeans, and cowboy boots. The men shifting in place like chicken-footed dumplings. Weariness on the faces of the adults, but the boy looking spellbound by the canoe hanging from the ceiling and by the liveliness of the circus colors gathered around the sandpit.

"Would you like to seat your family at to the bar while you're waiting for a table, son?"

The boy looked to his grandfather.

"Look at the gentleman behind the bar and answer him, son."

"I don't think I'm old enough, sir."

"Oh? How old are you?"

"I'm nine and a half, sir."

"Well, the *half's* real important. Last night we had a nine year old in here. Sat right up here at the bar half the night, drinking my free lemonade and talking my head off about skateboards." I finished dropping cherries into the last of the Shirley Temples. "Ate a whole basket of home-made buns too, come to think of it."

"With extra butter on them?"

"Hey, you're beginning to look familiar. You sure that wasn't you sitting here at the bar last night?"

"No sir, never!"

"What's your name?"

"My name's Gordon, sir."

"Well Gordon, here's the deal. No one seems to be leaving the dining room very quickly tonight. In fact, it's your good luck that these barstools are empty. As for you being under age, well, with the ferries running behind schedule tonight I don't think anyone will take exception. My advice, Gordon — your best chance of finding a seat tonight might just be to bring your family over to the bar, quick like. And while you're doing that and making the introductions, I'll fix your family whatever they would like to drink. On the house, of course."

"Home-made buns too, sir?"

"You bet, Gordon. Free buns, too."

"Can we Grandpa? It's free!"

Ten o'clock came and went and ushered in the fatigue of half past eleven. All evening Jill had worked the porch crowd, serving the rattled and the stranded as many cartons of macaroni-and-cheese and petite loafs of gingerbread as plates emptied of key-lime pie and berry cobbler she'd brought back to the kitchen. Jackie had handled the crowd in the dining room and lounge with her usual good humor and only two good hands, a brain like a calculator, and some thoughtful editing. And thru it all, she managed to make the flames in the stone fireplace behave like they were on the cover of a travel magazine.

At eleven fifty-five someone called up from the court-yard that two ferries had docked and were ready to begin loading vehicles and passengers. Hearing this, the porch crowd sent up a wave of spastic *hoorays* and began scram-bling to pay their bills. The dining room cleared in one great birdlike swoop — Claire's fifth-grade rainbow coali-tion of back-packs and marsupial radios, at last, unhitched. Bar stools and couches and coffee tables emptied. And the bands of cigar and cigarette smoke, which had been escap-ing out the bar windows all night to climb the canopy of a sugar maple, dispersed. Conclusions drawn on both sides of the screen door were set aside; the preposterous had finally given way to communal disbelief. School was out, and pub-lic manners and minimum standards of social decency had still prevailed. Hope had pooped its shimmering head up once more on the walls of *Jimmy's Campground,* and anyone still standing could see that it rested on the shoulders of a twenty-five headed, pasta eating grade school snake drag-ging its tail beneath the webbing of a pink moon and the arms of two slightly inebriated schoolteachers.

From the top of the porch stairs Jill risked her life with a verbal high dive into the hearts of a mass exodus. "People, except for the bomb scare doesn't it feel like we've all been to a wonderful church picnic!"

Ottava carried her Vodka glass with her on her way out, not so much as a skewer of interest in the man behind the bar watching her leave. Behind her the screen door spank-ing its jamb, beneath her the planks in the porch floor com-pressing under the weight of her red-heeled hammers, the oars of the clock over the fireplace mantle dipping into a new day and Ottava's face returning to press against the screen's circuitry.

"There's a stump in the water. Wants to come aboard your boat. Maybe more I can't see. Gonna feel like you're playing Ping-Pong on a chess board."

"Goodnight Ottava," I said. "Keep the glass."

"Watch the railing, Ottava." Jill's voice rang out over the porch like a lazy jazz tune. "It's sticky. Someone spilled peach brandy all over it."

Four bicyclists, and the heads of two chess players whose faces I'd not taken much notice of all night, were preparing to leave. Once these people were out the door the *Campground* would be comfortably empty. Jackie knew it, too, and had already staked out her section of solitude in the dining room, behind the fireplace, and begun the task of organizing tomorrow.

"Joseph is a friend of ours and we don't like the way you've been talking to him, especially tonight."

The man behind the threat, and another man standing beside him, had planted themselves at the edge of the bar in the narrowest slot of time in which I'd turned my back on the room. Both men stood in a stalking stoop, inspecting me.

"Excuse me?"

"Joseph — he's a friend of ours and we don't care for the way you're treating him."

The man had pronounced Joseph like *Joe-sefff*, and for a second or two the pronunciation threw me off.

I felt the room narrow. The clicking of kitchen silverware beginning to distinguish itself from Hazel's pots and pans and amplify the emptiness of the bar-stools and tables chanting behind me like muted cymbals.

"What of it. You're in my bar and I don't like the way *you're* talking to me."

The men stood shoulder to shoulder. Their bodies built like boxcars, their heads shaven down to their knotty scalps. A collection of colored animal tattoos collaring the bristle on the thick necks of both men. Eyebrows meeting at the bridge of their Mongoloid noses. A wormy puffiness about the eyes and temples of one man as though the skin has been stitched and re-stitched. Thick whorish lips on both men. A sizable gap between one man's two front teeth. Both men holding a soldier's bolted stare to my forehead.

"We don't have a problem with Jimmy. But we're surely developing one with you." The man reached out his hand, revealing more crayon printing on the backs of his fingers, and placed his dinner bill and payment on the bar. "We're not unreasonable men. We like to give a man, even one choked up as badly as you are right now, fair warning."

Windows on both sides of me disappeared to tiny tic-tac-toe specks and then sprung back like giant chalkboards to form coffin-sized walls around my vision of the two men.

"You're not standing on Jimmy's half of the bar." I said, staring at both men. "You're standing on my half."

"Know what we think?" The man's cubed head pushing a little closer towards me. His voice was calm, the delivery of his threats monotonous and rehearsed. "We think you should give Joseph the benefit of the doubt. You might start by taking some time off to think about what we're really asking of you. It's not all that much we're asking, not if you think about it properly."

A bullying at any age is a filthy thing to swallow. In the humiliating squalor of not knowing when it will end it brings forth a disparaging rush of all sorts of personal failings and painful regrets, each painful recollection all the more wrenching and paralyzing for not having been constructively confronted. Bullying by men is the cheapest form of currency on earth. You can identify it anywhere in the world, at any age, by its self-righteous charge. It has but one purpose: to leave the terrifying whip of aloneness forever lashed on the backs of the persecuted. Jimmy was right to have chased it down and twisted the life out of it whenever he spotted it prowling in the fields of high school; he saved me then, and his example has served my spirit well ever since.

"Know what I think, I think anyone looking for an education ought to get one. Your *kind*, especially." I spoke from a fever of anger and sequestered shame.

"Mister, you haven't a clue."

"Joey's a punk kid, same as you." Some rage older than me shed its frayed skin inside my chest and begged me to act, to harm these men that had lived so long and so well as predators. "Trailer-park's two islands over. You still want to fuck someone in the ass when you get there, maybe that halfwit next to you will oblige."

A hawkish silence caromed off the walls of the *Campground* and came to rest in the cube of space between us. Time stood still, and I watched how much bigger and more violent my words had become after I'd spoken them, watched how they swam of their own volition over the flashes of anger erupting on the faces of the men before me.

From the sandpit something oily fell from the lips of one of the cyclists, the other three cyclists grouping around him so that they could move as a single unit towards the two men.

"That's quite enough, gentlemen!" Jackie shouted. There was fury in her march from the dining room and a fist full of receipts in her raised hand. "Everyone just hold their point of view for two seconds."

Jackie took a little hop which put her in the narrowing space between the line of cyclists and the backs of the two men.

"I'm sure both Mr. Jacobs and these two gentlemen appreciate your willingness to intervene, but would all of you please step back for half a minute." Without waiting for a response from the cyclists, Jackie stepped around my attackers to face the men head on. "And I will ask you two gentlemen to give me your American word that this argument is over."

"Ma'am, we're here on Joseph's behalf —"

"Joseph is a grown man," Jackie's words cauterized the man's tongue immediately, "and he's an employee of this man. If Joseph doesn't like the way his employer is treating him Joseph can speak up or Joseph can quit."

"Who are you?" The man who had yet to speak huffed and widened his stance. His friend put his hand firmly on the man's folded forearms, as if to remind him that he was not to speak.

"I'm the manager. I'm the one who is politely asking you two gentlemen to leave. Now please go. Or would you rather I call the sheriff?"

"Sure thing, ma'am. But just so you know. In the future, I think you'll find us to be reasonable men when we're treated with respect."

I started to say something as the two men moved in unison towards the door, something ancient and unyielding and which could not accept the guilt that comes with turning the other cheek. But Jackie tilted her head back at me in disbelief, the caution her eyes were expressing enough to silence me.

Each of us stood like so many staggering by-standers watching the *Campground's* screen-door endure another thoughtless slapping. The bar dead quiet of all human voices. The noise coming from behind the kitchen doors so concentrated, breaking so crisply over the fire's pale crackle that only the sounds of steel mixing bowls and running sink water commanded our attention for a time. Finally, Hazel's radio leaked a long brassy human note that scratched softly at our rattled nerves like a bank of lifting fog. The boots of both men thumping the porch planking. Jill standing stiff as a board outside one of the porch windows, watching me.

"Manager, eh?" I broke the silence.

The cyclists laughed, faintly.

"It worked, didn't it?" Jackie blinked her words at me.

"Yes it did."

"No more of these personal confrontations, alright? If there is a next time, we call the police. Right?"

"Agreed."

"I think it best that you go talk with Joe right now."

"I will."

"Mark?"

"Yes, of course I'm going to talk to him."

"Can I give you a little advice?" Jackie said, pointedly.

"Sure thing, ma'am," I joked. "Right after I put my foot in his ass."

"That's not terribly funny, Mark. *Talk* to him. Get the facts before you go biting his head off."

"Treat him like he's a math problem, is that it?" I kidded.

Jackie's full hips angled away from me as soon as I'd spoken. I think she knew she had belted a home-run off a bad pitch by the way she had intervened and handled the trouble. And she knew we knew it too.

"Jackie?" My voice caught up with her half-way across the room. "Thanks."

"You're welcome. Let me know how it goes with *Joseph*." She disappeared behind the fireplace. "And don't put it off."

"We're out of here, Mark. Thanks for the sport's highlights." Rib cages and tendons shared a spot of humor with me as the cyclists clicked by me, bicycles in hand. "We'd stick around and walk you down to your boat, but we all agree you're probably a lot safer with Jackie by your side."

"Thanks for backing me up, guys."

"You want us to stick around, we will."

"No, no. Go on."

"Alright then, we'll see you another night."

The shortest man in the group held the door open for the others. When his friends were on the porch and lifting their bikes to their shoulders, he looked back at me. "Jackie's right, call the police on the fucking birth-defects next time."

I stood to one side of the kitchen door and waited for a break in Hazel and Joey's conversation.

"— Hazel?" Joey sliced another pan thru the soaking sink water.

"What is it Joe, I've got to keep my eyes on tomorrow's ingredients."

"Do you think some people only read the bible when there's a terrible fight going on inside them?"

"What kind of terrible fight, Joe?"

"Oh, the everyday kind we all suffer because of Satan running out on our Lord."

"Go on, Joe."

"I just get to thinking there's different kinds of evil living inside some people's heads. And, well —"

"And what, Joe?"

"And this evil gets the upper hand for a time. Makes a good person do something bad."

"Joe, I think you know my feelings on that subject. If someone is truly holding the teachings of our Lord in his heart, such a battle would never see the light of day on God's good island."

"I suppose."

"Joe?"

"Yeah?"

"You've heard me say this before, Joe. There's a ring of fire inside each of us called temptation. It's only when there's no battle between our desires and God's words that our minds can slip and do terrible things. I believe that."

"Like tonight's bomb-scare, Hazel?"

"Yes. Like someone trying to scare my Claire. Someone trying to scare our good friends and customers. And for what? For what? Joe, if you knew anything about this prank on the ferry. I mean anything at all Joe, you'd tell me wouldn't you? Like you tell me about anything that's bothering you and we talk it out."

"Hazel, that's not it. I've just been thinking a lot about Jimmy's daughter. I guess I really am kind of stupid about some things."

"You're not stupid, Joe. You're as smart as your brother."

"Step-brother, remember?"

"A brother's a brother, Mr. Joe. Neither half nor whole ever lacks a soul."

"Then how come, Hazel, how come I've never been able to understand how Jimmy's daughter came to thinking that way. So badly about herself, I mean. Hazel, you listening?"

"Yes."

"What kind of fight would have been so awful inside her that Jessie would want to do something like that to herself? To stop the battle inside her? You think that was it?"

"What brought all this on tonight, Joe?"

"I don't know. Guess it's in the air a lot more now that Mr. Jacobs is here for the summer."

"That really it, Joe?"

"Sometimes when I'm out training I stop at the cemetery where her grave is and pray for God to forgive her. For God to release her soul into the hands of Jesus."

"Did you know Jimmy's daughter very well, Joe?"

"No, I've told you that. She was nice enough to me in school though."

"See there, Joe. Some things you do better than your brother. Better even than Jimmy and Mr. Jacobs for that matter."

"How's that."

"I bet you're the only one who has spoken a prayer over that poor girl's stone in some time. This spring Claire and I went out there to pray. The grass was so tall you couldn't see her name or nothing. Yes sir, Joe, that's a special thing you're doing."

"Hazel?"

"Yes Joe."

"I'm not the only one. Mr. Jacob's wife prays for her there sometimes too."

"Careful what you wish for, Mr. Joe. You know what they say: God's ears are the sun and the moon."

"It's true. I saw her at the cemetery the same day Mr. Jacobs arrived here on the island."

"Mr. Jacob's wife?"

"Yes. Remember he came in the bar early that day. Before we opened up. To be by himself and get drunk?"

"Joe, I don't want to hear that sort of disrespect in my kitchen. You're better than that. And so is Mr. Jacobs."

"It's true. He does most of his drinking alone. I think that's mostly why his wife is always checking into that place on Depot Island."

"Joe, enough! I think it's much more complicated than that."

"I think he's the mental case, not her, because —"

"Joe! No more."

I'd paid a stone cold price for listening in on Joe and Hazel's conversation. I stepped away from the kitchen door and went back to my duties behind the bar, no longer feeling up to the task of talking to Joe tonight.

When I face my regrets, some dark virulent cocoon in my mind that I once promised allegiance to begins to unfurl and swallow all hope of making things right. I need only slip by Red's neon doorman, ambush my own boat, and before long the stone cold bitterness of a fisted shot glass will take me back to all that I've lost, all that I've wronged. Hope recedes, the truth nowhere to hide, and bitterness and cynicism become the singularly clenched eyes of God watching the world go black — the last thump-thump of the world's heartbeat soon left circling the last pounding sigh from the lip of a pasty shot-glass. In the wake of dawn, the worst of the fall will be over and the drone of reassembly will begin. And here, on a cold and murky and fowl tasting bed of one's own making, you begin to peel back the lies the world of men have perpetuated and you see that the truth lies always with a dark angel beyond the reach of our sifted doctrines. You've lain with this dark angel many times before. She is sure, this dark angel, she is certain, she does not waiver. You have carried this angel's wailing cry into any number of church pews offering the promise of forgiveness, but it is hopeless, for there is no shedding the feeling of complete aloneness that has been born of her revelations. It is a package deal the two of you have signed on for, and like so much of anything that is addictive, part of the value of its attraction lies in the suddenness of its departure.

Laughter, swaggering and hyphened and spurred on by Salvador's dissident accent, sprinted up and over the porch steps. Jimmy dropping his usual coined phrases on Jill's sleeveless shoulders, each of his one-liners pitching Jill's flowered skirt at a circus-act pace before he practically dances his way thru the tavern's door. Salvador trolling in right behind him, a thin frown clamped to his cheery face.

Where berry-stained sandals had bobbed under Jimmy's feet earlier in the day, a pair of honey-colored loafers brushed his tan linen slacks. A mustard-colored dinner-jacket draped his shoulders and opened wide over his olive-green pocketed shirt. The slash of his ponytail like a loosened banner about to come to rest at the bar.

"We heard," Jimmy said, taking a seat at the bar. "Everyone's okay though? Idiots probably on their way back to the east coast by now. Just the same, best to play it safe next time and do like Jackie said. Pour me a cup of green tea, will you? How you holding up, otherwise?"

"Where you been all night?"

"Playing jacks and hopscotch. You?"

"Yeah? Me too."

Jimmy seemed unsettled, his eyes preoccupied with his thoughts and the view outside the screen door. "I'm a little surprised you let them walk."

"I'm a little surprised they knew you."

"I don't know them. I know who they are."

Sally went to the kitchen.

"Well, one thing's for sure." Jimmy said.

"What's that?" I asked.

"Sure put the color back in your blue balls."

Sally returned with a bowl of macaroni-n-cheese and a small haystack of buns. He walked towards an unlit corner of the room by the fireplace, one hand cradling his bowl of food while the other worked at wiggling out of his jacket.

"Jimmy organizing a posse is he?" Sally asked, tossing his jacket at the arm of driftwood in the sandpit.

"Tomorrow maybe. So what else have you two been up to?"

Jimmy slouched back in his barstool, teacup and saucer in hand. He cooled the green tea with his breath, sipped at it, watched it ripple and throw off a little steam.

"Tell him, Sally."

"I wouldn't do the story justice, Jimmy. Hey Mark, I'll bring those shit-heads who were in here tonight up at the next town meeting. They've been spotted in town before trying to make trouble for folks."

Jimmy set his cup and saucer on the bar. He reached inside his jacket and pulled out a banded wad of cash and tossed it on the bar.

"Check that out, my man."

"Jesus Jimmy, where'd that come from?"

"Eight thousand, eight hundred and eighty-eight. First big hit all year. The eighty-eight dollars is my doing. Didn't actually win that part of it. But who's to know but you and me? I was trying to work it up to ten thousand and then leave. Leave for good, I mean. Quit the dice forever. Settle down somewhere nice with you. Hah! But the dice are demons sometimes, aren't they?"

"You had to be playing table max to win that kind of money."

"And your point is? Hah!"

"Just asking."

"Hey! We need more lumber before we can start the addition. This money will go a long ways towards that."

"Good on you, Jimmy." I said.

"You and Jackie take off. Go on. Sally and me will close up."

"What, now?"

"Sure, take off. Where she hiding, anyways? Or is she still out chasing down those white fuckwits?"

"I heard that. Watch your mouth, mister. Or out you go." Jackie's voice seemed to rise out of the flames. Her body still concealed by the stone fireplace.

"Get my friend back to his boat safe-like, will you Jackie."

"I can do that. Five more minutes."

"We gonna see you at her picnic?" Jimmy asked, lowering his voice.

"I don't know. Maybe."

"She's put a lot of work into it. You could at least make an appearance. Get you out of that sinkhole of a boat you've been tripping over every night."

"I don't know."

Jimmy folded his paperback book of cash back into the

pocket of his jacket, got up, and walked towards the kitchen. Before going in to see Hazel he rapped the end of the bar hard with his knuckles. "Kind of strange, isn't it? Those two men showing up in town same night we get a bomb scare on one of the ferries."

"Jim?"

"Sir."

"You really win all that money?"

"I did. Jessie's hard eight finally come around again. Funny night all the way 'round, huh?"

"Yeah."

"Hey? I got your back, you know that."

"Yeah. Yours too."

I waited for Jackie in the courtyard while she said goodnight to Hazel and Joe and put the day's receipts in the safe. Main Street looked deserted. The street lights with their hanging baskets of flowers like props on a stage awaiting tomorrow's performance.

I leaned against the courtyard's open gate and smoked a cigarette. Watched the moths circling the lights, as if they too had been sealed inside a glass jar.

When Jackie came down the porch steps, I put my cigarette out in a stone dish of sand. On Main Street we walked with some apprehension, for several blocks saying nothing about the bullying trouble at the bar or the scare several hundred ferry-passengers had endured. Jackie seemed refreshed by the walk and the night air. On the way, she pointed out a garden shop's bed of wild-flowers with admiration and a bit of envy and laughed a little at a one of Salvador's windowsill planter boxes he'd built with the rules of wind's winter-geometry in mind. On a corner, where a section of the sidewalk had been uprooted by a sycamore tree planted at the entrance to the town park, Jackie suddenly stopped and pointed at a dragon made of concrete and beach glass and we accidentally bumped bodies and laughed quietly about me calling one of the men a halfwit. We shared a few words about the night's pink moon and how wire-stained the sky was at this end of town, and for the few minutes in which we set all things significant aside it was pleasant enough walking with her thru town.

When a paper cup hopped off the sidewalk behind us and scraped across the oyster-shelled street my arm bumped Jackie's hand again and she abruptly asked what my take was on the trouble we'd had in the bar.

"I'm only here for the summer." I said, and jabbed my hand in the air in the direction of her candlestick island. "Got my own full-time problems right next door to yours?"

Some of the warmth in Jackie's eyes dropped away.

"Oh. And our friends and neighbors? How should we think about their safety for the rest of the season?"

"Hey, I'm sorry. All I meant was that tonight's scare is all bullshit if you ask me. Come on, let's cross the street."

"That's not what you told Jimmy."

"I don't ever tell Jimmy what I'm really thinking. Do you?"

"And that's supposed to appease me?"

"Maybe we could put this off for another time, Jackie. Today's been long enough, hasn't it?"

"No thank you, I don't take my work home with me. I live next door to all that people would put off, rather than, face up to. Oh no, I didn't mean — oh god, I didn't mean to say that. Mark, I'm so sorry."

"Aahh Jackie, don't sweat it."

I don't think it showed on my face, but Jackie had stopped me cold. It was as if her slip of the tongue had dipped into a fog bank of some far-off solution and scooped up a handful of it to show me what I was doing wrong.

"It's inexcusable what I've said. I am so sorry, Mark. I

meant to say what I've been holding back all night, that, that the wait is as bad as the outcome sometimes."

"Forget it, Jackie. We're all going to live a few more hours, a few more days —"

"Don't do that, Mark."

"Do what?"

"Dismiss the concerns of others. That kind of sentiment doesn't suit up well with your education. And it does matter to you. If it didn't you could have hibernated in Seattle all summer and avoided all this."

"Fair enough. Come on. Let's get a look at what's going on at the docks."

From the terminal's hillside scaffolding of wooden steps and railings, we started our descent. *The Grand Bryndeline* rested stiff and ungracious in the harbor, her exploratory surgery looking hours away from completion, what with several teams of centurion-clumped police uniforms and jacketed investigators still traipsing her lighted decks. In a fire lane bordering one of the emptying lanes of vehicle traffic, blue vans with idling engines ran their taped umbilical cords out the side doors of their command centers while more uniformed authorities moved about in teams of two between the last of the vehicles waiting in a holding lane. The uniformed men and women shining their flashlights on the faces of drivers and passengers, and sometimes instructing the occupants of a chosen vehicle to step out of their car while a canine unit inspected their coolers and camping gear. A string of orange flags flapped near the belt-line of an impatient officer waiting for the last of the foot-passengers to put the contents of their backpacks back in order.

"It's not this bomb-scare that alarms me," Jackie voiced more of her concerns, "these things always get plenty of attention. It's the determination with which those creeps wanted to hold you hostage that scares me."

"You make it sound like they were carrying weapons."

"That's just it, Mark. It's rarely the big bad pistol in your face, is it? No, it's always the little things you ignore that come back to bite you."

"Jackie, I don't think —"

"Really, that's often the case, isn't it? I mean, don't you find it odd, don't you, that those two men picked tonight to cry fiddle for Joey? Have you ever seen them before tonight?"

"Yeah," I joked, "in a Seattle soup line."

"Maybe I'll laugh with you on Saturday," she said, somberly. "I don't see a sniff of reason why we shouldn't walk over to the authorities, right now, and report the incident. Do you?"

"What, now?" I said.

"There won't be a better time."

"How about we talk it out tomorrow first, instead?" I hurried my descent. "I'd like to keep it between you and me and Jimmy for now. Alright?"

"May I ask why?"

"I don't want to see Jimmy fly off the handle and go and do something we might all regret."

"Like what?"

"I'd just like to just sit on the whole thing a couple of days. Listen, if you're not comfortable with it when you come back to work, we'll —"

"We'll what? Help you change your bandages?"

"We'll file a report. We'll make it policy. They show up again, we'll make sure everyone in the bar knows they're to call the police."

With permission, and under polite scrutiny from a state trooper, Jackie and I crossed the public parking area. I hurried the pace towards the road to Red's, hoping she would walk a little faster, pay a little less attention to a sheriff's deputy speaking with a state trooper.

Once we were over the first hill in the road, all the slivers of light shining in Red's backyard popped into view and the road dropped into a tunnel of maple and alder growing on the bank of a gooseneck cove too small for mooring boats. For another hundred feet or so the road to the marina would pinch a trail-like path between the base of a sandstone cliff and a bulkhead. The moon and the stars and the incoming clouds entangled in the spearing tree limbs overhead before opening into a grassy knoll roped off for guest parking.

At the end of the pier, Jackie knelt on one knee and lifted her cotton skirt so as to stretch her other leg into the spoon of her aluminum boat. It was an orderly approach to the tipsy boat, swift and defined, less sensual than safe, and reminded me more of someone accustomed to hopping into a city cab this time of night than into a rowboat. I kneeled and untied the boat's nylon ropes. The ropes new and cheap and twisting like pieces of licorice on the boat's empty seat where I'd tossed them.

The motor started and its little egghead shook off the day's long nap. Jackie put on her orange life jacket and pulled a neatly stored blanket out from under the seat and unfolded the red blanket over her legs. She said goodnight. I waved good-bye, whispered goodnight.

I don't know how much time passed before I let go of the image of seeing her go, maybe a couple of minutes while Jackie's teaspoon boat dipped and bounced in the lapping waters, maybe a couple more minutes listening to the pitch of the boat's engine yo-yo a rhythm across the channel. There were no other boats on the water, no friendly veneer from a passing ferry to divert my thoughts, just a faint mist of rain that had begun to powder the shavings of moonlight fading from the channel's surface. The frayed light from the cottage windows on the bluffs of Depot Island chasing a parting moon.

I showered and went back to my boat, crawled into my bed, covered myself with the corners of four different sleeping bags.

From a place where the polished silver light of an August morning once washed aside the imperfections in the glass door to the room's balcony, Jessie had promised me more of her life than was reasonable. I am not a heartless man, nor faithless, but I do not trust doctrines promising eternal intimacy. My choice, my marathon. I ended my sexual relationship with Jessie the day after I'd promised her half my heart, and the day after that she had set out for Depot Island, quietly and sensibly to collect her thoughts, I'd believed. Or maybe I wished it to be so — I'm not sure anymore. Maybe all that I've so delicately sectioned into slides of politely portioned temperance of the days leading up to Jessie's death is but a pocket of the truth I wish to face.

In the cold dampness of my bed, I closed my eyes and imagined a prayer, and still it was a jumbled mix of muted longings when I spoke it aloud...*could you have found your way again, Jessie, could you, if I had stepped aside more gently?*

CHAPTER SIX

THIS DAY WILL UNFOLD like no other, a day of purpose. Wheat fields and wicker lawn chairs will weave their dreamy vignettes into the neglected corridors of some *other's* memory, some other's *perceptions* not entirely of my own or Jimmy's making, and demand recognition.

The day will begin with the spectacular bloom of a buttercup sunrise and the playful pounce of a lost dream tugging at my body to get out of bed. This day mapped out for us like so many others before it, so long ago. This day of color, of powder blues and tongue-streaked reds crowning the snow-capped mountains to the east donning a needling light which is tracking the wings of skidding mallards about to iron the ocean waters of the channel.

This day of heightened hope which will dry up my runny nose, heal my hoarse throat, and generally disinfect the stale cabin air in my head. This day which may even stifle some of the unspoken claims by the minority mouths of my good neighbors in the marina that I am a scab of a sailor and an unforgiving husband. Fair enough, over the last couple of weeks I may have left a few thin slices of my personal history dockside. I'll admit to that much of Red's crude survey, admit that some part of my behavior has provided my neighbors with a small point of morality on which to stand and pass judgment. But all things considered, my fellow boaters know little of the lives I've lost or tossed aside.

I reached for my keys and wallet and switched off the lights in my moored jack-o-lantern. Jackie's barn warming was not until two o'clock this afternoon, so there's plenty of time beforehand to visit the empty *Campground* and make some breakfast, maybe wax and buff the hardwood shuffle-board, maybe even surprise Jimmy by hanging the door in the *Campground's* hole in the wall. At the very least, a work list of the *Campground's* backyard priorities needed to be posted out back for Juan and Danny to crumple up and disregard.

I wave to a circle of resident boaters having their morning coffee on the docks. Their undressed stares are less than neighborly, but I've no intention of permitting any of them to unplug my reservoir of denial or prod me into visiting Dianna's cottage window so early in the day. Not this day, this day my internal dialogue is as wrinkle free as the outgoing tide, and I will do everything this side of sober to keep it caged.

It is an easy jog up the steep trail of the bluff which overlooks the marina. At the trail's end, I take the path thru the golf course's stunted grove of shore pine, jump the ruts of a dog-legged stretch of golf-cart tracks, and make my way across a landmine of dog turds to a littered strip of sand and roadside weeds. From behind a blind of a hedge, I mistakenly rush too quickly onto Main Street and my feet are nearly drawn into the spokes of a racing bicycle.

"Pay attention!" The racing cyclist yells out. The rider swooping sideways to avoid hitting me but never once losing control over his machine.

"Sorry!" I yell. But my apology is a gnat in the wind to

the hooded cyclist, who has already taken back the inside edge of the street's white-striped bicycle lane and is about to disappear around the scalloped corner of a storefront's red and white striped awning.

Standing near a coffee cart on the other side of the street, a heavily pocketed photographer has been watching my near miss while slinging equipment bags from his shoulders.

"I would have warned you but there wasn't time." The man speaking to me had shed both shoulder bags and now his hands were engaged with one of the cameras strapped about his neck. "Wouldn't have mattered if there was, though."

Still breathing hard, I crossed the street.

"What's that?"

"*Time — wouldn't* have mattered if there was more time. I still wouldn't have warned you."

"No matter," I said, coldly. "Nobody's bleeding."

"See, that's what I mean though."

The man fiddled with some sort of setting on the camera he was holding, continuing to speak as often into the nooks and crannies of his camera as he did to my face.

"Your precious blood could have been spilled all over the streets and where would I have been? Right here, same spot you see me now, snapping pictures of your pain and agony when what you really needed was a helping hand. Bad habit of mine, I'm afraid. Atrocious."

"They say it's the thought that counts."

"*They? They* don't get out of their houses." The man extended his hand. "Anthony Flagg."

"Of no service at all, I suppose?" I said, half joking.

"What's that?"

"Forget it — Mark Jacobs."

"Oh!" Anthony chuckled. "Good on you, mate. Will you have a coffee?"

"Absolutely."

"We took our hot coffees a few feet away from the espresso cart, so as to see around the street's overgrown hedge and catch the water view.

"Where's home, Anthony?"

"Sidney. New York. Seattle, lately."

"You love to travel?"

"When I was younger, yes. Not so much now."

"I take it you're a professional photographer?"

"For the better part of forty years. Tell me you saw first sunrise this morning, Mark?"

"I did. Magnificent."

"You're fortunate to live here. Beautiful country."

"Where might I have seen your work?"

"Magazines mostly. Periodicals."

"What brings you to the islands?"

"I'm part of a love triangle — one writer, one photographer." Anthony took three short sips from his coffee cup, his bugle-boy eyes fishing for something moving around one wheel of the coffee cart. "Look there!"

Where Anthony was pointing a small crown of sand and duff twirled around one of the wheels of the coffee cart, the twirling duff mesmerizing a huge Angora cat.

"Who's the third party in this love triangle of yours?"

Anthony reached for his tobacco pipe and stirred his coffee with the pipe's stem. "Why you are, Mark — the public if our work has any influence."

"You could start a church with a doctrine like that. Might even be one I'd attend."

"I'm afraid we'll have to put our trust in the general public this time around. How's your coffee? Need a sweet roll to go with it?"

"No, no thank you."

Anthony took three more quick sips of coffee and asked what line of work I was in.

"I teach."

"Here, in the islands?"

"No, no. Seattle."

"So you're here on holiday as they say in Sidney?"

"I help a friend out in the summers. Gets me off campus for a spell. Gives my friend time to sail."

"You don't sail?"

"No. Not really."

"His boat or yours?"

"Mine when it's moored. His when the sail's up."

Anthony chuckled, and using two of his chubbiest fingers drew the outline of a sail in the air. "Each of you half of a love triangle?"

I smiled. "Your picture paints a thousand words. And most of them would come from my friend's tongue when he's trying to teach me how to sail."

"Passions are queer, aren't they? I was taught my craft by one of the best in the business. She was brutal whenever she critiqued my work. Publicly or privately, made no difference to her where she spoke her mind, she would show no restraint anywhere. If she saw any flaw in my work she went after it with blatant disregard for any artistic strength the work might have possessed. 'A good photographer learns to keep his mouth and his sense of morality in check,' she would say to me over and over again, 'moral distress has no place behind the lens of a camera — your only obligation to the public is to find and identify opposing forces.' She became even more critical of my work after we became lovers. And of course, having slept with her, I became more sensitive to the slash of her tongue. One day I struck her, in public. She'd taken a pair of scissors to my two favorite photographs at my first serious showing, everyone watching. It was not like me to do such a thing. In all my life I have never struck anything or anyone. Know what she said to me that night after we'd made love, after I thought we'd both made amends? 'I staged the lesson of a lifetime for you today and you blew it. You put your hand to my cheek when you should have been taking my picture.'"

"You married her?"

"No. That night was the end of us."

Inside the comfort and solitude of the bar, I removed the panel of plywood covering the opening in the back wall and let the island breeze rush in and brush the shadows from the room. With the warm breeze came all the best of Saturday mornings past, her neutrality, and for a moment the memory of the *Campground's* promise became an old dream come and gone come back again.

I went straight to work. I worked hard and gave no serious thought to last night's pimpled punks. Morning lifted and sniffed away a couple of gentle hours.

Before leaving I left a packed cooler out back for Juan and Danny. I placed it in the shade between a stack of lumber and four pallets of cinder blocks. Juice and soda-pop, bananas, chips, meat-loaf sandwiches, more chips, half a key-lime pie and one page of work notes. When I was done, and after I had fastened the sheet of plywood over the hole in the back wall, I locked up and returned to the marina for a shower.

Half an hour later, I was on my sailboat and motoring across the channel towards Jackie's barn warming. Another ten minutes and I was across the channel, my emptiness of stomach so squashed by the possibilities of Jackie's picnic that it seemed as if someone else had tied my boat off to Jackie's raft and rowed me ashore in my yellow rubber raft.

A few yards up from Jackie's beach a group of wiry children are performing a low-branch trapeze act. Scabbed and sunburned, shirtless and shoeless, the kids are toe-stepping their way along an apple branch entangled with blackberry tentacles and the whips of suckering apple growth as they try to reach a spot in the tree where the thick limb curls skyward. One of the boys in the group is first to reach the u-shaped turn of limb and, once there, stuffs another marshmallow in his mouth just as he's about to make a one-hand maneuver to grab hold of the limb's great twist.

Farther down the shoreline more children have staked out their shoreline claims. Some of the children have scraped out boundary lines in the stony shore for some kind of game about to be played. Others have found their bleacher seats in Jackie's grounded rowboat and are moving about like squirrels on a tree trunk. Two boys have just splashed three girls before noisily swimming out to Jackie's raft. The girls pay them no mind, more excited about the salamanders they've found behind a large mossy log than with the crazy *dares* from two crazy boys. Back at the rowboat the children are smacked with laughter. Each one taking a turn at stuffing more marshmallows into the lunch pail that has been passed around, until an ambitious toss launches the lunch pail out to sea and the pail coughs up a flotilla of marshmallow drums which catch the eyes of some trolling sea gulls. School is over, summer begins.

Some in these islands will tell you that the gender demarcation at a picnic rarely widens, that males remain on one side of the picnic bench and the females on the other. That suggestion, silly as it may sound, was once again being established along the shoreline where two young girls now gawked and mouthed their annoyance with a pair of bothersome twins daring them to wade into the stomach-slapping chill of a high tide. *No boys, your chances are slim to none —* Jackie's fin-less boat simply has too much more to offer a girl than any testosterone-laced bicep belonging to a boy. A tough-talking black-haired girl wearing candy-cane shorts is adding even more spice to the suggestion that there are distinct gender lines at an island picnic. Standing in Jackie's beached rowboat, the girl is punctilious in her instructions to the other girls on how one is to peel apart wet paper plates on a sunny day and properly place them on the boat's limited seating. She rolls her eyes whenever one of her chosen apprentices fails to properly space the wet paper circles on the boat's center seat, and she exclaims — "so as to dry quickly, Priscilla." Next in line to Priscilla is Sandra, and she's been chosen to split all apple atoms, polished or not, into skinless canoes. Samantha sits beside Sandra and is busy mashing some bananas, diligently unfocused. Laurel, with hands held high, squeezes a gasping and pirouetting syrup jug over the rowboat's centerpiece of wet plates and sliced apples, at the same time, mimicking the drizzling sounds of stringy chocolate by sucking on her teeth — after which, all five of these ladybugs simultaneously commit themselves to the club's memorized communal chant: "Lots of Chocolate Syrup, Darling!" Everyone giggles except bemiring Claire, the club's leader, who personally hands out each soggy plate of fruit casserole as if it were a sticky paper taco.

Feels like the bottom of the ninth on a knoll of grass just up a ways from the beach activities, where Red is playing talk show host to a gathering of wise-guys; a horticulturist from the Department of Forestry and a civil engineer from the State Highway Department. Accumulatively, the three men represent nearly two hundred years of island opinion shared weekly, sometimes daily, with the people of Seattle where two of the men work. I know this for a fact because I've been listening to these men talk about their commute to and from the islands for the past ten minutes, and because Red has been interpreting these facts to me for what feels like nine of those ten minutes. Mostly, I am quiet and respectful around these men. After losing my temper with Red, on *my* boat in *his* marina, I know he figures I owe him my silence for a while in social situations such as this one. He's wrong to think so, but the fact is I do owe him for many other blunders I've made at his expense. At an hour in which these men would usually be thinking about their coffee break, they seem mentally stalled here, becoming somewhat digitally cautious in their selection of subject matter and in their preferred choice of vocabulary. It is too early in the scheme of this day for these men to act boldly or to speculate, vehemently, on the possible outcomes of such controversial subjects. Whichever time zone the men have attached themselves to — morning or mid-day — the time is not yet at hand to passionately disagree or behave rashly. At an island picnic, heated discussions and instinctive posturing are best served later in the day with dessert and alcohol.

Red is an island wonder, a man of profound bluntness and almost no interest in visiting the past. Right now he is steering the two older men in his group towards a discussion on the science fiction possibility of bridging the San Juan Islands with a harness of concrete ligaments — an idea he brought back from a visit he and Anna once made to the Florida Keys. It is at this crossroad of possibilities that I decide to excuse myself. But before I can make my getaway Red grabs my hand, or rather, compresses it. He wants to thank me for the new garden hose I bought him and for repainting his *Quiet Time: 10pm - 6am* sign. He winks a grandfatherly admission that he understands I've probably learned my lesson about drinking so heavily in his backyard. I nod, and leave him to carry on with his friends, their inner-island bridge discussion quickly resuming before being suddenly brought to a halt by the interruption of a kindergartner's questioning on how best to retrieve a floating lunch pail of sinking marshmallows.

In the field which stages Jackie's big barn at the top of

the hill, Brynnie and Jenny are initiating gold-star children into the delicacies of dog tag. Already the children in the front lines have experienced some serious crossfire. Brynnie must have tagged a bantam youngster too hard, because Jenny is now whimpering and a group of fallen toddlers are yelping "surrender." Sally has made his way to the scene of the accident. First he will check Jenny's limp, console the dog, and then take the time to nudge the fallen boys to their feet. He now feels obligated to explain the English Springer Blitz to the lads gathered around his dogs, in all its intricate field dog variations, though it is apparent that the grass-stained boys need no further translation. What all players new to the game of *dog tag* don't realize about Sally is that he doesn't give a hoot or a holler if they play the game wisely or not. His slow and methodical instructions to the children gathered 'round him and the dogs is just picnic politics, branded public palliation, a smoke screen for the holders of patio seats and their sidelined pandowdies — the simple but effective disguise that is giving him the time he needs to be sure Jenny's leg is okay.

Picnics and patios, each one a stage for revisiting memories and rekindling old aspirations. A place where we eat and we talk and we dream of what we might take home come the end of the day. Our dead somehow with us, somehow listening.

On Jackie's patio, Hazel is marching with a bowler's precision towards the great line of food tables. Her wide rump covered by a new pair of loose fitting tan shorts, a black t-shirt covering her lumpy shoulders, green knee socks over her calves wide as a bison's head, her small feet stuffed inside the puffy tongues of her scruffy looking penny loafers. Hazel's ears are the tiny exception to her obesity; thin, sleek, a palomino coloring to them in the mid-day sun that is sensually palpable.

"Hello Hazel. I almost didn't recognize you out of uniform. Did that crank of a boss finally agree to give you the day off?"

Turning to face me Hazel answers exuberantly. "Yes, with pay! Can you believe it?"

Hazel's lips have been artificially sweetened today, made chubbier by carnival paint, so much of it applied that her lips now project new borders which carry the look of a crimped cap from a soda-pop bottle whenever she smiles. It's a bloody shame that she paints her lips so heavily because Hazel's natural smile, which is made all the more queerly attractive by such an abundance of gum tissue, is as big and beautiful as her heart is genuine and welcoming, a smile as persevering as an angel handing out popsicles in purgatory.

"Jackie told me you might have had something to do with it, Mark? Me and my Claire want to thank you for that. I ain't had a day off like this with pay all year long. Not that I've come to expect it, Mr. Jacobs."

Looking up from her baskets of baked buns while she foils a steel pan of berry crisp, Hazel thanked me again. There's a natural wave in her thick brown hair, pretty enough, but the soapy perfume oozing from her neckline possesses all the charm of a freshly cleaned lavatory. She pinches the aluminum foil over the blueberry-mortared edges of the crisp pan once more, her backside to me when she speaks more of Jimmy's reluctance to pay for her time off on holidays.

"Jimmy stopped giving me so many days off with pay this year, you know."

"Oh?" I said.

"What with his gambling and all the time losing lately, I guess he just can't."

I was considering how best to respond — my mind's eye remembering how Jimmy had smacked the bar with his wad of hundred dollar bills — when Father Jerald stepped from the barn's kitchen onto the patio and began an ensconced inspection of the tables of food set out before him.

"Such a feast!" The priest on the patio paraded along the line of tables as he spoke.

"If you ask me," Hazel said, ignoring the priest's arrival, "something's burning a hole in that man's good pocket besides a need to gamble."

"How about I talk to him next week? I think maybe we can find a way to compensate you a bit better than we have?" A big gummy smile returned to Hazel's face and she lifted her fisted hands above her head in silent cheer.

I know something of this priest on the patio, some of his doubts and those of one of his parishioners. He's out of uniform today, this confident priest. Black linen pants sluicing about his sagging horseshoe hips. The pleats on his pants ironed so often that a silvery sheen now perpetually creases the fabric between the pockets. A tartan belt, enough yellow and green color lacing the loops that he could well make claim to being a valley fan of college football in Oregon. His Irish tweed about to slip from his shoulders and drape his tattooed left arm, before he will give his blessing to Jackie's picnic.

"Jackie, the Milky Way has never held higher aspirations for man's evolution than your ambition and deliverance to our community. Truly an accomplishment. And the barn — your home, now — it looks luminous."

How this priest loves to sing.

"Why Father, you'll have me tripping in the dark tonight over such compliments." Jackie's sunglasses fall from her trickling hairline to slip-slide over the bridge of her nose when she walks across the patio to greet her priest.

"Mark, I see you've sailed your way over to Jackie's picnic."

Father Jerald extends his hand to my shoulder. He is as

tall as I am, as physically thin as my faith but by no means brittle. I smile and shake hands with him.

"And Hazel, you are a *rose* to do so much." Having become the character he was born to play, the priest knows he is cupping the very best image Hazel has of herself in his own posing, quiescent eyes. Out of the shade of an Irish grin, Father Jerald is about to pour on more praise. "And you've delivered all of us unto your famous buns!"

Father Jerald has always possessed a pitcher's fast ball for cutting to the chase where food's involved. But it's the charm of his timed release that is now drawing the other players in from the field to the tables, and he's not been shy about it, waving in half the outfield without first checking in with the manager.

Jackie laughs at how quickly a crowd of children have gathered around the priest, and suggests that he might give a fast-ball blessing before the food cools. Red seconds the idea, having bunted his way in right behind the priest by playfully bumping aside a loose knit line of elbows trying to halt his forward progress.

"Jackie, may we?" Father Jerald asks. "Before these blessed children bloody this fine table."

I smile and wonder if maybe I haven't just witnessed the priest's fast-ball prayer.

"The sooner the better. These children want to get back to the field. They're expecting a bloody fine ballgame from you after lunch."

"Yaaaahhh! Us kids against the older people." The children's chatterbox pitch is aimed straight at the priest, a hint of chicory in more of their vocal challenges as two barrel-shaped coffeepots begin to percolate at both ends of so many pinned tablecloths. The benches are emptied and Jackie's picnic is in full swing.

"Nothing like a ballgame to make a picnic." Father Jerald

says as the line moves along. "Wish we had a few more of them at our weddings."

"I'm afraid it won't be quite the ballgame you're accustomed to, Father."

"Oh?"

"The children and I have added a couple of twists to the game."

"And what twists of fate might us older people be in for?"

"The use of a tennis ball when the children are up to bat —"

"So that's the way it's to be, is it?"

"There's more. A downward lie for the kids, whenever they are batting and running the bases. When it's our *ups*, the grown-ups will be swinging at a Whiffle-Ball. And when the old folks run the bases it must always be uphill."

"Nicely done, you rascals. I've a feeling we're all in for a good go of it."

"Cross-dressing again are we, Father?" Jimmy's voice slid into the conversation like the uncomfortable weight of a counselor's intervention.

"Jimmy! You rascal. Where'd you come from and how are your idols treating you?"

Jerald's face loses some of its cheerfulness. He quickly stepped out of line and around the hard pick Jimmy seemed to have intentionally set, nearly dropping his sagging paper plate of food in the process.

"Something I've said, Father. Or something you've read on a telephone pole?"

"Tell me, Jimmy. This infuriating news — is it the lone hand of a miscreant or hell-bent radicals? It would trouble me deeply if it was the latter, more so if I were to discover that you have been withholding information from the authorities about their activities in the islands."

"Ever wonder what makes a priest ask what he already knows, Mark?"

"And Mark, it is my understanding that you are the one they accosted so maliciously." Father Jerald set his plate aside and tugged at a fold of paper protruding from the pocket of his jacket. "About the incident, which, as you can see was brought to my doorstep, I can only say what you surely already know — that those men are in no way representative of this community's heart."

Father Jerald's fishing. His clever Irish eyes jumping from Jimmy's disinterest in the paper he's holding to my own alertness.

"Ever read their mission statement, Jimmy? This is a copy. I've also given one to our sheriff. In turn, he's probably given copies to other investigative units visiting our islands."

The priest placed what resembled a folded paper airplane into Jimmy's hand.

Jimmy took hold of the piece of paper, crumpled it, and stuffed it into his jeans. "Don't pay much attention to that side of the island, myself."

"Well gentlemen, perhaps this unsavory matter is better suited for another day. After all, we're here to celebrate our new friend's first picnic in paradise, aren't we?" Father Jerald reached for his plate and stepped between us to find a seat. "Oh, and Jimmy, when you do read it, you'll find that at the bottom of that vile piece of paper I've written some of the names of their members. Know your enemies, Mark. Know them thoroughly."

For the next hour we returned to the pleasures of eating. We sat and were comforted by our foods, by the recollections each familiar spoonful delivered to us of picnics in the back yards of our own childhoods, black and white in our preferences for all that we remember to have been kind in the faces of our neighbors. And when our stomachs were full and our voices quieted for a time, Jackie stood and pointed to the place awaiting our rebirths. The children swarming after her motherly march into the green field like hatchery fish about to be fed. After all, for the children this was Jackie's long awaited picnic.

Jackie's fishnet hammock stretched its low-slung smile between two of Salvador's tripod lanterns. Inside the hammock's rainbow netting Jimmy rested on his back, his eyes closed, dozing or pretending to doze. Jackie set a pillow on his stomach and then flicked his earlobe with a snap of her finger before walking back to her chair on the patio. Jimmy grumbled something derogatory about putting an end to employee benefits for all new-comers, a bit of a wince twisting his smile short when he pushed the pillow under the weld of an old scar on his knee. Cocking his elbows behind his feathered ponytail, my friend created the image of a crossbow taking aim at the rest of us. The hammock began to swing.

"That was such a fun ballgame, wasn't it Hazel? The children had the time of their lives."

"Didn't they though?" Hazel's pineapple chest heaved.

"I never would have guessed a bunch of grade-schoolers could outrun me to first base," Jimmy's body shifted in the hammock's diamond webbing, "then humiliate me by hitting homeruns off every other pitch I threw at 'em. Claire, alone, must have bounced five of her six homers off of Jackie's raft."

"Seven out of eight was my count." Hazel corrected him from across the patio, where she was folding dishcloths and in search of more buns. "She's a slugger, my little girl. You surely brought out the peaches on all their cheeks today when you surrendered the last inning to them."

"And let's not forget about that crazy wager he lost to those kids." Red chided, to Hazel's delight.

"I guess I'll never understand a gambler's wager," Hazel dubbed. "But God bless one today. God bless 'em all today. And you too, Mr. Jacobs. A gift from God to see you enjoying yourself so much."

With a bun at last corking her mouth, and another in her plump fingers, Hazel finally stopped with the bloody blessings.

"Your girl beat us fair and square," Jimmy moaned. "The little runt. How she managed to hit that raft her last time up, after calling it, is stupefying. Hell Hazel, that's like jumping from a nickel to table max and then pulling a blackjack. Almost never happens."

"All the same, Jimmy," Jackie praised, "it was a saintly performance on your part to throw the game when Father Jerald was begging for the ball at home plate."

Jimmy adjusted his headband while performing half a sit-up from his swinging bed of roped diamonds. His face wincing again in profane admission of his aches and pains.

"And look what it's costing me. My damn knee feels like a crushed oyster."

"Would you like some ice for that old hinge?" Jackie asked, taking three or four sudsy swallows from her glass of ale.

"Ice? Noooo-ah. Don't need the ice, darling. Need the dice."

"Don't need the *darlings*, need the *farthings*." Jackie responded. Her delightful laughter skipping over the patio to join ours. She burped, unexpectedly, a tadpole of a burp which flushed her face and caused us to laugh all the more.

"'Don't need the darlings, need the farthings,'" Hazel munched on Jackie's words. "Good one, Miss Jackie."

Jimmy rotated his headband with his fingers and grinned.

Jackie held up her empty lizard glass to the sun and tapped at the reptile's coppery head. "Red, I'd say you've mastered the yeast. This is one of the finest ales I've ever tasted."

"Why, thank you. Best when it's warm, isn't it?"

"Purr-fect."

"Red makes a fine apple cider, too." Jimmy complimented. "Good as any Canadian brew."

"Better than us Canadians?" Jackie teased.

"As good, I'd say. Lot of years drunk up in the perfectin' stage, mind you." Red lifted his glass to toast the air with a high-pitched *uh-huh*. "Right Jimmy?"

"Try decades," Joe mumbled from the edge of the patio. After the ballgame he'd positioned himself and his bicycle as far away from Jimmy as the patio would permit. His bike stood on end now, its front tire spinning as slowly as a Ferris wheel, its paddling spokes clicking off their daily ritual of prayer and necessary lubrication.

"'*Decades.*' Good one, Joe-Bo." Hazel patted Joey's knee. "That's the way to wipe an old pan dry. No offense, Rupert." She had stopped grazing for the time being, and was now swirling some of her paint brushes in a paper cup of obsidian-colored water close to where Joey had set up his work station.

"None taken, Miss Hazel." Red answered, his arm shooting out like a hungry fish biting at the bread basket on the table. "But that snide remark gonna cost you another bun."

"Just one?" Hazel said. "Mine mostly come in pairs, you know."

"Hey, hey, there will be none of that." Red tried bucking back a big grin. "You know how married I am, young lady." He winked at Hazel's red-tide rouge, and took two buns. "Bet if I weren't though, you and I'd be on a rum boat to Jamaica by sun-up by-golly."

There's time to wonder.

"Jackie," Red says, "did you know these boys once towed a rowboat full of your orchard droppings into my marina?"

"My trees?"

"Same trees. Same two eggheads. Boat weren't no bigger than yours is. Brought 'em right up in to my Anna's doorstep. Looked like a half-sunk log coming across the channel."

Red looked at me from behind the food tables. His eyes squinting against the bright sunlight, the patch of sunspots covering his brow wrinkling to map sixty years of life in the islands.

"I forget, Mark. What was it you two boys were up to, anyways? I know picking apples was never Jimmy's cup of tea."

"Thought we were going to flood the market with applesauce, remember."

"That's funny," Hazel's paint brushes madly whisking the water in her paper cup, "'thought they was gonna flood the market with applesauce, Joe.'"

"That's right." Red remembered. "And that was the indisputable fact, Hazel. Pure stick-you-in-the-eye determination, these boys. Some of your Yankee cut-your-nose-off-to-spite-your-face stubbornness too, Jackie."

Red's head wagged from side to side remembering more of our youth.

"Yup. And cuss — these two boys could burn your face the color of an unpaid gill-netter come payday Friday."

"Tell her what Mark said after we'd skimmed out the last net-full?" Jimmy coaxed.

Holding his last bite, Red pulled the better half of a second bun from his mouth.

"Green apples floating everywhere, Jackie. On the dock,

off the dock. Bushels of 'em. Me and Jimmy scooping the ones kept falling from the little boat into the water out with one of my fishnets. And here's Mark, here's this new kid come to town looking me dead in the eyes. 'Hey Red,' he says, 'when they're running the channel like this, what's the legal limit on Gravensteins?'"

Everyone but Joe laughed a little.

"Had to hand it to him though, didn't we Jimmy? Back then when Mark made up his mind to go fishing for something you could pretty much figure the whole town was going to get fed. Hungry or not."

"When did you all first meet?" Jackie asked with a bright smile on her face.

"Now there's an introduction."

"Introduce us," Jackie said, filling Red's glass to the brim with more ale.

"Alright," Red says, "you don't have to twist my arm. That ah girl. See, Jimmy always started cutting my Anna's little fluff of a field about the first of June. You weren't here then, Jackie, but there used to be a cut of pasture that grew right up to the marina."

"Pasture, my ass," Jimmy interrupted, "it was marshland."

"Oh it was not, Jimmy. A little damp at times, maybe," Red turned to Jackie, "where the gravel parking lot is now, that was once a small field."

"Damp! Hell's Bells, Red. Smitty's milking cows used to come down off the bluff to forage for spring grass on that swamp of a field, and never see the inside of a barn again."

"Hush. You boys could pass a lawnmower over it without a life-jacket on, couldn't you? Oh I'll admit, Jackie, there was a puddle on occasion."

"On occasion that you could swan dive that little puddle all the way thru May and June."

Even Joe laughed a little at Jimmy's running commentary.

"Well sure," Red snorted a bit of his beer, "during the off season it may have been a wee-bit spongy. But you boys managed."

"Now he's making out like there were greens and a fairway down there, Mark."

"Shush you. Let an old man write his memoirs the way he sees fit?" Red grinned, but there was a bit of a glare in his eyes ready to pounce at Jimmy. "So anyways, Jimmy-boy here usually showed up alone around the first of June. Cut some campsites out with the mower. So as the fishermen have a place to park their rigs and spread out a bit, you know. Always mowed the whole field himself. Two days of cussing, swearing, and tossing boat parts into the sea to hear my Anna tell it when I got home. *You got a problem with my mouth, I'm walking,* he'd say to me whenever I asked him to put a lid on it." Red looked across the patio at Joey. "Do you doubt Jimmy's mouth was any kinder at fifteen than it is now, Joe?"

Joe kept his nose glued to the spinning wheel. Only when Hazel nudged him with one of her wooden paintbrush handles did he look up from his work.

"Take Jimmy damn near one whole day to sickle his way thru the thistle and Scotch broom. What, maybe two more to sled the lawn mower thru four feet of something I confess probably ought to have been bailed?"

"Don't forget about all the cow-shit we had to shovel."

One of Red's boots tap-kicked the patio stone as if the mere mention of cow-dung could cue an instinctive response from him.

"Yes, alright, I'll give you that. An occasional scrap of manure may have dusted the mower blades."

"So, what you're saying Red is that as a young man Jimmy was quite the little Entre-manure?"

"You're a woman ahead of your time, Jackie." I said.

"Hang on you two, I'm gonna getcha there. So anyways, this one summer here comes Jimmy bluebells with an extra set of shoulders with him. Come struttin' down to my marina with Goldylocks over here. Hair on him thick as my football helmet, Mark here. A chest on him that have made Tony Weismiller's trunks droop. Says to me, 'Jimmy and I will cut your pasture for half the usual price but, but we'd like your permission to peddle a few flowers when we're done.' Tells me the *establishment* is gonna get a dime for every dollar him and Jimmy make selling roses to the fishermen. If I knew then what I know now."

"Things not go so well for the establishment?"

"Put it to you this way — a trip to the dentist might have been easier than working with these two rebels that summer."

Joey shifted the pad in his bicycle pants and unexpectedly farted. In the chair, which she had set up next to his work station, Hazel squirmed and choked up a chuckle.

"Kah-come-on, Red." Joey stammered while hurriedly scraping up his tool kit from the patio. "Tell the story, will you. Fah-fall foliage is almost here."

"Nicely spoken, Joe." Hazel said, looking back at us while kindly fanning the backside of Joey's bicycle butt with a handful of clean brushes.

"Red's always been pretty good with kids." I said. "Kept at least a couple of them off the streets of Seattle that summer."

"Yes, and look what fine gentlemen we've become." Jimmy mocked.

"One of you, anyhow." Jackie chided. She poured herself half a glass more of ale. "So, back to the summer of your historic meeting. "Details, please."

"The fishermen all be gone by sun-up, you see." Red lifted his arm and used his thumb to draw a line across his view of the distant marina. "That's when these two boys did most of their sniping. Or was it *snipping*, Jimmy?"

"Come nine o'clock Sunday mornings we'd do a wee bit of pruning inside Petree's commercial greenhouses. He was a stickler for nine o'clock mass," Jimmy elaborated.

"An hour later the two of 'em would show up at my marina. Each one of 'em with a chokehold on a heap of Petree's prized, cut roses."

Red's chuckling grew more robust.

"The fishermen all come in off the water about the same time on Sundays. Every boat docking men wet to the bone. Some of 'em step off their boats two sheets to the wind and drop like sandbags on my dock. Buy more beer. Clean up. Check out. That's when my boys would hit 'em up with a dozen long-stemmed roses to take home to their wives?"

"And no one caught on?"

"Not for a week or two."

"Really?"

"Sometimes you're late setting the hook on the really smart ones, you know."

"Whose idea was it to five-finger discount Mr. Petree's roses?"

"Mine," Jimmy answered her.

"But I went along with it easily enough." I reminded him.

"True enough," Red agreed. "In those days you would have carved your own initials on your own balls, I'm afraid, if it was a dare from Jimmy."

"How'd it all work out?" Jackie asked.

"Broke half a dozen of his already broken windows."

"Why."

"For the fun of wishing we'd broken some of his new ones," Jimmy proudly confessed.

"Old man Petree made us pay for those, too. Remember?"

"That and more," Red offered further explanation. "Had to wash every greenhouse window Petree owned. Inside and out. Hundreds of them. All of 'em by hand. Took their punishment and moved on. Became proper gentlemen, both of 'em. That I know."

"Petree was an old cheat and mean to his animals." Jimmy said with disgust. "That's why we done it, mostly. Do it again if he weren't so dead."

"He may have been all of that and more, Jimmy. But you boys are better off for having crossed his path. Think what might have come down the pike had you gotten away with it? Besides, you boys still managed to come out of it a couple of hundred dollars ahead. And come to think of it, that was hundreds more than the measly Dixie-cup of dimes the two of you left on my doorstep."

"Seems to me," I teased him, "that I can recall a young marine and his curling irons making a few bills down on the docks, himself, that summer."

Red rubbed his kneecaps. He chewed at his lips and messed with his hair, rubbed his kneecap, rubbed the end of his nose and looked around for a proper spot to focus on, and finally, made his demurring announcement.

"Ah Mark, those days are long gone. Along with the rolling hay fields and all the pretty orchards."

"What's a curling iron?" Joey asked.

"Red's never told you about his famous curling iron?"

"No sir."

"An anchor, an eighty-pound anchor. He used to keep it chained to the edge of the pier."

"What for?"

"Exercise. He'd curl that rusty old anchor from sun-up to sundown. With one arm. One arm, Joe!"

"Why?" Joe asked, his interest a runway of empty landings at the end of the patio.

"So as everyone knew, up front, to respect his rules while they were staying in his marina."

"What was the other arm doing?" Joey asked, sarcastically.

"Why, reading scripture young man." Red answered him, equally sarcastically.

"Do you ever cease to marvel at your good fortune of having the ocean at your doorstep, Red?" Jackie sighed.

"Wait 'till you've yawned your way thru a winter or two of fishhook sleet and rain," Red said, "and you'll have half your answer."

"Sometimes when I cross the channel in the dark, the water feels like gelatin under my boat. Makes me dreamy and I almost think I could step out of the boat and walk my way home."

"Never you mind the rain when it comes next winter, Jackie." Hazel counseled. "You can always stop by my cabin and yarn your way thru the end of it. Beats yawning at the rain any dead day of the week."

"Aahhh. Pay no attention to either of these two natives," Jimmy swung back at their admissions. "Water has a weight all its own around here. Sometimes you carry it uphill, sometimes it carries you. Walk the shoreline everyday no matter what the forecast and it'll be spring before you know it. Water's edge is where life is in the winter. Am I right, Mark?"

"Absolutely."

"Besides," Jimmy added, shifting his knee in the hammock, "there's always plenty of rain skips between church bingo and parlor poker. Am I right, Joey?"

Jackie pondered Jimmy's advice. "I think the rain will be lovely. I won't have to shovel it."

"Amen," I said. "And come spring you won't be bothered by any of those black New England gnats. No maddening rash of mosquitoes, either."

"I've barely had so much as a handful to put up with in the garden, so far. Back east the bugs take half the joy out of gardening. And my god, Joe, there's no humidity. You must absolutely adore riding your bike in this climate."

"Hardly none, Miss Jackie." Joe's head, like his bike, was upside down. One hand on one of the bike peddles, the rear tire sprinting towards an imaginary finish-line, his wide eyes and nostrils studying a miniscule swagger in the wheel's whizzing rotation. "It's God's country for sure," he professed before turning his bicycle right side up, "only some don't know it."

"True enough, Joseph." I said.

Interest in conversation waned some, and for a time an old daydream called me back to the eaves of Jackie's barn. The barn's hay doors near the peak of its roof had been rebuilt and re-hung with two of Salvador's yard-long steel hinges; each of the thick, wood-plank hay doors half-painted in alternating triangles of mustard yellow and paprika colors, each as large and looming as the *cable crossing* signs along the Timberlee shoreline. These doors which have watched the sea fade to a thread and swell the black night with nameless grief.

The children are at play along the shoreline. They stand at the water's edge admiring their new beach of make-believe rooms. Broken pieces of apple sticks have been stuck in the sand to define the walls of each room; a kind of gnarly goalpost framing which seems well-anchored in the snow-cone mounds of beach stone the kids have piled around each stick in the sand. The children dancing and jumping from room to room, behaving like winning checkers about to shout "King Me" whenever their heels touch down in a new room of sticks and stones.

"Red?" Jackie's voice is like the hand that pulls you back from the abyss. "Think those arms of yours might be willing to curl one more anchor or two, maybe three?"

"One end of it, maybe." Red answers, almost dozing. "Why?"

"That'll work," Jackie says. "Won't it, Jimmy?"

"Might. If we can keep him away from Hazel's buns for an hour."

"Shall we break the news to them now, then?"

"It's your picnic," Jimmy shrugged. "Gently though, otherwise this crowd's likely to bolt on us." Wrestling with his knee he sits up in the hammock and points at Red and me. "We wait any longer, that one or that one won't be able to steer straight come sundown."

"What about your knee?" She asked. "Think you can push off with it a little?"

"Knee's fine, girl."

"What are you two blue birds up to?" Red asked.

Jackie stood and folded her hands. Her lips part and she curls her tongue behind her vanilla teeth, tilts her head back to follow the tails of two kites in the trailing sky. She's measuring us up.

"Jimmy thinks we can safely accomplish what I have in mind. But if anyone is hesitant once you've seen what we're up against, you're respectfully excused." Jackie's a little tipsy, won't stop showing her perfect smile and her perfect teeth. "After all, I certainly don't want to see the field littered with shredded body parts. Oh, that sounded dreadfully discouraging. Didn't it?"

Better pass me some ice water, Hazel." I had a notion of what was in store for us. "Got a feeling we're all about to step into the hoofs of Animal Farm."

Hazel was perspiring heavily and the moisture on her face was dispersing her make-up to places unintended. Parts of her face had dried like a skim-coat of plaster on a wall-board of this morning's colorful dawn. She passed me the ice water.

"Is the heat bothering you, Hazel?"

"Bless you, Mr. Jacobs," she said. "I'm fine."

So it began.

Our curiosity followed Jackie's copper ankle bracelet down a footpath which lead to three arched openings in the barn's lower foundation, where a cellar of foraged odors seemed to take us back in time. Crouching under the sag of a massive T-bone shaped beam, more out of cautiousness over what we couldn't discern in the seedy darkness of the barn's bowels than from fear of bumping our heads, we entered a cavern of half-lit echoes. The smell of the earth here wonderfully cooling, sweet, forgotten, like a birthing room or the drop of fermenting apples.

"Bet that smarts," Jimmy snickered.

"Jesus, what is it I've bumped?" Something monstrous and metal had rammed my shin as I had crouched to step under the forehead of another ceiling beam.

"Tip of the iceberg, old man." Jimmy's voice more comforting than usual in the half darkness. "Farm implements."

Jimmy helped Jackie remove a tarp which appeared to be as heavy and uncooperative as a frozen animal hide. In the darkness of the barn's cellar their efforts to remove the canvas looked like the stilted movements of amateur magicians.

"You probably know just how these dead fellows are feeling, eh Mark?" Jimmy squawked. My eyes had not fully adjusted to the light, but I'm quite certain he was winking at the tongue on the steel plow I'd rammed.

"It was an education," I said with a splintering smile. I was standing a few feet behind him, could smell his athlete's cologne and body odor, a bruising shin pain still wrinkling my face. "You'll see for yourself if you don't find us a light switch pretty soon."

The darkness receded to a brown light and one by one the tractor-less farm implements rose out of the earth like doused smoke. One chandelier-shaped plow the size of Plymouth Rock, one harrow with discs the size of Hula-Hoops, and one hay rake with tines large enough to pitchfork logs from a fire.

"For curling hair on a bad hay day." Jackie kidded with Red as he touched the large tines on the hay rake. And I thought to myself, *what were your blindfolded tarps protecting your rusty implements from, girl? Mites?*

"You tricked me, woman, calling these old hunks of rust anchors." Red's silhouette rose out of a deeper corner of the barn's cellar. He was inspecting one end of an iron skeleton whose slotted framework was connected to three or four offset rows of large metal discs.

"Field sculptures." Jackie answered, triumphantly. "Each one will eventually be surrounded by its own plant composition — and here's the catch guys — including its very own apple tree. Way down there."

"You mean to say, young lady, you want us to drag these monsters up and out of this hole? And all the way down thru the field? You serious? Just so you can watch 'em rust up some more?"

Red looked completely stumped by Jackie's concept of field art.

"If you've never known a New Englander, Red, you do now." Jackie preached. Hands on her hips, she was determined to try and teach Red something his head scratching couldn't quite unravel. "We're made of covered bridges and rusty hardware. It never leaves our blood."

"Guess I see now why you couldn't help but buy the place." I droned, trying to make light of the work ahead of us. "Red, be happy she doesn't want us to move her a covered bridge."

"I feel so fortunate. The owner actually gave them to me. Can you believe it? What are the odds, Jimmy?"

"On this island," Red answered for him, "about a hundred percent, I reckon."

Delighted with the trap she had set for us, Jackie presented her rudimentary plan. She highlighted the spiritual side of physical labor — "ball-busting," Red corrected her — and the "ambrosial sleep" that would come from a day of helping thy neighbor. She carried on a bit, finishing her soft sell by telling Joe how such hard work might lead to a revelation by Sunday services.

Jimmy and Red surveyed the resting machinery and suggested a few safety measures we all watch out for.

"Horrifying, absolutely horrible if those discs or plow blades find your toes when she's ah-movin' downhill." Red voiced his concerns.

Joey looked to Hazel and said something profoundly fundamental. "Remember to breathe out when you push off, Hazel."

Hazel nodded her head, her bottle-cap mouth pinching shut with a Friday-afternoon-in-Detroit determination.

We took some consolation that the three implements to be moved were mounted on their original factory wheels and that each one projected its own hitch with which we might use to steer, should steering be necessary.

"Snake tongues," Red called the iron hitching arms.

Rust painted every inch of each piece of machinery. It powdered the blades, the frames, the bolts and rivets, and gave the illusion that the grounded monsters were entombed, harmless. Once, I'd witnessed these very machines at work in what was now Jackie's playing field. Heard the clanking and grinding sounds of their blades striking beach stone whenever one of their cookie cutter turns crossed over the water's reach. Marveled at how much soil the machines could spit into the gritty air pursuing the tractor's pull, its loosened bolts and jumping-bean steel blades dancing a jig over rutted fields as hard and sometimes as impenetrable as the stubbornness of the farmer leading them on.

Some sounds you never forget.

Stepping out from the rumblings of Jackie's new chain gang, Joey was the first to bury his doubts and his heels behind a three foot iron wheel. Hazel moved in next to him, shoe-laced her dwarfish bowling pin fingers, and cracked her knuckles.

On the first great monumental heave nothing budged. No inkling of movement cringed under our physical and verbal whips. On our second attempt we all heard a steely creak. This ran excitement up our twisted spines and caused us to buckle down our positions. Slowly the glue of the Iron Age released an inch of Jackie's garden art, then another, and another. We heaved. We pushed. We lifted. We slued, slipped and farted, and once more repositioned our sorely urban bodies behind the beast. We tightened our buttock muscles and prepared to deliver the torrential blitz and, at last, watched the plow's spooky iron rims print the earthen floor with big brown flakes of rust.

The plow's bent tongue is the first to taste sunlight. Seconds later, the massiveness of the plow's flayed chest cavity rolls over the great line of daylight. She'd traveled an admirable distance. But there was still a considerable knoll to be overthrown before she could reach the prairie. A driveway-sized bunker of century-old manure and straw had turned into a podium of lumpy grass, stringy weeds, and chins of buried stone, all of which was blocking her path to the field.

Jackie wiped her hands on her shirt. "Perhaps it requires a bigger team of horses, Jimmy?"

Joey frowned at her, dismissing the idea of a bigger mule team. I could hear the angels singing in his head.

"People," Joey spoke to us without a stutter, "let's not

let that little mound of cow shit stop us." He crouched and fiercely repositioned the weight of his shoulder against the plow's wheel rim, his hands reaching inside the wheel to grab hold of the steel spokes.

Red is laughing at Joey's determination and surprisingly well-lubricated oration, when the same spirit which has moved Joey takes hold of Hazel's large rump and moves it towards the plow's other wheel. Hazel folds her weight over the wheel, her enormous rump now perched high in the air, suspended in the sunlight with a kind of handicapped sprinting-block preparedness to run the race. Joe looked up at Hazel and spoke something over her heavy breathing.

"Come on, Joe," Hazel says thru the wheeze of her asthmatic breathing, "you and me gonna bite this bun but good."

Red wants back in. He's pressed the bulk of his body to the rear end of the plow's pronged anchors. "Come on ladies and gents, let's roll."

The rest of us take up our stations, each of us radiating some metaphysical glob of Joey's faith.

"On three," Joey says.

"On three." We all agree.

It is the same scene all over again. We squat. We push. We stand and lift. We sweat buckets. But we are not up and over Cow-pie Hill, mercifully or otherwise. We do it all again, the same moaning mistakes, the same uphill convictions, the same summer heat once more christening our backs. We hump and growl and grunt back at our iron cast until her velvety howling surpasses our own. Rust dust smearing her cross-country tracks and her hoof-sized bolt-prints stamping our bellies and thighs sore with iron ore. We've done it. We've reached the top of Cow-crap Mountain. And Jackie's landlocked anchor is beside us, a forgotten plow no more.

We took five minutes to discuss the next leg of the race.

"What's the downhill plan?" Hazel asked, consterna-
tion dripping beneath her sweatshirt.

Jimmy suggested that Joey join him on the machinery's
tongue, actually called the boy by his proper name. The rest
of us are to hold our positions.

Jackie went back to the barn to fetch a couple good-size
chunks of firewood. "Just in case she panics at the sight of
so much water rushing at her rusted chin hairs."

"Good thinking, kiddo." Red says to her, panting and
grunting for more oxygen.

We prepare ourselves for the downhill push. Hazel takes
hold of her wheel rim. She's pushed it this far and won't
hear of any assistance. I take Joey's place on the other
wheel. Jackie's back with two worthless chunks of firewood.
She waits for Jimmy to take hold of the plow's tongue and
say the word.

"Hey, up front," Red repeats a precaution we've all heard
more than once since leaving the cave, "careful that old
snake tongue don't chew your ass when she starts to run."

For our first few hen-steps we mostly worked against
one another. Red a real inspiration to no one whenever he
mouthed off phrases like *slower than cold molasses running uphill* and *winter tomatoes ripen faster*. For Hazel the difficult
work seemed to exacerbate her irritation with the wheel's
constant propensity to prick her hands with rust slivers.
More than once she and Red snarled at one another over
the other's method of lending an ill-timed helping hand.
Sexual tension? I couldn't say. And when we needed Jimmy's strength the most to steer clear of a sizable depression,
he thought it the opportune time to complain to Joe about
something trifling, which in turn caused both men to lock
eyes in a yoke of silent prayers and curses and pretty much
gave the wheel of Jackie's plow free reign to find the depression in the ground all on its own.

"Hold up," Joey yelled. "Hold up!" He'd managed to dig his heels into the slippery grass and keep the plow's tongue from plunging onto his and Jimmy's feet.

The plow settled and we all stared at Joey in cow-eyed bewilderment. He released his grip on the flanged plow hitch and shuffled off to one side of the grassy dip. He closed his eyes and hung his head, a shred of his dismal sigh catching our ears. I wondered if he might be hurt and about to pass out.

"Dear Lord," Joe began as we watched and listened, "hear my prayer and smile down on this wretched team of sinners. Jimmy's knee is hurting him something awful. Miss Jackie's done nothing but show kindness to everyone since she came here. Lord, hear this prayer, and give us the strength to set aside our poor judgments on one another long enough to help her move one plow, one harrow, and one disc. Amen."

"Amen," Hazel said, happy to have time to catch her breath. "You never tripped on a word once, Joe. That's your faith, isn't it?"

"Amen," Jackie said, touching her heart.

"Amen." I silently mouthed the word at the grin emerging on Jimmy's face.

"Damn, Joe." Jimmy's voice sang in the fields of Joey's glory. "If that prayer of yours is answered I may have to put it into my summer exercise program."

Slowly we began to push the plow across the sloping field, the earth beginning to soften and spill a bit of her powder over two beautifully hushed tracks of fallen grass falling in line behind us. The path was anything but preordained, and occasionally a piece of protruding field stone would tip the swinging weight of the plow's suspended blades towards one side or the other, throwing the bible twins off their precariously balanced tongue. Somehow Jimmy and Joey managed to hang on when this happened, and afterwards, always hugged the plows hitch all the more closely against their thighs.

Jackie's harrow and hay rake we moved to the canopies of her apple trees in half the time it took us to push the plow across the field. Not as heavy? True. A shorter distance to their destinations than the plow? Also true. But each farm implement relocated in half the time, without an ill word being spoken? It was something to think about, Joey's prayer.

Beneath an apple branch, Jimmy sat in the slotted metal seat of the hay rake and took his sweet time massaging his knee. An arm's length away, standing in the nap of the branch's shadow, Joey combed back his short hair. This time when Jimmy addressed the kid he did so in a respectful, even friendly, tone of voice.

"Come on, Joe. We've one more tugboat to dry dock. Let's see what that prayer of yours is really made of." Jimmy wiped the back of his neck with a clean T-shirt and waited patiently for Joe's response.

By now the pride we took in moving Jackie's machinery into the field had been somewhat desiccated by the heat of the day, done so at about the same rate our passion for more physical abuse had curled and flattened our bodies around the hay rake. Hazel's hair looked like a mop with pasty highlights, her washed out cheeks sagging as much as her big wet breasts. When she heard what Jimmy was asking of Joey, she frowned, finding nothing amusing in his blue-gilled solicitation that we perform more work on her one day off. Red was panting in pantomime, his forehead and rust-streaked forearms only slightly less scarlet than his name. He, too, looked to be in no mood for any more of Jimmy's soapbox lathering. He quickly cast a salty glare as wide as his fullback's shoulders at Jimmy's iron throne.

Jokingly, I asked, "What's next? The Barn?"

Jackie was devouring the new prop-filled stage she'd constructed in the field. She patted shoulders and gave thanks to the shredded peasantry at her feet. Her smile the shine of the moon upon gullets of iron.

"My truck," Jackie peeped, snaring us deaf and dumb.

"Truck?" Joey said. The word he'd spoken sounding as if it had been choked up from a hidden megaphone in his larynx.

"What truck?" Hazel droned.

"It's an engineless '56 Chevy. It's going in my living room bedroom. Well, eventually. Come and see?"

"Consider it done," I dribbled. "Next month."

Red found my remark to be very funny and pointed to the beach. "That's right, consider it done. Only throw us the keys first so we can run it thru the carwash another year or two."

"Jimmy and I thought if we could at least push it up the side yard and around the back of the barn to the living room window it would be ready and waiting for all of you at our next picnic. By that time, I'll have a section of my living room wall cut out for her."

"No one's coming to your next picnic." I volunteered my regrets for everyone present.

"I'm already sorry I came to this one." Red said, nudging me in the elbow. "Almost un-American for her to call this a picnic, ain't it?"

We all drooped a little more at the thought of another pushing and shoving match, except Jimmy and Joe. Red ribbing Jackie's choice of remodeling styles by pulling out a couple of greenbacks and a few quarters from his pockets, and insisting that she take his money and call a tow truck.

In the end, we proved no match for the easterner's charm. We dropped our teasing and traipsed uphill after her lusterless ankles, reluctantly reacquainting ourselves with our own deadpan footsteps, another bay in the barn's cellar we had not taken notice of, and one more of Joey's prayers.

"Look," Jackie said. She had jarred the truck's green hood open for us to look inside. "She's got no engine."

"That's nice, Jackie," Hazel said, working her way in next to her, "neither do we."

"She'll be easier to move than the others, don't you think?"

"Easier, not easy." Jimmy replied, tersely. "We may need more horses on this one."

"Maybe even another picnic," Red said, limping his way around me to have a closer look at the truck.

"Look, I've put four new tires on her. Won't that help?" Before we could begrudge Jackie's considerations she'd latched the truck's hood shut. "She doesn't know it yet, but she's going to be my couch and canopy-bed all in one."

I never heard the schoolyard bell ring that recess was over. But one must have rung somewhere on the island, because as soon as Jackie informed us that she would steer our ears suffered a shelling of children's excitable cries. Their voices came out of the sunlight and into our shadow-less camp, poking us with their wishful raccoon eyes. Their kite strings still looped, knotted, and biting at their wrists, their cries raced by Joey, their bodies producing an odor that steamed within the barn cellar's cool air. The children bunched like unruly vines between us, their wet and sand-stained bums twining over defenseless door handles and into the truck's windowless cab. I saw at least six bodies climb into the front seat in as many seconds. They packed themselves silly into the truck's sponge cake seating; hands cranking, turning, twisting, and stamping at any knob, button, handle, or lever that could withstand the frightening power of their inquiry. Squishing, Thumping, Jumping, Rocking, bouncing the dashboard and the steering wheel of the engineless truck into a mashing medley of strangling song. God Awful Sounds! Heads popping and pooping out of the cab's rear-window frame like swallows from the cliff dwellings above Red's marina. More heads prairie-dogging the truck's windowless doors, each with a mouth run amuck with laughter.

"Stop!" Jackie commanded.

The toy truck ceased to rock.

"Enough, children!"

Jimmy spewed an instigating burst of snickering behind Jackie's back, and the wildness began all over again. The kids breaking out their Halloween faces when Hazel's daughter broke out in song. *"Row, row, row your truck, gently down the field...merrily, merrily, merrily, merrily, life is but a Splash!"* The friends of Claire soon bouncing along in chorus, *"row, row, row your truck..."*

By chance, while the children carried on with their shenanigans, I spotted a low-flying aircraft clipping a waving salute no more than a hundred feet above my boat's mast. A piece of the plane's passing shadow touched down on the wheel tracks in the field before the plane banked and circled back around. Jimmy had spotted the small plane, too, and when he did he let out a hoop and a holler and ran out of the barn.

"Come on, kids! Plane rides and boat rides for any one who dares!"

I know now how a flock of a thousand birds can change directions on a dime, at a hundred miles an hour, and not suffer the rolling wreckage of a mid-air collision — they're young birds, children, and because they were born stone deaf to all calls of caution they've naturally developed extraordinary eye-wing coordination. That same sort of bird acrobatics was now occurring in the barn's cellar; children abandoning their barnyard caroling by the truckload, their slip-slapping bodies making them appear to be treading water when they made their mad exit from the truck cab and banked their first horseshoe turn into the sunlight.

We followed the path of children under the barn's T-bone arches, up and over the barn's familiar knoll of decayed manure, where we watched Jimmy and his entourage running like wild boars towards the shore. Jimmy was more than halfway down the field — *bad knee my ass* — jumping stones and running towards the water pony he'd evidently hired, his heels kicking up all the joy of a kid racing after a vendor's last melting Popsicle. The plane now flying parallel to the shore, its pontoon landing gear just inches from imitating a mallard's perfect landing.

When the blue and yellow plane splashed down, the lone sister and brother kite team, which stood knee-deep in the shore's apron of water, let go of their chin-up hold on the long dowel of wood tied to the kite's line. The kite dive-bombed my boat's mast in a twirling, two-fisted, starboard-aimed summersault. There was the faintest clank of shroud-lines, and a screeching scream from the boy's sister acknowledging that her once high-flying diamond kite would dance with the wind no more today, after which, the waving hand of a young pilot stepping from the door of the plane's cockpit drew everyone's attention. From the plane's passenger side, another man emerged, older and heavier, and slinging a camera as identifying as his name was patriotic.

"Guess delivery on your canopy bed will have to wait," I said.

"Yes, I think so. It's been a fine time though, hasn't it? What more can a girl ask for than to live on a baseball diamond with an airplane at your doorstep?"

Jackie removed her gloves. "Shall we clean up and join the others on the beach?"

I'd hardly noticed that Hazel, Red, and Joey had taken

the footpath back to the patio and were about to take on the buffet's second seating.

"Think I'll wait here if you don't mind." I pointed to the plow near the low reach of an apple limb. "Had my eye on that spot of shade there awhile."

"Okay, mister. Feel free to shower after your nap. I loaded up the chair in the bathroom with towels earlier."

"Alright."

I walked to the tree that held the plow in its shadow, took hold of a tall wand of field grass on my way, snapped it free, quartered it, rolled a piece of its stem on my tongue, chewed at it and tinkered with my thoughts. The events which were about to unfold beneath this apple tree unimaginable to me a year ago.

The unsettling wonder of seeing Dianna's hips leaning against the arch of the barn's kitchen door, when I looked up from the plow. Her body lingering under the door's arch and between my skipped breaths in suffocating proportions. She moves. She passes under the patio's pergola to canter across the barn's jetty of stone. Her yellow summer dress folding about her knees, the dress retracing its own course the way a child's paper plane twists its flirtatious return after it's been released into the air. Her hands hiding within the colors of her sash. Her bare shoulders out from under the casting shadow of the pergola's patterned sunlight warm and waxed. A bold blush of strawberry, plum, and apricot cloth coloring the waistline of her yellow slip of a dress, and her colorful sash crowning the return of new flesh on her hips.

That the woman, whose hands gestured freely to friends on the barn's stone patio, now stood outside the forested confines of the treatment center was mystifying. The woman poised like the brushstroke of a painting to be studied, her priest the first to clasp her hands in approving admiration of her miraculous recovery.

I watched Dianna greet Father Jerald and hug the robe he's wearing that's not there. The exposed skin of her spine shining at me like cooling tallow. There is a new strength in her embrace, brighter, tighter than the talons of any of this priest's penthouse sacraments. The curvature of her spine so polished it seems vocal. Her shoulder blades dancing like sharpened machetes cuffing the humid air of a Honduran jungle whenever her speech pulls another smile from her pretty priest.

I breathe the stares of strangers returning to the patio and can almost make out the pitching palms straining to avoid the coming storm. Almost make out their umbrella fronds falling in the pine woods behind the barn and the shadowing lamp of a passing cloud about to cross the field like a crouching tiger playing with its newborn cubs. I have not wished these sentiments into being. They have come of their own volition.

Dianna's first step from the patio becomes a dancer's prance by the time her sandals touch the grass. Her long legs scissoring gracefully around a tuck of straw to take the quickest path across the field. The ageless eyes of her priest tagging after her as she walks thru a pleat of fallen grass that Salvador's dogs and the blankets of families have ironed in the field. The flesh of her sleeveless summer dress a hundred times more ensnaring than the disrobing, lamb's ear plea Dianna had last staged in her room.

Anyone who loved her as much as I would have rushed to take her in his arms and acknowledged her recovery.

Anyone with half a camera lens on us could see that I had been disfigured by Dianna's unexpected appearance. My body mirrored the slanted stance of a heron on the shoreline and, for a few seconds, remained as frozen to my spot of shade under the tree as the deathly blue in the bird's armor was to the water. When I move, it is to try and rub away some of the dirt and knife marks of rust from my arms. My forehead is hot. A streak of perspiration runs from the heart of my chest to the bareness of my grass stained stomach. In the time it takes me to clean up the best I can and to rethink all the things not to say to her, I become the beard of straw and crabgrass trapped between the spokes of one of the plow's wheels. A man trapped and afraid of what his tongue's anguish will spill.

Should I have rung the island church bells and sealed my belief of seeing divine forgiveness in the butterfly hand that Dianna was waving at me? Walked away from Dianna's rabbit-in-a-hat appearance? Avoided the sunny stares of all the happy picnic people beginning to take notice of the distance closing between us, and disappeared up the dirt road and into the pine woods beyond the treatment center? Admit that I was homeless, held to a spot of my own making and to the wonder of seeing so much of my wife in the sunlight, of seeing something so foreign to my wilted understanding of her depression. Wondering, too, if her appearance was another one of Jimmy's magic tricks, a ruse to pull me out, like the plane he'd pulled from the lollypop sky for all the happy children.

The almost imperceptible scar that bridges one of her almond eyes. A summer tan which has browned her high brow the lighter shade of a lion's mane. And when she speaks, her voice is oiled with ease and purpose.

"What do you think? Like it? It was Jackie's idea." Her slender fingers displayed the braids of her new hairstyle, a cajoling of golden beads and shimmering dreadlocks. The braids crisscrossing in her fingers like a shifting school of silverfish.

"You look well."

She looked radiant. My stares studying her body, tracing

the muscular trim of her copper colored shoulders, not so much because I was obsessed with the taut skin of its re-birth but because, for so long, I had known her form only thru the slaughterhouse windows of her helplessness.

One of her sandals gently tapped the inside of my ankle. Once, twice. She's forgiven me.

"Hey, it's me." Dianna tipped the flared tumbler of ice-cubes to her mouth, rolled the rim of the tumbler over her lips to catch a leaf of ice. "We're friends, remember?"

Only a very small part of me wished that she might make it easier for the two of us, click her heels together and fly away. Leave me alone with my crass silence. She must have read my mind, because she sucked on another leaf of ice until it seemed her silence and the shade from our daughter's tree had etched our silhouettes in the field grass. Somewhere, beyond our scope of caring, I could hear the shrill of Jimmy's children turning Jackie's raft into a ribbon of warm taffy and the roar of his chartered airplane begin-ning to plow thru the channel's chop. See Jimmy coaxing the last of the marooned children to board my boat.

"I believe I've finally mastered your great small skill of living alone with the past. I suppose I should thank you for that, before I go."

"That sound's like my voice," I said.

"Please say something more than that, Mark. You needn't worry that it's the medication you're talking to."

"Shouldn't you be resting? I could walk you back to your —"

"I'm going to ignore that." She tipped more ice to her lips. "Do you remember the first time I brought you here? Did you know that for years I've wanted to return to this old barn with you and talk with that young boy? Stand in this field and tell him, tell him that she was so much more than I could have hoped for. Such happiness just to feel his life in her little body. Tell him that I'm so sorry I let my life, our life, go away with hers for so long."

"I remember everything," I said, callously. "Remember?"

The slightest glistening swelled in her eyes.

"It's too much for one person to think about sometimes, isn't it?"

Dianna smiled and palmed my ear and began to cry a little. But there was no trembling taking hold of her. No distant island train whistle fell from a trackless bridge into the Sound. The ceaseless bellowing which had gnawed at our skulls all winter, all spring, had chosen to spare one of us.

"There's no crying at picnics." I said, and wiped the crest of her cheek with the last clean spot on my hand.

"No, there should be no crying."

"Where will you go?" I asked.

"I've a little more homework to do in Seattle. To be sure I'm not back-packing any more of your regrets."

"I deserve that."

"And you?" She asked.

"I guess I need to revisit some things a little longer than you."

The faintness of a sparrow's sorrowful smile returned to her face when she reached to wipe the dirt from my forehead.

"If I could, I would — stay with you, Mark. Love you again. But for us — I think no good thing will ever come out of these islands. If I thought it might, believed it could, I would gladly stay and watch you destroy yourself — have gone with you."

"We could start over." I tried to sound encouraging. "Go somewhere — somewhere, where there's no water."

"I wouldn't recognize you without water nearby." Her words annexed themselves to her hand of lures as she spoke. "And I think you would feel the same about me. And neither of us would ever admit it was hopeless, would we? So long as the other believed it might work."

"It's come to this? You're certain of it?" I wasn't convinced I'd spoken or that my words carried my voice if I had. "Next term's right around the next island, you know. I could give us both a failing grade. We could repeat the class."

"You would have me extend the larceny of our lives, is that it? Stay here and worship one of your precious pools of guilt — yours and Jimmy's?"

"That's not what I said. That's not what I'm saying."

"Our downfall has become your dream, hasn't it? You are happier here, in this, this place that you would hide half-lit candles in and have me worship with you. Would you tell me otherwise?"

"Probably not. Not today."

"Maybe it's another's narration you're waiting for. Is that it? Is it? Is it Jimmy's life you're after?"

"No."

"Jessie's?"

"Don't say that. Don't say it like that, Dianna."

"Like how?"

"Like she's, like she was a foolish young woman to go off swimming in the dark. That's what you're saying."

"I don't think that." She tucked the tumbler into the twist of her elbow. "I don't think it was a swimmer's sky Jessie was after that night, that's all."

I thought I detected a slinking off of her voice, a fear returning.

"Tell me something, Mark. When you're in the middle of a muddling math formula that one of your students doesn't understand, what do you do?"

"You've made your point, Dianna."

"What do you do?"

"I go back to the beginning. Same as you."

"Yes, to the beginning, where there is at least some mutual understanding. Where you're standing now, Mark, is there some beacon of light waiting for you that the rest of us don't see?"

"Yeah. Candles every which way I look, Dianna."

"Then you're alone with it, because I don't see it. And neither does her father. And he loved her, too."

"You've made up your mind. Now you can live with it, same as I've had to."

"Know what I think? I think you and Jimmy behave like lost boomerangs between these two islands just so you can avoid each other's guilt. I think each of you knows exactly what the other is missing. Buried your secrets from each other for so long that now you both, mistakenly, treasure them."

"Don't say that. Don't say that."

"You would refute it?"

"I think in the absence of the whole truth, each of us — every last pathetic one of us — swears allegiance to something lesser."

I watched her look to the western sky for solace, where I knew she would find none.

"Your heart is dead to all love but hers, isn't it?"

"No. No love is ever that pure."

"Mine was, once."

"No, I don't believe that."

"You were the only one, Mark, the only one who insisted on beating yourself beyond empty."

"It's called grief, Dianna."

"No. Yours is no longer grief. Yours is only a perverted strangling on something, something you believe to be living but which is not."

"And you were always real good at dismissing my memories of Jessie's life."

I kept on telling myself that to crawl was better than no

movement at all, that I need only find one place where no one recognized me and my secret would sustain me.

"Maybe you really loved her." Dianna said. "Maybe, I'm no different."

But Dianna was different. She was stronger than me. She was stronger because she was willing to confront all the faces of truth.

"Oh Mark, just this once, in the middle of this deaf orchard, can't you tell me to my face what I know!"

I couldn't. To say it, to hear it was to have nothing of my own left to hold onto.

"Not even a whisper of the truth, my love?"

I looked at Dianna's beseeching face. She had moved as close to my heart as my mind was to unleashing its tormentor. And the bellowing serpent, the one which had paced the margins of my wife's pillow for so many months, hardly a dithering trace of its tracks left in the pelting veins of her temples.

"Are we to become nothing more than phantoms to each other? Say it, Mark, if it's the wish you want. I'm well enough to hear what I already know."

There was crying which came with the pain of seeing her tremble, and it did provoke a deeper sense of shame within me.

"No," I said, "you will never be a phantom to me."

"Jessie was something special, I know that. She was, wasn't she? Sometimes I think her death has been all that's been holding us together."

I held Dianna's wishing well words in my head. Words I'd waited for three summers to hear drop from the arms of lawn furniture, words now as powerless over me as the reading of commandments from a dead religion.

"Where will you go from Seattle?" I asked.

"Away. Away for a while."

"What do you want to do about the house?"

"Sell it. Sell it quickly — to yourself if you want. Or to Seattle, I don't care." Her warm hand let go of my fingers.

Neither of us said another word, both of us looking away so as not to feel the other's good-bye.

I wiped my face with my shirt and then put it on inside out. After I'd hiked away from the picnic, I wanted to run back and put my arms around all I'd been afraid to speak of. Tell my wife that there were more words in her absent kisses than I cared to hear, tell her that her beauty was a wondrous thing to behold from a rocky plateau in the sky, from the seat of a tandem bicycle, from the barefooted wharves of foggy marinas or the deck of a flanking, starry-eyed ferry. But the words and the sentiments attached to them sounded clownish, even in thought. It was too late for any of that. I was already tracing her leaving thru a burning field of rain and snow and the watermelon blooms of next spring. It was a flavorless tale my secret had spun, nothing more than a mammoth and devoted evaporation on the highest of pantry shelves.

The dirt road at the edge of Jackie's orchard was like a new street in a new town I'd never visited, and walking it was like meddling in the middle of someone else's dream, my eyes following my footsteps and searching desperately for the sparkle of an oyster-shelled street. Jimmy's voice and wisdom in my head above all the others — *you feel hunted when someone is telling you they are leaving you...and when they've gone, well, when they've left you haven't even that construction of the mind to hold you up...and all the frantic searching thru dresser draws, for letters written and promises celebrated, it only embellishes that hunted feeling with more disease, more tumbling and disbelief.*

I made my way behind the old barn, beyond its new balcony, to the gravel road which would crest at the treatment center. At the top of the hill I left the road to find one of the facility's postcard benches. It was a fine bench with a fine view, as near to the grassy edge of the bluff as was safe. From the bluff, I looked out at the insipid Sound.

For a time, I held the sea and its islands in the realm of *another's* anger, moved its turbulence to the peppery beaches of Napier where Jimmy and Dianna might become soundlessly unknown. For a time, I sat on the wooden bench and indulged my perceptions, knowing of no power, no Word strong enough to reshape the shoddiness of my convictions.

CHAPTER SEVEN

I WATCHED FOUR OR five sets of mashed elbows slobbering the weight of their inadequacies on the railings of the ferry. Tight white T-shirted aprons over their protruding bellies. Black work boots a part of their tattooed uniforms. The men were hammer-toeing the outside deck of our ferry with their boots, shifting and stretching their elbows as though their T-shirt trusses were too tight or too starched by body salts. Each man stuck close to the man next to him, hoofing and snorting like a small herd of under-fed cattle. Their fathers shared some of the blame, their fathers had shit on the rich melting pot of America and now it seemed their sons felt obliged to do likewise by feeding freely on bigoted schemes and dreaming of a white-carded nationality. They were closing in on our island's best days, had already closed in on mine.

It was disturbing enough to see signs of this paranoid cult on the mainland, where they sometimes dumped their dim self-serving light upon black businessmen, gay-rights demonstrations, and any other perceived immorality. But to witness their beliefs row-boating an island ferry was enraging. In Seattle, on rare occasions, you might spot them strutting the malls or disrupting the city transit schedules with their shuffling crosswalk stunts. In the newspapers, their printed numbers seemed miniscule; their agenda more often shipwrecked by their own crew's pinpricking idea of God and his limited will. In Seattle, they maybe blotted our streets once a year with their halfwit parading. And, in the city, their presence seemed more safely contained or, at least, better monitored by the authorities. But seeing these fuck-wits here, on the decks of our ferries, their presence felt more obscenely statuesque and calculating. To the somber faces on passengers now shuttling their way back inside the ferry's tabled living room, these men were a threat to the peaceful soil of our campground fires and cottage marinas. Neighbors preaching a return to the sins of our fathers no one needs.

Jackie was sitting at the table with me watching the same group of men, watching them lift their shaven heads from the ferry's waterline in time to turn and find Jimmy poking his fingers at the tallest of these stump-heads. In his gambling uniform — sports coat and white dress-shirt — Jimmy had moved in on a section of their railing with his brazen ballroom etiquette, the slash of his fingers and something spoken daring the tallest man to dance.

From behind the ferry's windows the rest of us watched a few more of Jimmy's words cluster themselves around his pointing fingers. I looked around for Joey and Salvador, but then remembered they'd wandered off for cafeteria coffee. Red was on the deck above us, talking with the captain. Hazel had gone to one of the ferry washrooms. I returned my attention to the activity taking place on deck. Jimmy's mouth had managed to disfigure two members of the group of stump-heads. Except for the flashing reflection of the casino's neon sign on the window by our table, the mood on the outside deck looked as black and white and foreboding as the sea around us. A few more minutes and we would be docked at the casino's twinkling boardwalk — Jimmy's idea of the perfect ending to Jackie's picnic.

"I have no idea what I'm doing here, Mark." Jackie's sigh interrupted the haziness of Jimmy's plot. "It's not at all like me to go within a fogbank of a casino."

"I know exactly how you feel." I spoke to her without taking my eyes off the T-shirts outside my window. "Know what I do when I'm feeling like that?"

"What?"

"Tell myself I'm not going out to gamble but to see a bit of street theater — Jimmy's."

"That's even more pallid."

"Well," I said, "perhaps it will be our first and last binge for a while."

"They're not the same men, are they?"

"No — their offspring maybe."

Jackie pinched the air with her thumb and forefinger, making her hand into a kind of can-opener before bringing the pinch to the point of her nose. Lowering her voice, she mocked the stump-head warnings we had confronted in the bar.

"'That's only this funny, Jacobs.'"

"'Mr. Jacobs, ma'am.'" I played along.

Bending her voice tone so low that it sounded like an Irish-brogue-in-a-bottle, Jackie tried humoring me. "'I say, young fool, you're not standing on Jimmy's half of funny you're standing on my half.'"

Jackie rolled her lower lip inside out while extending her arm and squeezing out a thin crunch from an aluminum pop-can she was holding.

"Freeze that face," I said to her. "We made need it to stop this bunch at the door."

"Ignore them." She said, and abruptly changed the subject. "So how are you really feeling?"

"It hasn't hit me yet. In fact, I think maybe I'll join him."

As if he'd read my mind, Jimmy came thru the swinging steel door like a trophy ram, alone and in one piece, swooping in under the thunder of his smoking cigar to take his place by our table.

"What did you say to that beefy bully?" Jackie asked him.

"What else but the whole sad truth. That Mark here was a funny-bunny and had eyes for black boots with silver heels."

"Think they bought it?"

From across the aisle, Joey and Salvador approached our table.

The smile left Jimmy's face. "Just maybe."

Sally slid his body into the empty bench and sprawled out, his head resting on the window sill and his boots dangling over the seat's cushioned edge and into the aisle. Joey kept his distance from our cozy circle, but was paying close attention to Jimmy's watchful eyes on the men.

"What did you say to them, Jimmy?" Joe asked.

Jimmy puffed on his cigar and pretended to straighten his collar in the darkness of the mirrored window, before blowing more smoke in Joey's direction.

"Said tonight would be as good a night as any to find out what kind of a swimmer Mark is."

"I don't think that's what you said to them at all."

Jimmy ignored my hostility. He looked at Joey and flapped his mouth some more.

"Poke the biggest tub of lard out there in the eye, Joey, and the rest will cry lullabies to their mamas. There's maybe half a pencil-dick between the whole lot of them. And that's if the lighting's good. Excuse my French, ladies."

"You're certain of that?" Jackie asked.

"Totally. Too gutless to wear an American uniform. So what do they do? They T-shirt a crib sheet and recite cornball over the ballroom rails. Ain't I right, Joey?"

Joey's face soured, and his body seemed to grow uncomfortable with its newly positioned posture against the stairwell wall. He fidgeted with his Styrofoam cup, bending the rim of the cup with his fingernail and letting it snap back to form just often enough to annoy Jimmy.

"That's it, take your time. Think of a proper reply. Then make your choice, Joe. And try making the right one this time. Again ladies, excuse my tone."

"Answer my question, Jimmy. What did you say to them?"

"Been there, done that with you. It never sinks in."

Jackie rolled her eyes. Hazel nervously shuffled her new deck of cards. Sally was exercising his usual muted patience with Jimmy. There were no other ferry passengers in the immediate vicinity of our table.

"Alright, alright, I give up ladies." Jimmy said, looking thru me. "Regrets — told them mine, told them yours. Told them they'd be missed by many but not by most." Cigar smoke lifted his right hand to his heart. "Scouts honor, hope to die."

From the blue light of the steel stairwell, Red limped out onto the floor and approached us.

"Captain says he's gonna speak with the whole rotten bunch of them when we dock. Won't tolerate a stitch of misbehavior on his boat." Red's chest swelled. "Captain was watching your back the whole time, Jimmy."

"No need for recruits, Red." Jimmy's cigar hand slashed the air. "I'm a solitary force. Besides, Mark here had me covered. Always has, always will. You can bet your last dollar on that, Hazel."

"Alright cowboy, settle down." Red's good humor pushed in with a croupy laugh. "We know you can perspire, but can you inspire?"

"Yeah, come on *Young-man*." Hazel chirped. "We've all

pooled all the money we've got together. Show us how to count these cards so we can double it tonight."

The smoke from Jimmy's cigar perfumed a crude tango over our table.

"Yeah," Jackie jumped a little in her seat, "we've not much time before the last bell tolls."

"Yee-hah," Hazel hooted, her gumball knuckles fisting half a deck of cards in each hand. "What have those waxed-eared idiots got to do with you teaching us how to count cards, anyhow? I say time enough to thump 'em and dump 'em on the way back. Right, Miss Jackie?"

Sally's cowboy boots scuffed the underside of the table. He sat up like inspiration might actually be an ant in his bony ass. He threw twenty dollars on the table and voiced the same wish as our female choir.

"I'm with the French girls — think maybe you can turn that twenty into two tons of stainless?"

Hazel began softly pounding the table with a caressing "win, win, we want to win." Jackie joined in, tapping and chanting "yes, yes, why will we win — I mean yes, yes, when will we win!"

By the time three horn blasts signaled our docking, it seemed the only thing our table players had learned about counting cards was that, with a count of *minus nine*, not one of them possessed the funds to endure even an average night's losing streak. Hazel put the cards back in her seaweed green hand bag and pursed her lips, not the least bit shaken about her chances of winning. That is, until Red stoked the fire in her by hammering home the fact that it hardly mattered what the count was if she couldn't afford a get-even-wager after losing ten hands in a row.

"Am I right Sally?"

Sally seconded Red's point. "For the life of me, I've never been able to weld two back to back winning hands together."

"Me neither, Sal," Hazel said. "I'm usually either sitting on fourteen, fifteen, or sixteen, no matter what the great Count says. What about you, Mark? You know numbers better than anyone here, better than Jimmy I bet."

"No, never big money. Just might be your night though, Hazel."

We walked the boardwalk as a group. The casino's red saucer roof spattering its glittering spotlights on the stars like a probing flying saucer. With each step I thought of Dianna; where she might be at this moment, what she was doing, what she was thinking and how she might be thinking about it. For the first time in weeks, I would not be putting her shapeless robe to bed this evening in my mind, in the confines of her cottage on the bluff.

A thin strand of hemlock and fir, on the steep hillside behind the windowless casino, littered their swaying movements beneath the lumbering moonlight. A few headlights humped the speed bumps in the sodium light of a terraced parking lot. Red's picnic talk couldn't have been more right — all the showcase apple orchards that once grew rosy with fruit on this island were gone. Fertile tribal land had given way to asphalt and the whistling pews of fulgurating slot machines. No one came here anymore to be still and to listen to the sea.

At the casino's monolithic entrance we stopped, not to listen to the music playing from the pumpkin-ribbed rafters, thirty feet above the valet parking booth, but because Jimmy's entourage wanted a powwow before going in. Everyone but Jimmy had decided they'd rather people-watch for a while, have drinks in the lounge, and let Jimmy try his luck with their money if he didn't mind gambling alone. Joey was biting his lip, trying not to raise his hand too noisily in our soup kitchen of his imagined future.

No sign of the stump men, no torn remnants from their

T-shirted hides had settled on the limbs of the casino's parking lot trees. So where were they?

"Forget about those tadpoles, will you." Jimmy had read my face as I'd looked back for any sign of the men.

"I better not go in, Sally." Joey told his brother. "I'll wait for you guys on the dock."

"That's no good, Joe." I said, genuinely discouraging the idea.

"Whoa. You almost grew wings there for a second, Joe." Jimmy mocked Joe's change of heart.

It was tiring listening to the way Jimmy was always ready to pounce on the world's crookedness and hypocrisy, always he was the constant panderer eager to trace all the world's faults with too much condescending color.

"Suit yourself, kid." Jimmy shifted his gaze from the parking lot on the hill to the snaking walkway which led to the casino's marina. "Only don't let me see you with those stumpfucks when I come out with your winnings. I do, and I'll give your money to the whores with your name and number written all over the bills?"

"Leave him be, Jimmy. The man said he doesn't want to go in."

"Well excuse me. Didn't know you were back in the adoption game."

"Come on now, lads," Red intervened, "let's take this inside and turn it into a pile of chips. All this serious stuff will sort itself out tomorrow."

"That's okay, Mr. Jacobs," Joe said. "I've got plenty of stuff to think about." To his brother's back he said, "Have fun Sally."

"Big handfuls," Hazel coughed. "We need five big handfuls."

"Pyramids, five pyramids!" Jackie half of Hazel's choir.

"Come on, lads. Let's get this crew inside." Red coaxed.

"Red's right," Jimmy made us suffer one more of his

mothball prophesies before opening the casino doors for the ladies, "what's dead is gone and the living left to crumble?"

"Say it ain't so, preacher." Jackie tacked a cheerful leer to her jest as she slipped under Jimmy's arm and opened the doors to the casino.

"We won't be long, Joe. You want anything? More coffee?"

"No thanks, Mr. Jacobs." He'd already turned away from the group and was walking towards the tipping masts of sailboats. He looked like a man searching for something — a bicycle, perhaps, or maybe my wife — the shadows of streetlamps in the beds of roses quietly letting him pass.

Inside the casino the obesity of so much color and noise is unsettling. Feels as if we're being plunged into a window-less aquarium. The air smells stale. The noise an incessant ringing in the ears, an inescapable chirr. Air so starched with the droppings of human tantrums it scratches. Great clutches of waddling, pumpkin-assed gamblers bumping and grinding their way thru a maze of glossy machinery. Emblems of Diamonds and Monopoly Money tinkling ten-cents on the dollar on the screens of *slots* that will spin forever. The casino's architectural expanse combining the building styles of a bullring and a chicken coupe.

"What?" I shouted to Jimmy over the heads of a dragon tail line of name-tagged retirees that had separated us.

"The Garnish game! Buttering us up with sparkling light and color before the butchering begins."

We walked across an urban landfill of carpet, its mar-bled patterns of flattened elk and deer heads tracking our shoes most of the way. Tall stalks of bamboo wallpapered two concrete columns at the entrance to the main casino, where the ratcheting herd of retirees would choose one of two paths — either to take their places at the feeding troughs or to rush to the bathroom stalls. But for others, the earth itself became noticeably more flat inside a casino, and a gambler could idle in that knowledge for a time, curl the edge of the world's flatness all the way to the cliffs of their credit lines, and outrun the thinness of a crust-less dollar bill until it bit their hungry children in the seat of their frayed pants.

We hooked up with Jimmy again behind a half-empty, twenty-five dollar table. Jackie wished him luck and excused herself with the others to check out the band in the lounge. Before I could go with them, Red pulled me aside.

"Straighten things out with him. It's gone on too long — this blame game the two of you play at." Jokingly, Red added, "and while you're at it keep an eye on our loose change, will you?"

Ahead of us was a gorge of felted greenery where crescent-shaped mini-bars fondled a fleet of blackjack players only half mindful of the losses to come. Jimmy took his sweet time inspecting the play at the first cluster of tables, walking slowly enough for me to see four-inch stacks of red chips regularly being returned to the silverware trays of blackjack dealers. I saw player after player reaching for ashtrays, cup-holders, and requesting *another hundred in red chips*. I witnessed double-down losses, verbal dismissals, denial, doubts, disbelief, dubious decisions, and talk of insurance, insurance, and more *insurance*; clips from a scene so closely divided by tone and purpose as to remind me of the one my wife and I had played out earlier in the day.

At a twenty-five dollar table Jimmy stopped in heavy traffic. At the table's third base seat a gentleman unknowingly mooned the crowd from his stool. The man wore a blue pinstriped shirt, washed so many times that the cuffs now rested a shot glass length above the man's pale, paint stick thin wrists. Two seats away from him a woman in a marsupial blouse was fumbling to straighten four twenty-dollar bills on the table, her fishtail loafers tapping at the table's brass footrest while she waited for the dull-faced dealer to change her money into casino chips. One of the woman's painted nails was split, half of the heel of one her loafers missing, her eyes adrift in pink parchment coupons that smirked *bet two, win three.* Inside the woman's purse, which lay open on a stool next to her, tea leaves for the misbegotten in the form of a soda-fountain romance novel and a book of horoscopes.

While Jimmy watched the last cards of an eight-deck pile being shuffled, two other players approached the table. They gulped and quickly straddled two stranded seats until the chrome heads of each of their stools were swallowed up whole by the couple's pair-shaped asses, which, in the great slump of their cloned decline could have easily kissed the eyes of the carpet elk.

It was easy for me to shake off the mediocrity of the table games, their garrulous clutter which peddled the desire for money. I wanted to tell Jimmy this, exactly this, wanted to tell him I'd made a mistake coming along tonight, that I'd suddenly no stomach for this drab crawl and was going outside to find Joe.

"Look," Jimmy said, as if once more reading my thoughts, "let me put their money to work for a couple of hands and then we can talk. I know you feel like shit right now. I know my mouth hasn't helped you any. Alright? Couple of hands."

Jimmy moved forward after he'd spoken to me to shore up the open space at the blackjack table's first base spot.

"No red, I want all green." Jimmy said to the dealer. He pushed his stool in under the bar as far as it would go, stood behind it, and plopped the group's hundred dollars down on the table.

"I'm going outside to check on Joe. Good luck."

"Hold up. Five minutes, that's all."

"And how are you gentlemen this evening?" The dealer asked. His voice sounds cordially recorded.

"Couldn't be better." Jimmy said. To me he said, "Five minutes, ten at the most."

"Would you gentlemen care for a drink?"

"No thanks."

Jimmy put a twenty-five dollar chip in his betting box.

"Everyone ready?"

But before the cards are dealt, Jimmy drops another green chip on top of his first one.

When it's the dealers turn to show his hand he stays pat on seventeen. Two smiling face cards coffin Jimmy's wager— a suited King and Queen. Jimmy wins and presses up the group's next bet.

Next hand, dealer is showing an Ace. Jimmy's hand is showing two more face cards.

"Insurance anyone?"

No one takes the insurance bet.

Dealer checks his face-down card. No blackjack. No one at the table draws cards. Dealer flips over his face-down card, a black nine. Half the players at the table *push*. New hands are dealt.

Dealer is showing a seven. This time, Jimmy doubles down on his Ace-three.

"Doubling for less," the dealer dubs.

There are now six green chips in front of the group's blackjack hand — a four stack family and a marriage of two.

Unbelievable. Jimmy's hand has pulled a seven. Our friends are now sitting, comfortably, in the lounge on a pat *twenty-one*.

The dealer busts, and Jimmy's wager is paid with six more green chips. He pulls the three hundred dollars from the betting box. But he's not smiling. He's not stepping back from the table with the group's winnings. He's not cashing out.

The dealer wallets a slight smile, waiting on Jimmy's next wager. Jimmy's the only one at the table holding up the deal.

Jimmy slides the entire tower of green back into the betting box. Three hundred dollars.

"Table Max."

The dealer pulls an Ace, and so does Jimmy. Player's second cards are dealt from the shoe, the dealer turning over Jimmy's card ever so slowly on the group's lone Ace.

"Picture!" Jimmy yells out before he's seen the card, so loudly that everyone seated at the table jumps.

"Blackjack! Yeah, baby."

"Insurance, anyone? Even Money, sir?"

No one speaks.

"Good decision, people."

The dealer has busted and is paying all hands. He praises the table's play.

"Congratulations, Jimmy."

I'd just witnessed what Hazel had made mention of at Jackie's picnic, how easily Jimmy could jump a steady ship and enter the uncertainty of tribal waters. He despised money-for-nothing performances. Yet, here he was, a man in contempt of his own doctrine, tonguing his white teeth and tapping his fingers on the table's black belt like a blind man about to reach for the big handful of chips in front of him.

"That ought to keep the natives off my back and out of my play for a couple of hours."

"I would think so," I said.

Jimmy handed me the seven hundred and fifty dollars in black and green chips, and asked if I'd take them to the cashier's cage and deliver the winnings to the group.

"You don't want to be the messenger? You did all the work."

"Wasn't any work at all. Wasn't my money."

But I knew better. It may not have been his money but it had been his vanity on the line with each wager. I also think he knew that by making me the bag man he was giving me my opportunity to leave rather than talk.

In the lounge, I gave our friends their winnings. They behaved like delirious Christmas carolers and wanted details. I smiled and told them Jimmy would be around in a minute with a full report.

"I'm going outdoors to check on Joe," I said. "Enjoy."

"Give him this." Hazel said. She passed Joe's share of the winnings to Salvador.

"Are the dogs okay, Sally?" I asked, taking Joe's share of the money from him.

"Oh yeah. Probably got jobs in valet parking by now. Not to worry, Mark. The guys parking cars keep an eye on them."

"Alright then. I'll see you all in a bit."

Outside, near a caging footbridge which roped and bound a levitating parking area with the casino's own marina, I called for Joe.

"Joe. Joseph?"

"Down here by the water. Under the stairs."

"Got a little something for you, Joe."

I stepped over a drooping rope of a rail and made my way down the embankment of sharpened fill rock. There was plenty of light seeping between the drier stones to catch my footsteps, some of it dotting the bunted way to a ledge of packed earth under the footbridge. Where it was necessary to crouch to pass under the footbridge, the soil bank dropped off more steeply. A damp and barren grade of shadows under the footbridge, a few weeds, but still more pleasant than the valet parking booth where I'd checked on Sally's dogs.

Joe had taken his Nike shoes and socks off and made a lumpish pillow of them. He was soaking his ankles at the water's edge, his toes wiggling on the surface of the cold to peek at the winnings I was waving in front of him.

"Here." I handed him the money and a large cup. "Money for nothing, as the singer says. Got you a hot chocolate to go with your winnings."

Joe looked at the hundred dollar bill I'd jacketed around the five tens. But when he his hand reached out it took only the cup of hot chocolate, leaving me holding his money.

"Probably Jackie or Hazel ought to divide it up, Mr. Jacobs."

"They did. This is your share. I'm more stunned than you are, believe me. Take it."

I watched him fold back the hundred and look with surprise at the other bills.

"There's a hundred and fifty dollars here. Holy Moses! Jimmy turned my twenty into all this? I don't believe it. No fooling?"

"I kind of wish I was. He's probably gonna rub your face in it all summer, you know."

"That's okay by me. I'm giving it all to my church. So maybe I'll rub his face in it a little, too, I guess."

"You think?"

"I can't hardly believe it, Mr. Jacobs. A hundred and fifty dollars."

"How cold is the water?" I asked.

"It's not too bad, really. Feels like Mountain Lake at the end of August. I usually like to give 'em a good soak the night before a big ride. What with all the surprises God is giving me today, though, I almost forgot."

"Why not split the winnings with your church? Buy yourself a couple of new bike tires with half of it."

"No, Mr. Jacobs. That just wouldn't be right after all that's happened to make this money come my way." Joe exercised a single sit-up and held it while bringing the money closer to his eyes. "Me going to Jackie's picnic instead of riding today, then following Jimmy to this casino, this is what's made things work out so perfectly."

"How's that?"

"It wasn't really my twenty to begin with." He sipped his hot drink. "Mmm-mah, this is really good, really hot. Thanks. It's kind of funny, isn't it? I've got hot stuff going in my top and cold feet coming out the bottom. Hope it's not another sign or something."

"Me, too. Been enough for one day."

"Yes there have. Sometimes I don't think I can handle one more sign from God. Though, I always do." He slurped at the whipping cream before fingering a glob of it into his mouth. "Mmmm-ah, this hits the spot. Can I tell you something personal, Mr. Jacobs?"

The bobbing lights in the sparkling marina had lost some of their charm to the cooling night air. I closed my eyes on them before answering Joe.

"Knock yourself out."

"See, the thing is. The thing is, I've been praying for your wife's recovery every day ever since you arrived. This year, I mean."

"So you're to blame," I mumbled.

"What's that, Mr. Jacobs?"

"Nothing."

"Your wife, she's completely well again, isn't she Mr. Jacobs?"

"Well enough, I guess."

I rested my head on my crossed arms. It was irritating and unsettling listening to someone less than a friend asking all the right questions.

"I had real nice conversations with her today after you left the picnic."

"Good for you, Joe."

"She's got a very kind way of thinking about things. You know all about that, I'm sure. Funny thing was, she got me thinking differently about some things. And that's not so easy. I invited her to attend services at my church. Hope that was okay with you?"

My eyes were closed, my head at rest, and listening for Joe to sip more of his chocolate had become a mindless distraction to measure time and mistakes.

"Mr. Jacobs? You awake?"

"Yeah."

"Know what she said?"

"Make something up," I mumbled.

"She said, 'one day in the not too distant future I would like that, Joseph.' Something tells me she will, too. See, it was your wife's money that I gave Jimmy. She gave me the twenty. She said it was a gift for my church. That's why I thought, just this once, it would be okay to gamble it for the Lord. Like maybe He intended me to since it was a totally unplanned thing us all coming over here like this. Together you know, and since the money fell into my hand on the same day your wife was healed."

I was uncomfortably seated on the jagged edge of a boulder, my head cradled over my knees, my mind trying to grasp Joe's mathematical absurdities while acknowledging my stomach's growing nausea.

"And you think it's a miracle?" I said, rather sluggishly.

"These things *are* miracles, Mr. Jacobs. Your wife cured, and now all this money, all on the same day. How can you not consider these to be signs? I have to."

I rolled my head on my arm and opened my eyes without lifting my head. Joey was holding the paper money up to the night sky. It was like he was running a flag up a pole, insisting that I should salute it one more time to confirm what he was saying about miracles. I was too tired to disagree.

Joe talked on and on after that. For an hour or more his tongue netted other *signs* from his own special wilderness, pairing fields of skipping stone coincidences with ambrosial conclusions. Sometimes the rippling churn of an isolated current or the trickling birth of new wind on still water would rush the wooden legs of the footbridge and interrupt Joe's strangely fluid rhythm of speech. Sometimes, it was a gambler's crude laughter or the heavy heels of a boat owner snaking out a dark drumming hum from the steel ramp, overhead, that would cause the boy to pause in mid-sentence and stare up at the flexing grates, entranced and patient, as if aware that these passing interruptions could prevent his one shot at converting me while I was at rest in his underground pulpit.

"Those boots overhead sound like thunder, don't they?" I whispered to Joe. I cradled my head again, waiting, wanting daylight to come back around.

"I wish they'd move this bridge to London." Joe whispered back.

"That man's boots are sick from crossing the same old bridge night after night."

"Could be you're beginning to read the signs right, Mr. Jacobs."

"Maybe you're not so far off this time, Joe."

I spoke, but it was as if some other inside of me had answered him. Under that footbridge, I could hear the whole world's panting overhead, a grinding and exhaustive breath that spoke of life's futility. How close I was to allowing all language to become foreign to me.

"The Lord is around every bend in the road, Mr. Jacobs."

The minutes dozed by, some of them without the soup of desperation attached to them. I'd never known Joe to talk so much or so freely. Somewhere between the casino's entrance and the marina's footbridge his rusty chain of stuttering seemed to have been replaced by a clean oily one. His snowplow interpretations of events came with the same old divine signatures, but the contours of his new speech were impressive and hypnotic to listen to for a change.

"Mr. Jacobs?"

I thought I heard Joe uttering a name which sounded so familiar, a name which sounded like *Kowlong* or *Kowtong*. All evening language had been growing, frighteningly, more foreign sounding to my ears, more and more fatiguing to attend to. Had he struck two stones together when he'd spoken the strange name? There was more, more of this click-clock language being spoken outside my head — *Kownong, Kee-eh-na, Koonlong* — and the words were beautiful, like a mountain stream whose trickling call leads you out of the darkest woods.

"Mr. Jacobs? Mr. Jacobs, you trying to sleep?"

"Yes."

"Will you be leaving the islands now?"

"Why would I be leaving?"

"I just figured, well, because now that your wife's better."

"You're the miracle-man, Joseph. What do you think I should do?"

"It's a whole lot easier on my nerves when you're working the bar. So, I guess, I'd like to see you stay."

"Why do you stay, Joe?" My tone was disrespectful, and my question hardly as well reasoned as Joe's inquiry had been.

"Can you keep a secret, Mr. Jacobs?"

"Like nobody's business."

"For me, *Jimmy's Campground* has turned out to be the Lord's proving ground."

"How's that?"

"Well, Mr. Young doesn't know it yet, and I don't exactly know how it's going to work itself out myself, but he's part of the Lord's special mission for me. That much I'm sure of. See, before you started working the summers here, way back before I rode bike so much, before I came to

Christ, well, thing is, I was going to run Jimmy down with my truck up on Switchback road."

"No fooling?" I mockingly acknowledged what I'd heard.

"Yeah, I'd been planning it for weeks. I thought about it day and night from about November all the way thru to about most of January. It was like a thirst I couldn't quench. I wasn't out to kill him or nothing. Just wanted to clip him bad enough with the bumper so he wouldn't run straight afterwards for awhile. Maybe not ever straight would have been okay by me. I tell you, Mr. Jacobs, the fury inside me was growing so fast back then. That's exactly what it was, too, pure hate. You ever had anything dig at you so bad you couldn't think straight?"

"I suppose I have."

"Well, I have. I'd worked out a convincing enough plan, too, a plan that would have made it look like an accident. You know, for afterwards, when the questions started coming in. I diagramed my perfect plan on three weeks worth of his stupid little cocktail napkins. At night, all thru Christmas break, I practiced coasting my truck down from the parking lot. I measured how much time it took me to reach the first switchback, then the second, like that you know. In the mornings, before sun-up, I would hike back up the mountain. Hide out in the woods somewhere close to that last switchback and wait for his backside to show. He's one hell of an athlete. I learned that about him quick. He'd always come jogging around that last turn within fifty-five seconds of his time the day before. That's hard to do. Well, all thru Christmas break I kept on checking my truck's coasting time, then his, like that you know. When I was as good at timing my downhill coasting as he was about running uphill backwards, I made the commitment. It was going to be like the gong in a clock that goes off at the same time every day. Only I'd be the only one to ever here it coming. He'd never hear or see my truck coming, the way I figured it. It was going to be my masterpiece."

Joey's bare feet humped on the surface of the water as if he were pressing on the brake pedals of a sweet dream remembered, a bit of splashing and toe kicking while he continued to talk.

"Yes sir, January sixteenth was to be my day of reckoning so to speak. So, on the day before, I drove my truck up the mountain and left it running in the parking lot until it was out of gas. Then I pulled the battery, so as to have an answer to future questioning, and threw it off those cliffs up there. Did you know a truck engine can idle on empty for way over an hour, Mr. Jacobs? Especially if all you're doing is thinking about one thing over and over again? I had my own foot speed and Jimmy's pretty well figured in by then. Did I say that? Anyways, that way, next morning, actually it was more like the middle of the night, all I'd have to do is hike up around the backside of the mountain to my vandalized truck with a token can of gasoline, and do all this before Jimmy started out on his run up Switchback Road. No one the wiser. Nobody. Except for me and my demon thirst."

"This is what you were like before you found Jesus, that's what you're saying?" What do you say to someone's self-examination, someone's confession, at this hour of the night under what was becoming a bridge for the misbegotten?

"Totally. Your friend used to offend my spirit something awful back then. And I don't mind telling anyone that now that I've been saved."

"Wouldn't he have seen you coming and jumped out of the way?" I asked. "Jimmy, I mean, not Jesus."

"I thought that part out too. He'd always run up those last two switchback turns ass backwards. You know the ones I mean, up near the top of the mountain. Lit-troll-lee.

Always. You know, working his quad muscles when the weather was too cold for him to run with his little bullshit sprints up the mountain."

"Jesus, Joe. Weren't you setting yourself up for a hell of a fall? Considering you could have just pulled your truck over and told Jimmy you were quitting the *Campground*."

"I don't have Jimmy's gift of gab. You know how he is, how good he is at it. He would have talked me out of it right there and then. And like I said, he offended my spirit pretty bad in those days. I was going thru with it, that's the one thing I'm sure of now. The way my thinking was so tangled up wrong by the devil, oh yeah, there's no doubt in my mind I would of done the deed. Excepting for the Lord showed me His signs that day. I mean, sign after sign like nobody's business."

"How do you figure?"

"On the morning I was going thru with the real deal it was dark as pitch out, and beginning to rain a little. No matter, off I go, like I'm some joke of a paperboy thinking it's nothing but a little sprinkle. I'm so pumped up that I get to the top of the mountain way before I need to. I'm sitting in my truck forever, watching the rain making a puzzle out of my windshield, when my watch says it's time to get out and start pushing. I'm a little shaky when I hop back in the cab, maybe a little afraid, but I'm on time. Perfectly on time. Only one thing, the first thing, starts to go big time wrong."

"What's that?"

"When I'm coasting down that long straight stretch, the one where I should be seeing the backside of Jimmy jogging towards me, he ain't there. He ain't coming around the curve like he's supposed to. But I handle it, 'cause I'm not so far along that I can't pull off the road far enough up the hill from the curve to still get speed when he does show.

I'm waiting. Just waiting. You ever wait on something you just know in your heart is coming down the pike?"

"Once."

"I'm counting the seconds. Two minutes go by, three, then four, then five. I can't figure it. Ten minutes more, then twenty, then it's like forty-five minutes and no Jimmy. Now I'm truly getting petrified. Partly because I've been parked in the middle of the road for over an hour and now it ain't nowhere as dark as it was when I left the top of the mountain. And partly because I'm getting a little paranoid that somehow he's figured out what I'm up to. Next thing I know I'm getting absolutely piss-eyed at Jimmy for not following the schedule. I'm a real mess real quick about why he's not there. Tell you the truth, I think I flipped out a little up there sitting on the side of road up there for so long. Now I might have to walk another four miles back to town for more gas and another stinking battery, and maybe reshape everything I've worked out. Maybe I won't have the satisfaction of riding back to town in an ambulance with him. I tell you, I was really getting cold feet about the whole idea. Then, at about the exact time my mind's almost ready to erase the whole plan, the hood on Jimmy's sweatshirt bobs into view. And wouldn't you just know it, I'm hot as Hades again to go thru with it. I'm no more than a hundred yards away from him. Here we go, I say out loud. I yank off the emergency brake. Know what? Sign number two is coming straight at me, only I don't yet know it. You with me so far?"

"All ears."

"I'm coasting and picking up speed pretty quickly. What I don't know, until I'm all jammed up in the clutch of it, is that all that extra waiting must have given the rain time to turn itself into the Devil's black ice. To make matters worse for me, sign number three is about to rain right down on me too. For no good reason under the sun, none, right there just ahead of my truck, Jimmy comes to a complete stand-still. Can you believe it? He don't turn around. He don't start doing fifty pushups. He don't start back up the hill doing a hundred and fifty jumping jacks. He's just plain decided to stand there dead ahead of my coasting truck. It's like's he's waiting on something. And then, God Almighty, I spot what it is he's waiting on. My windshield's fogged up on one side and all greasy with rain on the other, but I see what it is that's holding him in one place. It's this big long rope, probably ex-actly sixty-six feet of it, knowing where I'm going. It's unreal what I'm looking at. He's got one end of this rope tied around his waist, but that ain't the real problem. The real problem is that on the other end of it, a ways off down the next turn, it's looped around a group of first-graders. Each one of them kids is tied onto Jimmy's rope like they was a string of dead trout or something. And me, I'm already committed, helpless and hopeless, and coming straight at all of 'em. And doing it with no lights on, no horn, and no way to get out of the mess that's developed. How come? Because my truck's already be-gun to slide out of control on a mirror of ice, I mean, a com-plete circle of a spin. And Jimmy with this dumb-ass rope of his tied around his waist, tugging at least twenty-five school children behind him. Him deciding that this is the one day he's gonna chaperone some sort of kid's daytrip."

I groaned. "They've cancelled school due to ice?"

"You got it. 'Course all this don't sink in until my truck's in the middle of my first spin. When I come out of it, there they are! No sooner does my truck spin around once when it starts in on another. I'm heading right at all those strung-out bundles of nylon and rubber boots like it's my final finish line and maybe theirs too. How many kids I'm going to pull in under my wheels when my truck snags their tow line com-ing out of my next spin, I only kind of want to think about. There's this other thought popping my brains out right about now, too. Even if I manage to miss every one of them, even if there's no more ice once I go off the road, it's likely my truck's gonna keep going for a ways. If this happens, I'm gonna probably roll. I mean friggin-fuggin right over the cliff right there below me. Or what if I miss all of 'em, but Jimmy's tow rope snags over one of my wheels? You see my problem? A couple of dozen cookie-kids gonna go right over the cliff with me, aren't they? I swear, right then I would have done anything to pull stupid back. All of it. The cocktail napkins, the stopwatch, all of it. I'll tell you how bad I felt, Mr. Jacobs, it was the last time I can remember saying the word *fuck* out loud. And that's saying something, isn't it?"

Joe lifted his soaking feet from water, leaving me hanging. "So what happened?"

Joe was about to put his dirty-white socks on his wet feet, when he stopped and folded the socks over his knees.

"Another sign, what else. I could see the faces of the children when I came out of that second spin. I couldn't hear a thing. It was so eerie quiet. But I knew they were screaming. I knew that much of the cloud I was in wasn't no dream. Jimmy's eyes ran right smack into mine about then, too. At one point, he was so close to me that I wondered how he'd gotten inside my truck so fast. Then I saw him on the outside of my window again. It was like he was twins for a while. I know he was yelling something at those kids right about then, something smart enough that they could react to almost instantly. And you know what happened? Yes sir, it's the truth what happened next. True as this night and this money is in my hand. All of them fell to the ground like one big beautiful human avalanche, the kids on one side of my truck and Jimmy flat on the other. And my truck slides clean over their rope-pull. And off the road I go. Only it's not over. There's still one more sign the Lord wants me to plug into."

"Don't stop now."

"I don't remember it, but I guess my truck rolled over at least once, once the gravel kind of slowed its momentum. I do remember looking over at the passenger's side when the truck was still moving and seeing the roof of my truck sitting in the seat beside me. It looked like the top half of a pyramid had climbed in upside down with me or something. I'm thinking it's that doorknob of a guardrail up there in front of me that must have done it. And if that's true, well, then I'm already over it and nothing left to stop me from going completely over the cliff. Next thing I know, there's this bruising pain in my hip and a tree trunk where my side window used to be. And I'm completely stopped. And you know what's hanging on that tree trunk, Mr. Jacobs, the one in my window, the one staring me right in the face? The happiest little *Jesus Saves* sign I'll ever lay eyes on. I swear it, you can ask Jimmy. I couldn't believe it either. I turn my head at the tree trunk in my window one more time, at about a hundred miles an hour, and there it is not moving. You know, one of those white plastic ones that invisible people hang on trees out in the middle of nowhere. Only, right under this one, right under the words *Jesus Saves*, someone, and you know who, had lettered in with paint, *and Jimmy Serves at Jimmy's Campground*.

A muffled, closed mouth chuckle lifted my chest a little.

"Know what I did the next day?"

"No idea," I answered truthfully.

"I went right back up the mountain with a hand painted sign of my own. Know what I wrote on it? I wrote —

> *Jesus saves the little children,*
> *myself,*
> *and Jimmy too.*

"And you haven't driven since?"

"That's the truth, Mr. Jacobs."

"Amen."

"Amen is right."

I rubbed my head and stretched my back. I was no longer tired or nauseous, I was angry. I wanted off this pin prick of an island, wanted nothing more from this day but to face the insatiable anger that rests on the bottom of a bottle. I shook Joe's hand and thanked him, and was on my feet grappling my way up the embankment before he had finished putting on his socks and shoes.

"You gonna go find Jimmy?"

"I suppose, though it might be easier if we left him here."

"If he's winning he won't come?"

"Want to bet that hundred on it?"

"— I wouldn't if I was you." Hazel's clunky voice had found us. She and Red were standing by the footbridge, both of them watching me climb. "And he's not, he's not winning."

I stepped onto the parking lot's spotty lighting, Joe taking his time to climb the slope.

"He's not winning a pickled penny."

"All the more reason for him to crawl back to the *Campground* with us. I'm hungry and I want my own food, Hazel. Your food. You two coming with me?"

"I don't think so. This old Robin and Rooster have to get home and get to bed."

Hazel spooned me a kiss on the cheek and said goodnight.

"Come on, friend," Hazel took Red's arm, "walk me to the ferry."

"How bad is he losing?" I asked Red.

Red searched for the right words. Hazel nervously tapped the sidewalk with one of her shoes.

"Insane amounts. And going out of his way to piss people off that are foolish enough to try and take a seat at his table."

"He bought the table." Hazel was quick to offer more

details. "When we left he was betting the table max in near-ly every circle."

Joe jumped into the lot's mercury lighting. He stretched his arms over his head until his bodily height towered over Hazel's flattened hair.

"Red?"

"It's true, I'm afraid. There's not a bit of embellishment in what Hazel is saying."

Red shifted his weight off his bum knee.

"It's not really any of my business, Mark. But maybe you ought to go in there and talk some sense into him be-fore he loses the whole goddamn Campground. I tried, and was told to go shuck oysters."

"That last dealer, she swiped four five-hundred dol-lar chips out from under his first four hands out of a new shoe." Hazel looked genuinely concerned. "Did it like she was enjoying stickin' it to Mr. Young."

"Five?" Red questioned Hazel's numbers.

"Five," Hazel punctuated. "Five pink ladies. Don't you remember? Soon as that dealer turned over her ugly black-jack Mr. Young's ponytail swung clear around and met an-other mouthful of more cursing."

"Are Jackie and Salvador still in the lounge?" I asked.

"They were watching Jimmy's play when we left, I think."

"Alright. Well, I guess this is goodnight then."

"Good luck in there, Mark."

"Yup."

Hazel and Red walked off bumping bodies and pock-eting their loose hands, the lamp of a docked ferryboat ahead of them.

Inside the casino, I picked out Jimmy's ponytail in heavy traffic. There was now a slight sag in the bones of his unnat-urally propped and stifled shoulders, a slump that wasn't there during today's ballgame or when he had dragged half of New England across Jackie's meadow. A cannery of annoying moaning was now gathered around him, cheerless and cornering. The people observing his play looked like cornered fishermen watching one of their own wiggle and writhe on a barbed hook.

At Jimmy's table I stood back and watched with the others as he coughed a forefinger tap on the table's felt. A discouraging picture card flipped its royal cape over his first hand and shattered another wishing-well wish. He played a few more disastrous hands, tidily winking from twenty-five dollar chips to sow-pink five-hundred dollar slices of micro-chipped wafers.

I stepped up to Jimmy's table and as I did another three-grand in stomach-lifting pink chips were swept off the table and into the casino's rainbow rack of promise.

"Christ Jimmy," I blurted out, "don't give this fucking church another dime."

"I'm working here, friend. You mind?"

"How much you down?" I persisted. The goosenecks surrounding the table seemed enthralled with the glamour of my friend's financial execution, and were quick to hedge-hop my outburst so as to keep watching the table action.

"Be a sport, Thomas," Jimmy said to the dealer, "tell my wife how much I'm down, will you? She's a math wiz. Maybe the shock of hearing the numbers will shut her up."

The dealer fingered his tray for a count. "Looks like ninety-four hundred, Mr. Young."

"Looks like ninety-four hundred, Honey." Jimmy winked at the small crowd behind him. "And counting."

The smell of stale beer and cigarette smoke gristles Jimmy's table of empty stools, Sally shrugging his shoulders and Jackie rolling her disbelieving eyes, and my friend unwilling to admit that the water is rising.

"The rest of us are catching the ferry back to the Campground." I said. "You coming?"

"Campground? What the hell you going there for?"

"I like it there. Beats watching you throw your half of it away."

"That a fact?" To the dealer Jimmy nodded and said, "And to think, Thomas, that the man behind me wrote his Doctorate on lost numbers. Hit me!"

Sally stepped up and put his hand on Jimmy's shoulder. "I'm with Mark. Come on Jimmy, finish up. Let's go."

"Give me a minute. Take it, Thomas. God damn it."

There's a glaring white line of anger in Jimmy's eyes that follows two more of his towering stacks of chips into the house's money tray. And there's more of a twist in his terse smile than was there when I stepped up to the table, and it's about to give the old man who's crow-walking around the third base stool an earful.

"That must have hurt." The old man lays his insult on the small crowd while placing his ring laden right hand on the back of one of the stools.

He's a clothesline bird, this old man. Speaks a language Jimmy understands and speaks fluently but doesn't much care for in others. Hangs his plaid sports coat over the back of a stool, a jacket worn to threads at the elbows, anemic tails, buttons cracked and dangling like the beaks of broken-neck chickens. The laces on one of his shoes are untied and dragging. The shirt he's wearing missing half of its ladybug buttons, no matter, he's shameless, proud of the wrinkled sheep-skinned chest he's showing the casino's cameras. Needs a haircut and a shave, some better manners.

"Money's water. That's all it is, old man."

And having said that, Jimmy placed his last stack of Angus colored chips in the betting ring and walked away from the table, butting Sally and me to move aside as he turned and walked.

"Come on, Sal. I'm ready to go."

"What? You've still got a standing bet out there."

But Jimmy had already slipped thru the meager crowd, not a scat of interest in the outcome of his abandoned wager.

That was the end of it. A half hour later we were all taking our places on the upper deck of a ferry, the dogs happy to be back by Sally's side, the others with us talking about ordering midnight breakfast at the *Campground*.

"Just like the old days, eh Mark. Count your losses and then bury them."

I refused to acknowledge his commentary. There was something hideous and repulsive about what he was saying, about all that I'd seen inside the casino and heard under the marina's footbridge.

On the ferry ride back to our island a foreigner's language drummed once more in my head. It climbed the waves and shouted from the valleys of thin water between each surge. At times, what I heard was hardly more than the strum of a hummingbird's flight, a beseeching call which soon faded in the twinkling wake of our tinkling vessel.

"Dianna told me everything this afternoon." Jimmy said, leaning against the railing next to me as we were nearing our home dock. "Are you staying on?"

"Oh Christ, Jimmy, what's it matter? Your daughter, your lover, your wife — what difference does it make — there's always one that walks away and one that stays behind and sinks."

I hated the sound of what I'd said and walked as far away from it as I could.

The porch light gold and fluttering when we walked thru Jessie's courtyard, but a ship's light come home from sea when Jimmy opened the screen door and unlocked the door to the *Campground*. He gave the heavy door an unnecessary toe-kick, and when he did I slid by him happy to make him wait. Sally and Joey came in behind me, and one of the dogs. Jackie lingered a minute on the porch stairs with Jenny, the two of them searching the stars above the banding fog and listening to the flutter of maple-leafed moths circling street-lamps before giving the dog a dish of fresh water and entering the quiet bar. It was late, sometime after midnight.

Time curls back upon itself, or maybe, we help it to do so. Dianna's voice whispered in my head, her skeletal sway gone now as I watched her body's new blood wave goodbye to all the pretty picnic people gone too. On the mirrored walls behind the bar Dianna is still here, youthful in the silvery-disked photographs which lapped their colors tonight from the rim of the *Campground's* porch light, soothing the *wishing-wall*s with her laughter and the pretense that there was a time when my trust, my loyalty, was infallible.

Draw the curtains on the bar's porch windows so my eyes might cloud the mystic stares of Depot Island, and believe, however irreverently, that there was time enough to wade back into the promise of Dianna. Time curls back upon itself, or maybe, some *other* only wishes it were so.

Jackie and Joe offered to make all of us something to eat. Jimmy followed them as far as the kitchen door, joking that Hazel's lunch-pail radio had to be on before the stove could be lit, and then walked to the *Campground's* new back door. He reached between the rungs of the wooden ladder which still protected the unfinished door and slid back the door's deadbolt. The pine door tip-toed opened like one of Sally's dogs stalking a bird and an aisle of light from the backyard spilled onto the room's wood floors. The light felt warm and lemony and made the gouges in some of the table legs in the room stand out. Except for a single nightlight hiding behind the fireplace wall, where it pitched a tiny tent of yellow on the dining room floor, all other lighting in the bar room was off.

Jimmy walked back to the bar and ducked in quietly under the bar's gate. I took a seat on the barstool nearest the front entrance. Sally had walked to the fireplace and started a small kindling fire, which soon settled low and smokeless with prisms of color that shrunk the room.

For several minutes Jimmy became engrossed with the writing and calculation of numbers on a pad. When he put the pencil and pad away the arrogance which had colored his face most of the evening had completely faded. He looked confused, worn down, half dressed.

"You know, Mark," Jimmy looked at me from his side of the bar, "people are talking."

"That's what distinguishes us from the other animals." I gulped the last of my ferry's cold coffee, and for a brief moment did not have to look at him.

"It's not Dianna they're talking about."

"Since when you ever bent a hair on your pretty little ponytail to public opinion?"

"Losing money ain't like losing a wife and lover though, is it?"

Talk like this had been the heart punch of Jimmy's counseling for the better part of a year. I was sick of it, sick of the rub of his handcuffs, sick of the sounds of slowing tires and the pop of street gravel outside. Sick of what was real and what was imagined.

"Wouldn't know. I ain't ever cried over money."

"Will you two drop it. This here's quiet time." Sally had moved from the fire to take up his usual residence on one of the couches by the sandpit, his feet up, his hands busy sectioning yesterday's paper.

"You like to kick people when you're down, don't you Jimmy?"

"If I thought it would make a dent."

"Been there, done that with you. Ain't ever going back."

"Hey!" Salvador tried once more to make peace. "One of you get over here and poke a fire that's not so hot."

"Ten grand down the drain and all you can come up with is 'money's water that's all it is.' About what I'd expect from someone who never came to his daughter's funeral."

"What you ought to be thinking about doing right now is walking on back to Reds and cooling off."

Sally tossed his paper aside and stood up. He walked back to the fireplace and pulled one of his pokers from the rack. Brynnie remained on the couch, patiently watching and waiting for Sally to put the poker back in its rack. Both of them, man and dog, listening to something outside of the other's reach. I'd heard something, too, maybe Jenny's nails racing a moth over a stretch of porch, maybe my own footsteps racing ahead of her thru the courtyard.

"Like to put cuffs on me again, would you? Be a whole 'nother kind of night this time around, won't it?"

Jimmy pointed his finger at me and my insides began to float. "I did what you asked of me. You hung that promise on my back. Remember?"

Sally put the poker back in its rack and made his way to the open door in the back wall. Brynnie jumped off the couch, stretched, and went with him.

"You think you're the only one who's living thru this mess, don't you?" Jimmy's gaze carried a ministry all its own. "The black man who lives all alone down by the sea and walks on water. Tell me something — in your house of sand and secrets, you and your wife ever talk about Jessie's activities in Seattle?"

"Jimmy —"

"What's the matter? Dead pussy got your tongue?"

"Jesus Christ, Jimmy." Sally spoke up from across the room. "Shut it."

"You don't know how it was between us." I stood up in anger, accidentally pushing over the barstool. "Wasn't the way anyone thinks it was."

"I wasn't given the chance to see it in any kind of right, was I? I had to see it and swallow it from a newspaper. God damn catholic priest stuck it in my hand. Then he kept sticking me with it all year, same as you been doing, 'til it's a living thing in my head all day, every day. You got regrets? Well I got 'em, too."

I felt the walls of the Campground closing in on me.

"What exactly did you read in the papers?" I asked.

"Jesus, just shut up."

"Tell me. Because I don't know."

"You fucking freak." Jimmy's voice a towering guillotine behind the bar. "You know god damn well what people read into her death. Everyone. Everyone knowing she'd have been at that picnic today if not for that cult's miserable hazing."

This was not the ending I had rehearsed. I had heard of this ending but I had not reasoned it, because in my heart I knew it could not be true.

"What are you talking about? What hazing?"

Jimmy's face sunk like a stone holding all the agony of all fathers still lost in the death of a child.

"The Jessie we knew would never have entered those waters in daylight, let alone in the middle of the night. Never. She'd be alive today if I hadn't pushed her so hard to tell me who the father was."

"Jimmy, I —"

I tried swallowing the sickness of what I'd heard. Tried breathing myself back into the body standing at the bar.

"You were supposed to watch out for her. You made promises, too. You made promises."

"I don't understand. What you're saying, it's not —"

"You think I don't know why Jessie tied in with those white shits in Seattle, but I do. I could write a book on what I know about them now."

I didn't know my secret could betray me with one of its own. I must have spoken. He must have heard what I could not — that, what he was saying was not possible. Not possible, because I had been with her the day before she drowned.

Jimmy hung his head over the bar sink. He looked like a boy studying the flatness of his likeness in a spring puddle, his ponytail feathering some part of him that was no longer connected.

"I loved your daughter. And I told her so every time I was with her."

"You never could see a thing for what it was." He spoke and gestured from a rolling deck. "That what you come up with at the bottom of a bottle? Might help me if I knew that's where it come from."

"It happened."

"Shut up. Just shut up."

I think Jessie could have walked into the *Campground* this night all open arms and forgiving, Dianna too, and neither of us would have taken notice. The room was orbiting. The cube of space where I'd reached for the fallen barstool — desolate and soundless.

Brynnie's head cocked alertness near Sally's knee, the dog's tangerine eyes opening wide on the *Campground's* front door and its ears pinching the darkness from all corners of the room. Even before their boots shook the porch, the dog had released a low-pitched growl and pulled back his quivering lips to show teeth that remembered the coffin cages of circuses.

I counted seven of them.

"Jimmy! What the hell you doing here this time of night?"

As if from some ghostly campfire, my friend's name had been called out by the tallest armband in the group of sculled men, and allowed to tumble onto my palace steps with no other purpose than to soil our confessional.

I could smell their spoiling flesh seeping salt from under their armbands when they marched passed my barstool. A bleached ball of cash rolled on the bar like a shriveled clump of grapes. The huge prosaic hand hovering over the wad of cash quick to hammer the green bills more paltry gray with his fist.

"Food and American beer. Please. As much as that will buy. And tell your city-boy friend — Mark's his name, I think — tell him not to think about telling us you're closed."

Moronic mumbling came from the other men as they spread out into the room. The sons of absent fathers, men whom had come to our islands beneath the cloak of a caustic fog, their hoofed snouts riding high off the water. Their sniggering feeding on itself and poisoning the light from the fire.

I looked at Jimmy and wondered if it was my dead secret that was now holding his spirit in check.

"Hurry up," the tall one spoke, "we ain't got time to wait for two old atheists to be born again."

Jimmy said nothing. He unraveled the man's money — seven twenty-dollar bills, one for each man now trespassing on my side of the bar. He placed the twenties on top of one another and rolled the dirty bills into the shape of an empty shotgun shell.

The room grew more uncomfortable from the sounds of chaffing chairs being pulled half-circle around Sally's fire. Some of the men put their boots into the backs of chairs, smirking at one another and casting stares at Brynnie who was facing down their white t-shirts with a glaring stare of her own from across the room.

"You deaf as well as mute today, Jimmy? I said hurry up with the grub."

It is amazing what choking things return to usefulness in the hands and movements of a coiling wrath, how convincingly memory can trigger the body to act. We had found amusement this evening in how much this banded infantry resembled rats perching on the beam of a fallen barn, Jackie suggesting that these men had been searching the fiery horizon in the east for the origin of the Great Bang which had toppled their reign. And now, two of the men, the same two men Jackie and I had dealt with once before, were worming their way thru the others to lay hold of a photograph of Dianna which hung above the fireplace mantle.

"Take your filthy — fucking — white hands off it!"

The tall man beside me reared back. Some of the others scoffed. One of the men seated by the fireplace kicked an empty chair hard into a table and stared back at me. A bulldog of a man with his back to me stepped into the sandpit and prepared to take a piss. One of the men crowding Sally's mantle, the one I'd quickly recognized, hacked violently and spit on the photograph he was rocking with his fingers.

"I think we're standing on Jimmy's side of the bar, this time around Jacobs."

"This whole island, and everything on it — it's all his fucking side of the bar. All he's got left. And you," Jimmy's words stone cold and determined, "you stinking little pricks — you think you're gonna come in my front door and spit on him. No."

"No need to be rude, Jimmy."

"Know what a hundred and forty dollars is to me, Trump?

That's your name isn't it? One percent. One percent of what I lost tonight." Jimmy's hand reached under the bar, and when his hand was visible again it slipped whatever it was he was holding against the back of his neck. "Not even enough to buy me one of your bitches for the night, is it?"

"Watch your mouth."

"You stump-fucks ever seen the way a real man lets his hair down at night?" There was the gentlest of scrapes from scissors cutting close to the hairline on the back of Jimmy's neck. When Jimmy's hands came back around the scissors he'd been holding slid quickly into his pocket, and his ponytail lay limp on the bar.

The pus of laughter came from one of the men moving closer to Sally and Brynn. "What the hell you do that for? 'Fraid we might do it for you?"

"Needed a rubber band, pup." Jimmy spoke without looking up from the bar. He twisted the tie from the amputated tail of hair, and the ponytail suddenly lay on the bar like the stems of so many plastic flowers.

Trump stepped towards the bar to take back his money. But before the man could grab the roll of bills Jimmy's hand had swept the money from the bar, tying the paper cartridge with the rubber band from his ponytail as fast as a cowhand ties a calf's hoofs.

A lance of a stare came from Trump as Jimmy violently threw the money across the room, every man in the room seeing it bounce off the fireplace brick and come to rest inches from the flames.

Trump's men stiffened and rose. The men stood like elbow-spaced buildings watching the fires of the homeless flicker below them. A few defiant stares before one of the men kicked at the burning with his black-laced boots. A few coals scattering and bouncing like marbled corks over the room's floor by the time the boy had grabbed the roll of bills beginning to burn.

Salvador stood tall. Brynnie held a half point, tasting the running blocks, one of his hind quarters quivering, his eyes waiting for Sally's hands to give any kind of a command.

The string of men grouped in closer to one another, angry and waiting for instructions from Trump who was facing Jimmy, their gluttonous faces hoping to taste an unprincipled glory. One of the men jumped ranks to lift an empty black picture frame from the mantle, the frame Jimmy and I had intended to put Dianna's picture in when she walked into the *Campground*, well again. A defiling smirk spun the frame by its corners on the tips of the man's middle fingers.

"How 'bout we put your face in this empty one first, Jacobs." The bulbous face spat its warning at me. "You might look nice hanging over the mantle?"

Jimmy reached under the bar, slid a drawer off its runners, and overturned the contents of the box onto the bar. I was dumbfounded. Piled like a small heap of trash over his lifeless ponytail, photographs of the men now standing in our bar were being shuffled thru by Jimmy's hands.

"Why don't you put one of these pictures in the frame —Christopher?" Jimmy flung one of the photographs at the group. "Or how 'bout this one. Here's one of my favorites, Jeffrey."

More photographs took to the air and spun a web of confusion in my head. The pictures soured the faces of Trump's men with the incriminations that trailed behind their flight, in the way the stiff photographs lighted upon windowsills and tagged the cloth of tables, and in the way the pictures sometimes struck the men they were naming. *Christopher — Jeffrey — Bryant — Ryan — Tate — Sage — Trump*. I would have wished for Jimmy's sake that these pictures, which kept soaring towards the fire like the jagged weapons of samurai, had come from a father's love that the fatherless can not know, that they were not blue and black and somehow staging a living vengeance to further darken a father's grief.

"My friend, Mark, he asked you nicely long time ago not to come back. Know what? Now you're not going anywhere."

Jimmy's eyes instructed Sally to go to the front door. Sally was there in half a dozen quick footsteps, closing and dead-bolting the door while Trump watched and nodded re-assurance to his men. Brynnie's eyes tracing Sally's march to and from the front door, step for step, waiting, anticipating.

There is no sound from the ladder which still hangs across the opening in back wall, until Sally tosses it aside and its wooden rails scrape across the floor like an empty crate.

"Sally, what's going on?" Joey walked out from the kitchen. He took but a single step before stopping to stand stunned at the sight of so many men in the bar.

"Either you're with me or you're against me, Joe." Sally words bit hard at his brother's disbelief. The kitchen door swung shut.

Trump's men spread their wings, eyeing one another's positions around the room.

Sally spoke a single word to Brynnie — *Circus!* — and the fiercest of growls erupted from under the dog's pinched lips, then faded to a quiver beneath the dog's stone-eyed glare. Sally's second command to the dog was voiced even louder — *Ready and Wait!*

Jimmy looks to be in some kind of trance. But for me every little thing that is moving in the room is bright and clean and connected to me. There is a tunnel of space swirl-ing outside the opening in the back wall, and another be-tween the yard's two stacks of lumber, which I take notice of. How neatly the handles of shovels have been lined up and how tightly an electrical cord has been laced over the arms of a portable cement mixer — each is a weapon, I see that for what feels like the first time

Jimmy's finger lifted him out of his trance. He pointed it like a bayonet in Salvador's direction. "Now you white shits gonna leave my church same way your whoring fathers thought niggers and fags should go out."

"You have no idea how far we reach, Jimmy. You only think you do."

I held my anger up to the eyes and skulls of the men around me, seeing a way out, a way to make amends. Dreamed these men to be crumbling, shelled-out buildings along the shoreline of Jessie's last swim. Wished it as my own ending because I saw how the filth in these men might escape the law, because I saw their hanging ropes swinging from the limbs of willows and desperate desert canyons forever beyond our reach. Because I have seen the nails and the hammers and the hatred of their fathers pooling for centuries behind their despicable white crosses. And then I struck at bone and the flesh of a man guilty and untouched for centuries.

The force of my sweep kick caught the lower part of Trump's calf and brought the man hard to the floor. There was the cracking sound of his elbows hitting wood and the smug look on his face changing to agony. Jimmy came over the bar like a gymnast to meet the next man rushing towards me, stopping him with an open-handed strike to the man's throat. The man reeled backwards and fell to his knees, frantically clawing at his injured windpipe before collapsing on the floor in a coiling of chilling, gurgling squeals as two other men charged us from across the room. Jimmy found his stance at once. I swung full circle before either man had reached us, coming out of my spin delivering a barstool blow to the skull of the man that had charged from the sandpit. My barstool struck at the man's eyes when he was down, and more pathetic cries rose from the floor. I let go of the barstool — Jimmy was yelling my name and tossing me the bar bat — and skipped back to catch the bat and avoid Trump's reach. In that same moment, the sound of an animal in pain rose up from some corner of the room. In a matter of seconds Jenny had somehow managed to crouch under my legs and was now shivering with fear. The dog's small body nearly ripped from her head by a boot kick that missed her but connected with the backside of my knee. There was time for me to see Jenny escape another vicious kick and run for the dark caged corner a table offered, before my bat struck Trump's hand and knuckles. Trump tried to stand and grab my groin, but Jimmy skipped between us to put the meat of his thigh into the man's forehead. From high above my head, I brought the bat down hard on Trump's spine for a second time. And still there was no sight of blood on the floor or from Trump's body to make what was happening seem deadly or savage.

I looked across the room for Sally and saw blades and whips and ropes chasing the mothers and fathers of terrified children, saw these instruments of fear dancing like playthings in the minds of the men struggling to take Sally down. I ran thru fields of rotting hay and stale white smoke, wanting to stab and spear at thistled teeth and gouge whatever flesh my hands lay hold of. Salvador caught the hook of the poker in the meat of his thigh, a savage axe-swing of a strike that opened his eyes wide with pain. The blow might easily have come down on Sally's skull had his attacker not been off balanced by Brynnie's running jump at the man's wrist. With a wedge of firewood, I struck at the ankles and spine of the boy trying to crawl out from under the jabs of Sally's ladder. In the punching and kicking that ensued I took but one lancing blow to my chest and, in the pain it gave birth to, grew more riotous in my pulling of the canoe from the ceiling and in its crashing collapse on the fallen boy.

Sally shifted his weight to better defend himself against another powerful swing of iron, but the ladder he was holding became entangled with the driftwood in the sandpit. Before Sally's attacker could complete his second strike I took hold of the man's bloodied arm and dragged him into the pit, caking as much sand into his eyes as I could fist once we had fallen.

From the sandpit, I could see Jackie and Joey spraying two of Trump's men with the kitchen's fire extinguisher. It was an odd sight, seeing both of them grappling with the extinguisher's trigger and nozzle, like watching children playing with a bell rope. Jimmy was with them, already in the mix of it, grabbing hold of one of the men who was blindly reaching for Jackie's arm and swinging her attacker thru the opening in the back wall. Before Joey's attacker could retreat, Jimmy rushed the man and collared him with his own t-shirt, twisting the white t-shirt blue around the young man's neck. The man's boots kicked at the floor, sheer panic in his eyes as he flailed and tried to break loose from Jimmy's one-arm hold which was dragging the man towards the back door. In seconds, the youth was tumbling thru the wall's opening like a dish of spoiling table scraps Jimmy might throw to the birds.

Unbelievably, Trump was back on his feet. His eyes a slit of scathing anger. Salvador yelled "Whip! Brynnie, whip!" and the heart of that dog's soul, which the circus could not kill, flew thru the air, all eighty-eight pounds of its tracking muscle and memory. Brynnie jumped over sand and body and the ache of all eyes watching in disbelief, and descended into the fat of Trump's forearm in a torrid purple rage. The dog's intent, unstoppable.

When the dog released Trump's hand, I thought that

might be the end of it. Then, something out of a dream — the dog hooking its front paws over Trump's leather belt to climb the man's backside as if the man's spine was a ladder. On the ridge of Trump's shoulder, the dog somehow held on and savagely dug its teeth into the crown of Trump's skull and the back of the man's neck and shoulders.

Maybe ten or fifteen seconds of Brynnie's rage orbited the room. The dog's jaws snapping violently over Trump's flesh, its teeth digging deeper into the viciousness of the attack with each second screamed out from the rafters. Under the severity of the dog's attack, Trump's body finally folded to the floor — the man's hands slapping at air as if his scalp was on fire, as he fell.

Nothing Trump's body tried to do to cover itself unbalanced the animal. The man's cries to his comrades incoherent, desperate, and unanswered. Brynnie's gnawing bites merciless and carrying the grating sounds of an un-soaped blade slicing its way thru granite. One side of Trump's lip already hung like a bloody earthworm over his snot covered chin. He tried to roll, hoping to smash apart the dog's mania, the fangs of our black angel now scraping over Trump's scalp as if trying to puncture a beach ball.

Only when Salvador yelled, "Down Brynnie! Down — Down!" did the dog free itself from its dome of terror and look to Sally for more purpose and instruction.

Trump crawled to the hearth of the fireplace where he continued to rabidly punch at empty air, his eyes and fists insanely searching for the breath of the dog that was no longer there.

I thought it was over, truly I did. I expected an exodus. I scanned the room. Everyone was resting their exhaustion. Everyone bleeding or bruising some hope of an ending, so I thought. Christopher was bent over near the bolted front door, clutching his belt buckle, his bloody nose the only

damage I could detect in the light of the wall lamp someone had turned on. Jeffrey groped for the windowsill next
to him, his belt fully out of its pant loops and its leathery
weave wrapped around his fist. Both of these men looked
like drunken schoolboys to me now. Two other men sat
folded near the feet of Joey and Jackie. These men panted,
chests tilted forward, faces covered. I heard no sounds of
life coming from the opening in the *Campground's* back wall.

But Trump had managed to climb to his feet. His huge
hands gloved with blood which streaked over his ears and
down both sides of his face. He seemed suddenly deaf, as
though he had fought the most insidious and penetrating
sound inside his head and lost the battle. His head rose to
the underside of the mantle, his chin arched, and his arms
took hold of mantle's edge to lift the bulk of his wild-eyed
body. Trump's voice scratched out at the paleness of any
goodness which may have once lived in him, shrieked out
at the core of our stares tracking him like the crackle of winter's thawing ice, each of us held back by the wounds of the
reckless violence all but Jackie and Joey had succumbed to.

Trump's shoulders braced against the stone of the fireplace, his one functioning hand slipping downward, fingers
fumbling and raking over the soot and stone until his hand
found the spiraling handle of one of Sally's iron shovels.

"Trump, let it go." One of Trump's men had voiced unbelievable neutrality. It had come without grace, and had
cost the man nothing, but it would live forever in the dust
of the room's furnishings.

Like a giant unbalanced fulcrum, Trump's pendulous arm
swung high as he mumbled something incoherent — the iron
shovel he wielded scrubbing a rafter with a spurring gouging
that was muted by the last of Trump's slurred words.

"I — I'ng going kill 'is dog."

The beauty of Jackie's coupled hands, their prayer-shaped

lull-a-bye moving to cover her lips. Jenny's muzzle tracking the arc of Trump's arm. Sally's face painted with a putrid shade of fear.

I yelled for Salvador to somehow command Brynnie to move.

In that moment of time that was to leave all but one of us still and sickened, in the terror of the room's piercing quiet, Jimmy's commanding shout floated from the bar to tag the dog's ear.

"Jump Brynnie! Jump!"

Trump lunged, and the heaviness of Sally's iron shovel whirled down on Brynnie before the man collapsed and flopped like a glob of wet paste against the sandpit. The dog's body wavered and came to rest against the driftwood and the ladder's broken rail in the sandbox.

For a few hopeless seconds, the dog struggled helplessly to stand on its own, its eyes locking with Salvador's and holding the look of a soul about to pass gently off to sleep. The clock on the mantle to mark the dog's gut-wrenching collapse, a sight made all the more sickening by a gush of blood from the base of the dog's skull.

The iron shovel would have missed Brynnie completely had Jimmy's command not placed the dog directly under the wildness of Trump's strike. The suffering in Jimmy's eyes, how it ran so far ahead of my pounding heart. How it perched itself so quickly in the coves of the *Campground's* wailing walls to look down upon the cribs of babies and prophets, that each might be delivered from the hands of fire — *and he shall send down fire and flame unto the wicked, and fire and smoke will be the glass they drink from and they will know the wrath of the lord once more.*

From the shallowest ledge of my deepest hatred for this breed of men, I drove my knee into Trump's ribs until the shattering within me could not hear his splintering, rolling prayers for it all to stop. Into the mouth of his acrid pleas, I struck without remorse. He sprawled on his stomach in a desperate attempt to grab hold on the rim of the sandbox. I pulled at his body until I'd broke his hold, pulled him by the ankles to the flaming hole of the fireplace, where the fire of coals and burning wood twisted his body and scattered his cries to the heights of an extraordinary hatred within me — a place putrid and intoxicating and which lives in all men long after the evil thing we fight has been conquered but not conceded.

I believe I would have remained with Trump, in the pain and in the fire, until exhaustion had lowered my fists. I believe, too, that what pulled me from that extraordinary hatred was Jimmy's voice and not the whipping belt buckles Trump's men were delivering to my legs. I don't know how my mind deciphered kindness from Jimmy's voice, or how his commands grew so much louder in my mind than the digging, burning sensation of belt buckles striking flesh and stone. But they did, his words finally breaking thru the heat of my hatred to yank me from the fire.

I released my hands from whatever it was they were choking and Trump rolled out from under me. Jimmy was kneeling beside me, holding me. Sally was cupping Brynnie's quivering muzzle, holding the dog's head off the sand. Trump's body softly squealing on the floor between us. For the first time since the violence had begun, I saw the carnage Brynnie had impaled on Trump's body.

Three of Trump's men made their way towards us. They picked up what was left of their leader and began to carry him towards the *Campground's* front door.

Jimmy stood and moved quickly to block their path.

"No sir. There's still only one way you're all going out."

The men glared at Jimmy before turning and hammocking their leader towards the back door. Trump's body sagged in the arms of his men like one of Anthony's poor seals.

"I would have killed you." My words smoldering from behind the shovel which was holding me up, before snaking across the room to find the eyes in Trump's tortured face.

I would have liked the prayer of my hatred to have come only from a place which inflates our last push at life so as to open the door to another, less troublesome room, and to have believed that the righteous violence I had promised to the soul of my enemy lived only to prevent a greater violence in a life to come for both of us.

Afterwards, after these men had left us alone with our wounded and only their boots on the path of gravel in the *Campground's* backyard suggested the quietest of prowling, every little sound inside the room came back in double time to haunt us — the water left running in the kitchen sink, the moaning of the refrigerators behind the bar, the pop of smoldering wood rekindled.

I don't think any of us knew if our friend was alive or dying at Sally's knees, no agonizing moan had yet to come out of the dog's mouth. Joey was crouched by his brother's side, crying and patting his brother's back and laying his hand to Brynnie's outstretched back leg. Jenny lay between the two brothers now, her nose brushing the hand and towel that was applying pressure to Brynnie's head. A few gummy and bloodied Polaroids stuck out from under the stillness of the dog's body, a nauseating sight that hardly elicited anything more from us except quiet, gruesome regret.

Jimmy had already gone to the kitchen and come back with a mop and cleaning bucket, and begun to scrub the floor of its blood and phlegm. It was bizarre — his mopping of the floor — as if nothing out of the ordinary had happened tonight.

From the low light of the kitchen door, Jackie stared at him. Then she shook her head at me with such anger in her eyes that I looked away.

"You and Jimmy got a fucking policy for nights like this one." Jackie's voice trembling as she made her way thru the room's overturned furniture to be by Salvador's side.

Jimmy looked up from his cleaning pail.

"We can't call the police, Jackie. We started it." There was gentleness in his voice, almost no meter in his strike.

Salvador stared up at him in disbelief.

"God damn it, Jimmy. Put that down and get over here. I'm going to need more than Joey's hands to hold this dog down. No. No! Not here. I'll work on him at my place, if he's alive when we get there. Jesus, Mark," Sally broke into tears, "look what we've done to my Brynnie."

Under specific instructions from Sally, I went to the kitchen to find two of Hazel's largest baking trays.

"Mark, hurry."

We inched Brynnie's body onto the double-stacked trays. Joey holding up the dog's lifeless hindquarters and Jackie pressing the blood-soaked towel to the dog's head wound.

I watched my friends carrying the limpness of Brynnie's body over the front porch, took one last look around the bar, and locked the *Campground's* doors for the last time.

The ricey morning light in Salvador's compound suggested the blessing of sunrise was not far off. Jackie and Salvador rested half asleep on the patio couch, under their blankets, each of them holding a hand to Brynnie's outstretched body which lay between them like something hopelessly trapped on its side. The dog's chest lifted the blanket covering its body with each distressful breath it took. Much of Brynnie's skull, and most all of the scruff of the dog's neck, Sally had shaved under the light of a lantern when we'd first arrived. He'd skillfully stitched the dog's wound — a tusked opening as wide and meaty as the strawberry-white belly of a freshly gutted trout — which had exposed bone at the base of the dog's skull and run deep into the thick flesh on the back of the dog's neck. The work had been exhausting for both man and dog, a feat requiring a full loop of suture thread for nearly every pound of the dog's body weight and, at times, requiring the assistance of several hands to help hold and calm the dog.

In the last hour Brynnie's breathing, though still labored, had not produced any of the convulsive choking we'd watched the dog endure thru much of the night. And it had been hours since the swift and violent tremors, which had briefly taken hold of the dog's body and caused a noodling of excrement to run down his hindquarters, had caused our own bodies to fitfully stir. For these improvements in our champion's condition we were grateful, though Sally took little comfort from these changes in the dog's condition or in the prayers which his brother initiated over the dog's body whenever he cleaned the savage wound. In carefully voiced admissions Sally had, understandably, begun to worry that what appeared as a stabilizing of the dog's condition might just as easily mean Brynnie was slipping away from us. As for the rest of us, we were too broken to know how to respond to Sally's assessment of the dog's chances with anything but our silence. Each of us had seen the ceiling to floor blow that had struck the dog's body. What word spoken could ever soften the man's memory of having created the tool that had become Trump's ironing weapon. Even the cavities in the gray canvas roof over Sally's work-stage looked weakened and silenced by its maker's agonizing, as monolithic a teardrop as any we might wish upon Trump's men at this unholy hour of the night.

It was almost five in the morning when the town's fire alarm went off. The ringing bell a sickening sound that cornered the mind like the cold sea filling a sinking ferry. Jackie and Salvador instructed us to go at once. Joey asked his brother's permission to go with us, and together the three of us left Sally's compound to see for ourselves what each of us refused to imagine.

By the time we reached Main Street we could hear the fire and see flame twisting from the smoke behind the hotel's roof. We hurried our walk up the middle of the street, our solitary parading carrying little more than our torn pockets and our jagged convictions, our welted faces unwilling to speak, unwilling to believe that the paste of smoke billowing over our town might belong to our beloved *Campground*.

"It's not possible," Joe the first to speak his disbelief, "I sa-saw Jimmy mopping up?"

The trampling roar and its tower of monstrous flame climbed from a gaping crater in the *Campground's* roof, and more smoke and fire billowed and slashed from beneath the roof's shingled eaves. The fire whining and spitting flame thru the frames of broken windows to trench a path across the painted ceiling of the *Campground's* porch, tempestuous in its charge before the mastodon form it had assumed was no longer distinguishable.

It was incomprehensible the speed with which the fire rushed over the Campground's crackling skin, consuming her.

We watched, helplessly, rubbing our arms and faces of the fire's firefly ash, flinching with some soulful part of her when the *Campground's* roof screeched and the highest of her timbers collapsed. The sweeping wildness of her back yard briefly exposed by the collapse of her roof and the skeletal shiv of flames which sprayed high above her chimney.

Under a rising sun, we cowered often in the street — the fire coughing at our anguish, singing all the louder, all the more bitterly, whenever we tried to look away. The morning sky opening white-eyed beyond Jimmy's wailing walls blistering with all the color of a child's last piece of ribbon candy. The hack sack bodies of a few firemen and their filigree of hoses circling Jessie's courtyard. The fire's thousand tongues slashing a thousand more devastating stabs at the morning sky.

We stood down from the fire as she commanded. Each of us, I believe, accepting as our own some part of the *Campground's* dismantling skeleton. Jimmy looking as if he were studying the street's new strangeness for clues or evidence or the sudden appearance of Trump's disfigured smile.

"She's gone, Jimmy." Some part of me relieved to have spoken it to his face.

"Let her burn for a week for all I care." Jimmy's words already swimming in the muck of another drowning. His chopped head of hair bowing its ache towards some more distant stretch of memory. His body doused and dripping with more unwashed blood and bruising and surrender in the cluttered street.

"We'll rebuild it." How I loved saying it, repeating it.

"You needn't worry yourself about it. You and I, we've finished with whatever it was we felt had to be done."

"Jimmy, wait —"

"Stay where you are. You've done enough."

There was no maliciousness in the way Jimmy brushed my hand aside and walked away, leaving me alone in the street with Joe. I think he was releasing me from any further moral obligation in his life, casting aside what was reckless in both of us, kicking it under the dirt at the end of the street as if we were both something ugly the other had stepped in years ago. Some of the neighbors and merchants he'd known since Jessie's birth separating from the animated crowd to file after him. He pulled away from their attempts to console him, his spirit all wrapped up in the building of a new cocoon and the suffocation that comes with such a construction, his body hardly more than a tourist's stumble in the fog and smoke making its way down to the docks. The chop of his amputated ponytail mouthing back at me *stay where you are, you've done enough.*

I would have liked to believe that the hobbled slump of the man, which I was watching disappear into the gathering crowd, was experiencing the final bonfire of a father's muddied grief, that he would come back to me whole again once the fire was out. But in the confessional born of this night and long since perished, I had learned just how well a father's grief could tend a secret of its own. What I could not know was how thoroughly my friend would map out another, and how well it would shadow and hide his righteous obsession in the weeks and months to come. In this long day's withering into daybreak, I faced the fire's birth, and did not see the signs of the madness which still awaited us.

CHAPTER EIGHT

W E BENT OUR WAY thru what was left of the fog-crusted morning, feeling the cold of its dew on the arms of Salvador's plastic patio furniture, our bodies siphoned of reason and explanation. None of us wanted to be indoors so long as Sally and Brynn remained outdoors; I think, too, that each of us wanted to delay the inevitable trek back to our own beds, where we knew solitude would likely corner us. On a flimsy chaise-lounge in a sandbox of shade, Jackie was asleep on her side. She breathed as quietly as a caged rabbit at the State Fair. A scrap of gray flannel covered her from the knees to the streak of maple in her hair. For all she had stood up against, in her freshman term at the *Campground*, she deserved the bluest of ribbons. An arm's reach away from her, one of Salvador's curtainless windows was propped open with a couple of sticks of welding rod. Beneath the window an oil drum turned rain barrel caught the quietest of drips from the roof. A few feet away, near the open door to the cottage's kitchen, Joey's body had collapsed on one of his brother's salt-stained couches and finally kicked its way back to sleep, the boy's long calves slung over one of the corduroy arms of the couch like a couple of listing buoys. Sally hadn't slept at all. Each time I'd opened my eyes to check on him he'd been seated on the concrete next to his friend, his body holding the same half-lotus position, his hands either petting Brynnie's hindquarters or applying a cool washcloth of ice to the dog's head.

For six hours we had listened to Brynnie's breathing growing more and more labored, watched the dog's chest and stomach appear to bloat whenever his breathing became more girdled. Six hours of the animal's hack-saw breathing piercing the damp patio air as if its body were trapped under a thickening pile of wet lumber. *Civ-fah, civ-fah, civ-fah, civ-fah, civ-fah, civ-fah, civ-fah, civ-fah...* At times, the dog's chest would heave and exhale a slower, more comfortable rhythm of breathing for a minute or two. But the relief wouldn't last. Instead, the ruptured filtering of the dog's lungs would return its horrible girdling sound to our ears... *Civ-phah, civ-phah, civ-phah, civ-phah, civ-phah...*

Six hours. Was unconsciousness only deepening the dog's pain, trapping him in a nightmarish dream that he'd never really escaped circus life...*sharpening the sticks that the pain man would use...cramping/rusting kennel/wire with teeth... pain man coming...no where to run...pain/pain smell/pain man smell coming back...cage open/run...*"Get Back!"... *stick/pain/ wet-hot pain...*"No Bite!"...*wet pain/hot/licking pain...Empty Dark...hard water/hard hunger/pain in food...*"No! God damn You! No more food"...*chew pain/hunger hurt...jump fire circle/ get food/pain man watching/people watching/hot/ hot/get food/ hot...*"No Food!"...*hot stick/wet pain hurt/licking pain...Empty Dark...people screams/hot circles/circle pain/circle people/pain... dark/wire cold/wire on pain/licking/licking bad skin/lick pain...pain man smell coming...run/run/run from pain man...Dark Empty... Empty Darkness...*

"Sally?" I gently tapped his hand.

"Who," his voice breaking as if the word had fallen from a pile of seashells only to be stepped on and snuffed out.

"Sally, I think we should take him in."

"No. No, not yet."

"He's surely suffering."

"He hasn't given up. So neither am I."

"No. No, no, Sal — to get help. A doctor. You said there was a good vet in Anacortes. Let's get him over there. Come on. Get yourself a shower while I call us a plane. I'll have it pick us up at Red's. We'll be in Anacortes in half an hour."

I could see that Salvador wanted to let go of the arm of Brynnie's lounge and do as I had asked. Why wasn't he moving faster? Then I realized it was the money that was holding him back.

"Come on," I said. "We're going to Anacortes. And when we get there, I'm paying for whatever needs to be done to help this dog. And that's the end of it."

"Mark, it's Sunday and that's an emergency hospital —"

"Listen to me, Sally." Dianna was in my head as I spoke, Jimmy's disappearance, too, and now Jessie was pregnant and somehow all wrapped up with the men we'd fought. "I don't know about you," I wasn't sure I could finish, "but I'm not ending this day with any more regrets. Okay with you?"

I made three phone calls while Sally showered; one for a seaplane, one to a Dr. Shukla at the twenty-four hour emergency veterinarian hospital in Anacortes, and one to Red's store phone. "Yes, an emergency," I remember saying into the receiver…"Two men and an injured dog… Mark Jacobs… Anacortes. Can you have a taxi waiting for us when we arrive at the dock in Anacortes? You're sure? Because we'll need transportation from the dock to the animal clinic on, let's see, 12th and Thurman. Yes, that's it…"

After talking with the veterinarian and Red, I called the Island Cab Company to taxi us to the marina.

Sally tapped his brother's leg and told him about our plan to take Brynnie to Anacortes "Jackie's sleeping. Don't let her leave here alone, Joe. You hear, in case there's more trouble, in case they haven't left the island. Keep an eye on Jenny. She might try to follow when we leave."

"Okay Sal."

We lifted Brynnie onto Hazel's double-stacked baking trays and carried him to the edge of Sally's driveway. When our cab arrived the driver was hesitant about transporting an injured dog in his car, until I handed him a twenty and reminded him it was a three minute fare to Red's marina.

Once we'd left Sally's place our driver wasted no time in telling us of the tremendous fire down on Main Street. He hoisted his hairy arm and elbow into the breeze, where the great smudging of army tattoos covering his sleeveless arm seemed to prompt the man's fat bubble-gum lips to roll his dirty dick of a cigar from one side of his mouth to the other. Salvador would have none of the man's talk.

"Jesus, Mort. Use your god damn rearview mirror instead of your mouth for a change. Can't you see who you're talking to back here?"

After Sally's remarks to our driver, there was silence in the cab and the breeze in the back seat became a wind that blew cold on us, until the driver slowed to allow the cab's tires to ruefully pass thru a shallow pond of wet ash pooling its sinking feeling over an intersection on Main Street. Outside the cab's windows, a tremendous hoop of jagged charcoal timbers rimmed a sinewy crater between Jessie's untouched bench in the courtyard and a neighboring, soot-streaked stucco wall. From our passing cab, looking at where the *Campground* once stood was like being forced to watch the execution of someone you loved.

Red was too upset to say very much to us, except that Jimmy had taken my boat out and that Sally and I should call to leave a phone number where we could be reached, should we not make it back from Anacortes by nightfall. For Brynnie, there was plenty of understanding and sympathy in Red's eyes.

Dr. Shukla met us at the emergency room door. The glass door of his clinic opened onto a brick alley strapped with hanging baskets of orange and yellow nasturtiums. An oxidized mural — Noah and his animals floating in hot-air balloons — covered the two-story brick wall of the animal clinic and the vet's apartment.

After lifting Brynn from Hazel's baking trays to a stainless examining table, a cheerless thought crept into my head and turned cold at the sight of the empty bun trays. For all I knew, Hazel's baking trays were the only remains of the *Campground*.

Dr. Shukla took note of our facial injuries almost as quickly as he began his examination of Brynn. But his only questions to us were of his interest in the animal's injuries.

"Do you know the dog's exact weight?"

Sally answered him. "Eighty-eight pounds."

Dr. Shukla hunched his shoulders as he spoke. His powerful looking hands moved from Brynn's white gums to the underside of the dog's rib cage.

"He's been seen by someone already? When was this?"

"No, that's my work. The best I could do."

"It's nice work. Couldn't have pulled a better stitch myself. I'll take x-rays, but I don't think his skull is cracked. But there's for sure at least one rib pressing on his lung. How did this happen?"

Sally told him the truth. His voice sinking to a dreary state of guilt when he described the fireplace shovel, telling the doctor of the bulky heaviness of the first shovel he'd made in his youth.

Shukla winced. "They've shown up here from time to time. Caused a bit of anarchy on the ferries last year. Sons of bitches."

By now, a technician was beginning to shave Brynn's front leg. Sally asked her if they wanted us to take a seat in the waiting room.

"Nonsense," Dr. Shukla answered. "Stay right where you are. Call me nuts, but I believe this dog's spirit knows you're here and rooting for him. Not every dog, this dog. Don't you, Trish? Which one of you did I talk with on the phone?"

"Me — Mark Jacobs."

"This your friend, Mark. Or your sparring partner?"

"This is Salvador, Brynnie's owner."

"Salvador? Why's that name ring a bell with me, Trish?"

Dr. Shukla's broad shoulders hunched to allow his large hands to squeeze between the examining table and the underside of the dog's body.

"Those stump-heads do this. If they did, I'll have a squad car up their communal ass tomorrow morning. Think I won't, Trish?"

"Dad, focus." The young technician inserted an I.V. line in Brynnie's shaved leg.

"My daughter. Thinks I'm too colorful in the examination room. I remember this dog, I remember this dog now. Four or five years ago, wasn't it? The two of you caused quite a fuss in town as I remember."

"Three of us."

"Three? That's right, there was another Springer. Quite a bit smaller than Brynnie here, right?"

"Jenny."

"Yes. Now I recall. Sweet Jenny. His sister, correct?"

"Yes."

"Brynn and Gin, that's right. Brynnie and Ginny, that's how I remembered. She was a happy pup, licked me half to death. But Brynn, I drank half a bottle of gin the night I work on him. And not because of his burns, no sir, because it was the night I wrote the most searing report of institutionalized animal abuse I've ever published. Son's of bitches. Our mule of a mayor, at the time, used to book that asinine circus here every year. How was it you came to their rescue? I forget exactly?"

"Ran on stage. Leashed and tied their trainer to his silly barber's chair."

"That's right. Your fifteen minutes of fame wound up being more like fifteen days didn't it? Remember, Trish? The dogs were under our care until the courts ruled." The hunch in Dr. Shukla's back rolled up to the back of his neck as he straightened. "Let's get Brynn into the operating room, Trish."

"It was your father's recommendation that cinched my case." Sally explained to the short-haired blonde tech with a knob of stainless steel pinned to one of her nostrils.

"That and the town raffle on Brynn and Jenny's behalf." Dr. Shukla added. He glanced at his daughter's long grey-hound face, an attractive compass of sharp dedicated directions now focused entirely on the dog's breathing. "Judge required that the circus be compensated for the loss, you see. Sons of bitches and whore-hounds every one of them."

For the better part of an hour we remained by Brynnie's side, relieved to see how much easier the dog's breathing had become at the caring hands of Dr. Shukla. Brynn's barrel of a chest now lifting in long rolling sifting breaths, breaths as beautiful as the motions of a storm-battered log finally treading the quiet surf of a long sought after shoreline.

After we'd left Brynnie in the hands of Dr. Shukla for the night, it was instinctive for us to head for water. We walked the wide cracked sidewalks of Anacortes, both of us trying to trust this new day.

"You're walking like a penguin with a groin pull."

"I am. But imagine how Jimmy's ponytail must feel right about now. How's that gouge in your leg?"

"Okay, actually. My arms feel like concrete, though, like they've been hardened with rebar." A leaf of swollen flesh over one of Sally's eyes had made his eyebrow look like a squashed slug seasoned with pepper hairs.

"What are you looking at?" I smirked, my hand wilting on another crosswalk knob.

"Your face. You've got burns the size of agates on top of your bruises. You're going to look like a slice of purple cabbage by the weekend, you know."

We walked the streets of Anacortes, feeling like our chests had been retrofitted with the noses of surfboards, our legs inserted with lead cow-magnets, our eyes salted with the burn of sleeplessness. I suggested we find a hotel and some food.

Crosswalks shined their equal signs at our tired footsteps and traffic signals shoe-laced long strands of roof racks, kayaks, and camping trailers. Summer traffic vibrated on both sides of us, on the streets and in the cloudy reflections of storefront windows. Car windows, stuffed to their roofs with compressed clothing and brackets of jeering faces, passed by us on their way to the international ferry wharves; wharves which bridged vacationers to the San Juan Islands, our island, and Canada. We walked by longhaired dreadlocks carving their brilliant white smiles on our bruised faces, their flat-footed sneakers easing by us with their unleashed dogs, Sally and I doing our best to match their friendly red-eyed stares with some of our own. Walked behind backpackers who had left the city curbs of California, weeks ago, to hitchhike their way here to see for themselves what their book shelves could only suggest, to taste the island waters and the hot mineral baths and the wood-fired saunas, and the bare breasts and sensual arches of bare bottoms ripe for eating. So many beautiful dogs on the streets to walk with us. Dogs on leashes. Dogs crossing traffic, stopping traffic. A well-fed mongrel taking a biscuit and the sweep of a broom from the outdoor mat of an antique shop. Once, a three-legged chow, tied to a lamppost and pogo-prancing at the sight of its owner stepping back from the closing door of a bookstore. We walked with the living and the useful and with voices that spoke to us of the beginning of things to come.

We checked into the *Happy Dolphin Hotel*. On the balcony of our one bedroom suite there was a candid view of the harbor's industrial edging. Beyond the bustle of forklifts and commercial fishing boats and warehouses, the view to the eastern skies was heavily wired, after which, an eleven thousand-foot snow-capped molar of a mountain piloted the evening sky. It was a brandishing postcard that would have singed us had we not fallen asleep in our velvety, rocking recliners.

It was shy of ten p.m. when I awoke for the second time. A red dot blinked in the darkness of Salvador's room like a distant radio tower. It took me a second to realize I'd fallen asleep in the bathtub and that the light blinking at me was the phone on Sally's nightstand. My tub-water was cool, cold by the time I'd fully awakened. Not long after I'd wrapped myself in a towel, I heard Sally dialing the phone.

"Dr. Shukla, please —"

It's so quiet on the balcony that I can hear a muff of dialogue surfing my ears from the other side of the bay. Sally is perched on a wire I'm not sure will support him. On the sidewalk below me, a woman's softly spoken words seem to idle with the slow draw of nightfall…"my sweater, darling"… an incantation which almost matches the evening colors in the sky.

"Dr. Shukla? Yes, it's Salvador. I'm calling about Brynn…Yes. Okay. I know. Yes, those are circus injuries. I know, there's no other like him on the planet. Yes, okay… Thank you so much. Goodnight."

I hear Salvador fumbling to put the phone back on its stand.

"How's he doing?"

"Doc says Brynnie is breathing fine. He's very optimistic. He's got some sort of drip line in him for pain. That makes me feel better."

"What about his head wound?"

"Funny, Shukla say's he's not real concerned about it. Can you believe that?"

"I know what we saw."

"Yeah. How are you holding up?"

I twisted my towel tighter. "I'm beginning to think it was me brought all this on us, not them. What I started? Was I wrong?"

Sally rested his hand on his belt buckle as if his stomach might be hurting him. "There's no locking your front door to fuck-wits like them. You know that better than me."

"Well, we'll see soon enough, won't we?"

Sally's body was blocking my path back into the room, his teeth scraping at his lower lip.

"Something else you want to say to me, Sally?"

"There is, but I want it to stick."

"Say it."

"What you said last night about Jessie, it was true?"

"Yeah."

"And you've been swallowing that secret for a year?"

"Yeah."

"You never spoke to anyone about it?"

"No."

"No one?"

"No."

"Your wife?"

"No."

"She knows now though, right? From the picnic?"

"I think so."

"You want to talk about it?"

I felt like I was on the witness stand, deservedly so, being tried for an old crime.

"I left it in the fire, Sal. Mind if I get dressed?"

"Hey, for what it's worth. I got no regrets about standing up to them. And neither does Brynn."

Sally stepped back from the door to let me in the room. I walked to the bathroom where my clothes were drying, not knowing what to say to Sally's gift or how to say it.

After dressing, I stood for a minute in the doorway of the room's bedroom, watching Sally pull the plastic from a package of new T-shirts.

"What's that, Mark?"

"You and Jimmy standing with me last night, it's worth everything to me."

"Here, take one." Sally winked. "Nothing like wearing a new white T-shirt in an all white town, eh?"

We ate at the *Happy Dolphin Restaurant*. The hostess took one look at us and went completely possum. I joked with her that we had been in a rollover accident and asked if she wouldn't mind seating us in the darkest den in the house. We followed the pudgy hostess to a duck blind of a booth, Sally smiling back at her while fingering his loose tooth when he took his seat. The salad bar now looked almost too far away to consider. When a biker couple walked by our booth and gave us the intrusive eye — their halfway house smiles brewing crooked, pencil-pointed teeth — I told Sally, "they think we're new club members."

We ordered *happy fisherman's platters* from our guppy-cheek waitress and ate in silence — spooky how so many places in Anacortes hang the ruse of the town's rainy reputation on *happy this* and *happy that* signs. After we'd emptied our plates, we reordered, splitting a small pan of the chicken and dumplings. We cleaned off our plates with mopping slices of bread, and still hungry, ordered milkshakes and Bumble-berry pie. It was all very good, all very soft and easy to chew. Sally insisted on paying our bill, after all, thanks to Jimmy he had his winnings from the casino.

"He should be here with us." I said.

"It's going to tear his heart out when it hits him, if it hasn't already."

I bought cigarettes and a bottle of aspirin from the hotel's gift shop, a room more hut than store, full of rubberized toy barnacles and tug-boat sponges and kites that would probably never touch wind except, maybe, as window coverings in the closeted lofts of Seattle.

I smoked my cigarette, telling myself it was all in celebratory praise of my other abstinence, hardly missing Jimmy's sardonic voice or his precious *Campground*. But halfway thru my second cigarette my mood sunk and I wondered if my friend was sleeping tonight, where he was sleeping, if my boat was in one piece and with him.

Maybe on the other side of the rag of rage — *I would have killed you, Trump* — there lies a presence so pure it knows no other, living only for the waking moment of our greater separation, a vein of complete resignation that lives and dies solely for the revelation it leaves within us.

From our balcony, some beached logs cradled the bouldering piano notes escaping from the *Happy Dolphin's* lounge, the sound of the piano the color of unwashed silver.

Near the logs, a balsamic black and white *no trespassing* sign rusted on a slimy spine of a fence post, a yellow-eyed dandelion growing from its spongy head. In the peeving of tidal muck surrounding the sign, the wet shine of a fisherman's folded-down waders saucered a chink of light from the hotel. His old dog following the familiar smell of its owner's shellfish boots. Man and dog heading home, the gulls diving for the last of his family's breakfast bread, the fisherman's daughter praising the end of this day with *"isn't the night lovely, mum?"*

In the lifting of the tattered dog collar, which latched the rear gate in an unmowed dog-pooped corner of Salvador's backyard, some part of me felt I was back where I might one day belong. The view thru the shoreline trees, beyond the pond, is restful and hushed, the southern sky over Depot Island holding its blazing blue line against a mantel of low-lying freight-bearing clouds, clouds that seem determined to smother the island in a fine drizzle before the day is over.

Inside Sally's compound, my fingers hook to pull the stiff leather collar over the gate's leaning fence post. How much every purposeful tool on this island would ride my images of Trump's combative face, for a time; the simple stretching of a dog collar turned hitch twisting in my head to become Trump's anguishing, gun-blue lips.

The canvas roof over Salvador's stage looks tired and anorexic in the shade. Some slight desecration to the sail has caused a section of its canvas to droop unusually close to the stage floor, the canvas muddied and jaundice looking along one of its rumpled and pleated lines. Some stones, small as potatoes, rest in a stretched pleat of the canvas roof, higher up, along with an uprooted azalea bush and a dowel of broken pipe.

Closer to the stage, I find Juan. He's working from the higher rungs of a telescopic orchard ladder. His back is to me, both his hands gripping a fully extended pole saw, which he's using to try and pull the mucky root ball of a plant from a pocket in the canvas.

"What happened, Juan?"

There's a saber-sized tear in the un-tucked tail of Juan's shirt. Around the shirt's tear there are grass stains and what looks to be dried mud or dog poop.

"Juan, where's Joe?"

"Riding."

Danny is stationed across the yard on the patio with Jenny. The boy is squirting soap into a pail by the dog's legs, Sally's garden hose bending its stream of water over the pail's metal rim. Jenny is standing, only half-interested in my arrival, much more interested in the rise and fall of the water running from the hose Danny has pulled from the bucket.

"Where's Jackie?"

Strange that none of Danny's usual excitement has yet to sing out across the yard.

"Red's," Juan answers.

Danny's face is egg-shaped — don't know if I've ever really noticed how much so — wide in the forehead, pointed at the chin, a blotter of freckles and rust-red hair coloring the somber face and protruding ears watching over Jenny. In a moment as fleeting as the cube of time measuring a yellow-to-red traffic light, the boy looks in my general direction but not at me.

"Juan, leave that be and come down here."

"Sure."

Juan drops the pole saw in a crease of canvas. He will take his sweet time climbing down from the ladder, enough time enough for me to see soapsuds overflowing from Jenny's soap pail and to notice that Danny is showing no inclination of either shutting the water off or beginning the dog's bath. One of Juan's boots touches the ground, just one, both hands holding onto the rails of the orchard ladder as if the boy is thinking about climbing back up.

"Look at me, Juan."

Juan turned and faced me. Across the thickness of the boy's upper lip the flesh was split and bloodied.

"Who did this to you? Did those stump-fucks come here? Juan, answer me. Did those men come back here?"

"No."

From the patio Jackie's voice is an interruption. "Welcome back."

"Why isn't Joe here? He was told not to leave you here alone."

"Calm down, I'm not alone. These two strong young men are here with me." Jackie's words snapping the air over the patio.

Juan brushed by me in an obvious show that he wanted no more of my questioning. He walked to the patio and took a seat on the wooden bench near Danny.

"What the hell's going on here, Jackie?" She's taken completely aback by the sight of Juan's cut lip and moves towards the boy to take a closer look at his injury.

"Tell me that you didn't strike this boy, Mark." A mother's fury in her eyes, the look of someone who has already sentenced me.

"That is a hell of a thing for you to even consider."

"I'm sorry, I'm sorry. I've been gone no more than a couple of hours. Sally's yard was not like this when I left."

"Juan —" But before I can ask the boy another question Jackie's hand slaps the air for me to hush.

Jackie went to the kitchen to towel some ice for Juan's cut. When she returned, Danny had taken a seat next to Juan. He's hunched his shoulders and crossed his arms over his unbuttoned vest, which now seems little more than a sling for the boy's ribbed scrawniness.

Finally, Juan spoke.

"Danny, you're going to have to tell him. This cut is never gonna close if I gotta talk."

Jackie's fingers reached for the back of Juan's inked hand. She rested her hand there for a moment before she spoke. "He'll do fine, Juan. You just sit here with him. Okay?"

Danny's face turned a new shade of pale when Jackie reached to put her hand on his arm. "Remember what we talked about earlier. No good thing ever lived inside a secret."

"Any way it comes out Dan," Juan coached, "will be better than us holding it another night."

"We did everything we was supposed to, Mr. Jacobs. We stacked the lumber like you asked. We shoveled gravel. We dug. We dug the ditches. Then we started to cut the ditch along the foundation. Just like your note told us to. All afternoon I didn't smoke once. Then we ate Hazel's food, half of it, half of what you left us. But after we ate I wanted to smoke. Juan didn't though. But I needed to. I smoked five or six menthols. One after another. Then two more regulars. Mostly I tossed the butts into the ditch behind me 'cause Juan he's there and because I know he's trying to quit. I saved a few smokes for the dance later on otherwise I gotta head down to the docks and get more. But I think maybe I can hold off. Anyway Juan says to stay put that we gotta get the ditch done. We didn't talk none for awhile after that."

Danny let his arms drop to his side and leaned back into the bench.

"Keep going, Dan." Juan encouraged.

"Then it was like six or seven and our shovels were clanking at the back door Jimmy been working on. It wasn't like we'd planned it. It was just kind of like a good feeling getting off on how much work we'd made happen. So I just looked at Juan and he just looked back. We was like twins right then, or, or maybe I was thinking we was something real close to you and Jimmy. I know I must of lit up another one right then 'cause I was just happy you come along and give us this job. It was getting late and we want to check out the dance. We shower though under the shower pole. It's cold but it's nice except for my ratty cloths I gotta put back on. Juan's thought ahead though he's got clean ones. He says we should leave a note by the back door and to also leave you our hours. But it don't seem right we did or we didn't now. When we got to the docks I already see my spot for the night. It's all grassy over on the hill by the road to Red's and no one's using it."

Danny put his hands in his lap and began to rub one of his wrists.

"Only one thing. Only I got this stupid problem, I know it. I've always had it. Even before I started. I gotta have more cigarettes. I gotta have 'em. I smoke two more right then. I thought I was finished and I don't know why I never didn't stop. We gotta catch the ferry home 'cause the dance was getting over and the band went packing like people say. We gotta catch the ferry home, I know, I knew that. So why didn't we, Juan?"

Juan removed the toweled ice from his lip. "Go on, you're almost done with it."

"We go back to the Campground for the rest of Hazel's food. We don't catch the ferry 'cause going home to nothing much anyhow don't sound like much fun. We don't even try. Then we hear you and Jimmy. You sound far off.

One of you does. We can hear Joey and Miss Jackie talking 'cause one of them opens the window. Then the screen door I can hear and my body jumps but I don't move. We think maybe you're on the porch awhile 'cause it's so quiet except for I can hear Miss Jackie talking to Joe from the window. It gets more quiet then. Then I know why. 'Cause there's a pair of black boots come to the edge of the door right over us and part of a boot is staring right down at us. Soon as those boots move back from the door Juan says take cover behind the lumber. After that it was the most terrible. Because why isn't anyone coming to help. Why can't they hear what Juan and me are hearing? I think they must be afraid. Then I know why no one's coming. It's 'cause I can't yell for help 'cause Juan's hand is over my mouth so hard I can't stand it. Then something I can't never believe. You say you're gonna kill a man or else you already done it. I want it to be over then. Only Juan's hand's making it so all I can do is watch. They walked right in front of us those men. Those men that fell thru the door and then went back in. Then it was done and those men came thru the door carrying the big one and went into the dark. That was the worst. I didn't know how to think about you putting Brynnie on a tray like that. I didn't want to.

"It could of been me that done it. I could have left my cigarette burning on the door's ledge after what we'd seen was over. Maybe I did, I don't know. We hung around awhile so Juan could be sure it was really over. All I wanted to do was smoke and not move. Maybe I left one burning on the wood pile we was hiding behind. I don't know, I might have. I could of."

Danny's mouth stretched wide and the tears came.

"Why'd you have to come back here, Mr. Jacobs? Why you'd have to be so nice to us and give us work? Why'd you do it when you knew this awful thing was coming?"

For half a minute Danny was inconsolably. He let out one last beseeching cry to his friend before turning his head aside. "We didn't even try to help Brynnie, we didn't even try."

Watching the boy break down was like watching a January wind shredding the last standing cornstalk in a field of winter's slush, a cold and raw and lonely feeling. Terror and anger and whatever withering innocence had cowered with these boys in the backyard of the *Campground* would now forever be a part of their spirit.

"You didn't start that fire." I said.

"I might have."

"No. No way, Danny."

"What do you mean?" Danny wiped at his tears.

"Sheew! More cigarettes have been left to burn on the Campground's floor than you or Juan could smoke in a week."

"But we was the last ones there. And maybe I —"

"Look at me. You didn't start that fire, son."

Danny stood and the spindly bench beneath him wiggled its painted blue slats. The boy's posture seemed to carry the bench on his back as he wiped his eyes and moved towards me.

"I'm sorry your place is gone, Mr. Jacobs." Before I could cover up Danny was hugging my sore ribs.

"So am I, son."

Jackie was next. She welcomed Danny's hug with open arms and told him how proud she was of him.

"Oh Jenny, I bet you're missing Brynnie by now." Danny buried his head in the dog's shaggy neck. "He'll be back, you'll see. Right, Mr. J?"

Jenny looked up from another one of Danny's hugs. The dog's bright-eyed tail-wagging brought on either by the boy's promise or by the smell of the boy's leather vest haggard looking as a biker's bra.

"He will."

"Jesus Danny, you gonna marry her?"

"I would if I could but I can't 'cause she pants."

Jackie shook her head and laughed, and suggested we eat something. So much food had been brought to Salvador's compound over the weekend by friends and patrons of the *Campground,* she said, that it would surely spoil if we didn't all start eating like Jersey cows.

"You and Juan stay put and rest. Danny and I will go fix us up some of the town's condolences."

On the picnic table Brynnie's collar lay cleaned and straight, its Aztec checkering looking as if it had just fallen bright and colorful from a cellophane package.

"Sally will appreciate that. Man loves his dogs, doesn't he?"

"Who wouldn't." Juan's tone grew surly.

"I guess you and Danny got a lot more questions about what happened."

"No more than you and Jimmy."

"What we did to those men, you mean?'

"Yes sir."

"You think they had it coming?"

"More."

"You don't think the right thing, the smart thing, would have been to call the sheriff?"

"My mom used to do the right things all the time." Juan spoke slowly, slurring his words but his sentiments crystal clear.

Jackie watched us from the kitchen window, listening.

"Cut hurt much?"

"Some."

"I imagine it makes it difficult for you to say all you're thinking? I know the feeling."

"Why you telling me?"

"Maybe I got doubts myself about what I did."

"You think I don't know you're trying to teach me something? Something the opposite of what I seen you do."

"Why wouldn't I? No one else around."

"Why *ain't* no one else around? Why ain't nobody ever around you?"

Juan was right. Who was I to think a boy could witness a monstrous thing and then walk back to his favorite fishing-hole, unscathed and skipping stones?

"You didn't do anything wrong. You did everything right. You stopped them and no one knows it. It's not fair. Not fair that they don't know. They should know. This shit island."

"You done?"

"Yes sir."

"Did Trump's men put that cut on your face?"

"It's nothing. I fell."

"Sure you did, right after you got pushed."

"Answer me, Juan. Did Trump's men do this?"

"No. It was Sally's torch handle got between us."

"Who? Who were you fighting with?"

"It was an accident. He was after the tanks. That's all. I just got caught up in the cables just when he was starting to get the maddest. That's all it was."

"Jimmy? He was here?"

"For a while."

"Would you tell me what happened, son?"

Juan removed the ice away from his lips.

"Something was wrong with him. He was just here in the middle of the yard all of a sudden. As soon as Joe went bike riding and Jackie left, he just showed up out of nowhere. He said he had your boat anchored just over the bank off shore a ways. He wanted Sally's oxygen and acetylene tanks. He was talking to himself, sort of giving himself orders. His hair was gone. His ponytail, I mean. His body was all grungy down to his beltline. Oily like. Not like from running neither, like from putting real motor oil on his body."

"Did he say what he needed the tanks for?"

"Not really. He was mostly talking crazy things."

"What? What things?"

"Kept saying 'got work to do' and stuff like 'got drums to beat.' I got sick of listening to him and just come out with it."

"With what?"

"That Danny and me were out back when the fight broke out. That we could be witnesses if he needed us to."

"That's all you said? Nothing about the fire?"

"Just that we'd seen the men attack you. There wasn't no time to tell him more. His eyes went wild after that. He started kicking stuff and yelling and cussing me out. That's how all that shit got thrown up there on Sally's roof. He calmed down a little while but then went looking on the stage for stuff. The tanks, I guess mostly he was after. But Sally keeps 'em locked up with a chain. When he saw that, when he saw the tanks were locked up he went crazy again. Then he had the bolt cutters in his hands. I guess Danny brought 'em over to him. And that's when I got between him and the tanks."

"And you actually saw my boat?"

"Yeah. I checked as soon as he said it was anchored over the bank. It was there."

"And he never said what he wanted the tanks for?"

"Just that he had drums to beat and work to do. That's what he mostly kept saying."

"Anything else?"

"When he was leaving, when he was rolling Sally's tanks over the bank, he said some stuff about his daughter."

Juan hesitated.

"Juan, I need to know how Jimmy's thinking about things. You understand?"

"Mr. Jacobs, he kept calling her a whore. He'd say it and laugh. 'Jessie's a whore, she died a whore.' That's how he said it. He asked if me and Danny — if we'd, you know, done it with her."

Juan patted the blood from his lip with his shirtsleeve.

"Why would he say those things about his own daughter, Mr. Jacobs?"

"I don't know. Anything else I should know?"

"Then he was gone. Loaded the tanks in the rubber raft and Sally's cutting torches too."

CHAPTER NINE

V OICES TAUNTING AND VULGAR and flightless.
Jessie was a whore, she died a whore. Anyone who loved me would take me in his arms and not let me go.

Voices determined to make something perverse or poetic out of something tragic.

All week I have made the pilgrimage from Salvador's compound to the earthen steps where the *Campground's* porch once stood watch over the harbor. A streamer of yellow taping straps the entrance to Jessie's washed out courtyard and continues up the sidewalk where it ropes off the muck of the service alley, the ground within now the unveiled face of a carnival that has come and gone in the night.

All week street-side services have been held outside the *Campground's* courtyard gate. People leaving their remembrances tied to the gate's iron ribs — wreaths of flowers and cards and photographs, a child's stuffed animal — and on the courtyard floor a pile of beach stones and driftwood grows bigger every day. An outpouring of such scribbled disbelief by the community for our loss, that, a public press conference might have been more fitting than my watchful silence from the top of a hill. But who would have held it? Jimmy was nowhere to be found, no ghostly amputee had been spotted rising from the fallen timbers to pace the *Campground's* bankrupt fairgrounds come nightfall. And after all, it is Jimmy the town is honoring at the gate. Jimmy who had attended their graduations and celebrated their anniversaries, contributed his time to their school plays and fund-raisers, and saved their children from almost certain death on the icy road to Mt. Constitution.

The authorities have visited the site of the fire also, done so with compassionate consideration of our loss when investigating and interviewing and indicating all that needed to be settled on paper by more paper. The reporters have come and gone, too, and made the suggestion in print of a possible connection between the *Campground's* fire and multiple eye-witness reports of Trump's men having been seen on our island the night of the fire; a half page photograph in the local newspaper showed *Jimmy's Campground* in a blaze of flames alongside another showing a black-and-white, clover-leaf arrangement of Trump's men stooping around a campfire pricked with marshmallow sticks.

But where were they, these witnesses, when we needed them? Why were there no strays on the streets after midnight that night, where Juan and Danny might have paged their neutrality, their dancer's shoes?

In the evenings gray and blue, I made an ornament of my star-gazing melancholia and began to hunt what my grief had caged. Tracked what was formless, wordless, over the history Jimmy had left behind him on Joey's mountain and Jessie's barefooted shores. And, for a time, I felt I was with my friend, living within the realm of some *other's* borderless dream where cliffs of sand spun the wings of angels from some *other's* bridge of clay and fire, where an ageless grief at last stands down.

The boats napping on both sides of my empty slip make it look as though a tooth is missing from one side of the pier. It surprises me that I find anything funny about my missing boat, but I do. Behind me, the leather strap of bells on the door of the marina store rings and Red steps out into the sunlight.

"Be right over, Mark. Don't go anywhere." Red stopped in mid-stride to rub his hand over a heavy crop of whiskers, and then pegged me with a dull smile.

Red's seventy-something body looks particularly potato-sacked today? His mustard-colored corduroy pant cuffs stuffed into his pickled-green gumboots, as usual. A crusty, cranberry-colored sweater piggy-backing a ride over his shoulders, sleeves so cloths-lined-stretched that Anna worries about him working around machinery. He's carrying a boater's shiny red gasoline can in one hand — the kind with an egg-shaped priming bulb and black siphoning hose attached on the top — and a blue-striped quart can of engine oil. In the deep pockets of his pleated corduroys there's a gummy red-handled pair of needle-nosed pliers, ruler-length nylon ties, a pouch of tobacco, tape for pipe-thread, boxed matches with a saucy swimsuit fingerprinted on its tin cover, aspirin in a tin, a black pocket knife with one of the tar-tipped points missing but otherwise sharp as cut-grass, a pen-light, and on most days, unless it's raining swamps, a package of pretzels for the gulls.

After he's filled the can and mixed the fuel, Red carries the new gasoline can to the end of the pier and lifts it into the spank of a new boat. Anna is with him, back from

Seattle for a time, hoping to be of some help after learning of Jimmy's disappearance.

Sip your coffee and smoke your cigarette...turn the lunch pail radio on and keep the boat afloat, Red used to say to us. Grab hold of any reliable thing that has wiggled its way to the pole position of another day, that's half your life in a marina he'd muse. And happy to have us around for the summer, he'd grip me and Jimmy by our teenage shoulders and say what he always said: in a marina, lads, time is leaking with changes, so grab a bucket and choose one.

Gumboots rooting their way back over the dock like the snout of a limping pig searching for truffles. Anna joining him step for step, the two of them closing in on me like a couple of rolling pins working a pie crust to the edge of thinness.

"Mark," Anna says with a clustering hug, "after all you boys have been through, now this..."

Under the cover of a sluicing rain, the casino's shuttle ferry chugged closer to the headlands of Timberlee Harbor. Most of the passengers onboard remained inside, their bodies squeezed into the boat's church pew benches like a package of store-bought crackers. On deck, oblivious to the bad weather, Juan and Danny drank their evening coffee and watched the line of light from the casino's wharf begin to pencil out a neon life raft from the lumpish fog.

"There she blows, Mr. J. Casino Island." Danny clowned from the safety of the boat's railing, the thin short-sleeved shirt he was wearing beneath his vest quickly soaked clear thru to his skin. "Where our dear sweet moms slave all night and can't wait to meet you. Ain't that right, Juan?"

"Cool it, Danny." Under a bit of cover that the steel door to the upper deck was providing both of us, Juan sipped more of his black coffee and scoffed at Danny's remarks.

Along the shoreline the waves and rain slapped the ledges of black basalt and a few tribal fishing platforms left to rot and splinter and turn gray as peeled potatoes. The wooden scaffolding of one of the fishing platforms hung from the shoreline ledge like a fallen capital A, its lashings of rotting rope swirling about the stone shelf like a dribbling of candle wax.

We chugged on. Our ferry rocking like a cradle in the wind to make its way around the dour headlands.

In the rain and the fog the casino's windowless shell donned all the flushed wonder of a muddied mollusk, its domed roof a prism of pulsating light flashing a swale of washed out pinks and blues over the hillside parking lots. *Stay and Play*. Blink, blink. *Hot Showers and Sauna*. Blink-kitty-blink. *98 % payouts*.

Blink-kitty-blink, blink, blink.

Once inside the mouth of the harbor, the ferry settled into an easy troll and came around to let a teaspoon current swing her stern closer to the dock. The engines knocked, grew louder, rumbled down and produced a sound like a fist of air working its way thru household plumbing, and the ferry began to track its own wake towards a line parallel with the empty docks. The crew tossed two lines over the anvil sized cleats on the dock, the engines powered down, and the ferry belched one more sullying thump against the spongy pilings. A decanter of cheers from the passengers inside erupted. And from the wharf, a gull flapped its wings and cursed us while trying to hold its mount on one of the pilings the ferry had just bumped.

"Danny, come on." Juan waved his friend to the front of the ferry and reached to take my empty coffee cup. Only a black thread of the cut to Juan's lip had yet to heal, thankfully, leaving the flesh above the boy's lip with only a pinstripe scar where once the cut had scribbled a barber's pole striped slashing.

On the wharf, Danny continued to clown with his friend. "You gonna play table max again tonight, Juan?"

"Cut it, Danny. Mr. Jacobs don't want to hear no more of your guff."

"You don't know."

"Yeah, I do. A whole lot more than you."

Juan had glared at his friend before walking away. After giving him a minute by himself, Danny and I joined him. He'd found cover from the rain under one of the boardwalk's steel-roofed advertising tripods.

"Everything okay, Juan?" I asked.

"Maybe we ought to hold off saying anything to our moms awhile."

"No thanks, we come this far. How much time before your moms get off work?"

"We'll have to go in and ask. She never knows 'til they tell her."

"Hey, look at me. I thought we had this all sorted out?"

Danny walked over and put his hand on his Juan's shoulder.

"He's embarrassed, that's all. 'Cause see, Juan don't know how to tell you that we don't exactly live in normal houses."

"That's not it, Danny."

"What then? Afraid Mr. J's gonna blow our wages on the roulette wheel or something?"

Juan's eyes held Danny's smile in check. Facing me, he pointed at the boats in the marina. "Maybe we ought to show you where he's been camping out first."

I looked where Juan had pointed. A streamer of yellow tape, like the one the fire department had used to fence off the *Campground's* ashes, flapped wildly in the wind from the mast of my boat.

"Jimmy can wait. How 'bout we check in with your mom first? Find out when she'll be off work."

Inside the casino, the kinetic crowd is behaving like sea lions spellbound by the discovery of tribal fishing grounds. One of the security guards on the floor will escort the boys thru aisles of slot machines and faceless puckering, a pair of white gloves and a big blue bow of velvet pushing a janitor's cart alongside them as the boys make their way to the kitchen.

There is no sign of Jimmy at the tables, and probably a shot in the dark to have thought so. Wait and watch for the boys, and wonder how many times this week the blackjack dealer eyeballing me may have heard *money's water, that's all it is.*

"My mom had a chance to work a second shift tonight. Danny's mom, too. They'll be going home in two hours for a break. So if you still want to talk to them my mom says to be up at the house on time."

Juan delivered his mother's message to me as if her words were to be the conditions of my surrender, and then abruptly stepped into the crowd where he weaved his way towards the exit doors. We caught up with him outside the casino.

"How far is it to your place?" With the hood of his sweatshirt pulled over his head, Juan's face looked as gloomy and irritable as the weather.

"What?"

"Your house? Can we walk there?"

"My mom don't really like anyone being up there when she's not home."

"Alright. But can we get there by foot in two hours?"

"Yeah. It's only just up the hill."

"That wasn't so difficult, was it?"

Juan's cheeks puffed out an irritable sigh. "You still want us to show you where we spotted him?"

"That's one reason we're here, isn't it."

Juan shrugged his shoulders but did not answer.

"Is it our houses, Juan? That what bothering you?"

"Mr. Jacobs, could we just get going if we're gonna go."

"Lead the way."

Juan set a brooding pace thru the casino parking lot and up the first hill. The hillside on both sides of the road thick with gorse and defiled by paper cups and tags of blue-inked Keno tickets. Below us the rows of parked vehicles looked like so many finless sharks about to be thrown back to the sea from Japanese fishing boats. The road ahead of us promised a steady train of traffic from the mainland for hours to come.

"I sometimes forget there's a bridge that connects your island with the mainland. Crazy of me, huh?"

"Yeah, the bridge. It was better here before they went and built it. But our moms get better pay at the casino than they did at the school cafeteria. So they like it. But more dogs get killed. And we were a real island before."

High above the deep and cavernous gorge, which now boiled with the movements of a treacherously swift tidal canal and was largely responsible for preserving the island's four-mile long sand spit, the bridge which Danny had spoken of, so wisely, joined the north shore of the tribal island with the mainland. Six tapered concrete towers carried the arched suspension bridge over the narrow canyon of water, each tower displaying the boldness of Art Deco in their design and visible for miles from the mainland highway.

"A woman lost big time and jumped off right after it was built, my mom says. But Juan says different. He says it was some drunk Indian woman fishing under the bridge when the tide come in on her."

"Your mom's got it right. The young woman that jumped from that bridge and died was a student at the university. Sad, huh?"

"Yeah. Hey Juan, hold up. Here Mr. J, I almost forgot."

Danny handed us big plastic trash bags which he'd taken from the casino and forgotten he'd stuffed inside the pockets of his sweatshirt.

By the side of the road we shrugged off the labeling stares of passing motorists while we tore holes in the bottom of the bags and slipped the plastic over our hooded heads. When Danny held open the bottom of his trash bag like a woman checking the hem length of her skirt, claiming that we would now stay completely dry, Juan pointed out to his friend that his socks and sneakers were already soaked clear thru to the skin. Danny countered by asking Juan for the bag back and calling him Cochise. Juan scowled and headed up the road, but he kept the plastic poncho Danny had given him.

"Way to make do, Danny."

"Be even better if we had rope to tie around our waist."

We gave Juan plenty of room to stew ahead of us. Danny mostly walked with me, but every ten or fifteen paces he made a game of falling behind to ask another question before running to catch up with me to hear my answer.

"Is Jimmy sick or something, Mr. J?"

"He is."

"Which? 'Cause why else hang out at the dump when he could live with you on the boat. That'd be what I'd do if I had the chance."

"That where we're headed?"

"Yeah, didn't Juan tell you?"

"What was he doing?"

"Picking thru an old burnt up truck and some junk metal and stuff that ain't worth anything. Not stuff like I'm after when I go out dump-picking. He was carrying this big old Indian rug on his back when we seen him."

"Wearing it, not carrying it." Juan cut in. "And you don't know if it was Indian or not. You were too far away."

"Who's telling the story, anyhow?"

"Then get it right."

"Either of you talk to him?"

"No way."

Danny pointed with pride at a yellow dead end sign posted to the side of the gravel road we were about to walk by.

"See there, Mr. J? We live up that road. It's a hike but you don't hear the cars or see the headlights from the parlor. Do we, Juan?"

I pushed back my hood to look up the mountain road. Not so much as a rooftop or chimney showed itself on the mountainside.

"Oh you won't see the Pillars of Hercules from down here, Mr. J. Will he, Juan?"

"You're not even a drop of funny in this rain, Dan."

The road climbed another hill, took a long sweeping turn thru a clear-cut section of forest, and dropped down into a small valley of planted fields and fenced pasture.

"That's the Evenson farm way off down there. We got to cut thru it to get to the dump."

"If you want we can take the road the whole way." Juan suggested. "It'd be a whole lot drier, but we might not get back on time. It goes way around before it gets you anywhere close to the dump road."

"That what you want?"

"I'm just saying —"

"I like cows. Rain's letting up. Pasture's fine."

"You better like cow flop too, Mr. J. 'Cause there's lots of it."

Hoof-worn and cow-dunged, the cow path was a kinder and gentler road, a trail of animal decency and discipline and absent of the highways boarded up fireworks stands and constant spray. We walked to the pasture's end where another fence line crossed our cow path and separated the roadside pasture from the farm's lower fields. Two sow-bellied cows grazed near a run of fencing where Juan wanted us to cross, but gave no notice of our presence when we stretched the barbed wire and ducked into the next field. A few pothole springs dotted the field's rocky slope, and at the bottom of the hill, where the cow path cut thru a straggling hedge of salmon berry to lead us around a bog of skunk cabbage, Danny spotted a lone mule deer. The animal's head and body still as stone. Its black eyes gauging our movements and distance from the edge of the pine woods on the hill we would have to climb to reach the dump.

We abandoned the cow path where it washed out into a honeycomb of hoof prints by a shallow stream marking the farm's property line, and crossed a rudimentary footbridge of split logs, strewn boards, and swale rock patty-caked beneath the stream's center-strung, cockeyed fencing. The trail thru the pine woods was no more than a hunter's wish. Steep, undefined, a tangle of shin-high branches dead on the trunks of pole pines. The perfect approach for an ambush.

Near the top of the hill a fire line had been cut from the woods years earlier, and farther up, at the very end of our climb, a bulldozed ridge of earth, crushed concrete, and broken bottle glass crested the dump's perimeter.

"Told you, Juan. See it, Mr. J? Way down at the end. Close to the old railroad bridge."

At the far end of the dump, tucked in behind a pile of dirt near the splayed timbers of an abandoned railroad bridge, a miserable looking shack presented itself with all the harshness of a stillborn birth. In the distance, beyond the shack and the canyon of alder and scrub sumac growing thick beneath the trestles, a train of automobiles could be seen stringing their tail-lights thru the trees along the mainland highway.

Up close, the shack appeared to burp from the seepage

of souring garbage and was little more than a gathering of splintered boards, junk pallets, and the stink of chicken wire secured to three upright car axles buried in the ground. Scrap pieces of two-by-fours, over-lapped and nailed together lengthwise to form twelve foot stringers, framed the flat roofline of the three-sided shack and supported a rusty sheet of corrugated metal. So much rope and coat hanger wire had been used in the construction of each of the shack's three walls — lashings which had been tied and twisted over boards staked, vertically, thru the slats of wooden pallets stacked two high, end to end — that the gray shack choked with the look of a victim of interrogation. As if blown in by storm winds, a stippling of tar paper, newspaper, oily rags, black plastic, mud, and pink insulation resembling spoiled cow's tongue plugged the chicken wire which wrapped the entire shack.

"Why's Jimmy trying so hard to keep the mosquitoes and the rats out?" Danny piped. "Aren't they gonna be the only company he's ever gonna get way out here?"

"You boys been inside?"

"We weren't invited."

An oily shower curtain served as the shack's door. We pushed it aside to have a look inside. Straightaway, two rats performed like racing squirrels looking for a way out of danger. Both animals dropping their kangaroo stances to scramble across a wooden utility spool, where they'd been nibbling on tabs of crackers. The rats ran from us as if fire were climbing the papered walls of the shack. The fur covering the animal's huge hindquarters shimmering over a flattened velvet headboard and blanket, before the animal's pencil-tipped noses stopped outside the curtain door to sniff the damp air. Juan quickly slapped the shower curtain with the back of his hand and the rats were gone.

On the wooden spool which took up nearly all the space

inside the shack, a ribbed flashlight lay on its side in a runny pool of scrambled eggs ringed by a hunk of half-eaten yellow cheese and some rat droppings. The flashlight dented but functional, and after wiping the gunk from its cylinder on his plastic poncho Danny shined the light up and down one corner of the shack and across the cluttered wooden spool. A paper plate of rat-scratched hardboiled eggs circled the stubs of two smoked cigars, which lay like two human toes in a nest of white eggshells. Boxes of saltines and single-serving packets of grape jam littered the shack's floor, the floor mostly made up of a few rough courses of broken asphalt shabbily covering a filthy braided rug. The velvet headboard turned mattress lay flat on the floor also, one of its pleated corners exposing its foam stuffing and jammed in tight against one side of the spool's cylinder and the base of a shaky wall. Some of Jimmy's clothing, from the day of the fire, pillowed the headboard. A Pendleton blanket from the casino's gift shop, and a melted picture frame somehow salvaged from the ruins of the *Campground,* the only neatly arranged items at the foot of the headboard serving as Jimmy's bed.

"There's Sally's tanks."

Juan words had trailed the flashlight's beam of light. He'd spoken with no animosity, his left side brushing my shoulders while his right hand reached out to test the strength of the shack's wall. The pallet he'd grabbed hold of wobbled in place and a few flakes of rust fell from the metal roof.

"Don't do that," I said.

Juan slid between the spool and the pallet wall, and patted the armless green cylinder. He lifted the nooses from the necks of both tanks, rolled each tank back and forth in place, and declared both tanks to be empty or nearly so. When Danny crisscrossed the flashlight's beam of light over the spool, Juan asked him to hold up while he reached for an overturned glass tumbler which looked to be protecting a handwritten note from the rain. Setting the empty glass upright on the spool, Juan removed the note and handed it to me. On the back of a stranger's halved birthday-card, printed in flourishing letters dotted with the blood of an obscene amount of mosquito squashings, was Jimmy's handwriting.

"What's he got to say for himself, Mr. J?"

"Get that light out of my face."

"Sorry."

"We probably ought to be getting back, Mr. Jacobs. My mom's probably got to get a little sleep before she goes back to work."

"Sure."

Outside the shack the rain had stopped. A few yards away, a blade of a creek slipped thru the mutterings of trash that had snagged in the clump grass along its banks. Across the creek, hanging from the limb of a tall alder, a metal cot had been hoisted with the aid of a pulley. The metal ribs of the folded cot crisscrossed and cinched with strands of barbed wire which hung like a cage from a low limb of the alder tree. A stack of roped pallets, and another of rimless rubber tires, corralled the base of the tree's trunk. Two fifty-five gallon empty oil drums lay side to side near a thicket of hacked blackberry canes, their lids cut away by a welder's torch. Both drums now half filled with plastic bags, torn shower curtains, a deflated beach ball, and the protruding corner of a nylon tent. The oddest item, a bar of soap swimming in one of Hazel's soup ladles, lay almost hidden in a pedestal of grass by a trampled section of creek bank.

Juan removed his garbage bag and stuffed it in with the others already inside one of the metal drums. I did the same. Danny wanted to wear his plastic a while longer. He claimed he'd not eaten enough food today and had gotten cold as soon as we'd stopped hiking. He hopped the creek, looked up at the stars that were beginning to pounce from a clearing in the night sky, then turned to face Juan and me.

"It's like the dark side of the moon out here at night. Flat out scary sometimes. Know why?" Danny pointed towards the canyon beyond Jimmy's shack and kept on talking. "'Cause of that canyon under the old railroad bridge. It was once the little brother of the water gorge on the other side, and now its spirit is lost and trapped here, so it howls at night trying to find its way back to water. Some nights it's like you can hear the voices of little children playing deep in the canyon. And sometimes the wind blowing down is like the death scream of a dying animal. And then all goes quiet. An old Indian taught me all that. Spooky, huh Mr. J?"

"You boys come out here much?"

"Danny does."

"Much as I can. Not at night though. Once school's out if I ain't at Red's I'm out here dump-picking. There's tons more decent stuff you can find, now that the casino's here."

"Your mother doesn't mind you coming out here?"

"She counts on it. There's a flea market goes on all summer out back of the casino. Me and my mom almost always sell whatever we find. We made a mint on some old playboy's one time."

"Does she know Jimmy's out here?"

"I guess."

"Juan?"

"Everyone probably knows."

"No one minds?"

"My mom says some locals tried calling the sheriff on him to get him kicked out. But the sheriff can't actually do anything about him being up here, because everything on this side of the railroad bridge is tribal land. My mom says the tribe doesn't much care that he's out here. Her and I both think it's got everything to do with keeping him coming in as a regular. More about his gambling than caring much about his losing the *Campground.*

"Those men we fought, have you seen any of them out here?"

"No sir. But I only been out here the one time since the fire, when I was with Danny. Jimmy was coming down off the railroad bridge. He was lugging a lot of trash bags full of stuff. I didn't know it was him at first. Not without his ponytail."

"Crackers is what he's gonna be if he stays out here." Danny announced, and put a finger on one side of his nose to blow a Q-tip of snot at the gullied ground.

I handed Jimmy's note to Juan. "Would you read to us?"

Juan hesitated, before taking the note from my hand.

"Knew you couldn't —" A new stain of somberness darkened the boy's eyes before he stopped reading.

"You gonna read it to us or paint us a picture." Danny chided.

"They are not your words, Juan. They're his. Just read it the way he wrote it. You boys got a right to know how he meant it."

"Knew you couldn't leave fucking well enough alone. Walking to Seattle for a descent cup of tea. Try and keep up."

"Can I see it?"

Though the rain had stopped, Danny protected Jimmy's note by squatting on the balls of his sneakers and cupping the card close to his chest. Half his face was hidden under his hood. The way the boy's body teetered inside the rumpled plastic bag made him look like an old man taking a crap while reading the evening newspaper.

"Walking to Seattle? From here? Now that's choice."

"We should head back, Mr. Jacobs."

"Yup."

Juan led us out of the dump on a more rugged route than the one he'd brought us up on. He took us over an embankment of large boulders, where hundreds of broken whisky and beer bottles had scattered their caramel-colored chips in the crevices between the rocks. We had just begun to make our way down the trail when the briefest shrill of a human whistle halted our descent. The sound had come from the tracks of the old railroad bridge, which had been all but swallowed up by the darkness of nightfall, and was followed by a pinprick of red light, or flame, moving in tandem with a stooped and hooded figure that turned and ran atop the trestle bridge just as we had looked up.

"Keep moving." I told the boys. And following them down the embankment, I realized how blatantly Jimmy's note had tapped the time when he'd done all that the note in the shack was promising, and more. Remembered how he'd once told me, that, on a grade milked of all its natural sanctity everything on it eventually runs downhill.

Once, when Jessie was two, Jimmy had walked these same island rails back from Reno, Nevada. Seven hundred and fifty miles of hobbled steel rail and a story only ever half told. He'd walked a line of track which had taken him north thru the ranch country of Susanville, Klamath Falls, and Medford, thru September's first snowfall that had traced the branches of ponderosa pine in the mountain passes near Bend, thru the flatlands of Madras, westward now, towards The Dalles and the scorched hills of Goldendale, where the bellies of salmon and apples grow big and ripe as watermelons and the Columbia River maps a great line in the earth for the migrating geese. Northwest, thru the shipyards of Seattle, onwards to Anacortes, where the last of the rail's pitted silver would deliver him into island waters.

Eight weeks earlier, Jimmy had left Jessie in our care and taken a bus bound for Reno to look for her mother. He'd returned to us alone and on foot — sun-shackled, blistered, and broke — but a strand of the man that had left believing there was a reasonable explanation why Jessie's mom had run off. Not a cathartic cinder of emotion would he share with us about what had happened in Reno, except to tell us that Jessie's mom would not be coming back. For the remainder of that year, at Dianna's insistence, Jessie came to live with us at our home in Seattle.

That same year, a few days before the Christmas holiday, Jimmy received notice of his wife's death from the coroner's office in Reno. The coroner's letter stated that his wife's death was most likely an overdose; her bruised and needle-marked body had been found in the back seat of his gold Mustang, beneath the snow and ice of a December cold snap. A few days after Christmas, when we'd brought Jessie back to the islands to begin her new life with her father, Jimmy finally told us what had happened in Reno months before.

He'd found his wife between the sodomizing clutches of two men, both of whom had been more than willing to support her growing habit of cocaine and amphetamines. It is one kind of pain to be told of a betrayal, quite another kind to be called, by name, into a curtained room of a trailer and see the flesh of such a betrayal forever staged in your head. In the sleepless hours and days which were to pursue and defile him, he replayed the images of his wife's infidelity raw in his mind until the pain of it seemed unbearable. When he was done with it, he'd gambled away gut-wrenching amounts of cash and credit advances, enslaving amounts, money lost forever over days and nights of frenetic gambling.

In her final hours, Jessie's mom had managed to core some vein of atonement from agony's pith, putting her sorrow to words on a picture of her daughter that the police found tucked inside a Gideon bible by her side. Jimmy never gave his wife's last words a sniff of respect, but he framed the picture on which she'd scribbled her love for her daughter and husband. Jessie kept that picture front and center on top of her bedroom dresser all her life.

The following spring, on Jessie's third birthday, the four of us purchased the bar.

Following the boys along the shoulder of the highway, I recalled the memory of watching Dianna place little Jessie into Jimmy's arms at the end of Christmas break, how he'd held his daughter's sleeping body against his chest and told Dianna, with stone-cold somberness in his eyes, that the truth never set anyone free.

"Guess Jimmy bought in early before the gold rush, huh Juan?"

"Son, your mouth's been running my friend into the ground just about long enough."

Danny's footsteps flattened. "Sorry Mr. Jacobs. I'm sorry."

We walked along the white stripe on the highway until we came to the dirt road Danny had pointed to on our way to the dump. A chain with a *no trespassing* sign lay in the wet grass on one side of the dirt road. Two white posts marked the road's wooded entrance. Some round stones painted white circled the ground around each post. Fresh tire prints in the mud.

"I guess she's home," Juan said. "You still want to talk to her?"

"Jesus, will you stop."

Juan kicked at the chain in the grass and walked away, his body behaving like a ship captained by a pilot trying his best to ride out a circling storm. Near a sawn log the size of a small car, Juan stopped. He stared at the house numbers that had been axed from the log. The numbers had been painted white under a goblet of deer fern growing from a mossy crack which ran end to end in the fallen giant.

"Like I been saying, Mr. J. Juan and me, thing is we don't live in anything like normal houses."

"What part's not normal about them?"

"Well, for one thing, the hole in the ground they're sunk in."

"Juan?"

"Yeah."

"We came here to talk this thing out with your mom. Best we get it done, don't you think?"

"But I didn't do anything."

"And no one's going to ever say you did, son."

"No, you're not listening! I just froze. I just watched when those men were beating you so bad."

"So that's what's been eating at you all night."

"Mr. Jacobs, I don't think I can take hearing about it spoken out loud. Not in front of my mom."

"You protected Danny."

Juan's head rocked from side to side. "No, I just put my hand over Danny's mouth and did nothing."

"You protected your friend. You've nothing to be ashamed of."

Juan turned and planted a heel-kick high up on the house numbers on the log. From the branches of a cedar, a couple of crows jeered down at him and cawed at the sound he'd struck. He kicked the log a second time, and when he was done with it a deep closed mouthed yell of exasperation had spun his body around and planted both his feet in the tall grass. He put his back against the log, looked thru me with his tired eyes, and began talking of a line his father had crossed with him.

"My father used to kill everything that walked or flew or tried to swim away from his aim. He thought he was clever about hiding it from my mom. It wasn't like he was out killing for food either. To him it was like the animal he was shooting was just something inside a picture frame, just something in his sights that he could take. Something always needed to be dead before he could appreciate a new gun he'd traded for. He took some puppies once. Put them in a burlap bag. All of them just stuffed down inside. All of them screaming inside that dirty grain sack. Took all nine of

them out in our row-boat. Out a ways from where the neighbors couldn't hear or see any of it. Tossed the whole sack of
them in the water. A real all American shit, ain't he?"

I nodded.

"You know what else? He thought that by taking me
with him he would make me feel partly responsible for what
he was doing. That part of him knew me real good, and
for that I'll always hate him. He made me drink beer with
him while he was doing it. Him telling me how everyone in
these islands did this sort of stuff with dogs and cats. But
you know what. Even a little kid knows when he's being
lied to. Know what I mean?"

"One of the puppies got away though, right Juan? That's
what you've always said."

"For awhile, Dan."

Juan pushed away from the log.

"I don't exactly know why I just hung all this on you, Mr.
Jacobs. It just sort of all of a sudden seems related to those
men. Like I know my father would have been one of those
men. Like I know I could have done more to help you."

"You protected Danny. That's as much as anyone could
ask. Come on, let's walk up to your house and get this
thing done."

We walked.

Juan's uphill pace soon became a march. Does this boy
know that the agonies the three of us have shared have
tied some part of each of us here forever, on these island
roads, that what is to become of that bond has already been
mapped out for others to feel in the prints his red sneakers
are leaving in the damp earth? For that, I'm sorry Juan.

The road takes a sharp turn, washes itself of the corner's
bathtub gully of stone, straightens and levels out along a
section of clear-cut forest dotted with tree stumps and the
Appaloosa shadings of wildflowers. On the drop off side of

the road, a shallow landslide has all but buried a dozen or so stumps. And at the base of the slide, where a bog of skunk cabbage has been cut in half by the runoff of soil and small plants torn from the slope, the slash of a windowless, rusted-thru car door juts out of a stagnant pool of water.

The road narrows, becomes a wood road with a lush band of green grass and shut-eyed white daisies growing up the middle. Danny has stolen the lead. Walks the softened road like a blind puppy on a leash. Wants to know if I'm staying for supper. One of us is a stranger in this homecoming parade, doesn't he know that? And one of us not here will scavenge the dump floor for the wings of a headless angel, before this road ends.

"Now you can see why we don't have you over for dinner too much." Danny announced with a big smile.

On a cut of earth taken from a hillside, the foundations of two capped cellar-holes protruded a couple of feet above grade.

"Juan's always saying how people feel sorry for us. But except for windows, they're no different than any other house on the insides. Up close and down deep, that's how my mom says we live. The ceilings are low though. Red says we don't know it yet, but we're being groomed for the good life aboard a boat when we grow up." Danny tossed a pinecone that caught the back of Juan's head. "So that being the case, we don't really have nothing to complain about do we kid?"

A working stovepipe flagpoles each of the flat roofs on the cellar-holes, and over one end of one of the cellar-holes a mountain of black plastic has been pitched. On a mound of dirt dumped between the two foundations, a mashing of tall grass and weeds is smothering an island of knee-high cornstalks. A dozen bullet-riddled wheelbarrows, arranged on wheels-end against a bank of clay below the corn, forms a long row of handles behind two parked cars. Can't call the strip of grass and bark chips the cars are parked on a drive-way. Got to call it something that can't be mowed without sending a stone thru one of the car windows.

"Why all the wheelbarrows?"

"My mom grows annuals in them. Marigolds, Salvia, fluffy stuff like that. She wheels them down to the docks when they're ready to be sold."

"She sell many?"

"Sells them all." Danny stomped a heavy footprint next to a toad that had jumped in a tire track of one of the parked cars. "Otherwise she wouldn't bother with it."

A cord of driftwood is piled high in front of the wheel-barrows. Each piece of wood as gray as a hunk of spoiled spam, some as thick as a side of beef, some as long as a car bumper. On either side of the pile, a patchwork of broken boards and old car mats checkers the ground where two footpaths wind and roll their way in different directions over the knoll in the side of the hill.

"Danny's house was never framed but ours was. Clear up to the roof joists anyhow. Halfway thru a three day drunk my old man knocked all his own hard work to the ground by putting a chainsaw to that big oak stump you can still make out in the dark up there. All because my mom locked him out of the basement the night before. It was the only tree like it we had growing around here. My mom's and everybody else's favorite."

Juan stops at the first of several pallets which have been sunk up to their decking in a long bed of crushed gravel. The pallets and gravel make for a crude but solid patio leading up to a set of wooden stairs staked out by a handrail of drift-wood. At the top of the stairs, an A-framed mudroom sits like an ice-fisherman's shack on one corner of the cellar-hole roof. A narrow door, with a scratched and clouded piece of Plexiglas cut into its top half, takes up half the A-frame's entrance wall and is collared by two diamond-shaped paned windows. As far as I can tell, this is the only way in and out of Juan's cellar home.

"Got a hose?" I ask.

In an apparently random run of dribbling seaming, some sort of ugly bird-poop-white patching compound had been applied at regular intervals over the tarred roof and allowed to harden in long lines of broom-swept ridges. Along the back edge of the roof, the profiles of some old benches and the legs of a toppled sawhorse have been hobbled with rope, a twisted tarp pulled tight and looped over two of the upright saw-horses.

"Here, you can use this towel to wipe your boots off with." Juan stepped from the stairs and handed me a bath towel and tossed another to Danny. "We shouldn't really use the hose. The well's not very good. If you wouldn't mind, Mr. Jacobs, when you're done wiping your boots good, would you mind rolling up your pant cuffs? My mom hates mud."

"Hates it." Danny echoed.

Juan hopped the stairs and took hold of the puny knob on the door. The door opens with a muffled pop and its cracked bottom panel shakes like a snapped spring for a moment. He's holding the door open, waiting for me to take my eyes off the two beams of white light that are criss-crossing the night sky like a pair of giant suspenders.

Inside the mudroom, a bare light bulb with a pull-string dangles from the ceiling's peak. Its back wall bleeds with bent nails that have hooked wool caps, windbreakers, a leather dog leash with collar and tags, an extension cord, a child's red pail filled with rainbow-colored clothespins, a clean cat box. In a corner of the mudroom some fishing rods, a couple of umbrellas, and a pair of yellow rain pants with an onion-sized tear in the side of the crotch. Shoes and boots on the floor next to a paper sack of empty soda bottles. In a pan, under the window by the door, three top-less coffee cans; one of the cans holding screwdrivers and assorted pliers, one half-filled with silver coins, and one can snow-coned with wood ashes. We wipe our shoes one last time on a remnant of carpet so shredded that to clean it would be to erase it.

Juan closes the mudroom door. On the back of the door there is a long string of chalk thumb-tacked to a calendar-sized, cork-framed chalkboard which hangs below the door's window. The printed lettering on the chalkboard reads: *REDS, DWM.*

"Who's D-W-M?"

"Huh?"

"Your chalkboard."

"Oh that," Juan answers. "Danny's with me."

Stepping down the cellar stairs is like entering my grandfather's potato cellar. A latch of sour-sweet odors and stale air the deeper underground we go. At the bottom of the stairwell, Juan opens a second door and the light from a floor lamp rushes up the stairs. On the last stair step, the toe of my boot catches on a flap of gray felt and kicks loose a spoon of mud from my heel.

"I'll get it." Juan bends his way under the stairs, and comes back with a dustpan and broom to scoop up the poop of dirt resting near my foot.

"Happens all the time. Usually, it's Danny's shoes."

Juan's mother is washing her hands under a gushing stream of water in the kitchen sink, under a shade-less bulb, in a far corner of the basement. The glare of light above her head seems better suited for the duties of a car mechanic than for preparing an evening meal. Some flinty particles of dust swim in the bulb's cast of light. The particles swirling over her long thick black hair — hair as black as a raven's wings on the tail of a hawk's flight — and falling to darkness in the water splashing in the sink. Hair down to her hips, with a fern of darker, more richly, textured hair tracing the curvature of her spin — its blacker hue as dark and tangled as a child's fright. Hair that seems to swim with the changing colors of a candle's flame set out in a dish near the noisy sink. The candle's flickering light sometimes swelling, sometimes scattering, her human form on the white walls of her cellar home.

Her cotton blouse, as wrinkled as any bow-tied sail, bunches up along the roll of her shoulders and clings to her bra strap where a tapering pleat of her wet blouse exposes the curvature of her ribs. Her ribs like shards of ice folded within her paper napkin of a blouse. Black stretch pants, flared a bit at the frayed cuffs. Black penny-loafers.

She rinses the bulb's cone-shaped shade and sets the glass shade to the side of the candle dish. Lifts her wet fingers to loosen the collar of her blouse, scratches her neck, and shakes out her fern of hair until it floats like a wave of black velvet down her backside. She looks tired for having stood in one place for so long, for having waited for so long on so many long awaited things.

"A ways away from your own neighborhood, aren't you?"

Her pool hall welcoming feels harsh enough to extinguish the menorah of electric candles on a shelf above the television, in the living room.

"Mom, please. He's a friend and a guest."

I wait for Juan's mother to shut the faucet water off. Wait for her to roll down and button the ruffled sleeves of her blouse. Wait to hear if another slap of her tongue is coming my way.

"Mom, this is Jimmy's partner — Mark Jacobs."

"Ma'am —"

"Hold your own hand, Mr. Jacobs."

"Yes ma'am. No problem."

She's lifts her work frock from a kitchen stool. Holds the thinness of the fabric up to the light, like it's a dead chicken about to be plucked, and puts her hand into one of its tinkling pockets. Out comes the silverware she's probably boot-legged from the casino; a couple of knives, two forks and two spoons. Opens a drawer from under the linoleum countertop. Noisily tosses the silverware into the tray.

"I've seen you before. Where?" She won't wait for me to answer. "In the casino about a week ago. Right? You win?"

"I don't gamble."

"Sure you don't. Everyone gambles here. Why else would you come to this piss-pot island? Juan in some kind of trouble with you?"

"No ma'am."

"He about to be in some kind of trouble?"

"No ma'am."

She's looking at her son when she asks, "Am I gonna get an answer from this man?"

"No ma'am, not while I'm being interrogated."

"My house, my rules."

"Ma'am, I'm cold and wet. And I'm tired, same as you. Cup of coffee would go a long way to getting me started on what I come here to say. If you've the time, ma'am."

"Alright, but you best get on with it. I've a long night ahead of me."

"About a week ago we had some trouble at the bar."

"Yeah, yeah. Know all about it. Don't hardly care. So what's my son got to do with your fire?"

"Jesus mom, what's wrong with you? The fire cost Hazel her job, you know."

Juan's mother shrugged her shoulders, and moved to turn one of the stove burners on.

"Your son's right, Mrs. Rodriguez."

"Don't lecture me, Mr. Jacobs. And you'd be wise to remember that you're in someone else's campground at the moment."

"Mom, would you please let him talk."

"Instant's all I got. You alright with that?"

"Yes, ma'am."

Mrs. Rodriguez took hold of the fry pan's handle, empties some of the pan's water into the sink, and places the pan back on the stovetop.

"Well, go on. I'm listening."

"On the night of the fire some other unpleasant things took place. Maybe they were the cause of the fire, maybe not. Your son was a witness to some of it, most of it, most all of it. We only meant to defend what was ours, Jimmy and me. We didn't know your boy was there watching. Didn't know he was there when things went down the way they did. And now, well now —"

"And now tomorrow's come and you're not so sure, that it?"

"I'm quite sure what Jimmy and I did was the right thing, ma'am. I just wish your boy hadn't been there to see it."

Mrs. Rodriguez turned the stove off, put one hand on the counter and the other on her hip, cocked her head back, and looked at me as if this *thing* I'd so vaguely spoken of was now circling me.

"Seen some of your trouble last summer, Mr. Jacobs. Bet you didn't know that."

"No, ma'am."

"Well, let's just say whatever happens when your man Jimmy's around doesn't surprise me. There's your coffee."

For a moment, I was buried in the past and did not move.

"I ain't walking it over to you mister. Come and get it if you want it."

Before I could take a step Juan walked over to the counter and picked up my cup of coffee.

"As for why you're really here," Mrs. Rodriguez continued, "I don't need the details. How 'bout you just say this thing my boy is supposed to have seen straight out, and how it is he came to see it."

Juan handed me my coffee.

"Christ, it must have been some kind of wicked that ended with some kind of guilt to drop two grown men on this poop of an island. Both in the same week."

"Let's just say that I've —"

"Know what, changed my mind. Not sure I want my boy around your kind no more. Think I'll ask you to leave right now."

"Mom, it wasn't his fault. I was there."

It's funny, but now that I've been asked to leave, I don't much feel like leaving.

"For what it's worth, ma'am. We didn't start this trouble. They've been flashing their ugly heads in these islands for over a year now, and up 'til now no one's lifted a goddamn hand to them."

"You a vengeful man, Mr. Jacobs?"

"No."

"But you embraced the rage of one who is, didn't you?"

"I closed the gate on the cage their kind would put us in. All of us, Mrs. Rodriquez, if that's what you mean."

"So you're cleansed of it?"

"You think they would have stopped with me, ma'am? Is that what you think? Think they wouldn't make their way over to your island, set up camp in your backyard? No ma'am, I've no intention of letting myself be cleansed of it."

"Lucky for you they didn't have weapons."

"Lucky for them it was my Sabbath."

She swiped at a strip of dish-towel which looked to have been cut from a man's bathrobe. It was a vicious swipe which almost tipped over the chair.

"I don't care to bandy with you anymore. You may not know it, Mr. Jacobs, but yours is the only name my boy mentions at the supper table. Attaches the same fondness to your name as his talk of fishing. Maybe my boy's nothing to you. Another Lopez deck hand that doesn't know spic from span, *who* from *whom*. But he seems to think you're something special, something come around once in a lifetime. Guess he sees something in you that I don't. Guess maybe some men can fill a boy's ears with ideas. Same as they can get away with telling a bold face lie to a woman, for a time."

The dish towel Mrs. Rodriguez is holding between both fists is as stretched as a bird dog's point.

"Just so we understand one another, Mr. Jacobs. If you've set a silver spike in my boy's head, that, the kind of shoveling hatred you dished out to those men is the only set of tracks life's ever going to hold for him — I'll go to the police myself."

The seconds cowered away and reappeared, more dangerously postured, in the glare of Juan's eyes and in the lap of Danny's nervous page-turning.

"Tell me something. Why isn't your friend here with you?"

"He's taken the loss hard."

"Don't we all?"

"Well, I've taken enough of your time. I'll be heading back to Seattle soon."

"You come all this way to make amends or to tell me that?"

"Honestly ma'am, I don't know any more. I knew when I started out, but now — I don't know. I've tried to make amends with the boys. Best I can anyhow."

"You really want to make amends, Mr. Jacobs?" She's daring me to take a stand and I know she's gonna hold me to it if I do.

"You take my boy with you when you go to Seattle. And

when you get there you skip the sideshows, the ballgames, the space needle, the bullshit. Don't bother with the record stores or Jimmy Hendrix. You go straight to work, to that school of yours. You sit him down with those teacher friends of yours, let him listen in, and you make sure some of what they have to say sinks in. I know they got classes there you can audit in the summer. You take him to some of them. I don't want him back here talking Mariner games. I want him back breathing your people's ideas about things. He's got the brains, and he'll listen to you."

Hair like a black shawl when she turns her back on me and walks to the kitchen sink, where she folds the lifeless dish towel before setting the cloth close to the candle on the counter.

"But hey, if you think I'm asking for the moon — well, well then you have a nice boat ride home. By yourself, mind you. And when you come back, if you're coming back, you stay the hell away from my boy. Stay the hell away from him all the way to your last breath. Got it? Got all that in that want-to-do-the-right-thing head of yours?"

Mrs. Rodriguez made her way across the concrete floor to a curtain of a bed sheet draping the opening in the wall of her bedroom.

"Make your new friend feel at home Juan. And tell him he's got about half an hour to make up his mind. 'Cause that's how much time I got before my next shift."

So there it was. I had her stone-cold blessing spoken for the whole family to hear. The whole town. Well lucky me, Mrs. Rodriquez.

Juan studied me as the shine beneath his mother's long black hair folded itself, cunningly, behind her bedroom's curtain of cotton. The sofa squeaked when Danny stood to walk towards the pile of magazines crisscrossing a coffee table in front of a rabbit-eared Motorola. Orange and green extension cords are roping the ceiling above the television set, the cords stapled and coursing the exposed ceiling joists. So quiet in this hole in the earth that Danny's unfolding of magazine pictures takes on an eerie pacing around the room all its own. No secrets in a cellar-hole, I guess. No privacy either. And no way out of here except the way I came in. And I can't carry that hole in me around no more, I can't.

"You really gonna leave here for good, Mr. J?" Danny asks on his way back to the sofa. He sniffed and wiped his nose, and the whiff of another magazine page turning the room on its side snaked thru the cellar-hole house.

"You gonna miss me, kid?"

Lots of unfinished work everywhere I look. Metal boxes housing uncovered light switches and plug outlets between the skeletal stud walls. Coat hangers of clothing strung along one of the ceiling's electrical lines. A few colored bed sheets all that are providing mother and son a degree of opaque privacy.

"Sorry about my mom." Juan put his knee on the arm of the sofa. "She's pretty beat by the weekend."

Danny tossed his *Playboy* aside and picked up another issue. "Not as much as you're going to miss us."

"Don't take what my mom said too seriously. She was just being she-dog that's all. You know, looking out for one of her pups. Plus she's always had a really hard time being around people that got more than her."

Danny unfolded the magazine's centerfold over the sofa cushions and moaned dismally.

"You gonna do what Juan's mom told you to? You gonna take Juan along with you?"

"Hush Dan, you're being rude. Mr. Jacobs has a lot to attend to right now. You'll be coming back though, right? Soon as you can?"

"I've got a house to sell. Don't want to but looks like

I'm gonna have to. Won't leave much time for anything else, Juan."

"You want to sit at the table and have a sandwich with me and Dan before you go?"

"That be nice. I wouldn't be taking from you and Dan, would I?"

"Got lots."

"Like to wash up first."

"Right thru there. Don't mind the washing machine. Always shakes around a little. But it won't bump the toilet on you."

When I come out of the bathroom a spread of paper plates covers the kitchen table. On the plates are thick slices of bread piled high with ham and turkey and tomato and two strips each of cold bacon. A bowl of mayonnaise, a bowl of pickles, a bowl of potato salad, and a bag of b-b-q chips rings the center of the table. The boys are standing like attentive waiters behind their chairs.

"Want to say grace for us, Mark?"

Juan's question brings on a slump in my shoulders.

"Just kidding. Thought you needed a little break from all the seriousness."

"Nicely done."

In the time it takes us to take our seats at the table there is snoring coming from his mother's bedroom.

"Your mom, she must be some kind of tired."

"All the time. The crowd's are bigger than ever this year, she says."

A sheet-rocked wall, taped and mudded but not primed, separates the small kitchen from the bedroom and affords us some privacy while we eat and talk and sometimes laugh quietly at the gurgling, pulpy sounds of a woman's sleep. She's something this woman, leaving me with her boy, leaving me to face something inside of me she knows has given up, given in, give out.

Between bites Juan tells me how his mother's overtime pays for the property taxes and, most years, bought them a long weekend in Victoria over Christmas break.

"Maybe he wants you to follow him someplace." Danny spoke up, his mouth chewing the edges of his bread crust while his body stirs in his chair.

"Who's that?" I asked, and spooned more salad onto my plate.

"Jimmy, who else."

"The thought's crossed my mind."

"Follow him where?" Juan asked.

"Duh, wherever it is he's walking to." Danny answered.

"And where might that be? In your speculative opinion, I mean."

Danny opened his mouth and dropped a gob of crust onto his paper plate.

"Train tracks. He's probably walking on the train tracks."

I grinned, and took another big bite out of my sandwich.

"On foot? On the train tracks?"

"Is there like an echo in here or something, chief?"

"Eat your chips, Danny."

"What are you suggesting? A high-speed foot race?"

"If that's where the case takes you."

"In my condition. Chasing an athlete?"

"You're tougher than Jimmy, Mr. J. We seen it."

"Eat you chips, Dan."

"Or you could take your boat. Follow the shore line where the train tracks run mostly. The tracks stay pretty close to the water all the way to Anacortes. Tell him, Juan."

"That true, Juan?"

"Those train tracks up at the dump, they're not used anymore. But a couple miles out, on the mainland, they hook up to a mainline. From there the rails go north. You can either to Bellingham or all the way to the Canadian border. Or you can go south on the same tracks, near enough anyhow. Those are the rail lines that Danny's talking about. They do follow the mainland shoreline all the way to Anacortes. Pretty much so, at least. After Anacortes, the rails cut inland."

"Where to from Anacortes?" I asked.

"Mount Vernon. Then south or southeast a little to Seattle, I suppose."

I extended my arm and patted Danny's bony shoulder. "We don't know how long ago Jimmy set out. Or if he's really left the islands."

"Rest is yours if you want it." Danny wiped his chin and pushed his sandwich plate towards Juan. "But that's the beauty of it, Mr. J. The whole chase is sort of on your way home anyways."

"Trying to catch Jimmy at anything — anywhere he doesn't want to be caught doing it — is a gambler's long shot. Trust me."

"Yeah, but it's not like you would really have to catch him or anything. Not even bring him back to his crummy new oasis up the street."

"Danny. Shush."

"You'd be watching out for him, that's all."

"And what makes you think he needs keeping an eye on? Jimmy say something to you I ought to know about?"

"No, but — but he's still your best friend, ain't he?"

The bulb over the kitchen sink spread a blue-banded rim of light over the bridge of Juan's nose. Behind him, on one of the cellar wall's few window sills, the colored water inside a corked vodka bottle holds an opaque line between wonder and darkness. Holds a boy's hopes and dreams regularly marginalized by a father's drunken footsteps falling from the cellar stairs. The man who once lived in this home no more a part of something whole than the carcass of an animal he'd left to rot after the savagery of one of his kills. *Number the days of such men, let them become old and weepy and bound by what they've done.*

"Either of you boys ever been to Seattle?"

"No sir, never been to Seattle." Juan answered. "Anacortes. And a few trips to Mount Vernon. Twice we went to Oak Harbor for the air show. Seattle's expensive."

"I'd have to have help. Not only with the boat, but in Seattle, with the house. There's some painting needs to be done. Some yard work. I'd pay you, of course. But as to making any other promises to you, I can't. You might never see a ballgame."

Danny looked dejected. He slouched deeper into his chair. His vest looked like the torn wings of a butterfly, his bloodshot eyes about to stain the tablecloth. He's listening for my voice to swing his way and pull him off the rock he's certain he's gonna grow old on, older than the sea, before he ever sees Seattle.

"You either, Dan. We might never see a ballgame. Work's why you'd be going with us."

"You mean it!"

"If your mom can see her way past what I still gotta tell her."

"She'll be easy, way easier on you than Juan's mom. She catches spiders and lets 'em free outdoors."

"One more thing. Once we set out. Don't want to ever have to tell you something twice."

Danny held his hand out for me to shake. "Agreed."

"Whole thing's a little bit crazy, us going. Long as it'll take us to get there we'd be better off taking a seaplane."

But that wasn't the whole of it. The whole truth was that to rush off to Seattle would have meant a lockdown of more dead time and emotion when I got there. And to stay on in these islands — truth was I'd no stomach for digging in and cleaning up a fire's stillborn birth, so soon, or for facing down a town's gawking eyes and the rubble of public explanations.

"You want we should pack up tonight?" Danny asked.

I looked away from the joy on the Danny's face and moved my eyes towards the cool blue light in the Vodka bottle in the window, telling myself the mind need only keep the body busy to avoid making a bigger mess of things with a bigger bottle.

"Your mom, remember?"

"Yeah, I gotta get moving don't I?"

"Better pack up whatever you think you might need Juan."

"Alright. What about food? Want Danny and me to bring our own stuff?"

"We'll buy whatever supplies we need at Red's in the morning."

Both boys got up from the table. Danny headed for the door at the foot of the cellar stairs, and Juan stood and walked to his curtained bedroom. At the stairwell, Danny hesitated.

"Thing is, Mr. J, I got land under my feet where there's gonna be water. And I can't hardly stand staying with one thought now that I got two. Hey, you think Brynn's come back?"

"Could be."

"He's the best, ain't he?" Danny's voiced slowed and softened. "Taught those idiots something, didn't he?"

"That's behind us now, Dan."

"Hey, I got my own life-jacket. You want for me to bring it? Makes for a good pillow if nothing else."

"Your mom — best you tell her I'm here first."

I put the food away, trashed the plates, and after washing the silverware sat at the table and sipped my cold coffee. For a few minutes, I succumbed to that cubicle of space where language cools for a time, where the ravaging etchings of a lynching read about, talked about, gagged about, ceases to carve the face of its victim upon another of choking rage.

"Trudy, it's me. Not to worry, we've plenty of time. Oh!"

A woman's voice had crept out of the stairwell to move like a trance thru the room, a voice as affectionate and specific in its delivery as the passing of a church collection plate.

It is work to do more than look at the thin figure hunched at the bottom of the stairs. I swallow the last of my coffee and set the mug aside.

"You're Mark? Mark Jacobs, do I have it right? Oh, don't worry about waking Trudy. She's a log when she sleeps. I'm Lorraine."

"Nice to finally meet you, Lorraine."

"So you're my Danny's angel. I only wish we could have met under happier times. Hang on. These boots — Trudy's a little obsessive about her floors. How'd you manage to keep yours on? There, good Lord, I don't know why I bother. Loafers would be easier. Females and our fashion. Weird stuff, aren't we?"

"Maybe we could talk at your place. Don't know as I'd feel right saying my peace twice in the same house."

"Nonsense, there's nothing to talk about. You haven't done anything wrong. Danny shouldn't have been anywhere in the vicinity. 'Life's lesson and God's protection,' that's what I say. And if you don't mind my saying so, seems that's just how the Lord played it out." Lorraine gently put her hand over her heart. "Tomorrow, at services, I'll have our minister say a prayer for you and Jimmy. I can also talk to the tribal elders if you like. They sometimes will give a blessing over ground that's been desecrated. It wouldn't hurt."

"Danny's told you, then?"

"Danny tells me his entire day, every day. He's a talker, that boy. So whenever he comes home quiet as a clam I pretty much know something's wrong. Not Danny's style not to talk, surely you've found that out. If he's not talking he's probably bothered. Probably my fault, I probably developed that in him. He went to your friend's Salvador's place every day for three days, I think it was, looking for you. Seeing your friend's dog injured that way, how awful. How awful all the way 'round. Danny, he loves all animals."

"He truly does."

"But you're not to trouble yourself with what my boy saw. Danny's mind doesn't hold onto pain the way we grown-ups do. Not even the way most boys his age do. He's remarkable that way. Oh, I know he can get hysterical about things for a time. But then the injury just flies away from him, just flies away from him." The second time Danny's mother said *just flies away from him* she did it with the flourish and animation of a magician releasing doves from a hat. "You've not damaged Danny, Mark. You may rest assured about that."

"There's more to it than maybe he told you."

"Oh, to be sure. But I don't need to know any more of it. It's done, isn't it? Isn't that what you told Danny? Good, good then. Done is done. Whatever else you've attached to it, that's between you and Danny. I'm full up, know what I mean. That's why I won't have television in the house. It's all too much, too much for the world to ask of a mother. Know what I mean? Just too, too much. Look on the bright side of things, I say. Is it true, you're taking Danny and Juan with you to Seattle?"

"With your permission." Was this to be all Danny's mother wanted from me? A letter written but never read?

"Yes, of course. Is it true that the fire took everything?"

"Pretty much."

"I'm sorry that you and Jimmy have to bear this injury alone."

From the bedroom a mattress squeaks and Mrs. Rodriguez

sneezes. The coupling sounds from the heels of loafers hitting the concrete floor in her bedroom, and Juan's mother steps out from behind the curtain and walks towards the kitchen sink. A stiffness about her gait that was not there earlier. She reaches for the faucet without so much as meeting my eyes or acknowledging Lorraine's presence. Buttons her shirt sleeves and reaches for an empty shot-glass with two curling fingers. Takes hold of the handle on the metal pan and finds the running water and then the stovetop's branding iron. The pan water sloshes and hisses on the back burner, and comes to a full boil almost as quickly as she pours cough syrup into her shot glass.

"Got the fight back in you, Trudy?" Lorraine asks.

"Two minutes, Lorraine."

Mrs. Rodriquez sprinkles baking soda over the sink bottom and begins to scrub, her black hair tied back like a steam-rolled ponytail, her head slung over her elbow which now rests on the edge of the sink. When she's finished she pours the hot water in the sink and speaks into the drain.

"So what's it going to be, Mr. Jacobs?"

Lorraine pats the stamped mail atop a pile of clothing catalogues on the kitchen table into a tidy square. Pleasantly, meekly, she extends her hand.

"I'll leave you two for a minute, Mark. It was nice talking all this out with you. I hope the boys are not too much trouble for you in Seattle. If Danny gives you anything more than a headache, why you just treat him like he was one of your own. He's a good little worker, a wonder really, but sometimes you've got to keep a stick after him."

Lorraine squared the stack of magazines and patted the thin pile of mail, before addressing Trudy's backside.

"Well Trudy, I guess I'll see how our two travelers are coming along. See you outside when you're ready. Alright then."

"Two minutes, Lorraine."

"Be safe, Mr. Jacobs."

"Yes ma'am, we will."

I watch the feathering of Lorraine's shadow vanish up the stairwell. It's over, all but the trace of an ending.

"It's a fine home you've made here for Juan. Feels safe here. Quiet and safe."

Mrs. Rodriquez shuts the water off. Pushes the faucet aside. Pinches out the candle flame. Pops a pill in her mouth while she twists 'round to face me so that I might know something more of what she lives with, that I might see how she swallows some of it, that I might read the lines on her face and see the chance she's taking and know that she requires nothing more from me, expects nothing less, from *my kind*.

"It's dark and it's paid for. That's enough these days, ain't it?"

There's hardly more than knife-throwing distance between us, and Mrs. Rodriguez has just snatched up every inch of it except the box I'm left standing in.

"Juan?"

"Yeah mom?"

"You staying or going?"

"Going mom. Danny too."

"Exactly when will you be sailing for Seattle, Mr. Jacobs?"

The colored water in that bottle on the windowsill is holding back time. Behind me, there's a stuffing taking place in Juan's bedroom and talk of a snagged zipper, something mumbled about a better pair of shoes and a better belt.

"We'll take my boat back to Red's tonight. I need him to look it over good before we cross open water. If Red says the boat's good to go, I expect we'll be on our way by tomorrow afternoon. I'll call when we reach Seattle. Probably be at least a few days. If you're having second thoughts about all this after were gone, Red's got a radio. He can reach me on the boat or at my house."

"What about your friend?"

"If you should spot Jimmy in the casino, I'd appreciate you calling Red. I don't take chances on the water, Mrs. Rodriquez. I sure won't take any with the boys aboard."

Danny's been listening from the stairwell, but when Juan steps from the bedroom he skates across the floor to join his friend. Both boys walk to the kitchen and stand beside me, luggage in hand. Juan's carrying his gear inside a wide canvas duffle bag, golden tan with bulging sides, brown leather handle-straps on top, stiff leather bottom. Danny's luggage is more basket than baggage; an over-varnished, yellowing webbing attached to a frame of metal rods with handles on it like those of a fish-basket. Standing so close together, the boys reminds me of the black and white pictures of soldiers I've seen in history books; brothers anticipating their orders to climb my wall of worry, or swim the channel, or take the graveyard watch in the midst of a fog so thick it will conceal a barge about to knock-you-bottomless if the angles of our kindred stalking cross.

"See you outside," Juan says to his mother.

The boys pat me on the shoulder before leaving, first Danny, then Juan, Juan taking the time to mimic his mother's posture while his hand rests on my shoulder.

"Two minutes, Mr. Jay—my mom's answer to everything."

Mrs. Rodriquez waits for the voices of both boy's to reach the outdoors, before she speaks.

"There is one more thing I'd ask of you, Mr. Jacobs," she pointed her toweled thumb over her shoulder, "concerning your friend up the street."

"Anything you want to ask of me, ma'am, I suspect I'd consider."

Outside the cellar-hole, the maples have been painted quiet by the passing rain. The night sky pushing out a wider ring of clearing over the islands. The air temperature has cooled considerably and the boys are anxious to lead their mothers to Lorraine's car. It's already been too long a goodbye for the boys. Bus-stop benches and the tiled walls of a train station might have been easier on them. A string of pearls were not, but we're on our way now, the boy's mindful not to let the swing of their luggage bump the legs of their mothers along the muddy path.

The luggage is stacked and banged inside the dented trunk of a '65 Ford Fairlane — *it's tan and it's paid for* — before I can lend a hand. In the front passenger seat Trudy blows her nose, tosses her hair, and flicks ash and sleep from her blouse. Napping on the bridge of her nose is a pair of lime-green, cat-eyed, wide-stemmed eye glasses. Juan is saying something to me that sounds as far away as Red's voice the night he pulled my knife from my boat's vinyl. The boy is holding the door open to the rear seat of the car while Danny translates, telling me to *"get in and slide all the way over 'cause the other door don't open."* Soon as I'm in the back seat, Danny's sitting beside me going to town scratching the skin around a new scab on his knee. Juan muscles in beside Dan, closes the car door so quickly and so hard that the air inside the Fairlane compresses my eardrums.

It's uncomfortably tight inside the car, everything too close, too loud, too final. What's worse is no one's talking about our odd allegiance, our ratting out of one another's wide-eyed wishes. The new neighbor has come from across the channel for dinner without the company of his second-story wife. He's peppered their kitchen table with too much of his unsolicited history, but he's finally leaving, so it's only fair that any reprisal from the hostess be put aside for now — inside this classroom of kidnapped chances to change my mind.

Danny and his mom are already holding each other at the waist by the time I step out of the car and onto the casino parking lot. Bouts of hugging are followed by a crack in Lorraine's voice, which she will address by probing the pocket of her turtleneck sweater for a bottle of pills and a cigarette.

Trudy's racking a thin smile. She presses an affectionate kiss on Juan's forehead, closes the car door, and extends her hand to me.

"Watch over our boys, Mr. Jacobs."

"Yes, ma'am."

The women walk away. They take a path behind a parked bread truck and reappear at the casino's opened delivery doors. One more Gatling gun goodbye from Lorraine and it's over. It's done.

The benches, the bushes, the street lights that showcase the foraging truck campers and abundant Camero on the hillside lot —and more of the same on the way to my boat — all of it is echoing the leash of Joey's truthful confession by the time we cross over the marina's footbridge. Everything about the way we're leaving this place feels like it has happened a thousand years ago, or yesterday, or both, as if all time merges — as if all I need do is peer over the railing to see Joey's truck plowing deliberately towards Jimmy, as I play in the snow with Dianna and Jessie.

I looked up from the rocks and the water's edge, hoping to find Jimmy had tracked our departure all along. But no sound rose from the black ice-water under the footbridge. No sighting of Jimmy's ice-sheathed chaperone's rope snaked the casino's striped pavement.

All boats but my own seem at rest in the casino's marina. Some of their round-faced windows brewing a hypnotic light behind the margins of their stiff curtains. At the end of the dock, the movements of puppets pass like possibilities behind the banded yellow light of a galley window.

"You want us to help you or stay out of the way?" Juan asked, once we were onboard my boat.

"I'm comfortable motoring out of the harbor. But once we hit current I might need an extra set of eyes."

Juan nodded and suggested that if we waited for the casino ferry to leave we could follow her wake all the way back to Red's.

"Guess it would save us the trouble of watching out for storm debris, wouldn't it?"

"That's what I was thinking."

Juan tied off the boat's rudder handle and asked if he might give the motor a pull to see if she'd start.

"You know how?"

"Sure. Prime it, choke it, and yank. Red used to have me do it all the time. When you weren't going to be around for a spell."

"Alright, give it a go."

"Dan? Can you check under that torn seat and see how much gas we got in the tanks. If at least one of 'em is full then go ahead and prime the line."

"Good job, Juan." I said. "I wouldn't have thought of that until my right arm was falling off."

Juan sat and pulled on the engine's cord. The motor rumbled thru a brief cycle of vibrations before idling smoothly. I switched on the running lights. Danny fumbled with the anchor line, until his hands slipped and the line's slack dropped back into the water.

"No problem, Dan." Juan assured him. "Rope's just been left in the water too long. Use one of those cleats by your knee to tie some of it off. Or better yet, can you help him Mr. Jacobs?"

I checked the running lights and double-checked the fuel levels in each tank Danny had checked. I dug out the life-jackets and then stored the anchor Danny had managed to pull up. Within minutes we were motoring between the marina's two fish-stick banks of anchored boats. Juan stood in the cockpit, one hand on the rudder arm. Danny was on the bow, ready to keep a lookout for storm logs once our boat entered the chop of current.

"Ferry will probably move a little faster than we can." Juan said. "But I bet we can tail her wake most of the way. Easily, I think."

"If you got any doubts about going back in the dark, Mr. J," Danny called back to us with his two cents of wisdom, "there's a lot less idiots on the water. Least ways, when Juan and me take the ferry home late, there is."

I had some doubts. I'd seen how long nightfall could take to turn daylight loose in these islands. But all I voiced to the boys was, "put those life-jackets on. And strap 'em on you good."

"Mr. Jacobs? You want to steer? Want me up in the bow looking out for stuff instead of Danny?"

"No. Stay where you are. I trust your judgment."

At the end of a day unplugged of so many of its miserably misunderstood mandates, it surprised me how quickly and naturally both boys understood the momentum of the moment at hand. Danny seemed at home on the water and much more focused. He clung to the bow's railing like a raccoon sniffing out food, responded respectfully and with a gathering sense of an apprentice's duty whenever Juan asked something of him. I think, too, that each of us knew how much these open waters could shield us from some of what had been chasing us, watching us, all day by land.

We motored in the plane of the ferry's wake. When the ferryboat turned her runny nose into the wind, we did likewise. Her hull trenching a course for us all of the way back to the island, except for the last thousand meters when it was necessary that we cross her tepid wake to enter the chilly dreaminess of the marina. Red's neon sign the flag home of another leg of our journey.

"Red light running, green light moored," Danny whispered to himself from the bow, as Juan and I tied off to a pier cleat.

"Don't sweat it, Dan," Juan spoke as quietly as his friend had, "it'll stick come Seattle."

We showered, and sometime after ten the boys took the shortcut up the marina's bluff to make their way over to Salvador's. Once there, they were to set up the tent they'd found onboard my boat. If Sally was home Juan would inform him of our plans. I'd told both boys I'd be up within the hour.

On the waterfront, my walk across the public docks is quick and watchful. The house lights on the harbor hillside voiceless and welcoming. No sign of the usual Saturday night crowd. No chatter from musicians hustling equipment back inside their carpeted vans. No breezy flashes of young party-goers noisily brushing by me. None of the running weight of stragglers to shake the column of wooden stairs leading me up to Main Street. A new kind of curfew has been posted on the docks, on the telephone poles, and on a wagon-train of a banner strung out over the parking lot. *New Dance Hours — 6pm to 8pm.*

Up on Main Street, the worming light of a spiraling barbershop candy-cane has been left on. I know this shop's owner, many times have watched him closing the door on a tingling bell, jingle his keys, put on his barista, and cross

Main Street to catch the casino ferry. *Business is good*, I've heard him tell his customers, *dreams are better*.

I walk close enough to Jessie's courtyard to smell an undamaged Daphne blooming, and to wonder how many other shop owners would pass judgment on my morning departure. Time curls back upon itself, it's true, and the thought of going back to Seattle is clouded with things undone, unsettled. To sell one's home seemed to be to sell one's history, and I'd never done either, never known a home without the twang of hearing both their names spoken, without knowing the certainty of seeing their colors linger on the path to Dianna's garden or *Jimmy's Campground*.

On a knoll of grass, on the far side of Sally's pond, the flashlight inside the boy's tent goes out. Down the hill from where they've pitched their tent a piping of cattails and iris grow along the pond's edge. There is breeze enough tonight to cut the pond's surface. A few scant clouds trace the night sky.

On the patio, my eyes blink back the heaviness of the day. Jenny stretches and moans by my side. She lifts her head and cocks her ears and pinches off the last of my thoughts. I'm asleep by the time the dog's speckled nose has nuzzled under my chin. Asleep before my next thought can triangulate the girth of Hazel's warm quilt, asleep on a couch lucky enough to have found Salvador's patio.

Morning. Across the street from the *Campground*, near the alley to the bakery, Father Jerald's quick stride is interrupted by a jostling handshake from a blue suit and Sunday hat. We've caught the priest's eye, the boys and me walking side-by-side on our way to the bakery. He waves us over.

Once we're all inside the bakery and seated side-by-side at the counter, Jerald begins the slow preach. Listening to his gibberish today will be like watching a velvety caterpillar trying to cross a street. *Ain't this cozy and going to be a fond farewell?*

"And to think, lads," I say to the boys when the priest turns to greet another one of his parishioners, "we could have slept in."

"That man, Mark, have you heard him play? A ruffian to be sure, but truly gifted. Plays the most delicious Al Jolson you've ever heard. An indulgence of mine, I admit. But hell's bells, man, this is a life of taste and touch too, is it not? Plays up at the hotel's lounge for two more weeks. You should join me there next week."

Finally, the priest cleared his throat and came down for air. "Any sign of him, Mark?"

"Yeah, signs everywhere. Matter of fact, right now he's getting cleaned up for Sunday mass."

Father Jerald lifted his water glass, sipped, and set the glass aside.

I ordered green tea and a bowl of strawberries with granola and yogurt, and to go — two loafs of Como bread, a dozen ginger-molasses cookies, a frozen loaf of pumpkin bread — and gave no more thought to the sarcasm I'd directed at Father Jerald than the boys do to the size of my order. The boys order strawberries, and with very little coaxing, pancakes and sausage and chocolate milk. Jerald orders hot chocolate with whipped cream, asks that a teaspoon of chocolate ice-cream be put in it. Our waitress places our orders with the cook, Jerald interrupting her to add a slice of chocolate-hazelnut cheesecake to his drink order. *Sweet Jesus, ain't he a Sunday surprise.*

Jerald sucked on his swizzle-stick and swiveled his stool so as to take in the view of water outside the baker's window. Swivels back around and leans back to study the faces on each boy. The mood of an inquisition straightening his shoulders and deciding for all of us that maybe it's time these boys tell the world everything I won't. For another sip or two this priest will quietly set the stage, hold his mug of chocolate with a glove of a left hand, slurp more of the whipped cream and melting ice-cream, and raise the mug to the skunk-striped ponytail of the young baker smiling from behind the kitchen's service window.

"Damn it." Jerald says, slapping his free hand down on the countertop. "Why are you running off at a time like this? Are you scared, man?"

Becky, our waitress, approaches carrying three bowls of fruit on her arm. She sets the bowls in front of the boys. It's and interesting stage, this concrete countertop the three of us are resting our elbows on, a forest floor etched with the images of leaves, sticks, shellfish, and the flattened bodies of insects.

"You won't answer me because you feel I've betrayed you. I haven't."

I make every effort to eat with ease and not respond — my jaw hurts, and whenever I chew too quickly, or keep my mouth closed over my food for too long, the pain increases and lingers there for half a minute. What I really want is to scoop up the fruit and yogurt with my fingers and suck it off my fingertips and chew with my mouth open. It's the only way I've been able to eat comfortably all week without my jaw wrapping the pain clear around to the back of my neck. I swallow and brace for the pain that's about to erupt just under my ear, brace like a makeshift tent staked out against a cold wicked wind.

Jerald knows well enough why I'm leaving. Knows that if a man can't fix a thing he's failed that thing.

"Do you really believe Jimmy will come out of his self-imposed sentencing unscathed?"

"Tide comes in tide goes out is what I believe. Plus or minus a little evaporation."

Jerald dipped his soup spoon into my field of strawberries. *Son-of-a-bitch he's an arrogant skiff, ain't he?*

"Of course, you know he won't. He's doing to himself what any troubled soul does when it's lost what it loves. But he'll do more of it than most. You know that."

The other diners in the room are about as insulated from Jerald's preaching as Jimmy's shack is waterproof. Too many eyes on my cuts and bruises, too many ears to say everything I'm thinking. There are fine men who choose to wear the robe, I know that, but this one next to me seems to think his title grants him passage anywhere. Got it in his head that he can dip his wick and strawberry spoon in my misery hole any time he feels like it.

I leaned sideways over the countertop and into Jerald's space. Put my hand over his wrist so that he won't be able to lift his cup of chocolate up to his sermonizing mouth when I speak.

"Stay the fuck out of my bowl of strawberries, father."

"Oh, I see. Why stick around when you can dump your troubles into your neighbor's yard."

"You haven't a clue."

"If you really believe that then you are brooding with anger and ignorance, Mark."

He's still waving that spoon of his in the face of what he believes is my conceit.

"And you are arrogant to think so, Jerald."

Jerald got up from his stool and walked to the cash register. On his way out he walks behind me too closely, stopping to place a hand on the shoulders of each boy and to pickup his boxed cheesecake.

"Bring no harm to these young men, Mark. They're a loyal crew. Enjoy the ballgame, lads."

At the marina, we find Red hobbling up the galley stairs of my boat, a bag full of trash in his hand. In the freshness of this bright new day, the boat looks new again.

"Got your note this morning. She appears no worse for wear from Jimmy's hijacking. She's full of fuel. Did the best I could for you for grub. You got ice enough for a couple days. Plenty of bread and tuna and soups. Couple of jars of peanut butter. A sack of potatoes in there. Eggs, some cheddar, couple cubes of cookin' butter. Anna packed you a few extras. Some of her own canned peaches and some of her homemade applesauce. Yeah, and some crazy-odd trail mix she swears will keep you regular as a duck. Make sure that you get your share of the peaches. The boys here eat 'em up like they was candy. It's the truth, ain't it Juan?"

"I guess it probably is."

Red swung his bad leg aside and made his way back down the galley stairwell. "Give me just a minute. There. Alright gentlemen, come on aboard. We've a few things to cover before you set sail. Sleep well did-jah, Mark, up at the mansion? Sally called. Be back sometime today. Said if I was to see you, to tell you Brynn is back on his feet and eating like a horse. I told him that's ah-good because his pantry and my freezer holding enough donations to feed a ranch full of 'em."

Back on deck, Red sits and takes a minute to catch his breath. The boys want to know if it's alright to go buy something in the store — *we've got our own money.*

Red waits for the boys to leave our sight. His lungs drawling out one long fitful wheeze before he's physically comfortable enough to say what's been pressing on his mind.

"Not to worry. Got half the town keeping an eye out for him. I'll radio you if I hear anything. You just go and do whatever it is you got to do in Seattle and get yourself back here. Lot of summer ahead of us, you know. A lot can change. Lot of things got time to turn themselves around."

Dawn shuttered across the bow of our boat like grated slivers of frost, and with it came a scuttling mist that gave us goose-bumps and made our noses run. The mist lifted the stones from the shoreline and gave the beach the appearance of a piece of cheesecloth being pinched from the frothy ambush of sunrise. It's quiet out here, anchored on the water, not so much as a hum of engine noise hiding in the grainy bank of fog separating over the outlying waters.

"Here you go, Mr. J. This will help you to think. Know what I mean."

"That it will."

Danny's head is hooded. He's barefooted and cold. His shivering body cooing a look of danger about him as he hands me my cup of morning coffee.

"You two are a matched pair." Juan says to his friend. He raises the cup of coffee he's been warming his hands with to a blue-hooded heron painting itself out of the cove's misty fog.

Danny smirked, and pulls one of his hood strings tighter with his teeth. He looks a little purple around the lips. He's jiggling an empty coffee cup in one hand and holding the acrylic handle of an oxidized coffee pot in his other. While Juan gives advice that maybe his friend should go below and warm himself over the stove awhile, Danny tops off my coffee mug.

Juan looks rested and happy. He's wearing a clean long-sleeved white shirt, collar pressed and buttoned, shirttail out.

He's barefoot, one foot squared up against the knife cut in the cockpit's vinyl. He's made a table of one of his blue-jean thighs on which to rest his coffee elbow. Still got his eyes on that shoreline bird poking its pipe-cleaner legs out from under a lampshade of mist. It's a fine pot of coffee. Dark as ink and piping hot.

"In case you haven't figured out already it's about impossible for Danny to sit still. See there," Juan pointed close range at his friend, "even standing in one spot he's got to shiver to be himself."

"Juan Valdez is right. It about ruins my whole day if I can't keep on the move. Say, you got a radio onboard Mr. J?"

"Calling in a mayday, are you?"

"I mean a music radio. For jah-jah-jammin with when I'm down in the cellar fixing you kids breakfast."

"I guess there might be one inside somewhere. Look around. Here, let's have some more of that good coffee before you go. Close the hatch cover behind you. You'll feel like toast in ten minutes."

"That's the perfect approach to take with him." Juan tells me after Danny's gone below. "Send him off in any direction to get but one thing done."

"You think?"

"I'm serious. With Danny, it's best just to point and let him figure it out. Otherwise, you never get a moment off to yourself."

"How long you two been friends?"

"Since grade school. I pulled him out of his locker first time we met. Him and his mom moved in next to us a few days later. He caused me a bad bruising from the get go."

"How's that?"

"The Chickweed brothers. The three of them was the ones stuffed him into a locker on his first day. Ugly, ugly twins."

"You said *three brothers*."

"The twins had a sister."

I grinned and spit coffee grounds over the rail.

"Danny's lucky to have you for a friend. It was a little like that for me on my first day."

Juan set his coffee aside and swept his hand thru his hair. His front teeth scraping at his lips until a question slides out.

"So, you and Jimmy were friends even before you owned the bar?"

"High school. My family lived here for a little over a year. We had to move back to Seattle when my dad had his first heart attack. A few months after that we left Seattle to make our way back to New England."

"Why'd you go back east?"

"The heart attack frightened my mother something awful. I think she wanted her parents and sisters around her for support."

"What kind of work your old man do?"

"Worked in the shipyards. Was a welder."

"Bet he had to smack you around some every now and then, right?"

"My dad? No, never. Never."

"What, you didn't give him no cause to I guess?"

"I'm sure I must of. But I don't think it was in my dad's nature to be violent."

Juan reached for his coffee mug and looked away from me.

"My dad was always building us things, Juan. Anything we'd ask for he'd eventually get around to building for us."

"Like what kind of things?"

"A basketball hoop, for one. Best ever."

I tilted my head back to pluck more of the memory from the blue hole opening up in the sky and to acknowledge with wonder how patiently my father had withstood my relentless *suggestions,* suggestions as to where the best place in the yard might be to put up a hoop. Suggestions I continually plugged at his tired eyes, for weeks on end, whenever he was trapped on my side of the dinner table for one hour each night.

"Looked like a headboard for a tall skinny giant. From the hill overlooking Crawley's Pond, a thousand yards away from the house — way across the farm's hayfields — I used to think I could put a bullet thru that back board with my rifle. That hoop had legs of steel. Two massive pieces of pipe sunk in the ground on the edge of a nice green lawn that ran smack into a half-baked cow field. Imagine two pole-vaulting poles standing straight up, side by side, three or four feet apart. And on the top, a square frame of more steel that the backboard was bolted to. Couldn't break it, couldn't crack it. No way, no matter how hard you slugged the ball at it when you were pissed off. Tons of work went into it, midnights of it. How many? Don't know for sure. I know I watched my father work thru plenty of midnights, and then some, from my upstairs' bedroom window."

The flashing outline of my father's blue coveralls crimping lines on the face of darkness, electrifying a fog filled dome of hairless trees and hunkering metal farm implements all around his tilted space helmet each time the tip of his welding rod would torch his staging area in a spray of sizzling white light. A light that formed, in my mind's eye, a blinding force-field around his crouching, dissecting body. To me, my father was a scientist working an atom-splitting light that popped and spit its living current onto the smoky-gray trunks of sugar maples, where it amplified its frying x-ray powers into gaseous plumes. The flash of my father's world extinguished, instantly, when the sound of his dying welder-beast settled and roared its last hollow moan for the night — the clashing neon shadows of tree branches toppling the moment the rainy humid smear of a purple darkness returns to hide my father from the family that slept while he worked.

"When my dad worked late into the night the darkness around him had a smell to it. Kind of a clean, healing bridge of blue smoke that would ride the sweaty air up to my room's open window. Out there all alone, wrapped up in his work, my dad was a magician. No one could touch him. No one could hurt him. He was all ours. And me watching over him, standing on my bed in my second-floor bedroom where it's so hot I'm already on my third pillowcase wiping away a flood. Wishing he'd be done tomorrow. Hoping he'd stay up all night to finish it. Back then, when I was a kid, I thought it was effortless for a man like my father to work so late. At your age, Juan, I wasn't as thoughtful as you. Not even something close to you. Not thinking at all how hot my dad must have been inside that astronaut's mask. And those coveralls he's wearing. And a leather apron over all that. Probably wearing padded gloves, too. Man-oh-man, think of it, the fumes and the smoke and the furnace roar of that arc welder in your face all night. And on top of all that, his body's pumping out salt and water in the drone of an August heat wave. That's what August is like in New England — one hell-of-a thirty-two day drone. That, I know."

"God."

"Did all that work for us. For me and my brother. And my sister. And did it all after working his ten hour day job. Ten-hour shifts. Christ Juan, I don't even remember saying thank you to him."

"Probably still standing, right?"

"Absolutely."

Danny reappeared on deck with a fresh pot of coffee. The bottom half of the aluminum coffee pot is fluted with a thin skirt of soot I don't remember seeing before. Happens when the pot is placed on the burner too soon, before the propane flame has been given enough time to burn itself clean, something my father would take notice of and comment on.

"You turn the gas off?"

"I did."

"At the cylinder, after you turned the burner off?"

"I think so."

"Double-check."

"Okay."

"You go back and see your dad much?" Juan asked.

I emptied my old coffee overboard. "Your turn Juan. Did you know Danny's father?"

"I never met him." Juan took a slurping gulp from his fresh cup of coffee. "Can I ask you something, Mr. Jacobs, aside from all this?"

"Where am I gonna run off to? I can't walk on water."

"You think there's more prejudice here than where you live? More, I mean, in a small town. Then say, in Seattle?"

The hatch cover opened and Danny's tangled head of hair bubbled up. "Are we awake yet? God Juan, it's campy down here. Seriously nice. Hey, you guys care what I fix up for breakfast?"

"Just so the boat's afloat when you're finished."

"It'll be good for sure. See you in fifteen!" Danny slid the hatch cover closed. The boy's high-pitched, incomprehensible chanting chasing after him down the galley steps.

"There's prejudice in each of us." I said. "Size of a town has got nothing to do with it. Size of your education does. Know what I mean?"

"Not really."

"Every one of us can grow hate inside of us. But to know why you hate something or someone, too many people don't. Those people become the numb and the ignorant, people stuck on chasing down a target that's got nothing to do with their own bad luck and their own poor choices."

"I think maybe my old man had a degree in that."

"Son, some of the worse prejudice in the world lives in our own homes, where, too often, it is never really confronted."

Danny called for us to come and eat.

"Jesus, did he even have time to crack an egg? Come on, we'll talk more about this later if you want. Let's see what the kid cooked up."

Below deck it's warm. Danny's working two pans on the stove, wearing an apron that almost touches the beaded bracelet around his ankle. The hand-painted apron is awash with fish prints; pink salmon, rock-fish, flounder, and the rarest of all species — the artist's ingenious but delusional *Hen-fish*, a comical creature half bird half fish.

"Batteries in your radio got all corroded, Mr. J." Danny's talking to a fry pan bubbling with scrambled eggs, salsa, and corn chips. "So no music is what I'm getting at. So my rhythm's all off. So, so some of the food's gonna be real hot and some of it's gonna be cold. But it's all gonna be good. Toasty down here in the dungeon, ain't it? Hey, you sorry yet Mr. J? Sorry you asked us two heathens along?"

"Ask me after I've tried the eggs."

By midday, Juan has taken full ownership of the boat's rudder arm. He stands tall against the moving shoreline of limestone cliffs and rock slides, seems to favor the responsibility of steering the boat. He navigates with confidence, keeping a watchful eye on Danny's dangling technique of cleaning the bow and another on the lookout for the smallest of eddies, which swirl and stalk the hull's shoreline course and give notice of cut-throat rock resting just beneath the water's surface. And always, when responding to my inquiries as to when we might first catch a glimpse of those train tracks, he is cordial.

In the afternoon, we retraced a few miles of our morning course, in the remote chance that some dark and spotty movement in the trees might bestow Jimmy upon us. Juan navigated the short but constrictive passage we'd come thru earlier, where thick stands of blackened hemlock pushed the boundaries of the mainland out over a rising tide, where no movement of shadow tacked the boat's progress. But we saw no sign of him, only the eerie faces whirling in the channel's deep swift water and the occasional pinging sound of the boat's depth-finder.

Juan became more talkative as the day wore on. He tried engaging our cook, our janitor, our brass-and-polish man in the basics of sailing. When that didn't pan out, he jokingly admonished Danny for being overly obsessed with what Juan considers to be little more than "the cufflinks of sailing." But Danny was neither interested in sparring nor in listening to any kind of badgering talk whose aim it seemed was to make him feel he was pinned down in a classroom. After all, this was the middle of his summer vacation and he'd finally found work that suited him — what more could an island boy ask for. By the time Juan had navigated another narrow passage and turned the boat into a wall of sunlight, all he'd managed to pull out of his friend was the crack of a smile to go with Danny's mocking salute.

The train tracks finally appeared on a cut of rocky hillside below a cliff overlooking Doubtful Sound. But after running only a few hundred yards of shoreline, the tracks quickly disappeared into a tunnel in the cliffs and did not reappear on the hillsides, or along the shoreline, again that day. It seemed a gambler's fruitless wager to continue our course along the mainland shore much longer.

"Juan, slow it down."

"Why?"

"Salmon. Big ones."

"We ain't got time."

"I'm not fooling. Slow it up."

"More," Danny's voice ramped up his excitement, "slow it down more."

"Take it easy. Boat ain't a bicycle."

"Over this side, Mr. J. They're swimming inside our shadow. See 'em?"

A sniff of a splash, off starboard, caused Danny to go fetch his fishing pole from the cockpit.

"Here, don't forget your net." Juan says, breaking out in one of his ivory smiles while poking Danny in the back with the handle of the net.

"Shoot, I catch 'em, I clean 'em, I cook 'em. All you got to do is steer."

"That's because you catch 'em, clean 'em, and cook 'em."

"Listen to him," Danny says to me, "like he's talking back to some old Yank down at Red's."

"Juan, sass someone? I don't believe it."

"You ain't never really heard him mouth off, have you?"

"That true, Juan?"

"I do get fed up with them sometimes. All their jabbering about how much cash they got sunk into their big boats. Their sweet cottages by the sea. Always complaining we're not fetching their fish fast enough. It does get to me sometimes."

"That's about when Juan can usually just lose it. He'll just say it right out loud. 'Piss on it, it ain't me.' Wish I could, but I ain't him yet. One time this fat old turtle looking guy took hold of Juan's arm 'cause he said it to the man's old lady."

"That was years ago, Dan."

"Oh, Mr. J ain't never gonna go tell no one. Know what it was he done then?"

I bit. "What?"

"Chinooked him. Chinooked him real good!"

"What's that mean?"

"Know what that is? That's putting an illegal size salmon in the old turd's boat. I was there when he did it. Juan caught it himself and put it inside one of Salvador's dog kennels to keep it alive in his pond overnight. Then the next day he put the salmon in the guy's big yellow boat before anyone saw. After he done it he waited for where the fish warden's been hanging out all week. Case closed."

"Quit your cawing and catch us a fish."

"I got one!"

That evening, in a cove behind an arch of island rock which supported a few windswept trees and offered a bit of privacy and shelter from the open waters, Juan cooked us a beautiful dinner. Salmon fillets dipped in egg, breaded with cornmeal, and grilled alongside some sliced yellow potatoes. Cooks all of it up to a crisp on the barbeque and serves it to us on pottery plates heaped with brown rice and some of last night's leftover carrots. A pan of warm cornbread cooling on the table. A silver stenciled water pitcher stands like an obelisk on the edge of the table-cloth, until Juan remembers that he's seen a bottle of lime juice somewhere onboard. *"Red's wife packed it for us remember."*

We eat like kings and wash our food down with glass after glass of water poured from Dianna's dolphin-snout pitcher. We wipe our plates clean with the last of the cornbread. We leave the remnants of our chiding talk on our paper napkins, Danny talking of chef school in Juan's future and, for the time being, suggesting we handcuff one of Juan's hands to the door handle of the boat's doll-sized oven for the duration of the trip. We finish off our meal by opening a jar of fresh figs — the boys have never in their lives tasted such sweetness — and a box of store bought mint cookies. In the comfort of one another's company, we have become the Sound's new breed of fishermen; two fatherless boys and a drifting plank, and out there somewhere, one homeless widower. For the briefest of moments, we are the Sound's wealthiest of strays.

Juan and I take our coffee on deck, leaving Danny to clean the kitchen in the company of his radio and his own free will, which all too soon seemed hell-bent on switching stations every other song.

"Danny?"

"Yeah."

"See if you can find us a ballgame on the radio, will you. Might catch the last inning."

"Oh yeah. You got it, chief."

"Sorry you found him those new batteries yet?" I asked.

"We may have to put him ashore tomorrow and you and me go on without him." The tip of Juan's clove cigarette grew red against the wall of stars and water and black wonder behind him.

"You funny, Juan. Real funny. You one of those funny Tai-Juan-go-guys, ain't you?" One of Danny's wet cleaning rags flew up from the galley hole and landed at our feet.

"How much food and water you figure you're going to need 'til me and Mr. J get back from Seattle, Dan?"

"Ha, Ha," Danny belched. "You're a regular after-dinner mint, you two are."

"We'll have to leave him a couple sacks of coffee beans. Otherwise he might get the D-tee's and die on us."

"Funny, funny. I get it. Some peoples got clocks that need more winding than others, that's all."

"Where you'd pick that up? Red?"

"Maybe. But I don't hear anyone complaining about all the cleaning up I do."

"Pay our young captain no mind, Danny. Best this boat's looked in years."

"That's what I been saying to myself all day. Hey Mr. J? You gonna let us talk you into playing cards with us tonight?"

"No, no thanks. I think I'm going to call it a day and turn in. Juan?"

"Yeah?"

"If you're up late playing cards, keep the radio and your voices low. Couple of house lights up there on the hillside."

"Sure."

"Goodnight."

"Night, Mr. Jacobs."

The first hour in my bed is a crushing coronation, bides its bitter time passing, circles the room with the same thought that's dogged me all day — that there's a bottle of bourbon, unopened, under the sink. I repeat my silent prayer to my own higher self, ten, twenty times, until I fall off to sleep... *Don't let me linger. Don't let me fall. Turn my eyes away from all that is missing...*

Tomorrow comes and the first pictures floating thru my mind, when I awake, are of Jessie kissing me; once on the cheek when she was a child, once as the woman whose bed I shared. Outside my window, the ocean is as glossy as a snifter of apricot brandy. The boys are up and shuffling about. I can hear the rise and fall of their voices on the water.

On deck, Danny is one big smile chasing after another. He's shuffling across the bow like a plastic bag blown onboard by the wind, coffee in hand. Juan waits until I've had a few sips of coffee before telling me what's on his mind.

"There's another trestle bridge up the shoreline a ways that we could check out today, if you want. We might be miles ahead of him. We could anchor there for another day or two, and wait and see."

"No. It was a sketchy dream, at best, thinking we could spot a man traveling a few open stretches of hillside track." I tossed the rest of my coffee overboard. "Probably ought to pull up anchor and head out, Juan. Using up a lot of daylight."

There is more daylight and starlight and another day on water to come. The wash of tides and more miles of trackless shoreline. Land miles that twist and turn away from us and mark each hour that our sun-glazed eyes fail to find the chop of a man on the run, or even the apparition of one. Nothing will come of our drifting efforts. No silver streamline train will coast by us with its dinner hour boxcar. No hint of Jimmy's melodious limp rattling our shoebox glimpses of knuckled track. Only the dusky shoreline woods running breathless towards another soundless, foreboding tunnel.

One more day to hold all the others before it. How we watched with wonder to see it perched on the bow of our boat come the twitching cape of twilight. How it took our breath away and some of the hurt, carrying us all the way to the highway-hobbled splendor of Seattle's skyline.

Even when there appears to be no bodily movement, we have thoughts. And these thoughts have consequences; either we drift in the rowing weight of their repetition or race ahead to prepare for their ending.

Our house.

Our house is a jackknife version of a two-story New England colonial; white paint, black shutters. Forest-green front door with a brass kick plate. A border of red brick frames the landing to the front door, the had-to-be-green front door. More red brick, dressed down with green moss, edges a slanting cobblestone walk to the city sidewalk. Shake roof, heavily grooved and steeply pitched. No pretty white picket fence, instead, one of clear-grain cedar allowed to weather to a whale-grey color, allowed to lean towards the neighbor's yard from the weight of an untrimmed Seattle spring. Near the sidewalk, the gate to the front yard is made of rough-hewn cedar; a thick, wide, chewing of splintered boards and black strap hinges. Every one of the gate's natural knots punched out by the weather. Two flowering floribunda roses climb the gate's rotting wooden arch. Between the garden gate and the row of street trees, several squares of city side-walk have cracked and lifted, been pushed up and aside by the roots of the Sweet Gums. More dilapidated picket fenc-ing follows the sidewalk to the end of the property. *What to remember, what to forget.* A few spindling green vines stick out from the hedgerow of roses Jessie planted years ago, and are blooming buckets of yellow curls along the top of the fence. The far end of the rose hedge so deeply shaded now by the yard's three dogwoods, so tangled in with the neighbor's jail of a quince hedge, that one seldom sees a pretty bloom in that corner of the yard. The fence-chasing, faceless noses of all our beautiful dogs are long silent beneath the hedge of roses, too. All I have for their faceless wonder are more questions for them.

"Come on, I'll show you two the guts of this old hotel."

Before darkness fell, the boys made toasted sandwiches with the bread and cheese we'd brought up from the boat. It was all the food we had in the house, and the sandwiches were dry and butter-less like everything else standing stale in our stone and maple kitchen.

After they'd unpacked their things in the bedroom next to the kitchen pantry, the boys walked around the outside of the house with me. I pointed out the areas of the house I wanted them to begin working on in the morning.

"If I'm not here when you get up it's because I went for groceries. Concentrate on the first-story windows, the trim, and the shutters. Wash everything good. And rinse everything good. Buckets and hoses are in the greenhouse. Ladder's in the garage. Use whatever soap you can find in the kitchen or the laundry. When I get back we'll start scraping and sanding. Any questions? Good."

Back inside the kitchen, the boys went to their room and flipped a quarter for who would get to sleep in the bed closest to the television set. Last thing I said to them, before heading upstairs to my own room, was to be sure and lock up if they stepped outdoors for a smoke.

"Hey, are you two listening?"

"Yes sir." Juan answered.

"There are two locks. One on the kitchen door, one off the back porch. Lock them both."

"I will."

"Goodnight."

"Mr. Jacobs?"

"What is it?"

"Thanks for bringing us along."

"No problem."

Hours after I'd fallen off to sleep, I was awakened by the sound of a car pulling up to the curb. Dianna's letter lay atop the coverings at the foot of the bed. On coveted paper black and white and left behind for me to find, she'd shared volumes about her resilience.

I sat up in the bed. From the drift of bed coverings, I pulled

Dianna's letter to my chest. There was light enough from the street lamps to make out the words I'd already read.

Dear Mark,

Know as you begin to read this letter that it is love governing my heart and my pen as I write.

Soon enough I will open my window from some new bluff and look out upon another world, where I will search for the words you might hear tomorrow or some other day. I would ask of you one thing before I go — that you trust that it is my voice you are hearing now, not some desperate voice whispering to you from the sadness of Depot Island.

By now, I am so far away from the islands that I am tempted to believe you could not reach me, not with all the math in the world placed at your fingertips. It is not to torment you that I speak of the place I am in, but to remove any burden you may feel of following me there.

I am alone, you may trust in that also, and comfortable enough with the solitude of this island, even solicitous of it. Yet, I know in my heart that your lovely voice will soon enough consume my nights. And though there is no darkness in my head now, when my heart calls out for your heart from the dream of a night sleep yet to come, my tears are a joyful sorrow in this empty four a.m. hour. Call my name from any island's shoreline, where a passing ferry might recognize us, and know it for yourself — trust in a love which does not consider endings.

My love

A rocking of kindness. A hushed canvassing scream which opens and points the way back. I'd listened, and heard both these voices while reading my wife's letter. Have I known one voice more intimately than all the others, walked with its whispers into *another's* life or with another lifetime, a thousand, two thousand years lived out? Have I known each of these lives more than once, witnessed a thousand crucifixions, and buried the disbelief of what I was seeing in some unfathomable beating of my own — knowing, for all time, that a vessel which could love so unselfishly was also capable of such human atrocities? Could any of us be born unto another's consciousness, from another's conscious-ness? Did we perform this life for ourselves, a lifetime earli-er, and not heed its foreshadowing warning?

And you will stand down before me or you will witness a fire and rage that will know no name but my own. And my name will consume your defiling presence. And there will be no will conceived within you but my own, no pain suffered or vanquished but that which I choose for you.

You really believe that?

In marriage we stage the time given to us, the language changed by our interactions.

The Hopi-Indian rug on the bedroom floor, on the bath-room side of the bed, plays like a red violin on a round solo stage, plays the same open-mouth sensation between my bare feet on my way to the bathroom every night whether I'm here or not.

It's dark as pitch in the bathroom when I close the door behind me. Tiles blue and turquoise, imprinted and cornered inside my head by any shifting light trying to enter this cube of a room. A shower wall of glass block illuminates the room's surfacing light. I palm cold water from the faucet, drink until the photographs on the walls lift and play back a larger body of silvery pleasure. Colors like those lent from a dream; climates and celebrations and costumes, framed, dated, lost or remembered, made glossy or dull by the garlands of time. Maybe it's not so dark, maybe it's darker.

Outside the bedroom window, the streetlights look dim and souring in the rain. There's a taxicab steaming in the street, its peanut-colored parking lights close to the curb. The cab's passenger-side door is open, its black vinyl gleaming from the raindrops falling from the ribs of leafy tree branches. And beyond an arm's reach of the door's handle, a man — not the driver — is standing on the sidewalk. Standing stiff as cold, hands in the pockets of his dark hooded sweatshirt. The man's head tucked deep inside his hood and holding still within the arch of space above the gate, but mostly, the man is obscured by the hood's dark cloth and the shadow he's taken refuge in. Standing, almost motionless, a drooping harness of contemplation or maybe indecision or maybe misunderstood reconnaissance. A quake of bleakness pulls the man's hands from his pockets, pulls him just out of reach of the gate's nightlight before I'm able to open my bedroom window and rid what I'm seeing of its drizzle. The street light in the tree limbs over the cab calling the man back to the cab, lifting his leg into the cab's passenger seat, closing his door, becoming a part of the cab's moving advertisement and phone number.

In the morning, the first thing I do is walk to the garden gate to inspect what is mine. Plugging a square of the gate's lattice, as if placed there by the hand of some half-committed solicitor, is a yellowing photograph of Jessie climbing from the water onto the stern of my boat. The white borders of the photograph have been intentionally damaged by a row of cigarette burn-holes. In the middle of the photograph what appears to be someone's vandalized initials — O C T — have burned away much of the image of the boat.

From the side porch, Danny's head bops into the front yard, an aluminum ladder in his arms which he's enthusiastically pumping towards one corner of the house. Behind him, Juan comes out of the garage with two buckets and some rags in his hands.

"Crap, do I feel like painting a skyscraper before breakfast? No. Give me a hand with this ladder, Juan. I'm going clear to the fuggin top."

"You'll be spent before noon, the way you been jacking off every night."

"Jack-Jack-Jack, Jackie." Danny looked over his shoulder and growled. "Right, like you'd rather give it to Hazel instead."

"Hey!" I shouted. "This is my home."

"Sorry Mr. J. I thought you'd already gone to the store."

I walked back to the house. A minute later there was a knock on the kitchen door.

"Door's open. Yeah Juan, what is it?"

"Can I take some soap from the sink for the windows?"

"Help yourself. In the garage there's a can of gasoline. When your soap bucket's full, put two tablespoons in the water and mix it up good. Rinse each window off good before moving on to the next one. The woodwork, too."

"Alright. Did you see him?"

"It's a good idea to change the water in your soap bucket every two or three windows. Be sure to mix in a little gasoline each time. Got all that?" I opened the yellow-pages of the phone book and let my fingers mar the pages of realtors. "See who?"

"Last night. By the gate."

"What are you talking about?"

"Jimmy."

"And how did you manage that?" I pushed the phone book aside.

"I was up late watching television. Afterwards I went outdoors for a smoke. I'm pretty sure he didn't see me. After he left I locked both doors like you said."

"You saw Jimmy standing at the gate? In the middle of the night?"

"That's what I saw. But more like he was squatting. More like he was looking for something he dropped on the sidewalk or something."

"And you didn't think maybe you ought to come wake me?"

"I thought he was gonna come in when he stood up. He acted sort of like he was coming thru the gate a couple times. Then I guess he decided to leave you a note or something. Least wise, it looked like he did after he stood around awhile, after he looked up awhile at where your room is."

"Danny see him?"

"Danny didn't see anything. He crashed as soon as his head hit the pillow."

"Anything else you want to tell me before Christmas?"

"He got out of a cab. But, but how could he have done it? Got here to the city so fast?"

"He's hardly human anymore."

"No shit. Sorry."

"Best you shrink whatever you think you saw last night."

"Seeing him here — it was almost like I think I could of dreamt it."

"You didn't see anything. You listening? Juan?"

"Yeah, I'm listening."

"You didn't see anything. A cab pulled up, maybe checked a house number. Maybe flicked a cigarette at the gate before driving off. That's all you saw, if anyone asks."

"Just the way my old man used to think."

"What?"

"I only meant —"

"No, nothing at all like your old man. No one's guilty here. No one's running off on you."

"Trying to protect us, right? Cause you think he might have come here looking for those men?"

"Shrink it," I said. "You saw a cabby looking for a house number in the dark, that's all." I didn't wait for him to acknowledge that this part of our conversation was over. "I'll be back in a couple hours. Best get started on those windows."

Turning away from me, Juan mumbled "how do you shrink something big as that?"

From our house to Seattle's waterfront there's paint to buy, food to shop for, a realtor's pen to borrow, and when I return, a neighbor to inform that the light bleaching from our second-story windows at night is my doing. Of all else the less said the better, not a word about our house going on the market, nothing about Dianna's remarkable awakening and her subsequent flight.

By the time I return to the house the day feels nearly over. In the driveway, I remain in the truck and let the engine idle. I scan the blank face of the house, its patchy front yard, the stepladder that is now folded like an accordion under the heels of Juan's sneakers. The boy has benched himself in a shaded corner of the fenced yard, one hand extended high above his head and gripping a gnarly dogwood branch, his outstretched legs resting on the stepladder which parallels the line of sunlight crossing the yard. Harnessed in Juan's other hand, which rests in his lap, is an open paperback book.

"Hope you've got a strong stomach," I call out to Juan from the truck, "you're going to need it to finish that book."

"I feel like I know these people," Juan answers.

"I can see how you might."

"I never read anything like this. It's like somehow I already met these people for real, and now I'm reading about them."

"I think he'd like hearing you say that."

"I guess you've read it a bunch."

"Oh yeah."

Next morning the boys are up at sunup. By the time I come downstairs, Danny has set the breakfast table and Juan is busy poaching eggs and stacking a tower of buttered toast. The veined and ragged jacket of Eugene O'Neil's *Moon for the Misbegotten* rests on top of Juan's empty coffee mug.

"He's not easy on people, is he?" Juan says to me while pointing at the book's gaping jacket.

"No. No sir, he's not."

"He doesn't lie."

"That's for sure." I pour myself a cup of Danny's coffee and walk back to the breakfast table. "Not many young men your age connect with O'Neil's work."

"Some of the time, but I'm only part ways into the reading, sometimes I think the people in his story live right on our island. Sometimes, when I'm reading, it's like some of us are playing these parts."

"O'neil suffered. It opened him up. Then he wrote about it. Wrote it like no one before him ever did."

Juan took his seat at the table. He set the book on the tablecloth and tapped the curling jacket with his fingers. Danny seemed to take Juan's finger tapping as his cue to sit. He walked quickly to his chair, sloshing a bit of hot coffee onto the floor on the way.

"Morning Danny." I raised my cup to the boy and smiled. "Coffee's exceptional today. Think you might remember the recipe for one more day?"

"Doubtful, Mr. J." Danny tucked his chair in under his

butt. "Hey, can you sit down. We got a little something to say. It's not a prayer or nothing, so don't go getting worried or anything."

Juan's fingers stroke the cover of the book, as if its paper jacket is an injured animal he's trying to comfort. He waits for me to sit before speaking.

"We just want to say how grateful we are you took a chance on us. And that we know you can get thru this, Mr. Jacobs. Dan and I, we know you can."

"If I don't, maybe I'll write a play about it."

My response to Juan's wish of a prayer sounds trite. What do you say to a stranger offering a helping hand from across the sea? The toaster under the kitchen window is smoking more breakfast bread. If these boys are men, they're saying what men won't. Not often enough, anyhow, not in time. Breakfast is over.

Outdoors, everything but the view of the house from the front yard looks brighter. The house painting can wait. The garden, too. Time to go to school.

We've taken the city bus, the university run. It's the middle of the week and summer in Seattle. Not many class offerings this summer, so there shouldn't be many riders boarding the bus this morning. Halfway to campus only ten other riders have boarded the bus. Most of the riders tote an empty seat next to them, except for Juan, who has comfortably taken the seat next to mine. Across the aisle, Danny's taken up a curb side window seat in the back of the bus. His hands are folded unnaturally in his lap. He's wearing a white short sleeved shirt, his wrist bracelets all shiny and clean, clean feet, clean sandals, clean black jeans, a striped cotton belt, his white shirt buttoned all the way up to his black string necklace, hair combed. He's holding the tense posture of a first-day freshman commuting alone, and the snap of his blue-ribbon smile is tagging us from telephone pole to telephone pole.

Danny's having the time of his life riding the bus. His terrier eyes are galloping at all the city sights — the pawn shops, the sweeping female arms of passing roller-bladders, the leaving-nothing-to-suggestion posters that smear the window of an adult video store on the corner of Fifth and Clay Street, the chicken and rice vendors and the cheesy hotdog carts. The sidewalk-to-balcony television screens propping a storefront's window-wall of wine-stomping segments of *I love Lucy*. A quick stream of canvas strollers and hooded infants dragging stuffed giraffe and lion. Young sweat-suited athletes eager to cross a meter-less car-lined side street, their twitching tennis rackets swiping at car fumes and tagging the branches of maples once they've crossed over to the shady side of the street. The braids of a woman's auburn hair romp playfully around a lamppost. The young woman's eyes glistening and telling, and holding a forged gaze to her lover's clasping hand.

The bus slows often. But more times than not it throttles and slurps up another hill or turns down another narrowing ivy-banked corner, rather than, taking the time to stop at each empty glass hut. Danny says it faster, says it better — "pure luxury riding this bus, Mr. J."

A landscape of shaded fountains and sweeping lawns runs wide as a river between the city street and the school's historic buildings. The morning sun is warm and streaking with color against the peeling bark of my favorite sycamore tree, where we've stopped so I can think things thru one more time.

A salutary-branched Monkey Puzzle tree faces the sycamore tree. In the distance, the third-story windows of my office stare back boxy and dull from the blockish sandstone building which houses the math department. So much policy and predictability behind those office windows. So many dead lines hovering on black and white chalkboards.

"Feel like seeing the cafeteria first? Food's pretty good."

"Sure," Juan answers.

Brick upon brick, walls of it, each one chasing a climbing line that is dripping with forever-white windows. Pitted waves in much of the window glass that marbles green the sunlight coming thru the trees to brush the wooden tables in the cafeteria. The paint on the windowsills and sash of the cafeteria hall thick as Greek yogurt, chipped and scraped, thawed and repainted for a hundred years.

All that we gather and collect comes and goes on the high notes of a piercing change, painted and repainted by the vessel of our disfigurement. Sounds like something Metheny and the boys might compose under a musician's moon.

Alongside today's lunch menu, which is posted in chalk on a wooden easel beside the chocolate milk dispensers both boys are eyeing, there's a poster announcing an afternoon auction at *Overton Field*. It reads:

Three o'clock at Overton Field: "Seniors for Seniors."

A silent auction will be held at Overton Field. All proceeds to benefit Erickson's Rest Home. Athletic gear, art work, food and clothing coupons, big bell and lots of whistles.

All four stories of the new science building carry alternating crosses of chocolate brick and aluminum windows. A muted hissing from the cylinder on one of several glass entrance doors introduces a curved, three-story wall of glass serving as both curtain and stage for the extraordinarily large works of art performing in acrylic, glass, and steel.

The boys are left in the hands of Peter, one of the university's science students. He's a bright student, though a bit of a ham around people.

"Peter Moore. And you are?"

"Juan Rodriquez."

"Danny —"

"Interesting sir name. Not easily forgotten. Well gentlemen, shall we hike the halls of learning and visit the chambermaid's quarters?"

Walking alone on the campus lets me feel how many legless years have gone by. Years graphed and mapped out like the traceable light of an extinguished star — untouchable. Walking measures everything — time taken, loves lost.

Time to make a choice. Time to choose an ending.

Riding the crowded city bus back to the house, the boys are worn out quiet.

"Either of you hungry?" I ask.

"I could eat." Danny answers.

"Pull that cord for the next stop, would you Juan."

Off the bus, we walk for several drab blocks. The sidewalks wide and sterile and treeless. The streetlights measuring the stale lumbering movements of swing-shift workers on break. Another couple of blocks and we leave the concrete parkway behind us to climb three flights of plank stairs up a terraced block of bonsai gardens. None of us have spoken much. It's made for a nice walk.

A is for Amelia's," I say to the boys once we've step from the last stair tread and into a neighborhood of street trees, boulevard beds of roses, and long runs of clipped green-leafed boxwood. "Eh, *A* is for *Atalian*," I joke. "And *Amelia's* serves it up like you can't believe."

"I'm with you the whole way, Mr. Jacobs."

For the next three days we take the bus to campus. We eat lunch in the campus cafeteria, sometimes sitting with the students, sometimes at a table with other teacher's. An afternoon spent in the library's magazine room, another watching a National Geographic film in the science building, another in the theatre arts building watching a stirring rehearsal of *Long Day's Journey into Night*.

On the bus ride back to the house each evening, we detour. Take our dinner beneath a few painted stars and two copper moons on the *Amelia's* high blue ceilings, couples quietly choosing their words in the yellowing corners of the dark dining room, the boys behaving like gentlemen. From the restaurant, we walk to house each night of those three school days. Danny says the whole week's been like a dream — *"like every day I'm having the same great dream."*

Our house, how dark it looks in the daylight.

Days and days to paint a house. A house of colors once. Colorless now.

From the top of the stairs Juan shouted down to me. "Need to brush my teeth and comb my hair, that's all."

It's another five minutes before Juan comes down the stairs with Danny by his side. He's changed from his work clothes into a new pair of black slacks and put on a mango colored sweatshirt. Danny's wearing his new red sneakers, white socks with a collaring of two black stripes at the top of each sock, long black swim trunks and a long black T-shirt.

Stepping outside onto the brick entry, Danny asks how he looks. "The shirt will shrink," he says. "And anyways, I like 'em big and baggy."

"Swell Dan, you look swell."

"Yeah Danny, *swell* as in *swollen*." Juan joked.

"What's wrong with black? I love black." Danny begins tucking his long T-shirt inside his trunks, making his new swim suit inflate and look as if it came equipped with its own inner tube. "Hells bells fish-eyes, where you been? Ain't you ever noticed Mr. J wears all black all the time?"

"Some guys can pull it off, some can't." Juan answered, smiling at me.

Mariner's eleven, Texas Rangers seven.

A desperate thing a finish line. Two weeks dug in and dug out of Seattle, and half a minute, half a key turn to close the door on this ending. At last, one of you crossing the slick fluttering tape of a dark, rainy, and desolate marathon run from home.

The sight of the arriving ferry stirred the mulling crowd. Behind the narrowing crown of foot-passengers, campers and cars and the dullness of the dock's sprawling wire fencing began to vibrate. The streets trickling with rain. The water-view condominiums, with their spilling rooftop gardens, sniffing out the last of the grey mist. The city's stilted freeways throwing down a cantering roar on the roof of our idling cab. The avenues of hi-rise hotels, head shops, favored restaurants, and now, the finger-printed rear window of our departing cab will be the last of the city's props to dim the picture of our "home for sale."

Before we'd locked the doors to the house, I'd asked the boys if they wanted to spend our last hour in Seattle at the market. I'd winced and closed the gate under the freshly painted and pruned arch, watched the ocherous morning light lift our chimney from the last of the passing storm clouds. And now, now we were at the ocean's edge, our mired obligations over with in the swash of a loaded paint brush and a few more of my skinless signatures.

On safe seas, on a quiet boat pushing the bushings of wind and water, so much of what is unpleasant to think about can be left onshore for a time. On water, to cling to any construction suggestive of a beginning, middle, and end to all things living seems a useless sentiment? On water, even the darkest night becomes the moon's mascara. And to sell one's home — wasn't that the same as giving up some part of one's personal history? Never to see my wife's slender leg rising from the slip of her teasing bath water. Never to see Seattle in the same light again. The city's vacillating face of noises no more the path home than the ephemeral Sound could take me back to the kiss of Jessie's breath.

In the tow of Juan's eyes, which had been patiently watching me remember what I would not speak aloud, I knew I had chosen to go back to the islands. Juan had been right to say so all along, to have implied, with brutal accuracy, what his youth could not or would not articulate — that, after all is said and done, we own what we break, own it because the desire which leads to the hand's reach, its validating touch, is our inescapable nature.

"Mark!" My name slingshots from the market crowd.

"Mark Jacobs, it is you!"

There was no mistaking the commanding English accent making its way thru the crowd. The man who had captured Trump and his pagan men in his photographs stepped from the mulling crowd to greet me.

"Mr. Flagg. How are you?"

"Yes, yes, it's me. What in the world of man and beast are you doing on the mainland?"

"Shopping."

"I doubt that is *all* you're doing. Look at you — you've shed a few pounds. I can see it in your face. That's something I ought to think about doing. Won't happen in this arena though, will it?"

He's wearing one necklace more than when we last met. It's a chain of blue beads and orange cork that looks like a choker under his sun-sage double chin, a loop in the chain hung up on his grisly whiskers. I can hardly see his eyes thru his black machete shades.

"Not likely." I abruptly turned away to look for the boys. I wanted them around me. They're my way out if Flagg asks too many questions. "Looking for seal pups at the market, are you?"

"Why be harsh with me, Mr. Jacobs. I was only doing my job. Come, let's have a crepe. They're wonderful today, the best."

"I'm here with company."

"No you're not. Come now, let's find a bench and be friends again."

"Another time."

"Don't be that way. Come. I'll answer your questions. I imagine you've got a few."

"You're mistaken."

Trays of queer looking fish are racked under bins of shaved ice close to where I'm standing, the missing eyes in

their heads giving their faces the look of an apple twice bitten. Floppy sun hats dipping to go around the leashed faces
of four pugs. The market streaming with the chatter of all
the pretty shoppers and two mouthy pricks clothed in pin-
stripes and wooden clogs pushing to get by us.

"Your partner's a tough nut to crack. I'm still not convinced the photographs I took for him were what he was
really after. But that's another matter, and better left to
someone who knows him. As for your nature, my guess is
you've questioned pretty much everything your entire life."

The camera case strapped over Anthony's shoulders
dangles forward like a goose heading south when he leans
into my space to ask what kind of crepe I'll have. I've spotted the boys. They seem well enough occupied. Juan's examining a telescope near a warehouse-sized window that
clouds the view of Bainbridge Island. Danny's listening to
the astronomer talk about the making of the lens he's holding up to the sunlight.

While Anthony places our order at the crepe stand,
I scrape out a seat for myself at a plastic table. In half a
minute he will bring our coffees to the table and begin the
interview, under the pretense that it is he who is allowing
himself to be interviewed.

"I gather that in the weeks gone by you've wondered
what I know. Am I right, my friend?"

I sip my coffee and study Flagg's face of jewelry, but I
ask nothing.

"My crew figures there are about twenty-seven of them
that visit your island with some regularity. Least wise, until
the fire. Call their new recruits *hobos*. Every species on this
planet produces a few mutations, that, you and I already
know. But these guys, these punks are about as anti-Amer-
ican as any imbecile anarchist can grow up to be. Here, see
for yourself."

Anthony's pickled fingers handed me a rumpled roll of blue-lined notes.

"Bunch of whacked wankers. Hate the Jews, the gays, the black man, anyone and anything smarter and kinder than themselves."

"What do you know of this founder's day crap coming up?" I asked.

"It's all in there, in my notes."

"I haven't the time. How 'bout you tell me."

"Alright, in a nut shell here it is my friend. Once a year they celebrate their founder's birthday. Some idiot that was evidently pooped out of a cow barn under an October sky. Thinks he's God's little man. A real zealot who can quote scripture better than the devil himself. The rest of it, I'm sorry to say, you know more of than I."

Hearing his name called, Anthony excused himself to go pick up his crepe order.

"How is it you came to work for Jimmy?" I asked when he returned to the table.

"You're mistaken."

"I don't think so, friend."

"You say *friend*, but you mean something quite different. Oh, oh, my mistake. I misunderstood you. You meant the *stills* I took for your partner's legal case. So he showed you the pictures after all, did he? I wasn't sure he would go down that road with you quite so soon." Anthony took a large bite of apple compote and crepe, which quickly had the effect of tossing aside the ceremonious beginnings of his sad smile. "It was a bit of a beating for both of you, I suppose, having to look at so many of their despicable faces. See what I mean, though, about *thinking* being a polymer?"

"You've enough film in that flight jacket of yours for a documentary, don't you think."

"No one's interested. No offence, Mark, but it's the truth."

"Why not make them interested?"

Anthony sighed. His body shifted and angled in his flimsy chair for the right repose, for the right response.

"Friend, I am sorry. But what you're suggesting, that is a feat of talent I'm no longer capable of. I came here for the story, just the one story. But, as is so often the case, another story crept in. It was no skin off my back to throw your friend a few hours of my time. No, no, I'm not your man. Documenting times and places, the people I found there, that's the work I do. No conflict of interest to worry about, you see. Maybe someday, another will pick up where I left off. Perhaps, one day, many more will come and go from the places I've named and go on to tell the same story, tell it better. No, my friend, my work here is done. Incomplete as it may always be."

"No one last safari for you?"

"I've done what I could. I was fair and exacting about it. Now it's up to the community."

"Right — our reliable community."

"People rarely know their neighbors. Takes a crisis sometimes to open their stone doors. Do you know that almost everyone I interviewed told me that your tavern was everything your partner ever loved? I don't believe it. I spoke with your friend many different times, on many different subjects, and what I witnessed was a father who was looking for a way out from under the crush of grief. But hey, you know me, always looking for opposites. And what's a few hours spent in another man's life to say you know him, anyway? But I've told you all this before."

Anthony licked his fingers, wiped his hands on his flack jacket, and dusted the powdered sugar from his bristled chin with the edge of his folded paper plate.

"Insurance will replace what you've lost, I suppose?"

"We talking people's lives, or stone and wood?"

"See what I mean — *thinking*, it's definitely a polymer."
Anthony extended his hand. "Well sir, I should be going.
All the best to you. Keep an eye out for your partner, and
another one on those boys you've befriended."

Anthony made his way towards one of the market's garage door exits, where he removed his sunglasses and stared
back at me with the eyes of an old bird dog. Before he drew
the shades down over his untrimmed eyebrows, his orangey
eyes seemed to take a couple of smiling postcards of me
holding my farewell cup and saucer up to him, as if acknowledging that this was probably the last time we'd see
one another.

"Flagg!" I shouted.

"Sir?"

"Those men. They were not innocent seal pups."

"No sir, with that I've no quarrel."

Dockside, blocks away from the happy bustling of ferry
traffic, we loaded our groceries and four blocks of snow-
blue ice onto the boat. The last item to be loaded, which the
three of us somehow managed to hoist into the boat, was a
soundless piece of bronze caged in a large wooden crate —
Danny's impulsive purchase from the school auction.

Juan primed the fuel lines and within minutes we
were motoring away from Seattle's terraced eyesight, her
asthmatic harbor, her ear-minded euphoria and her pony-
tailed vendors. A great stumbling of red brick, sea-gray
cobblestone, and patched asphalt streets shunting the ivy
nested foundations of houses pinched on the harbor hills.
Pill-shaped rooftops mere inches away from the blur of waterfront linen and the candlestick masts of moored boats.
Her disfiguring bars stippling the train tracks that had once
lit the way back, the way home for Jimmy. And the ramping
of Seattle's freeways cooing like roosting chickens over it

all. Dianna would miss this city. Miss its pedaling colors so much more than I.

Tucked away with everything else on our humming boat, our thoughts were hidden from one another as we left the harbor. Seattle's hovering skyline waning into a noise-less mirage.

We motored northwest along the shipping lanes of Admiralty Inlet, thru wind cut waters doused with small boats like our own, Danny waving on three cruise ships that moved like great icebergs across the white cliffs of Whidbey Island.

"Slow her down some, will you Juan."

"Sure."

"Can you take us closer to that bluff? 'Round that way, towards those sheds about to drop into the water."

Danny cocked his head at my interest in the weathered out-buildings. He swallowed the last gulp of his bottom-of-the-cup coffee grit, winced at the taste of it, and offered a rather accurate description of the out buildings on the little house on the bluff.

"There she shits. Somebody's dream home."

The old sheds were part of a potter's compound that had been built back a ways from the grassy edge of the bluff, up wind from a corral, a barn, and a pocket of pasture surrounded by a few strands of barbed wire that kept the feeding goats from taking a deadly fall into the sea. The pale red barn is a one-story, paper-roofed, windowless endeavor, its low-pitched roof extending beyond its foundation to cover a corral of stacked pottery to set a profile of a carpenter's crippled square as our boat makes another pass closer to shore. A scrappy line of apple trees — strung trunk to trunk with wire, fencing boards, and foam boat bumpers — marks the property line of a neighbor's star-shape configuration of galvanized steel and tempered glass stuck on a pillar of cement. The compound's cottage, white and windowed, faces full sun most of the day.

"Gee-ezze, the place looks crapped on next to Daddy Big-Bucks. Don't it?" From the bow of the boat, Danny once more pointed out the obvious, the tip of his fishing pole slashing the wind in a futile attempt to scare away a couple of sniping gulls. "Either of you men gonna try and deny it? No way, I don't think so."

The compound on the bluff drifts by us like a curling string of dead fish baking in the sun, like a scene pulled from a subtitled film in which the approaching boat makes its protracted swing around the swallow-plugged bluff. Makes me remember so many of the poets and potters and the weavers I've met on Whidbey Island over the years. Makes me acknowledge how much respect I have for their firefly occupations that toast life in the islands. Makes me think of the smell of good Scotch.

"Maybe you and Jimmy ought to make the saps on the hill an offer, Mr. J. Kick out Ma and Pa and put some life back into the old place."

"Danny! Quit your yakking and hang on." Juan quickly steered the boat away from a pimple of a sandbar near the beach.

"Hey! Why's it me always got to drop what he's doing?"

"Because your tongue's got a longer reach than the boat's depth finder, that's why. Yackety-yack-yack, the whole way coming and going. Give it a break."

"Why we stopping here, Mr. J?"

"A potter I used to know lives here. Used to make these beautiful cattails out of clay."

"What do you do with 'em?"

"I thought maybe I'd tie a few to the gate Sally made for my wife. Look even better with a bit of color on it, wouldn't it?"

"If you say so."

One thing I know is that time heals nothing. It passes and fades and curls back on itself, forever splitting and separating our grief into smaller and smaller pieces but never erasing it. My cabin, my cave, my marathon.

"The hell with it. Forget it. She can sell it to Seattle along with all the other shit." I spit the words out angrily and pushed off hard from the boat's railing. "I'll be in my cabin if you need me."

Juan's voice is my father's voice when he approaches my bedside.

"You've been out a spell, Mr. Jacobs." One of the boys is speaking to me.

"Um-mah — I don't know." All I want is to be out of hearing range of all voices but my own.

"You fell. But you're back in your own bed now. Are you thirsty?"

Thirsty — what a beautiful word when you know you can remove it from your thoughts with the reach of your hand.

"Please. Some water."

"Dan, get the water jug."

"We in or out of Seattle?"

"You can see the lights of Seattle, but we're a good ways west. We expected it would be a zoo of a marina here. As nice as this place is, I mean. But it isn't. Maybe not half full-up."

"We by ourselves?"

"No, sir."

"Anchored out somewhere?"

"No. Like I been telling you, we're in a marina now."

"Know what," Danny's voice fumbles in, "this one fellow helped guide us in when I let off a yell for where we was supposed to go. It could have been a different kind of hairy coming in here in total dark, though. But we came in way before that."

"It's real nice here." Juan's voice is back. "Private like. Same fellow Danny's talking about, he says we don't have to pay until morning."

"You want another blanket, Mr. J?" Danny feels so god-damn close to my face he's an annoyance. "Here, you ought to take another blanket."

"Please." After wrapping myself in the blanket, I ask if he might look around for another one.

"The man that helped us dock says it's gonna be cold for another day."

"Cold as a witch's tit, he said it like that. Right Juan?"

I rolled on my back, so as to try and put their bodies with their voices. "Turn the stove on. I'm so cold."

"Can't no more. Before you passed out you kind of went crazy on a couple of the burners. After you busted it up good you came back in here to sleep. You were breathing alright at first, but then you started having some real bad coughing spells."

"We didn't want take no chances getting too far from help. You getting sicker, I mean."

"You did good. You boys did good."

My throat was on fire. Danny kept inching closer to me than I was comfortable with, the eyes in his bony body finding new ways to fill up the narrowing gap between my bed and the paneled ceiling of my sleeping berth. Finally, I understood, he was trying to hold a jug of water up to my eyes. I reached out for the handle and it became one of those wishful prayers people sometimes dream have been answered.

"Yeah, you just take it Mr. J. Don't wait for us to find

you a glass. You just drink it right out the top like Juan and I do."

Some of the water missed my mouth and washed my chin and chest with a burning cold that woke me to the feeling of something harnessing me, something strapped to my skin but also tied up in the bedding — a lifejacket — I was wearing a lifejacket.

"You want to try and eat something?" Juan asked. "Dan cooked up a mess of food while you were out. It's pretty good. I had to take a twenty out of your wallet to buy bread and stuff. Just so you know."

"We got plenty," I said. "Plenty food. Plenty money."

"Honestly, we don't. You tossed most of the food over-board. For a while there, Dan and I thought maybe we were next. We weren't about to try and stop you."

Juan motioned for Danny to go after something. The boy returned with a paper plate of food which he set on the bed.

"What is it?"

"That's priceless," Danny belted, and punched his thigh with his fist. "You must be practically your old self. Ain't he, Juan? Ain't he on his way though?"

"Those are salt pills and magnesium pills on top of the peas," Juan explained. "They were in one of the boxes of stuff Red loaded. My old man used to swear by them for fixing a hangover."

"Alright. Thanks. Thank you both."

With most of the weight of my upper body resting on one elbow, I mouthed a spoonful of pills and some buttery peas. Washed the mixture down with more ice water after I'd sucked on the pills for too long. I ate all of the rice and black beans and asked for more. I guzzled more water and gave my paper plate back to Juan. I remember closing my eyes on Juan's tight-lip smile, as he was leaving and closing the door to my berth.

After a prayerful minute had passed, I spoke from the darkness of my bed.

"You there, Juan?"

"Right here, Mr. Jacobs."

"Metheny and the boys, that man can pull running water from a guitar can't he?"

"Yes sir, I think so too."

"Seeing Metheny's soul play Seattle, that was something."

"We'd go back to Seattle with you anytime, Mr. Jacobs. All you ever gotta do is ask."

And knowing where I was now, what I'd come back from, the color of Seattle came back to me. She forgave me my relapsing fall, brought me music from her waterfront markets, gave me back the jeweled faces of all her pretty picnic people — all the pretty girls kissin' their morning coffee black and gold and breathing life into the maps of their dreams — all this while I listened to the cut of the boy's voices fade to a drizzle and then disappear into the cold mist outside my cabin door.

Deeper into the night, I was awakened by the boys talking and by what sounded like glasses clinking inside a metal trough of rising water —

What are you doing, pervert?

What's it look like I'm doing? I'm putting a message in a bottle.

Jesus, he's gonna kill you. And not with no shovel neither. More like with his bare hands.

No, he's never gonna know. Remember, he won't touch the hooch no more. That's what he said.

Yeah, but why test the waters? God, you're gutsy though. He's gonna know your shit from gin, ain't he though?

Who's he going to tell without giving himself up? 'Morning boys, I'm drinking again. By the way, have I told you boys how much I love your eighty-proof piss water.'

God, you're gutsy.

My guess is he's done with it for a while. Here. Take it and cap it, will you.

Where's the cap?

Right here between my big blue balls.

Shut-up.

Here. Put it on plenty tight.

Want a swig before I do, Blue Balls?

Bugger off. Cap it. Don't drop it, Dan. Hurry up.

God, that's gutsy.

Dan?

Wha-aat?

He's done us right. Well, hasn't he?

Better than alright.

Okay then, no joking around on this one. Not a word. Agreed?

I said I'm onboard.

Maybe this buys us some more time with him. We deserve that much. Well, don't we?

Alright already, I said. Geese.

Wrap that towel all the way around the bottle. Wrap it good. Use the white one. That's it. Now put the bottle on its side so that just the V across the label faces straight up.

Like that?

Well done, brother. Now close the cupboard door on that latrine. Quiet like.

Nightfall crept up on us the following day. Long strings of pearly headlights pushing north from Seattle on a Sunday night, their circles of crystallized light shadow-boxing behind the highway's distant guardrails. And the breeze of some ghostly passing whispering beneath a sudden gust of wind.

By now, I thought, Jimmy might be locked up or shut down or buried up to his pounding stomach in nettles and thistle on the formless land which lay like a sleeping dragon across the channel. The trail ahead of him mocking and endless. I know my friend is out there somewhere, kneeling to mend his fishnet or skimming the iron rails from Seattle to his shack in the woods. He's tracking a familiar beast for sure, trying to coax it back from those bruising tracks he left in the hills of Reno. In the absence of things loved and gone missing, he will look for something to lift his heart out from under the misery, the burning. He will carry his sadness into the creation of some new construction, that I know, one that is so moist of birth that no history yet lives to defile its beginning.

"Why are you coming back to the islands?" Juan asked from the dock, his arms folded over his chest. Danny's by his side, watchfully tired, his body still as the sea.

From my seat in the cockpit, I stuck my spoon into the lumpish heap of beans on my supper plate. Jackie's voice is in my head —the one she leaned on to tell the boys how *it's a pestilent pus that ripens the fruit of our secrets* — and if it were any louder, I'd have heard its chime scrape out another lesson on the chalkboard she's pegged to one of her apple trees a world away.

"Some debts you can never repay, Juan. About all you can do is nick away at the time attached to them."

Danny smiled at me, sheepishly. Juan took a good long drink from his water bottle. He looked out at the rows of bronzy masts in the marina and said nothing for a time. A slip of a moon about to be cushioned by the clouds in the evening sky.

"I don't know how you can think about it that way. Dan and I sure don't see you like that. All we ever seen you do is the right thing."

CHAPTER TEN

THE TRAIN TRACKS PARTED a scorched mountainside of blackened pine standing thick and branchless. Where the fire had burned the hottest, torrents of bright green growth had re-established and were now running rampant among the charred trunks of pine and a scrambling of jack-knifed madrona. In this ancient afterlife of a lightning strike or a matchstick long since extinguished, some of the mountain's brown stone had loosened and fallen to crest at the base of a landslide high up from the tracks. The landslide marked the farthest reach of the fire's burn and seemed, in the most natural of ways, the perfect gravestone to mark the hillside's golden death. It is as solemn a feeling to walk these rails thru the fire's wake as any failure revisited, and all but sheds a week wasted in recovery, all but moves the sun's midday ratcheting closer to the remains of an irrepressible, star-punched night.

Stop and rest out of sight of the track's ominous tunneling. Bottled water and tasteless tuna served up neat and extra dry near a decaying stump protracted by the bushy edges of a juvenile forest — "planted 1960." The stump alive with ants that march thru their own tunnels of moist red decay, wet webs, and ferns with antlers that could fit in the palm of a child's hand. The stump, which today I've chosen to rest near, is as large as Joey's flattened truck bed and cut about as high off the ground as his once crushed cab, a vexing thought.

Come nightfall my backpack empties its shell of a camp; sleeping mat and sleeping bag, and some of the wonder of how Jimmy could have fallen, so cleanly, from his year of standup grace. Roll out my thin wafer of blue sponge onto a new green tarp that crinkles like a breaking potato chip in these peaceful woods. Try to sleep, after leaving more thoughts of my friend's ordeal in the dark spaces of jeering salal bushes. Lay alone with a withered tree stump hidden by huckleberry bushes and the smell of wild mint or something similar to its nose-piercing pleasure which settles in with the clouds, and the last of the stars, and the peeping sounds of crickets or something closely akin to them.

The treetops in the canyon beyond the dump's trestle bridge tossed in the morning wind and threw down a lacing of sunlight on the iron rails. Last night's morose downpour had let up come dawn, and now, all that stood in the way of a sunlit day, and the final leg of our journey back to *Red's*, was the appearance of my mutinous crew in the channel a thousand yards down the mountainside. That, and a bit of a coyote hike so that I might join them when they showed themselves.

From the trestle, one could see most all of the gooseneck configuration of the channel — a brooding body of deep canyon water which separated the tribal island from its uninhabited sister island — and look south to a string of islands that skipped and rolled its forests like flattened hedges over the dark blue waters. The sky overhead pale with naval aircraft out of Whidbey and the faint cast of a moon regenerating.

Some figurant movement along the fringe of a boat's stern, followed by three faint blasts of an air horn, and another, longer blast — when I signaled back by waving my white t-shirt — soon put me back on my feet and swung my pack over my shoulder. Watching how my boat's piddling wake was so quickly swallowed up by the larger body of the channel's sparkle, I shook off how easily June had tramped deep into the month of July since the boys and I had left the islands for Seattle. Made me wonder what else had taken a deeper hold on these islands in our absence, what rumors may have ruled the taverns and the Sunday services and picnics, what charges lay in wait for us?

Below me, a spot of a world away from the abandoned train tracks which I stood on, the filth that had piled up around Jimmy's tilted shack hardly warranted a second look.

By nightfall a string of white light bulbs had talked us quietly into our slip at Red's marina. It was late, and except for the few boat hulls which traced the blue and black gauze of cabin lights on their waterlines, most of the boats moored in the marina were colored blind against the bannering light of Red's neon storefront. On the surrounding dock, a slouch of a man forked a steak from a garbage can for the dog by his side, both animals giving us three shags the stink eye on our way to the showers.

Red's store is as busy as a Saturday barber. Boaters in and out of his half-opened door every five minutes, the door's clanking bell announcing every sale. Inside the store everything looks different, cornered. The aisles are full up with people pulling loaves of bread and jars of peanut butter from the shelves. People tapping fingers on the canned goods they're coddling in their chest and arms, while reaching for bags of candy and chips and tuna and big jars of pickles. Up front, at the cash register, Jackie's hands are busy putting pop bottles, bagged snacks, and a few cased fishhooks into a paper sack. In her sleeveless white blouse her tanned arms and neck seem to shine with more muscle than I remember. Her reading glasses — black and gold frames with a loop of green twine riding the back of her neck — are crouched halfway down her peeling nose. When she sees me her lips part, and her eyebrows lift, and a welcoming word that's sauced with one of her lacy smiles reaches me from the hubbub at the cash register. I smile and nod and gesture to her that I'm going to the back of the store to talk to Red.

"Yo mister, you gonna milk this cooler all day? I got fish to catch." Red is restocking the cooler shelves with beer and soda pop, wheezing just a little each time he lifts another rattling case from his orange hand truck. I pick up a case of Beck's beer for his arms to reach for.

"Mark! You're back." Red pulled bottles from the case I was holding — two at a time, held between the swollen fingers on each of his hands. "Fish to catch? You? Fish to fry, maybe."

"Store's so busy. How come?"

"You been in Seattle so long you forgotten?" Red wheezed and reached for two more handfuls of bottles. "Fish tournament. But, I'll tell you something, the crowd this year seems to think it's more about *swishing* than fishing."

Red's wheezing crackled and cleared when he straightened and stretched. I opened another case of bottles for him.

"You better or worse off for the trip to Seattle?"

"Jury's still out." I tightened my stomach and lifted a new case. "You seen hide or hair of him?"

"No, but others have. Making quite a squatter's home for himself out there in that dump, I hear. Been putting off going out there to see him until you got back. God knows I've seen this life smack you boys around a time or two, but never like this." A sad glare crept over Red's puffy eyes. "You never once run into him coming or going, I suppose?"

"No. If he really did walk to Seattle and back, he must have done it in the middle of the night."

"How 'bout the boys? Behave themselves, did they?"

"No problems. A couple of the king's men, those two. Anna around? I'd like to thank her for all the food."

"Seattle. I sent her back to see the kids. Nothing more here she can do for either of you boys. He's got to find his own way home. Same as you've had to."

Red closed the cooler door, and put a cold and comforting hand to the side of my neck before pushing off.

"Come on, kid, you've got mail." His wheezing returning to churn up a little coughing spell, as we made our way to the front of the store. "By the way, some of us are curious what kind of bait you used to land that big church bell you got in your boat."

"That'd be Danny's fish tale to tell."

"Oh, is it now. Well, I guess I'm in for a gill-full today then aren't I?"

I paused by one of the store windows to finger a pocket view thru its shuttered wood blinds. Juan was standing on the dock with his coffee. He looked to be enjoying how Danny had snared a couple of wincing and laughing fishermen with his bell-ringing demonstration.

"That's all of it." Red handed me my mail and walked to the door to see what all the commotion was about.

"A gill-full is the least of your worries, old man. Your ears are gonna be ringing red come sundown."

"Yup. Like watching you and Jimmy grow up all over again, ain't it?"

Both boys stood in line to take the ferry back to their homes. Each of them carried one hundred and sixty-five dollars in his pockets.

"You both earned every penny of it. I'm only sorry it's not more than minimum wage. Tell your moms, tell them I'm grateful for their trust. Tell them I can be reached at Red's if they've any questions about you working for me next week."

Juan extended his hand. "Thanks for taking me, Mr. Jacobs. I'll come back soon as I can."

Danny pinched and patted the lump of cash in his pocket. He seemed to feel the need to flatten his public bulge while he waited his turn to say good-bye.

"Thanks Mr. J. This ain't goodbye or nothing. This is just a deposit until we come back. You won't forget to cover up our bell if it rains, will you?"

"I'll wrap it like a sandwich tonight if it does."

From the deck of the raucous ferry, Juan rapped his heart with his fist and stared back at me. I waved back. Danny slapped his swollen pocket of cash, hollering *"see you on the pass line someday, Mr. J."*

"Not on your life!" I countered.

On the first of many such evenings that would mark the beginnings of a new order, we stood worshiping inside the ribs of our fallen *Campground* — Jackie standing hands to headstone with Salvador's blackened fireplace, Salvador kneeling on his welder's apron to collect a rippled hunk of steel, Brynnie sitting, stoically, by his hip — each of us recalling the viciousness of the brawl and the *Campground's* sweltering end. We called back the many voices of our beloved *Campground,* lowering our eyes and opening our hearts to honor what was left of her neutrality. We were no longer cornered by her fate, not by the savagery of belt buckles or the puckering smirks or the cursing tongues of Trump's white whoring friends which resounded from the untouched cavities in the piles of ash. We recalled the viciousness of that night and the helplessness that punished us in the hours which followed us back to Sally's compound, more clearly and in greater dimension, whenever our boots and shoes stubbed some of the *Campground's* silverware which lay coiled near the melted racks of Hazel's disfigured dishwasher. We called back the *Campground's* cast of porch light never to shine again, where so many moths had circled wildly the night that would forever mark our disfigurement, and spread the memory of its buffering lamp over the purple-streaked firings entombing Salvador's mantle. We called back the very hour of the fire's smothering spillage, but we were not cornered by the memory of that chiseling hour. We were not beaten back by the gaping mouths or the pock-marked faces whose desperate coughing we would always carry in our heads — whose chummy names and droopy eyes and charred tongues wished to bubble from the gruel of a chair leg which lay dead-still on the edge of the *Campground's* hearth — our heads ringing with the queer names of men whose broke-back beliefs we had confronted. The living pleas of these men wicked, and cold, and clustering in that soupy mix of fear and hatred which now ran from the *Campground's* grounded gutters to the cave of Jessie's courtyard. We called back the faces of most everything that was horrific about our last night in *Jimmy's*

Campground, but those faces did not corner us. They did not defile our spirit. Not once.

Night became day and a new evening of obsessive inspection for each of us. Scattered about the trenches of standing water on the *Campground's* floor, the cleats of missing bar stools sometimes rolled about whenever we poked and kicked at the piles of ash. Near a hole in one of the charred floorboards, Sally kicked at a shoebox-size piece of mortared slate that dangled from a galvanized-now-vulcanized nail — the nail bent but still attached to an overturned table's mangled metal top. Under the table's only remaining corner the handle-less head of a shovel had somehow scooped up a strapless belt buckle, making for a grotesque and unmerciful presence which Sally quickly remedied.

We hung two tarps — green and grey and made stiff by Sally's rope and pulleys — over our customary perches. Bales of wet hay surrounding us as we sat in witness of all we had endured, all we had escaped. The sagging bales smelling of the *Campground's* sour runoff, or like the blanket that had once covered one of its owners. From our paper sacks, we brought out our coffee and chocolate, and biscuits for Brynnie and Jenny. We talked quietly into the night, our eyes soothed by watching Sally's long fingers rub the white star on Brynnie's head and from listening to his subdued voice retell the story of their great escape from the circus.

All the next day the rain drizzled late into the evening. The clouds of clay baptizing another of Sally's canvas tarps, which he'd strung from the *Campground's* standing chimney stone, the rain trickling its way down the grimy lines of mortar holding onto the Montana stone, stone that now sweated more mud and soot than natural coloring beneath a lantern's light. In Jessie's courtyard, the rain spattered the strands of pink and pea-green fiberglass insulation that had feathered among the trampled ferns. And on the poles of streetlamps, beyond the courtyard's gate, the rain shredded the paper notices announcing that the summer schedule of evening dances would be suspended indefinitely.

All week, the rain continued to fall from the neighboring rooftops and onto the sidewalks and gargling streets. It pelted the channel with unusually strong winds for summer, often pushing the struggling ferries off their determined course, and raising havoc for their captains during docking and departure maneuvers. But the harbor seals seemed to enjoy every minute of it, lifting their heads and their catch to watch the candle-eyed vessels roll from the sea's crest of black rain.

When the wind and rain at last died down, the faint lights of the treatment center on Depot Island emerged. I'd almost forgotten the facility was there, but seeing the lights shine from the windows was suddenly like hearing a child's lost voice call out from within a great wind. From my buttoned back pocket, I pulled the second of two letters I'd received from Dianna.

Dear Mark,

Jackie has sent word of the awful fire. Our beloved Campground gone. Gone. That the fire consumed our most happiest of times, and that you bore the pain of it alone, brings me even more sadness. I say this, knowing Jackie's words to be true that Jimmy is nowhere to be found, having "disappeared from the island after the terrifying fire had left all of us emotionally exhausted and numb." That the community had to endure the staining of such men on our beautiful island to begin with, and now, suffer all the more because of their vicious criminal behavior brings me the greatest grief that I could not be there for you.

Is it cruel of me to wish to return, so quickly, to the heart of this letter which had pressed me so relentlessly before the news of the Campground's fire? In a single sentence, to pass over the most recent days of your life, imagining but never knowing the brutality of your hardships? I am sorry if the timing of what I'm about to say seems cruel to you, but I think it best that I speak it…

With this prayer, Mark, let my will reach yours from across an ocean we've never known together. From my heart to the heart of all the sadness you have ever bore, my voice as you read be carried with it, and the heart of the only doctrine I know to be true find your forgiveness.

If I feel anger, Mark, I won't feel love. If I feel betrayal, I won't feel love. If I live any longer with this grief, I would lose all love of ever having known my beautiful husband. Such a grief would split the mold of us I've tried to mend. It would return me to that bleakness and suffering you have witnessed in me so many times, and have me erase everything of the life we've shared.

If there is a single thought left in the mold you've made of me which might touch forgiveness, chase its ending in the life of a new dream. In the rebuilding of Jimmy's Campground, forgive us both.

Dianna

So, she knew.

I sat on the Campground's hearth stone a while longer, and wondered if the septic smoke from all that Jimmy and I had tried to squash that night could have entered Dianna's thoughts the moment each of us had painted our choices in blood? Was the gash of the *Campground's* burn in our island skies, that day, more compass than I could have known at the time, a watch-fire lighting my wife's way to a life that my math could not reach? And was it possible that Jimmy and I had, callously, begun to will Dianna's departure the very day Jessie had died so as to one day fuel our own righteous vengeance?

I miss my wife.

In the reach for the metal lip of an overturned shovel, I let go of Dianna's hand and began to work. Nails and staples, tile chips, and the occasional stump of a castor and table leg all helped to clear a shovel-swept path to the ragged corners of the *Campground's* foundation. The shoveling took hold of something once honorable within me, and soon the snouts of fallen roofing timbers pivoted in my arms and had begun to drag a quiet line thru the debris and into the backyard lot. It was difficult to keep at it, the work being so shabbily attacked so late at night, but a noiseless piling of progress did begin to build around me. On occasion, a speechless pedestrian would scuffle by on the street below and take notice of the sounds I was making, the woman's hands snagging at her shawl and shopping bag but otherwise paying no interest to the janitor at work on the hill in the dark — both of us soon faceless to the other's witnessing while night eked out its eternal tolerance.

In the wake of dawn, my push-broom had swept the last of its tired line of ash towards the *Campground's* higher ground. Another stranger's kindness surfaced and shadowed between the amber streetlights outside the courtyard, his whistle halting to ask if I've had my morning coffee. This stranger, this prayerful embodiment of a word, brings me coffee steaming and strong and leaves with a hurried wave that pulls a smile from my sleepless eyes.

Later in the morning, there is the gift of a new shovel and wheelbarrow from the town's only hardware store. And before it can be filled with its first load of rubbish, a bandanna-clad employee from the bakery is handing me two bagged lunches thru a cloud of ash and sheetrock dust.

All morning, my work is flagged with the encouragement of strangers to carry on and not give up. The largest and loudest of encouragements coming from the hydraulic slam of a fifteen-yard dumpster — a gift from the hotel manager up the street — maneuvered in under the *Campground's* yellow taping by a delivery truck and dropped a half-step away from the heap of Hazel's canoe-shaped ovens.

"Anyone with half a hook in 'em might think they were luckier than you," Red pitched from the courtyard. "But they'd be wrong to think so."

"Bottom fishing again are you, old man? Wait there. Easier for me to come down."

"The hell you are, I'm coming up."

"Don't you even think about climbing up that hill."

"Don't you tell me what I *can* and *can't*. I'm coming up the front steps, same as I always have."

While Red was struggling to climb the hillside, Salvador and Brynnie appeared on the street. Sally pointed and the dog eagerly left his side and trotted into the courtyard, jumping the first little berm and fast as a fish saddling up alongside Red's bad knee.

"Help that old lion, will you Brynnie." Sally called after the dog. "Fetch and Pull. Go on, fetch and pull old Red. Good boy."

From the courtyard gate, Sally tweaked out a tender smirk and watched Red struggling to climb the muddy slope.

"Not his tail, Red. He's not an elephant. No, no, don't grab him by the collar. He'll tear your tongue out."

Red froze in mid-step. The hand he'd been readying to reach for Brynnie's collar now suddenly stuck in mid-air as if it was measuring the distance to the ground.

From his perch on a courtyard boulder, Sally let out a strong laugh.

"I'm kidding, Red. Rest your hand along the scruff of his neck. Go on, put your hand there and put some weight on it. He'll steady you and stay dead-center under your weight the whole way up. That's it. You set the pace. Brynn will stop and go accordingly."

Sally's face is polished and gleaming, and has set a smile from ear to ear at the human leash Red has allowed himself to become.

"Ain't he something, Red?"

"Yeah, he's something." Red scoffed in good humor, his body capitulating to find stable footing. "Something I don't want biting me."

At the top of the hill, Red tapped the crown of Brynnie's head.

"Thank you kindly, Brynn."

I crouched to give Brynnie a gentle rubbing. "His eyes look bright as ever, Sal. Doc feel certain he's out of the woods?"

"He does. And he's got his appetite back. Sleeping regular, too. You know, on his back dreaming like he used to. Legs twitching and stretched to the moon."

"That's good, Sal. That's good." I gave Brynn the last quarter of my sandwich and stood to face Red.

"So what brings you up into the hills, Red?

"I got to sit a tad before I talk."

Red stepped onto the foundation and headed for one of the lawn chairs under Sally's tarp. But before he'd taken a seat, a fully-loaded flatbed with an extended blue cab rolled up bumper-to-gate to the open courtyard, braked and rocked with a jolt, and rumbled to a stand-still idle. The truck's engine sounding like a chained beast teething a bright yellow backhoe and bucket loader on its mud-splattered deck.

"Oops, there's Ike and Tom. Guess I better get at it, hadn't I?"

"What's going on, Red."

"How 'bout you come over here and listen to what a wise old man done cooked up in his head while you was away. Maybe that new math of yours can make some sense of it for me."

Sally and Brynn had taken seats on the hearth. I joined them.

"Ike and Tom Kelton played ball with me, years ago." Red began. "Out of the blue they show up for this year's fishing tournament. Can't believe it, but you can see for yourself there they are. Been more than twenty years since I seen either of them. We've been catching up all week. All week we been chewing up old times. Funny, ain't it Brynn? How after a bad thing has come your way life will on occasion throw you a decent bone."

"I see where you're going with this Red, and I appreciate it. But this here's a mess. And it needs to stay a mess awhile."

"Now just hold your horses, Mark. It's just talking I'm staging here, not scaffolding. This here's your business, I know that. Before and after it's your life, I know, I know that. Ike and Tom and me, we just got to talking that's all, about what has happened to the *Campground*. And Ike, well, he took some genuine offense at this town not lending you a hand. Mine, in particular. Says he saw you out here late last night working by yourself."

"What of it?"

"Well, as Ike put it, for some of us in this town to have

not taken the Christian time to help organize a work crew for you was a sin. And he's right about that. And I can tell you there's a bit of shame going around this town because of it. Now, those boys you see standing out there on the street by that flatbed, they're damn good lads. Ike's a licensed electrician and his brother Tom's a licensed plumber, but mostly they're builders. They've a garage they're supposed to start building for a cousin of theirs out of towns away, but they can put it off a while if you want. They'll do part or all of most any kind of cleanup or construction you want 'em to."

Red rubbed his beard. So much talking seemed to have exhausted him. "Did I do wrong?"

"Hell yes, you did wrong. Where are your manners? Go on back down that hill and invite 'em up here."

In the few seconds it took him to stand and wave his friends up the driveway, Red's croupy laughter had turned into one of his usual coughing spells.

The two brothers climbed the slope. Ike took a seat under the tarp with us while his brother took a look around. No more than ten minutes passed, before Tom returned to the foundation to sit with us.

"We could get your place cleaned up pretty quick I think, Mark. If you can stick around and help, I think the three of us can haul most everything out of here by the weekend. Ike can put up a power pole, set you up properly with juice for power tools. If your budget allows, I'd like to suggest you let us grade some of the earth out back and throw some gravel down around the foundation. That'll leave you with a clean slate to work off of, and some decent drainage."

Ike spoke up. "He got water, Tom?"

"That water line to the shower pole is undamaged," Tom spoke directly to his brother, "but every line inside the foundation looks like fried eggs."

"Man ought to have some water when he wants it, shouldn't he?" Ike asked, throwing me a wink.

"Well, until he knows if he wants to rebuild we might just tap that shower line and leave him with a spigot for a hose."

Tom turned to me. "Would that help you out, sir?"

"It would. What's the math look like?"

"Three days or four?" Ike asked of his brother.

"Four —if we gotta go off the island for gravel."

"We do," Ike reminded his brother, "this isn't Seattle."

Ike pulled a business card from his cash-laden wallet and set it on the arm of the chair, the wallet's two folds of floppy leather sandwiching what looked like the innards of an old roast beef sandwich. He rubbed his ear between his thumb and forefinger, stared at the printed card for nearly a minute, exhaled, and finally pulled a pen from his pocket and wrote a number on the back of the card which he handed to me.

"How much more should I figure for gravel and dumping fees?" I asked.

"That number includes all supplies." Ike winked at Red and fanned a slight smile.

"When can you start?"

"Soon as you shake my hand, sir. Tom's too, of course."

While Red walked with the Kelton brothers to the foot-ramp at the back of the foundation, Sally walked to the fireplace and unrolled a camper's bed mat.

"Taking a nap, Sally?" I joked.

"Brynnie's bed for the afternoon, while I help you."

Minutes later, Ike and Tom's truck and trailer skidded up the side alley and rocked to a stop.

By the time Sally and I had dragged our first armfuls of wood to the dumpster, Ike was gloved and lumping heavy chain from the flatbed, and Tom was leveling a thumbs-up sign at his brother from the seat of a throttling backhoe.

"Have Jackie and Hazel been by to talk to you about their grand summer scheme?" Sally asked, gunning his wheelbarrow full of ash and stubble up a wooden ramp and onto the front slope. "Hey, all this ash and wood charcoal you can till into the hillside. Do your garden some good, I think."

"I've been meaning to go see Hazel."

Sally walked his wheelbarrow backwards. He gave the handles a quick jerk and made the wheelbarrow's tire hop the foundation.

"Here's your chance."

From across the street, Hazel thundered to life on her march towards the courtyard. She held a large tray of what looked to be picnic supplies in her arms, her legs carrying her with stamping precision up the sidewalk and thru the garden gate, her bowling-ball shoulders stifled by a scarf the size of a tablecloth, and her waiter's arms adjusting the tray's weight each time her talking head slung some hashing commentary at Jackie's open notebook. Whatever excitement was stirring Hazel's dictation seemed also to be instigating great urgency in Jackie's pen to get it all down on paper.

"If I didn't know you better, Sally, I'd figure you and Red been holding hands today."

"Want the watered down version, or the stampede version coming up the hill?"

"They gonna kiss me or kill me?"

"Let's just say that while you were in Seattle, one of those ladies found the streets of Paris."

Ike and Tom were as fascinated with Jackie and Hazel's request as the rest of us. Tom walked back to his machinery, muzzled the roar of the backhoe, and grabbed a bundle of two-by-four lumber while Ike ran a hundred foot extension cord from his truck's cabled generator to the arms of the courtyard's bench. After the two brothers had planked the arms of Jessie's bench with two-by-fours, Jackie and Hazel went to work setting up their mobile kitchen and, in a matter of a single ferry docking, the girls had succeeded in bringing a taste of Paris to the islands.

Over the course of the next hour, everyone but our exuberant caterers feasted on hot vegetarian and fruit crêpes. Ike and Tom playfully trying to overpay for everyone's meal after we'd stuffed ourselves and after Jackie had asked what we thought people would pay for such a fresh delicacy. Red, poised in serious consideration, first praised the flavor of the asparagus and cheese crêpe, then, with a new ripeness to his pleasant smile, dryly answered: "twice the price of a new boat." Sally agreed with Red, and experiencing a rush of ideas on how their makeshift kitchen could be made more efficient and a bit more stylish than Ike and Tom's two-by-fours, pulled a tape and sketch pad from his pocket and took some measurements. When Brynnie barked for the last folded cone of my strawberry crêpe, a deal was cinched and I'd gladly agreed to Jackie and Hazel's business proposition of setting up a crepe stand in Jessie's courtyard.

The casino lights flashed red and white and blue, and seemed to smirk at the wiggling flesh of newcomers coming ashore. From the upper deck, I watched the ferry's unloading ramp slump beneath the trampling sounds of tourists hurriedly admiring the pots of so many red, white, and peppermint-blue petunias scattered about the boardwalk and staked out like wreaths beneath the community bulletin board. The bulletin board displaying the island's latest headlines in bold newsprint, one of which was a colorfully framed, panoramic rendering of the casino's proposed hotel which saluted each passing gambler's rising pitch of faith.

On land, I walked with the hoofing crowd which was making its way along the boardwalk's planking and its borders of scruffy landscaping, stuck for a time among the ranks of something that felt like a sticky pilgrimage. Witness to a flower-tied world of rainbows where money games teetered on the legitimacy of sport, where players quickly learned to find nervous comfort in the root canal withdrawals of a second, and sometimes, a third *cash advance* — where the belief that *the only way out is back in* unquestionably reigns. But what was troubling me most, what had brought me back to Timberlee Harbor, was the phone call Red had received earlier — the one in which Danny's mom had expressed concern that Jimmy had been playing the tables for hours, and had been flushing *thousands* down a bottomless hole of green felt.

"Mr. J! Wait up."

Standing outside the casino's arcade doors, Danny pulled his hands from his pockets and waved at me, the boy eager to jump a set of steps and make his way towards me, his thinness side-winding thru the crowd's wide caboose of wasp-nest hairdos and closing the distance between us.

"Wow, I thought it was you. Juan's inside. He's made almost twenty dollars busting guys up on the pool table. Wha-cha doing here, anyways?"

I extended my hand. "How you been, Danny?"

"I been alright. Sorry we ain't been back sooner. We got waylaid with our moms. Today's the first one we've had to ourselves. Want to come in and watch Juan. He's deadly right now."

"No thanks, Dan. Gonna take a walk in the woods."

"Jimmy's left the house already, like they say around here. I seen him go up the road awhile ago. Hey, you want me go up to the dump with you? Juan won't need me for awhile, 'less he gets hungry and decides to eat. That's his style when he's playing for money. Hey, there he is. Be right back, Mr. J."

Juan appeared outside the arcade doors. In the shade of the arcade's stubby archway, Juan's face looked dark as molasses. He lit his cigarette before handing money to Danny, and before he'd spotted me and waved. A switch of wind tumbled over the casino grounds as soon as we started to approach one another.

"Hi, Mr. Jacobs."

"Hi Juan. Danny says you're in the zone."

"Not really, just lucky I guess. Want to come in and play a game?"

"No thanks. Gotta talk to Jimmy and then get back. I hear he's running an illegal rat race on the other side of that hill. Thought maybe I'd go out there and try and revoke his license."

"Only you could say something like that to his face." Juan's smile withered as quickly as it had erupted.

"Good seeing you, Juan. Give me a rain check on that game of pool?"

"Sure. Anytime you want to play, that'd be great. Honest, anytime."

"Alright."

Juan stuck his cigarette in an ash-barrel. "Thanks again for Seattle."

"Yeah, thanks loads, Mr. J."

"My mom's been talking about the trip more than me." Juan elaborated. "Practically everyone working the kitchen knows your name."

"Thanks for the warning."

"No, it's a good thing. Inside, they all got a bunch of new nicknames for Jimmy. But they ain't got but one for you."

"Oh? Let's hear it."

"*Father Jacobs*. My mom and her friends, they call you Father Jacobs."

"Mom's are like that sometimes. Seeing things that aren't there."

"Yeah, all week long our moms been drilling us on how we gotten this gift from you and how it's gonna change us. It's sad, Mr. J, how far gone our mom's brains are sometimes. But we put up with 'em anyways. We keep on telling them —we know mom, we was there with him."

"Alright, I gotta walk. You're welcome to come along if you want."

"Oh, I don't think that's us. Maybe if Juan was going, I would. You want to go, Juan?"

Juan frowned and offered a surly explanation.

"I'm not afraid of him. I'm not. Not no more. Not since that book you gave me to read."

"Don't you think Jimmy ought to hear that from you?"

"Waste of time with him."

"Juan, I can assure you Jimmy won't lay a hand on you. He even sneezes in your direction, Danny and I will jump him."

"See Juan, I told you. We'll push his rat shack over if he tries anything, right Mr. J?"

"And bury his sorry butt beneath it." I sneered, menacingly, at Danny's smile of puffed up freckles.

"I'm not worried about him." Juan said.

"Come with us then."

"Alright, but I'm not saying I'm sticking around when we get there."

"None of us are committing to that."

From the casino parking lot, we took the wooded trail which followed the road as far up as the first hill. From here we could drop down into familiar pasture land and not be dogged by traffic and road noise.

It was an easier hike to the dump this time, and we were

crossing the pasture's rotting footbridge in no time at all. Juan was in the lead and quick to point out to Danny and me that the odd courses of roofing shingles, which were now tacked to an outside plank in the footbridge, had not been there on our last hike.

"A welcome mat for the farmer's cows?" Juan scoffed at the wet planks of shingles. "I don't think so."

Halfway up the backside of the dump's embankment the remnants of years of decaying trash burped from the soil. Kitchen sinks, car engines, piping, motors, refrigerators, the arms of furniture all regurgitated beneath a massive slide of bottle glass. Nearer the top of the hill, the sunlight caught the corner of a buried mattress damming a potato sack of rotting sausage and cartoons of broken eggs. The meat and the stew of it had attracted a patron rat, the animal's tongue and front claws spooning at the mess until the nearness of our climb spooked him.

The dump's plateau of freshly bulldozed earth and scattered tags of garbage gave the shack at the base of the trestle a degree of self-respect. But the wind became more fitful the closer we came to the shack, sweeping down from the canyon to gather its full force over the openness of the dump's central ground. It tea-bagged the puddled ruts of tires that had come and gone, gusted, and turned back on itself to scalp the flattened burns of papery trash and oily garbage. It riled the great plain of matted newspapers punched wet by the recent rain. It blew wild and unchecked over the dump's chowder of odors leading us toward the shack. It thickened the air with images of unclean privies strung out over a deserted fairground, and reshaped the shack's jittery imprint holding its ground near the trestle. It buckled the black pipe of kerosene smoke coming from a twisted car muffler, on the shack's flat roof, and buried all but the most concentrated of fumes and flame rising from the crude rubber wicks of Jimmy's mosquito torches — this wind from the canyon.

"There's Sally's tanks." Danny said it with a hiccup and then took off running. He'd spotted a skittish grey cat and was off to meet the animal, or try to help it.

"She's getting by, Dan." Juan called out after his friend. "She don't look half as skinny as your bony butt."

Danny's determined sprint had ended near a stack of tires piled high near the dump's creek, where his sneakers were now working to flip thru a pile of plastic and a few flimsy, crisscrossed boards full of protruding nails. A loud, fractured hiss came out of the pile of boards, which quickly repeated itself and this time bore teeth and spitfire, before the lanky stray scrambled out from under the plastic and made a run for the creek. The cat jumping the little creek and vanishing into a bungling of grass shoots and blackberry, so fast, that Danny's jaw dropped in eye-popping surprise of the animal's feat and nothing more than the cluck of a hiccup escaped from his mouth.

The morose shack displayed signs of having been worked on since last I'd seen it from the trestle bridge. A new layer of chicken coup wire and splintered, moss-pimpled fence boards had been added to its flat roof, much of the chicken wire twisted and secured with strips of torn cloth to each of the roof's three rickety corner posts. A chin-up bar dangled like a coatless hanger from one of the shack's corner axle post, and a beat up metal sign — its chipped lettering reading *no swimming after dark* — hung from one of the shack wall's highest pallets. Hanging near the curtained door, the halved hands on a cracked myrtle-wood clock pointed at midnight's brass star. On the ground beneath the clock, a few clumps of dandelions had been transplanted to wilt over their spotty mounds of loosened soil, a ring of fertilizer pellets and a few stretched out slugs circling the exposed roots of each plant. Several yards away from the shack, three wooden crates lay stacked on their sides alongside a smoldering fire pit. The shelving of one of the crates holding a clean and capped mayonnaise jar with some seeds and thumbtacks inside. Beside the mayonnaise jar, another container stored a fork and knife, a toothbrush, and a jungle of burnt and stubby cooking sticks.

The shack's yard expanded in size, too. A crude paddock had been hacked out from the blackberry canes, on the far side of the creek, and the taller grasses between the creek and the berry brambles trampled. A large alder tree shaded much of this newly claimed area, its trunk chained with a six-foot high rope, which stretched over a shallow trench dug perpendicular to the creek, before being tossed and tied off to the flowering blackberry. A muddied stack of rimless tires stood close to the tree's girdled trunk.

From out of the stand of blackberry which had swallowed up Danny's cat, Jimmy staggered into the clearing. His head lowered towards the patch of mud at his feet, he coughed and spit up some yellowing and living thing at the creek bank. A sorrowful looking rug wrapped his bare shoulders and, as he took his next step towards the creek, the rug's tail of loosened braids began to drag thru the grass surrounding his unsure footsteps.

For a few agonizing seconds, we watch as Jimmy's body moaned and braced for another coughing spell beneath the weight of the rug. Though he had looked up at me, from across the creek, he seemed not to have recognized me with the boys in tow. The rug about his shoulders looked heavy and wet, and twice his body jerked to better center the weight of it over his back, and to lift it higher about his neck, and to free the growth of his ragged hair out from under the snag of the rug's separating braids. As he walked, he coughed a little more into his fist working to hold so tightly the rug burying his chest, his free hand struggling to cinch tighter the knotted rope he'd made into a belt for his raggedy cutoffs. A paring of an amorphous smile, after he'd accomplished the task, made him appear somehow organically damaged and maybe even dangerous. The suddenness of his running jumps — first one, followed by a second, more aggressive leap — carried his caped body first to creek's edge and then over it. Both of his jumps tracked by the tail of the braided rug, which had stirred up a cloud of murky water to sift thru the creek's tussocks of grass.

"Burying your troubles, Jimmy?"

"I'm sick — not so close."

Jimmy hacked out a long deep whooping cough before walking by me, his mouth open and his puffy eyes glued to the ground. His breath smelled as foul as the old rug he was dragging. He headed for an old truck seat that had claimed a piece of wasteland by the fire. When he'd reached the fire, he let his caped body collapse onto the seat's bench of exposed springs and matting, rocked forward and blew snot onto his knee and, with a violent jerk of his head, hacked up more mucus to spit into the camp's puny fire.

"What's it matter where any of us have been." Jimmy's proclamation came with a handful of scrap construction lumber tossed onto the coals. "The family's all back, safe and sound."

Danny's search for the stray had taken him across the creek, but Juan had stuck close to the fire. Three large wooden utility spools pinned the ground around the fire pit like points of a compass. Juan brushed away the smoke from where he was standing, scoffed, and walked behind the grounded truck seat before taking up a seat on one of the smaller spools positioned closest to Jimmy.

"Bring any gingerbread with you?" Jimmy smirked.

"Whole pan of it." Juan answered with rancor in his voice.

"Yeah?"

"Yeah. Ate it on the way over here."

"Guess I'll go to bed hungry."

"Guess maybe you will."

Jimmy straightened his legs and held them over a whiff of flame beginning to circle a crusted can of tomato soup and another of brown beans. His toes wiggling to snatch any ingot of the fire's escaping heat. His ankles and feet trickling with the dump's filth. The man's eyes big as grapes and straining to watch the new flame pucker from the coals. A flaking of sunburned skin splotched his cheeks and forehead. His hair, singed from some earlier fire, fanned out over his ears like the chop of a sea breaching in every direction. He pulled his feet back from the fire, coughed his croupy cough, and spit phlegm or some other discontent at the bleeding coals.

"My friend resurrect you, did he? Put some ice on your lip and find you a new voice on the streets of Seattle? Mark your new vessel of exaltation, is he?"

"Leave him alone, Jimmy."

"You don't know me, bub. None of you do."

"If we don't, it's your own doing."

"All this my doing, is it?" Jimmy's eyes locked with mine.

"Best you shake it off and come back with us."

Jimmy crumpled a sheet of newspaper into a ball and let it roll from his palm onto the coals. He opened his palms to the surge of new flame, staring at the fiery paper ornament like a blind man trying to decipher some sound outside that of the fire's gulf — the fire tearing charcoal tags from the paper ball and casting them into the air to fall on the dump's distant ground, where they fluttered and gathered the attention of two gulls scraping food from a stuffing of black plastic.

"Think you're out of the cage, son? Off leash? Forgiven?"

"I never talked, except to Mr. Jacobs. Never will and never would have." For the first time since he'd taken a seat next to Jimmy, Juan looked shaken. "So what's there to forgive?"

From across the creek, Danny called out to us. "He must be one whacked out cat."

"Be a good boy and go off to bed," Jimmy called back to the boy.

Danny went cross-eyed. "In the middle of the day? It's not even suppertime, Jimmy."

"Don't sass me, son. Get over here and sit your little rooster ass down. Don't come empty-handed, neither. Bring something with you for my fire, I'm freezing. You look like one you know. Like a rooster chasing after some little feathered whore in my barnyard."

"And you look like shit." Juan shifted off his spool and stood tall to throw down a vicious hate-stare on Jimmy's head. For the first time since sitting by the fire to challenge Jimmy, Juan's voice had cracked.

Danny's jaw dropped at the nerve of Juan's remark.

"God Juan, are you going crazy?"

"Hold on. Hold up! You want me to say I'm sorry for giving you a little smack a thousand years ago? Is that it? That what this is all about? Alright, I'm sorry. Why, just look at me, I'm so silly with sorry I've made myself sick over it. Think that will do it, Rooster. That going to be enough *sorry* to satisfy your brother in arms? It ain't, is it?"

Danny made his way around the stack of car tires and an empty, overturned fifty-five gallon oil drum. By the time he'd jumped the creek and edged closer to the fire, the newspapers he'd gathered up on the way had been rolled into the tight shape of a dowel and tucked up under his armpit.

Like a man peering over a pair of reading glasses at

something fast approaching from across a wide expanse of prairie, Jimmy lifted his eyes to face Juan's anger.

"I admit I've lost my sparkle, chief. But that's no reason to be rude. I've set up house here. You and your little Rooster been snooping around my camp long enough to know that."

"This is tribal land." Juan defiantly reminded him.

Jimmy pulled the wrap of his rug tight to his chest. He sniffed and put a knuckle to his nose, before placing a finger over one nostril and blowing bloodied snot onto the rug.

"Like I was saying, pup, this here's my home now. That being the case, I think maybe your bunghole of a mouth has dumped about all the trash I'm gonna tolerate on my white carpet. You want to apologize, then maybe I invite you back for next week's Powwow?"

"You first." Juan stuck the words hard to the back of Jimmy's seat. "You've given up. Mark hasn't, but you have."

My boot pushed the flame of Danny's newsprint back into the heart of the fire. "What the boy says is the truth of it Jimmy. It is."

"Fuck you both. I'm too sick to come at either of you." He gathered the tattered folds of the rug over his legs and dug his heels into a bit of sand around the fire.

Danny was fireside now, and his knobby knees and legs had not stopped kicking at the fire and smoke since he'd taken up Juan's seat on the wood spool. But now, watching his friend's anger, Danny's hands nervously reached to hold his legs in check, his fish-eyed stare at the fire's slashing rainbow moving from Juan's anger to Jimmy's sloshing head which had begun to gently bump the back of the truck seat.

"Hey Rooster, you remember Trump don't you?"

"Who?"

"Trump! Trump the chump with the fat fiery rump."

Danny belched a nervous laugh at Jimmy's loud portrayal of the enemy.

"Come on Dan, let's go."

Jimmy let go of the rug and dug his hands into the front pockets of his greasy cutoffs. Out came two banded rolls of cash, one in each hand, which he waved at Danny thru the smoke of the fire.

"Got all this peddling bibles in Seattle. *Book of James*, mostly. Know what I mean. Plenty more to be got where this come from. When we need it, not now."

Jimmy slipped a hundred dollar bill out from one of the rolls of cash and held it over the fire for Danny to see.

"Here Rooster, come get yourself a big green egg off the top shelf."

"He doesn't want your money. You won't take his money," I instructed Danny. "Understand? You take money when you've worked for it. Same as Juan, same as me. No other way."

"Yes, sir."

Jimmy put the two rolls of cash and the loose bill in his pocket. He slouched back, clearing his throat with a groveling moan, and began to gently thump his head against the torn greenery of the truck seat.

For a time, there was no more talking, and the boys and I lay in wait watching one another watching Jimmy become transfixed with the thumping trance his gentle rocking seemed to be putting each of us under. The spotty rain returned, cool and menacing and without pattern, and for a time it too strengthened the spell of our uncomfortable trance in Jimmy's camp. The raindrops pattered the sheets of newspaper that Danny had draped over one of the wooden spools. And some of the rain quietly splotched the oil-stained clubs of firewood stacked near Jimmy's bare feet.

"Little rain ruining your appetite for a picnic?" Jimmy

broke our silence. His torso sawing at the words which rolled from the seat's ticking.

"You done clowning?" I asked.

"Yo Rooster, I ever tell you how much I love this old truck seat? Used to make love on it to Jessie's mom." He stopped his pathetic rocking, leaned forward until his fingers had grabbed hold of his toes, and tilted his head sideways as if looking for something hidden under the truck seat. "Guess she ain't there no more, Rooster. If she ever was?"

Once again upright in his seat, he pushed the filthy rug back from his shoulders some.

"Thought about getting this old box spring reupholstered before you all come up to the house. But shit, the damn cats around here want to scratch the wool off everything. Know what I mean? Christ," his torso twisting and turning from the fire for us to look at, "why just take a good look at my backside. Am I'm lying, Rooster?"

Over the skin of his shoulder blades, a glistening sheen of sweat and grime covered a barrage of cuts and deep scratches. More cuts and bruised abrasions, inflamed and colored purple by the rug's grit, flanked the flesh and muscle along his spine.

"Come on, Dan." Juan spoke protectively. "We gotta get food in us."

Jimmy pulled his knees up under the raunchy rug and began to rock softly. The seat's leather squished and moaned over the muffled squeak of springs each time his head thumped the back of the truck seat. His rocking made him look all the more pitiful, juvenile, a man-child dressed from neck to navel with movements suggestive of someone trying to skirt a sickness or delirium. Had the sounds of steel springs oozing from the truck seat not been so grating — noises not unlike those of two disinterested lovers humping a weakening headboard tune — his catapulting rocking might have come off comical.

"You want us to bring you some supper back before dark, Mr. Jacobs?"

"No. I won't be staying much longer myself."

"You want us to we will."

"Considering the garbage you'd have to put up with again," I thumbed my hand towards Jimmy's rocking, "I could hardly ask such a favor."

The truck seat thumped out one last head-pounding skid and stopped, giving us back the sputtering quietness of the campfire until Jimmy's poker stick stirred up more sparks and more coughing.

"We'd do it for you."

"I know you would. If you've got it in you after you've had your own, I guess I wouldn't turn it down."

Juan gave Jimmy's fiery poker stick a thoughtful stare before half-heartedly waving goodbye to me. Then the boy turned and headed out across the dump's dismal landscape. Danny already about to run ahead of him.

"You planning on carrying on like this all summer?" I asked, once the boys had disappeared over the hill.

"I don't know. Are you?"

"We've both lost about everything we ever cared about. Can we agree on that much?"

"Why wouldn't we."

"Alright. So what say we try and salvage what's left of you and me?"

"What's left of you and me is the whole problem."

I could hardly argue with him. I stood and walked to the shack's entrance. Thru a slit in the curtain, I could see mail on the spool table inside the shack.

"Where did all the mail on the table come from?"

"My house, mostly."

"You've been back to the island?"

"I might of."

"Any of it I might be particularly interested in?"

"Lots. But the really pressing stuff I burned."

"How come?"

"Seemed the considerate thing to do. Any word on the insurance investigation?"

"Why would there be? A few hotel guests complained about some noise that night. But those that did checked out on the day of the fire. Best I can figure."

"So no one's the wiser?"

"I guess. Unless those fuckwits decide to talk."

"They won't. Half of them got criminal records. Besides, talking might get them connected to that bomb scare we had awhile back."

"Do you think the fire could have been my fault? There were coals scattered everywhere after you pulled me from the fireplace."

"The less said the better, I think."

"I suppose. Mind if I go inside?"

"Be my guest."

Inside the shack, the light was poor and the air oppressive and smelling of sulfur or something like it. More chicken wire had been attached on each of the three truncated walls. The wire tied and gagged with bulb-sized wads of crumpled newspaper and serving as lath to scale the walls. On the shack's food-stained spool table, a small canister of soil and earth worms had been tipped over onto a plate of tortillas and dried cheese, much of the soiled mess appearing to be on the move.

"Did you know that mail has its own unique smell when it's burning?" Jimmy's voice raked the earth outside the shack. "Every little piece of every little message seems to give off a little different stink. When it's from the people we owe money, well, well then it smells rather sweet. But the *dear Jimmy* kind — that kind of sweetness has always been a souring message that stings my nose. Nothing at all like the smell of Trump's curly locks all afire, is it?"

"What the hell are you talking about?"

"There was so much of it. And all of it taking up so much space in my head. Too much dead news fighting for my a-ah-attention," a coughing fit had clipped his last word, "none of it worth saving. Hey? What do you think happened to old Scalp, anyways?"

"Who?"

"Old Scalp. Why hasn't he come back to pay us a visit?"

"Don't know, don't care. Have you actually slept in here?"

"Old Scalp. Good a name as any for that piece of shit. Where do you suppose the rest of his men are hiding?"

"They left the islands. I told you that."

"That wasn't very neighborly of them, was it?"

Jimmy was rubbing his eyes with his fists and whispering to himself when I stepped from the shack. His voice climbing and sinking within each swipe the fire's smoke took at his face. His words scratching for some wisdom too quickly crimped in mid-sentence for me to make any sense out of. Sentiments of the heart, perhaps, left to resonate in the deadened earth beneath his bare feet. Feeble sounds which served only to mold him into something foreign and ruptured under the wrap of his rug.

"Maybe we ought to look him up. Give him Jessie's final farewell blessing. She might like that."

"We've other responsibilities now."

"Says who?"

"Says me — the only family you got left. Hey! I'm talking to you. You listening?"

"Part of me might be."

"You so full of anger that you've forgotten how many

others have been harmed by the loss? You got to do more than just breathe yourself sick over what's been taken from you. You've got to help me."

"You must be crazier than I am, thinking I'll ever go back to that prick of a town. You forgotten we fought that fight alone?"

"I won't ever forget."

A violent fit of croupy coughing took hold of him. He doubled over and nearly vomited before managing to suppress most of it. He groaned and sat up, wiped his mouth, and hacked up a marble of phlegm which he spit to one side of the truck seat. A long, beleaguered moan seemed to put him more at ease.

"We should get you to a doctor for that cough of yours. When that part of you is fixed, we'll find you somebody in Seattle to look inside your head."

"Maybe I do go back with you, what then?"

"Nothing needs explaining — not between you and me. Not to anyone. Not anymore. Come back and you can get well on my boat. Red and I will see to it that you're left alone."

He choked back a couple of sputtering coughs, then his head and shoulders lunged into another wicked coughing spell. When his coughing had quieted, he spoke into the fire.

"I need to lie down. Inside. It's too cold for me out here. Or hot maybe. Sorry friend."

"Jimmy, listen to me."

But he'd have no more of my trying to reason with him. He stood and threw off the rug and walked an angled line to the shack's opening, where the cuts and scratches on his back and shoulders disappeared behind the slap of the curtained door.

Minutes later, I folded back a crease in the shack's curtain to check in on him. His hands were grappling with one of the shack walls to keep the weight of his collapsing body from falling so hard to the floor. It was a desperate sight, and when he slumped to the floor it was made all the more desperate to watch by the muted cry of Jessie's spoken name. On the floor, Jimmy's body curled and sniffled over the water bottle he was holding with both his hands. His voice funneling some prayerful thing into the mouth of the bottle about a child's stolen violin and a lost pink leash that once belonged to Jessie's dog. His hands twisting the neck of the water bottle as if it were some pagan idol his pain might coerce.

"There was no other like her, Jimmy."

It didn't hurt me to speak the words into my friend's darkened well. And hearing my voice speak of his daughter, a happier piece of her life was returned to me. But it was agonizing to watch her father, someone living, someone you love, falling so far so fast in the prison I'd helped bury him in.

I stepped away from the shack's opening. Near the measuring fire, I drank from my own bottle of water. A long powerful guzzling which did nothing to take away the howling shame I felt for having contributed to a father's nightmare.

Later, Jimmy stepped from the shack to stump-walk his way towards the campfire.

"Do you think we're cursed?" He asked.

"Stop it." I told him, and watched how he kneeled so as to reach deep into the open stomach of the pleated truck seat. He pulled a few hidden stones from the gutted springs, and stood to toss them viciously at the leafy branches of the alder tree across the creek. The stones caused a hutch of perched, red-winged blackbirds to scare and fly away.

"I love to watch how they all fly away in one big red and black sail. Keeps the fire in me alive. Hey, where are your offspring?"

"My what?"

"Your boys. Where are they?"

"Casino. Or maybe they're home by now. Juan offered to bring us some dinner."

"I'm not hungry."

"I am."

"Why the hell you dropping so much time on those two?"

"They're both smart and they're both loyal. What fool wouldn't reward that with a little of his own time. And maybe, just maybe they're going to help me rebuild the *Campground*."

"You ain't going to rebuild shit. She's gone. And she's gonna stay gone."

"You gonna piss your pants all summer here — in your Garden of Eden? Or are you going to come back and help me?"

He sat and actually seemed to be considering my challenge.

"I would have liked to have seen her swim ashore and spit in their faces. Wouldn't that have been just like her? Where might she be now, if not for their brainwashing?"

"She was beautiful." I said to him. "Mixing in with those stumpfucks was just a dumb mistake. She was hurting. She was angry."

"Shut it."

"Christ almighty, she was her father's daughter. Why didn't I remember that, and know she was capable of something so punishing?"

"Shut it."

"No. No, I won't shut it. One bad impulsive decision doesn't summarize the end of all she was to us. In your heart, you know she was so much more than that. In your heart, you know it!"

There was no anger in the way I'd spoken to him. And, in the way he had stared back at me, I felt I had at last reached him with the only truth that should ever have mattered to either of us.

"Your daughter was a delight. She was my ally. The only thing worth remembering now is that she loved both of us."

"That's too much fabrication even for you, Jacobs." He spoke with a great disgust milking his words back from the fire, but then looked up at me with an unexpected fondness in his bloodshot eyes. "Maybe, maybe if the baby she was carrying — if it had been yours — maybe I might have gotten back to your side of things."

"That's not possible, you know that."

"But, if had been yours."

"You're trying to take us both to a place where there's no life. Where there never could be, Jimmy. If I go back to that place, alone, or with you, I'll kill. Do you understand what I'm saying? I will kill."

He threw some scraps of roofing paper into the fire. The paper curled and blistered and erupted into a ribbon of black smoke. He began to speak from a place beyond the shadows the fire had called from the pine woods.

"I wake up feeling the same as you. Cheated. After all we did for her, all those years together, this is the thank you note she dropped at our feet."

"I'm not sorry I loved your daughter. I'm sorry I denied it so horribly, so blindly."

"My thoughts swung that way once. But that man, he's come and gone. For me, there's no flavor in any part of her memory no more."

"That's just black-ass regret peeling the skin off you. Don't cover her face with that crap no more. The world came and wept, and buried your daughter. You and I don't have to."

"You think your grief is my grief. Don't you?"

"I do. Ours is a grief that sickens the mind. It's always been that way with you and me. First we turn on ourselves,

and then on those around us. Just look at how we abandoned Dianna."

"We didn't do that to Dianna."

"Yes we did, and don't you deny it. We shut her out.
We kept our pathetic secrets. And for what? What higher
ground did they ever take us to?"

"Tell me something, was I good to her? As good as you,
I mean? I mean, when you were fucking her. You know,
when Dianna was doing your laundry and I was tending
your bar and you were fucking my daughter, did my name
get the same respect she was giving your body?"

As whimpering as it was wicked, Jimmy's weakened
voice managed to ride his obscene questioning a little deeper into our wounds.

"Did she, Mark? Did she ever mention her father's
name, his love for her, with, with the same kindness she
was holding out for you on the tip of her tongue?"

"Shut it."

"Ever?"

My eyes ran the edges of the dump — searching for the
missing boys, looking up to the stars, looking anywhere but
back at my friend's cruelty — knowing that I could have
searched for any prick of light on the horizon or in my mind
for another hour, another thousand thoughts, and still not
found a way to parlay a fraction of what I was feeling into
some tool of forgiveness. When I came back from the emptiness, the blood-lined whites of a father's eyes were shaking something unspeakable at me. Something uncompleted
to his idea of a true and transforming fall.

"Every day feels a little heavier to me." He spoke as if
he were standing graveside and trying to comfort an inconsolable friend.

"You're skin and bones —"

"I'm not talking about my body. I'm talking about my soul!"

The sullen tracks left behind by his words fanned out angrily over the last of the burning tar paper. His body bending to cane the fire with a few splashes of sloshing kerosene he'd cupped from a can onto the fire.

"Then take hold of it, god damn it!"

There was more of our shouting to come. More of our anger and blame and the sickening underbelly of a grief revisited to churn our stomachs. And when it was over, when the fire's squalor had worn down our words to an echoing curse, both of us had retreated to a more desolate place by the fire.

We spoke nothing more of Jessie's death or of Dianna's depression, though, for a time, Jimmy's sunken eyes seemed to pocket the look of a man possessed and fighting some treacherous thought. Eyes that groveled with the evening star, as if trying to etch out some fizzling commandment from its light, some whispered and whimpered muttering to further punish me.

Later, we watched in silence the light of more shadows cross over the flattened earth of the dump. Situated halfway between the shack and the dump's pole gate, a chest high pile of lathe and plaster now held the muzzled movements of a foraging rat. The animal's rabbit-sized haunches shifting to find solid footing, before raising its head and forelegs into the newborn wind coming down from the canyon, as if expecting some avenging thing to wander onto its mealy turf and disrupt its search for food.

Jimmy had spotted the rat, too, and rolled from his seat to walk to the back of the shack. He came back around one corner of the shack, his arms holding a couple of sacks of something which he held close to his hip as he headed towards the pile of plaster. The rat spun 'round and bolted from sight. Climbing to the top of the pile, Jimmy emptied the contents of the first sack; a nauseating and yellowing tangle of plastic glue-strips strewn with the bodies of dead flies. Over the tangled plastic strips, he emptied the contents of a bag of *Purina Dog Chow*. A weakness of hand shook the wet paper sack before his arm extended and waved the bag over his head — the last of the food pellets drawing a tail in the air before dropping like rabbit turds onto the scattered fly paper and plates of plaster. He climbed down from the pile and crossed back behind the shack, no sound but the canyon wind pursuing him.

To our fire, he brought with him a tube of hard cardboard and a few flags of roofing paper which he threw onto the coals. A great weariness moved the rack of his body once around the fire's ring, before both his hands swooped hold of his poncho rug and wrapped his half naked body in the shake of its braids. He began, once more, to circle the fire that now whistled with a new torch of flame, his stone-eyed glare sometimes goring me to stand and move away from his child's play. A snow-cold hoarseness groped his shackled voice when, at last, he spoke — a voice of desperation and prayerful plea which whispered that I should leave and not return.

From a cavity of space in the debris pile, the rat lifted its lifeless laminated eyes into the sunlight, scouting the dump for predators and some deformity of spirit only the abandoned and betrayed have come to believe in. A body bigger than Danny's feral stray, the rat's tremendous hindquarters twitched with shadings of brown and black fur as it ascended the pile and grew to its full size and sentinel form. Scratching. Sniffing. Claws like shiny headless nails typing at the sticky fly strips so as to loosen the nuggets of dog food. The depravity of Jimmy's fire painting some invisible stalk of darkness over all that consummated the animal's wretched scavenging.

Jimmy hacked up more yellow phlegm and walked away from the fire. His hands grappling with the dead weight of the rug, until he'd reached the bank of the creek, where his body found some balance nearer the ground in which to kneel and lay claim to his despair. His fingers scratched to take hold of a torn braid, tossed aside the effort, and fumbled for an apple which lay on a tuft of grass edging the creek. The scar of his ponytail a severed hackle facing down the fire's pith. He lifted his gaze from a shallow wash in the creek water to watch the rat eat, put the crest of the apple to his mouth, and nibbled at the skin of the fruit with the same mechanized teething with which the rat was nibbling on a pellet of dog food. The eyes of both animals looking thru me to something ancient and worshiping in the other's stare.

The lint from the last of the fire's unburned fuel fell from the air like wingless paper airplanes upon my fallen friend.

The boys never returned with dinner.

CHAPTER ELEVEN

Danny and Juan were each nursing their second cup of coffee when the north wind picked up and the long scribbling rain clouds, which had worked the island skies over Depot Island all morning but not threatened our own pocket of blue, dropped in low over the channel. Within minutes, the outside temperature plummeted twelve degrees, and Main Street became a dancing current of pelting raindrops and pedestrians running for any awning or porch offering cover from the downpour. The rain fell cold and heavy, and chained the boys to their coffee mugs and one of Sally's sagging tarps. I kept my head down, my hood cinched, and my cold hands glued to the pickaxe I was using, happy to have work that suited the foul mood I was in.

For an hour, the rain fell with a thunderous chatter. And the wind which came with it battered our cold faces and soaked our bodies with crowning, boisterous gusts. In the trench, which the boys and I were digging for the *Campground's* new drainage pipe, the heavy rain caused us to move a little like mice checking for traps their enemies may have set out for them; our hand tools scraping, shoveling, and piling to the low side of the ditch the soil which each of us swore we'd already twice dug. In the passing of just one hour of rainfall, it seemed half the slop of soil and stone, which we'd piled up against the *Campground's* foundation, had slid back into our drainage ditch. All of our trenching efforts about to become a swollen creek of silt and mud on a run-away course to the courtyard, and maybe onward, to the piers in Red's marina.

Danny was wearing a green sweater three sizes too large for his body. The sweater was one of mine, and beneath the long green sag of its waterlogged cotton, which stretched over the boy's muddied shorts and hung past his kneecaps like a grotesque pannus, Danny's bearing looked more shapeless and scrawny than usual. The work at hand was difficult, and whenever Dan lifted a shovelful of muck from the drainage ditch his wet sweater would swing from side to side, making his ribbed body look like that of an old woman struggling to keep her dog from pulling on its leash.

"You're gonna sink in that bathrobe you're wearing, if you don't finish up and get out of that ditch."

"You think so, chief?" Danny plucked a spot of mud from his lips and flicked it into the channel of water rushing over his ankles. "I go under, and you're gonna have to give old Gene Kelly mouth-to-mouth re-Suck-ah-tation. Don't I look just like him, though? Don't I?"

"Who?"

"Gene Kelly? You know, that digging in the rain guy?"

By early afternoon, the sun had returned to wash the islands on both sides of the channel with brighter skies. The air warmed, the boys changed their shoes and socks and put on dry T-shirts, and we washed for lunch.

Juan knifed three slabs of white cheese off our lunch table's cutting board and placed each slice on a piece of brown bread. He folded and pressed each half sandwich, taking a big bite out of his own sandwich as he tried passing me mine.

I waved the sandwich away. "No thanks. Tired of white cheese and white bread."

Danny walked under Sally's tarp to pour himself the last of the coffee pot's cold tar. He sat for all of two minutes, then stood and surveyed Hazel's crepe cart. A line of customers had formed from the courtyard gate to the pole of a streetlamp up the sidewalk a ways, near the *Campground's* service alley. At the back of the line, the hungriest and the coldest rubbed their hands and shoulders while shuffling in line. The street bordering them steaming in the drying sunlight.

"Say cheese one more time Juan, and Mr. J's gonna staple your lips to the back of your head." Danny joked. "When he does, know what you're gonna look like? Like one of your cruddy open-faced cheese sandwiches."

Juan smirked. "Suit yourself, ladies."

"Want to hit the crêpe tables, Mr. J?"

"You're singing my song now, son."

"Ready, set, let's go." Danny sang his words confidently. "Come on Co-cheese, you too. I'm buying."

Jackie and Hazel had made a serious go of it all week. On opening day they'd surprised me by showing me their vendor's license and their food handler's permits. And every day since then, the boys and I had watched Hazel's station wagon pull up to the curb in front of the courtyard and watched the girls unload coolers of prepared vegetables, cheeses, and fruit. Always a small crowd awaited them on the sidewalk, eager to help the girls unload, and biting at the bit to place orders for breakfast crepes. Word was out, and the excitement attached to it had reared its banner of syncopated anticipation from the ferry docks all the way to the state campground on Joey's side of our island.

After Danny had placed our order, Jackie pulled me aside to ask if she might replant Jessie's courtyard. What she couldn't safely transplant from her place, or find in the wild, she would purchase. All she asked in return was permission to use the courtyard space to sell her flowers, herbs, and excess vegetables — *"oodles of flowers coming on like Chicago gangbusters in my garden."* She said *Chicago* with a gangster's sarcastic smile twisting the sound of it.

"For sure much of it needs to be replanted. But —"

"But what?"

"I'd like to do the planting myself, that's all. I could use your help though. I'd pay you for your plants and your time, of course."

"Of course, Mark. But your money's no good here."

"Jackie —"

"Shut-uupp."

"Alright, I can do that. We can do that. So, tell me something. How's this town taking to the influx of French cooking?"

"We're quite pleased. You may have to talk to Ike and Tom about adding a wing onto the *Campground* for a crepe franchise."

"That's good to hear, Jackie."

By late afternoon the boys and I were carrying our tools and pushing our wheelbarrows pretty much wherever Ike and Tom pointed. We swept up pounds of jack-knifed nails, did loads of raking and shoveling, lots of lifting and dragging burnt wood to the dumpster, and a fair amount of just plain staying out of Ike and Tom's path.

Ike regularly took time away from his own work to show the boys how to use a carpenter's square and level, how to set a proper plumb line, the importance of accurately measuring a piece of lumber to be cut so as to avoid the carpenter's cardinal sin of having to cut the same board twice. Ike explained to the boys, only once, how a dull saw blade was a dangerous saw blade. But more than once, I caught him catching each boy's attention by touching the three burly scars on the knuckles of his left hand with his one good forefinger. Come dinner break, and only after we'd promised to keep it a secret from Ike, Danny told us his new nickname for his new carpenter friend — *Ike the mike* — "as in he's a broken microphone about all this safety stuff, guys!"

Tomorrow comes, and with it comes a brandishing sunrise to wash our breakfast of white cheese and peanut butter and banana sandwiches. Main Street is empty of moving automobiles, dispatched of its out-of-bound golf carts, but its sweeping downhill curve shoulders the footed pistons of a dozen racing bicyclists, all of whom are here and gone again fast as I can sarcastically compliment Juan on the breakfast he continues to serve us every morning.

"At least, the breakfast you've been dishing up every day is never any colder than the outside temperature."

"That's why I'm here, Mark." Juan says, and throws Danny and me each a red apple. "Good cold nutrition. Eat up, gentlemen. Might give one of you some ambition today."

"One thing about Juan's killer brown bread and cheese, Mr. J." Danny talked and chewed while his sneaker drew a line in the pile of sand at his feet. "Kind of puts a little fire in your intestines, doesn't it?"

"Sure does."

"It's been making my dumps humongous all week."

"And we needed to hear that, did we Dan?" Juan stuck his knife in his apple and finger-snapped Danny's ear.

"Alright Juan, what say you and I get to work? We don't, Danny-boy here's gonna run what little appetite I got left for your commando breakfast into the ground."

"Mr. Jacobs?"

"Yeah?"

"You think maybe it would be okay with you and Sally

if Dan and I was to camp out at his place sometimes? We could get a lot more work hours in if we didn't have to take the ferry back and forth so much."

"Don't see why not. How is it you got here so early this morning?"

"Because we never went home last night," Danny answered.

"We'll run it by Sally this afternoon. If we can't convince him it's a win-win situation all way 'round, then you boys can sleep work nights on my boat and I'll camp out at Sally's place. Provided you're in bed, quiet, not smoking, and lights out by nine."

"That pretty much cinches up our camping reservations up at Sally's place, eh Juan?" Danny joshed.

I gave Danny's earlobe the slightest of snaps, as I walked by him on my way to look for my shovel.

For the next four hours the docking ferries would become our sun dial, our lunch whistle, our call to break from work and catch some of the dockside chattering spilling uphill and into Main Street. And after dozing in the pleasant murmur of commuters climbing Main Street, after watching the churn of each ferry docking, always the opium waters on the far side of the channel mirrored the quieted bluffs of Depot Island, and gave no hint of having ever been shaken by Dianna's sudden departure.

"Want some help, Juan?" Danny asked, stepping out from a patch of shade. He looked eager to reach for the wheelbarrow handles resting by Juan's side.

"Not if you're going to shovel it at me from both ends?"

"You're a sharp kid, you are. Head of your class, I'd say." Danny smiled and took hold of the wheelbarrow handles. "Could have been a contender, a guy like you. But instead, you're a working *stiff* working for *legal* tender."

Juan stopped his shoveling. "Feeling a humongous dump coming on, are you Dan?"

Danny exhaled. "I could push twice this load. Oh yeah, I'm as big as you today."

Danny heaved and ground his teeth. His face reddened. His cheeks puffed on a cigarette that was no longer in his mouth. When he managed to lift the wheelbarrow's metal feet off the ground, Juan piled more sand into the metal tub fast as he could shovel it. But Danny hung on, his spindly legs dancing in the sand as he tried to maintain some semblance of balance, under a load which Juan was making heavier and more lopsided by the second. In a last ditch effort to push the mush of the wheelbarrow's tire over a lump of earth, Danny's wiry body wavered like a mosquito that's taken on too much human blood.

"Set it down, Dan." Juan said, finally tossing his shovel aside to take hold of the wheelbarrow's handles. "You're shaking like an old man."

"No, I can do it. Just get me over the hump, ass-wipe."

"What about the cussing?" I asked. "Think you might push some of that aside too?"

"First things first, Mr. J."

"What?"

"I'll try, I'll try."

Juan gave Danny's shoulder a little hold-up tug. "That's far enough."

"I can do it."

"Set it down, Dan."

"No-ooh! Gonna give it the old college go one more time. Ain't I, Mr. J?"

"Juan?"

"Yeah?"

"You and Danny feel up to taking the boat over to Jackie's place this afternoon?"

"What for?"

"Wrong answer."

"Sure we're up to it. But I still gotta ask what for."

"See Jackie before you and Danny head down to Red's. She'll fill you in."

But Danny hadn't heard a word I'd spoken. Soon as he'd about ruptured a kidney pushing the wheelbarrow's tire over the bump of earth, the wheelbarrow had taken off on him and he spilled the load.

"Good job, Dan. Right where Mr. J wanted it."

"Promise me you won't steer my boat like that."

"Never Mr. J. This here was just a dry run."

In the courtyard, a small parish of hugging, handshaking women was saying their goodbyes to Hazel and edging their way up my hill. Church-folk for sure on my doorstep. High-heeled, sweater-bunched women suffocating Sally's steel roses in the courtyard with their over-the-top, straight-up, mud-in-your-eye whale oil perfumes; two of the women palming their mollusk hairdos as they try to keep up with the forced march of two others ahead of them. Watching these woman struggling to conquer the hill, one thing I know, gonna be too many questions for anyone's front door to withstand. The women climb and voice a fondness for Salvador's artwork, have probably contended with Jimmy's contentious doubts over the years, but they've no idea who the man on top of the hill is.

There will be others to trespass and climb my hill today. A parade of grade-schoolers, two teachers in tow, will rush the *Campground's* hillside of quaking milkweed and floundering sentiment. The children will climb towards me like jumpy toads, like soldiers dressed in creamy polo shirts and glad-plaid skirts twirling blue knee-socks, each girl wearing a yellow ribbon in her Scotch-colored hair. All classes of higher learning have been erased clean off their chalk-boards today, all but mine. When they've captured my hill and have begun their inquisition, I will inform their teach-ers that if cutting off his ponytail had represented Jimmy's first physical corruption of severing ties with any sense of community, if it had been more premeditated than I knew or had yet to discover, then it followed that his status as squatter in the tribal dump was to become his second best corruption of spirit. Tell them to their faces, I will, in words not at all like these, that to my friend the spoken word has become a smear of trackless points, that even the heartfelt words of his priest could not chip away the understand-able ache of his daughter's death, that my best friend was bound by an inconsolable grief which wrapped his body like a molten cape. But it is a gentler kind of truth that I will share with these spidery young students. For them, in a voice only slightly louder than a whisper, they will hear that my friend has gone to live in the dump in order to mount his prophetic insurrection, to bloody himself on pastures of trash plowed deep with remorse, that my friend has made a new life for himself in a puddle of rain that allows him to keep alive the oldest of cradled memories. That he's grown wings of anger and vengeance that stretch over the skies of the casino like willow branches fishing for trout in the hazy afternoon sunlight. That he's made friends with the grinning snouts of Norwegian rats, whose monstrous pitted faces have been striped with peach-peeled burns caused by the enemy's many exploding aerosol cans. That my friend has become a man stripped of his vanity, that he's infected and blistered with bugs and bites, and eats with his fingers from soup cans, that he cinches the belt loops of his soiled cut-offs with a dog leash and uses duct-tape to pull the hair off his legs and arms in the darkness of a moonless night. I will tell these children, for their own safety, to steer clear of my ghostly friend, that you cannot whisper the word *ghostly* too often to describe such a man as my friend.

The church bell in the town square will ring out the ending of still another class on my hill. And after the bell's final toll, some of the children will wring their hands and exchange exaggerated facial ticks, while others will softly giggle and tie their hands with their fingers in disbelief of all I have shared with them. But two of the more precocious children will speak up to challenge the accuracy of my reporting. They will insist that my story is all fabrication, share with me that a *figure of authority* has informed their parents that Jimmy has found *Christ our Lord,* and claim that other friends of the family have also witnessed Jimmy singing hymns around his stinky campfire, all this while their families were dumping their weekly trash at the tribal dump.

Before they descend my hill, children will ask my permission to fold their hands in prayer. They will shuffle like penguins and find their new order before me, their polished penny loafers settling in the sand and stone like a slinky gesturing of grasses in a breathless wind. Children singing their song, folding their charitable banner before passing it on to the owner of a flagless country.

There will be others come singing their mourner's song. They will climb my hill all week to deliver their sorrowful words. Strangers bearing gifts and letters and noted treasures, delivering more spotty sermons, more fretful remorse, more of the town's deep-seated worries for our safety. Long after the coals of my evening fire have collapsed in the *Campground's* fireplace, the shunting kindness of my neighbors will call on me to step forth upon the hill and witness their condolences, their regrets, their unexcused absences the night of the fire.

On Monday next, I accepted Ike and Tom's second bid to

post and beam the *Campground's* new design. Two days later, the posts and beams arrived on site. A day or two after that Ike and Tom's sons showed up, making Ike and Tom the crew of four they had been waiting on before beginning the task of setting the *Campground's* twelve, eighteen-foot perimeter timbers.

When Danny saw the *Campground's* new timber construction finally taking a foothold on the old foundation, he stuck his shovel into a pile of swale rock, put his hands on his hips and proclaimed: "I guess we'll be rebuilding bigtime, once Jimmy returns from hiatus."

"Where did you pick that word up?" I asked, impressed.

"Well, won't he? Won't he want back in once word gets out we're doing all this for him?"

"No, the word *hiatus*?"

"College, my good man."

"Where?"

"On campus, Mr. J. You forgotten? Peter kept using it. So I kept asking until I knew it was sort of like a vacation. Only I guess you're supposed to be doing something important when you're gone, not just fluffing off."

"I'm impressed. But I'm afraid right now Jimmy's tripping on something that sounds closer to *He-hate-us*."

Juan stood scanning the *Campground's* new beams, one hand on his hip, the other fisted and pointing at a lone cloud in the sky. He thought it was time we found a place in the *Campground's* new construction for Danny's mission bell to hang.

Danny threw up his hands. "Now you're seeing it! Haven't I always said this town could use a decent dinner bell?"

"You want us to put your bell on the porch?"

"No, that's no good."

"What'd you have in mind?"

"Couldn't Ike build us a real bell tower?"

"Whoa, Danny's been thinking."

"Why not, Juan? It'd make it a little like Monterey up here, or like one of those other mission bell towns Mr. J showed us pictures of."

"Mission San Juan Bautista," Juan put a name to a memory, "that's the one you're thinking of Dan. Where Mr. Jacobs got married."

"It'd make for a radical change. Well, wouldn't it? Be like having sunny California around us all the time."

"A bar and a church bell under the same roof?" Juan sipped his coffee and seemed to consider the future merits of such a concept, rather sentimentally I thought. "You might be on to something, Dan."

"What happened to 'piss on 'em, it ain't me?'" I asked.

"Seattle changed me some." Juan jingled a few framing nails inside one of his pant pockets. "You changed me some, Mark."

"On a first name basis again, are we?"

"For quite a while, actually."

"And I suppose I'm to call you Mr. Rodriquez from now on?"

"If you got it in you."

Come morning, Salvador's compound is a rush of racing sound and light. The door to Sally's kitchen is open and out walks Danny with a full pot of coffee. All smiles, he brings the coffee to the patio table and pours me a cup, talking to me the whole time about how "we're all definitely on the mend."

Where does this kid pick up these phrases?

The coffee is good and strong and rubs away the veneer of so much sleep. There's a polished stick on the table, which Danny takes hold of and places in front of Jenny's panting mouth. The dog inches forward to bite gently on the wood. Danny hangs an empty wash pail on one end of the stick. He couldn't be more pleased with Jenny's ability to hold the pail steady.

"Ain't she something, Mr. J?"

Jenny stands on the patio like a hobo ready to break camp soon as this kid's prattling waves her on. I'm all for going with them.

"Keep an eye on these two today, will you Juan?"

"Sure thing," Juan answers, poking half a donut into his coffee cup before turning to Jenny. "Say, Jenny? When you're done teaching little brother here how to carry a pail up the hill can you remind him it's his turn to peel potatoes?"

"Where's Brynnie?" I asked.

"On stage with Sally."

From across the yard, Brynnie cocked his head out from behind a stack of pallets teetering on the edge of the stage. Sally's body stooped and working close by, the screech of a disc grinder sending a spray of sparks out over the work floor. While I sipped my coffee and watched Sally work, Juan brought up more unanswered questions about the *Campground's* fire.

"My answer's still the same, Juan. We don't know how the fire started. Not really."

This was always my response to Juan's questions about the fire. But privately, I'd considered the same two possibilities we'd all considered; either some of the coals Trump and I had scattered across the floor, during the fight, had been missed during Jimmy's mop-up, or else Trump's men had come back and started the fire. Yes, there was a third possibility that had crept into my thinking the night Jimmy had appeared in my Seattle yard. But it seemed too repulsive, too disheartening, too much an act of betrayal to seriously entertain.

When Sally set his work aside to join us for breakfast on the patio, there was more speculation about the cause of the *Campground's* fire.

"When he was putting a name to each one of those pictures — the ones he kept tossing at Trump's men — I didn't, I didn't really give it much thought. But now, now I think about it every night. I guess, maybe now, I figure he did some homework on those men and never said a word to anyone."

"Like he was waiting for all of them to walk thru the *Campground* door that night."

"Exactly. Like maybe when he was dancing with them on the ferry, maybe he invited them over."

"Lately, so much about that night strikes me as more than just bad luck and coincidence."

"Well, time will tell."

"God, I hope not. I'm full up with revelations. Know what I mean?"

"Yeah, I do. But Jimmy, him I don't think so. He's dead set on chasing down more pain, if you ask me."

"You passing judgment, Sal?"

"I am. Everyday, like everyone else."

"You've never known the grief of losing a child."

"True enough. I've only ever lived with dogs. Though, I would argue that grief does not distinguish one life form from another. I think it knows only the immensity of the loss of a love taken."

"Perhaps."

"I read a book once of a veterinarian who had lost both a child and a beloved dog, one lost about a year after the other had died. He said that the grief he felt was the same for him. That the loss of each love taken was immeasurable. I believed him — I believe his story. Love is love, I think — it has no interest in measuring the shape of life's infinite forms so as to calculate its tailoring. It recognizes only the weight of its attachment to another, I think."

"I suppose that's true enough for some."

"Wouldn't you say grief is a blade to the belly of any caring spirit, Mark? And that it is a lie, most of the time, for people to claim that pain makes us stronger."

"For sure."

"A month before I met those two trouble-makers over there," Sally lifted his coffee mug to his lounging dogs, "I had to put down my fourteen year old Collie. The grief that followed cut me as deep as any parent's loss, I would tell you. No one will ever tell me otherwise. I was there, sickened by its empty weight for months. And then some. Same as you, I think. Same as Jimmy."

"Point taken. I meant no harm."

"Know where I never see you questioning your purpose, Mark? Those boys."

"That's because I've no history with them to foul it up."

"A year ago that argument might have been true. But not today, friend."

"Time will tell, Sally. No way you'll change your mind about going over with me to see him?"

"No, no way. I'd do most anything either of you asked of me. But not this."

"Mind if I ask why?"

"I won't be a moth to his flame. When he's thru feeling sorry for himself, he'll have my full attention."

"Alright then. Well, I better let the boys know I'll be gone most of the day."

In Sally's kitchen, I told Juan I had business that would keep me away most of the day.

"You think you and Danny can keep busy on your own today?"

"Yes, sir. Anything else you need from us?"

"Keep little brother from falling down the hill with his pail and shovel, will you."

"I can only promise you I won't push him."

"Good enough."

"Be safe, Mr. Jacobs."

"Why wouldn't I?"

In the jag of each breaking wave the coldest of melodies brought back Jessie's face. Her arms struggling to fight off the waxy pulse which hung within the crest of each new wave. The edge of her ending opening her eyes white with fear, her breathing so panicked, so far away from the shore-line's black porridge, that her body had been reduced to a single breath to swallow all other desperate voices within her. Taken from us. Taken into that unknown bleakness where no language speaks to us of a rebirth.

Until I revisited the body of water where Jessie's body had been recovered, on the far side of Depot Island, so much of my fiction had sustained me. It brings to mind a belief that in the making of all things read and witnessed a vanquishing of so many other constructions must die. Is it the same for my wife?

Dear Mark,

To tell you of the richness of my days here, to speak of the turquoise colors which wash each breaking wave, there is not enough ink in my pen. Could I bottle the Tasman Sea's earliest light, toss it thru a canyon of tree ferns to the other side of the world, and find you

*reaching for it on a beach of your own choosing? It is a new begin-
ning for me here, Mark.*

*The variety of plants and birds to be found here are simply
amazing. Crocheted sails of every shade of green imaginable. Giant
palms and tree ferns wrap the trunks of California redwood trees
like bracelets of jade! Tell Red and Anna that no sail and mast has
ever been better matched, or more oddly united, with the world of
water than on this South Pacific island of opposites.*

*I have rented a small cabin at the bottom of a canyon of spin-
dly tea trees, and each morning I step onto a crib of a beach. The
cabin is called a bach and intermittingly has running water and
working electricity (Peter, the property's caretaker, is working diligently to fix the frequent and startling surprises of 'cold-cold' water
which come from the outdoor shower and often stay cold for days
and days). Peter and Gwenda live in a splendid house on the rim
of an amazing canyon of tree ferns overlooking the sea, and when
the wind blows down thru the canyon the groves of giant ferns
practically swallow my bach whole. Their house becomes a living
mezzanine of plants and birds when they fold back the home's floor-
to-ceiling doors, and you cannot imagine a better view in the world.
The ocean shines green and blue from every perch and window, oh,
and the feathers of 'cheeky' parrots pull more colors from the ocean
waves than words could describe. Tomorrow the three of us may fish
together from a line that runs first to a kite in the sky, and then to
the water line and places below, which Peter tells me "only the fishes
and me-ancestors have ever visited."*

*How to say this? How to shape the heart of this letter without
hurting you? So difficult for me to put the past in writing, for once
on paper it speaks with an agony not entirely of my own making.
Do you think that way, too?*

*It has been a year of secrets for each of us. Too much of our
loving history has been buried by the carrying of so much pain. I
would ask, as you turn the page, that you remember our history,*

remember all that binds us and trust that there is only love and kindness in my heart for you.

About a month before her death, by chance or fate, I happened to run into Jessie at one of the malls in Seattle (I've often spoken to Jimmy about that chance meeting, and neither of us believes Jessie had any association with those thugs prior to that day). She was passing out flyers of hatred for that despicable cult, flaunting the whole idea of being seen tramping about the mall with men preaching bigotry and racism. She actually pretended not to know me. The anger of witnessing such a betrayal, the scar it has left on my memory of her, the scar it has left on me. I slapped her, Mark, slapped her repeatedly until she had fallen from my anger and my blindness.

I knew of the two of you long before the tragedy of her death. Your mood would darken like a stone whenever I was in your presence. But Jessie, she could lift you out of a slump and put a shine in your eyes whenever she was with us. Your betrayal was difficult enough for me to bear, Mark. But Jessie's, her betrayal, so close to the time of her death, was insurmountable for me.

Dianna

In the deep channel of ocean water, which was cutting its tidal course thru the mountainous cliffs and high bank terrain of two islands, far below the squalor of Jimmy's encampment, I pointed the bow of my boat away from the channel's main current and towards the neckline of a sheltered cove. Once inside the cove, the sea churned more quietly against the boat's hull, breathing out wide pancake waves that barely wet the enormous ledges of surrounding shoreline stone.

In the cove, the boat was hidden from all sight lines the dump's trestle bridge may have offered an observer. And sheltered behind the cove's cape of pine-topped rock, which separated its nested waters from the channel's chop, any boat anchored here was not easily spotted from the decks of any ferryboat making passage thru this deep water inlet.

After anchoring the boat, I rowed the small rowboat that Red had outfitted my boat with to shore, and tied off the sailboat's bowline to the trunk of a saw-cut madrona. A steep, shadowy, rudimentary trail had been cut from the thick shoreline salal, since last I'd hiked down the hilly mountainside from Jimmy's camp.

At the top of the trail, the stale day-old breath of the dump feels like the treasure hunter's fished out pond that it is. Tires scattered everywhere. Tractor tires, lawn mower tires, plastic tires snapped from lawn furniture warped and oxidized by a summer's yellowing. A wheelbarrow tire, dead on its side against its sleeve of warped steel. Toy tires, broken and burnt. Two halves of a playground's warped merry-go-round. The tires on the spoke wheels of a baby carriage looking as thin and hardened as segments of old putty peeled from a shaky windowpane.

At the shack's entrance, a piece of chain-link fencing has been strapped to the opening's wooden header and then rolled across the blue tarp covering the shack's flat roof. A piece of galvanized roofing gutter has been squashed flat, unfolded, and used to make a sign of warning. The flayed metal sign looking as if it's been formed in pounding, hurricane preparedness. Nailed to the sign's metal lettering, a severed top from a soup can forms the letter 'O' in the first word. Two snap-rings from soda pop cans have been used to dot the eyes in the sign's second word. Three feet in length and a foot wide, the run of letters waffle its melancholic warning with a green and white finish of spray-painted penmanship. All this mindless work so that Jimmy's idea of island folk art can post his bitterness: *No swimming.*

More knee-deep trenches had been dug around the shack's footprint of a foundation, most all of them connecting with the cheeriness of the creek. The creek water, which had filled one of the larger T-bone trenches, looks to have been polluted and painted with kerosene oil. And, in one of the half-finished trenches, nearest a tilting corner of the shack, the surface water endures the drubbing of two, quart-sized oil cans — each of the oil cans punctured numerous times and about to sink to the bottom of the stinky ditch.

Inside the shack, I placed the supplies I'd bought for Jimmy on the large wooden utility spool, covering the grocery bags with the clean new tarp I'd brought with me. It's hot and fly-ridden inside the shack. The air parched and brown and streaked with a current of ash and fiberglass filaments. Squashed and cornered by the shack's three walls, my body feels like it's a tin thermometer that's here to measure the sticky highs of my friend's day. The flies buzzing my head move like skaters thru the air's glaze, pitching and swaying, or suddenly lighting and climbing the wobble of a dark corner like smelt laddering the shallows of the Sandy River. The flies crawl over the plugs of crumpled newspaper on the shack's chicken-wire walls, tracing the sugary scents of something old and musty and fried, their marbled bodies lazily performing a kind of injured and intoxicated traipsing as they pick at the occasional microbe of suspended nutrition. Flies hovering above the wooden spool in orbiting clumps of scouting, conjuring, antagonizing spins and circles. Bulging, helmeted, green-eyed aliens — these flies — each one keeping tabs on any decomposing thing that might be born of Jimmy's trail.

Outside the cell walls of the shack, the dump feels like a sanctuary.

For the better part of the afternoon, I wait for Jimmy's appearance to rise from the smear of sunlight and dust twirling over the floor of the dump. Watch the same two trucks regularly returning to rumble their loads thru the dump's open gate. The cabs of each of these trucks bearing mostly the drab colors of primer paint, their damaged beds rattling clear down to their rusted-thru fenders as they bounce and roll across the rutted dump, their clutches slipping and grinding after emptying their loads and winding their way back to the gate, where, for some reason, the trucks will jerk to a halt just outside the dump's entrance, and always, the two young drivers laugh and switch trucks.

With each passing hour of the dump's quiet life, I watch the same two trucks come and go. Watch the tires on each truck deepen the trenched trails in the dump's earth, as their heavy loads bounce like floating shanties on a flood-crested river. Watch the trail dust, about to gather voice and direction outside the rear window of each driver, rise and fall over the dump's trash whenever the truck tires spin and sing.

By four in the afternoon, both trucks are back again. Each driver jostling one arm over his steering wheel while leaving his other arm to hang from the truck window — arms like tree limbs about to sweep an endless ravine of human debris. Both trucks loaded and roped from cab roof to earth-scraping trailer hitch, their jittery truck beds humping up-ended handlebars, ski poles, mattresses, some pitted and peeling red-rusted barbeque lids, one-half of *Dusty's* dog house, and a mountain of rimless tires. One driver raising his arm to half-salute to me, as the two trucks race to cross paths in a clownish game of chicken. This will be their last load of the day, and in their National Guard uniforms both drivers look overdressed for what has been a clanking, pouncing, tire-vaulting party of a shift.

After the trucks had gone, Jimmy appeared bareback and squatting on the trestle bridge. In his hands is a long piece of steel pipe, which he is holding like a kayak paddle and alternately tapping against each iron rail until it seems he is satisfied that I have seen him. Rising to his feet, I watched him step closer to the edge of the bridge's wooden ties. Standing the pipe he'd been holding on end, he took hold of it with both hands — the way a parent might hold onto the swim shirt of a child about to enter the precipice of his first dive — and let go of the pipe. Both of us as still as perched hawks watching the long tube of steel topple from the bridge, end-over-end, soundlessly falling, until it landed straight up in the stony wash of the creek bed like a hunter's spear.

A goat trail, cut from the trestle's embankment of gorse and thistle, led Jimmy back down to the dump floor. He headed straight for the creek, made his way up the middle of a shallow current as if he were trying to conceal his tracks from something chasing him, avoiding my stare, eyeballing the dump's new playing field of Saturday trash as his footsteps splashed against a new bend of rippling current. In one of his hands, a rope I'd not seen twisted up and around one of his forearms. An orchestra playing inside his head.

"What else you learned how to do out here this week?" I called out to him. "Your cat and your rat gonna jump thru a ring of fire for me tonight?"

From the creek, Jimmy feigned a disfigured smile but would not answer me.

When he hopped out of the creek bed, it was to walk to the backside of his shack and take hold of his chin-up bar. He looked in my direction long enough for me to mark the dark color of his mood, then he jumped and took hold of the lashed chin-up bar.

Jimmy's body strained to finish his first five chin-ups,

his biceps swelling to hold the seamless line of his levitating body, a greasy sweat running like a line of marching red ants over his sunburned cheeks and temples. He turned his eyes on me, briefly showing me the teeth of his strength, and performed the next twenty chin-ups effortlessly — the skin on his neck and arching throat thumbtacked with radish colored rings and blisters from what appeared to be self-inflicted burns. Closer up, an embryo of a blister covered a clover-shaped burn beneath his right ear, and another covered a four-point burn on the back of his right hand. He'd torn away the penciling scab on his right cheekbone, and the baying flesh had become sunbaked and was now displaying a slat of pink, unhealed skin beneath his cobbled beard. Eyes drooping with the crust of some sleepless time revisited, his cross-raked brow carrying the pulp of dirt and rubric rubbings of dried blood, Jimmy coughed up three more chin-ups.

A few yards from the camp's fire, a small portion of the creek's course had been asked to alter a new line away from its central current. Water now circled the rocks that Jimmy had placed in the center of the creek's shallow course, in order to help channel some of the creek into his foolish irrigation ditches. Center creek, on one of the wet and nested stones, a pair of socks rested in a kind of poisoned fetal position. The stretched socks looking as worn out as the papery guitar case that lay inside a child's broken rainbow crib Jimmy had placed up stream. The wind, too, seemed to have been aggravated by the new presence of so much human lingering in its path. It had washed the reedy grasses along the creek bank with so much dust and ash it seemed snow had fallen, or that more fire than was customary in the dump had ignited.

"You start this piddling-ass fire?"

"How about a cup of coffee and a piece of pie?"

By the fire, Jimmy lifted his rug from the back of the truck seat, folded it some, and tossed it over the seat's exposed springs. He looked across the creek at the slashing of blackberry vines, then at Sally's tanks and torches he'd strapped to the alder tree. A padlock secured the chain knot holding the tanks to the tree's moss laden trunk.

Closing in on his truck seat, a cumbersome chainsaw lay on its side on one corner of a wet and paltry mattress. The saw looked like a tired beast digesting last night's kill. Its loose chain stretched out over splinters of bone and mayhem, its belly sloshing and excreting body fluids when Jimmy moved to kick it upright. The cap on the saw's punctured fuel tank had been screwed on cockeyed and looked chewed. A mixture of oil and water and gasoline had leaked from the tank's wrapping of electrical tape, and soaked thru much of the mattress.

The old rug formed a mealy pleat, giving it the look of a blotted bandage, when Jimmy slumped back into his seat. A smear of green paint on his chest had dried and had clumped some of his chest hair. Over his cutoffs, and along his dirty thighs, a few more finger-strokes of the paint had given his legs the caged look of a vandalized Pollock painting. He shuffled in his seat and sat up, and after tossing more wood onto the fire, reached under his seat for a wrinkly plastic bag which he threw onto the mattress. He smiled watching how I was watching him, then whistled a series of sing-song notes at the passing wind. As soon as he'd stopped, Danny's stray crawled out from the blackberry. The cat hopped the creek, sniffing its way towards the grubby mattress, studying me, sometimes skittishly side-winding if my body made even the slightest of shifts. Once the cat had found the bag of food Jimmy had thrown on the mattress, the animal began pawing at the plastic slit in the side of the sealed bag, the stray's efforts pulling electrified snapping sounds from the bag which seemed to put another smile on Jimmy's face. In half a minute, the cat had widened the slit in the bag, and managed to carry away the chunk of half-burned charcoal briquette wrapped with a leaf of fish skin and the severed head of a fish.

"That cat needs a home."

Jimmy fingered his matted hair. "Are you black or blind?"

"There's cat food on the table in the shack. See that you share some of it."

"You going to try and save us both now?"

"Those burns on your neck, you put them there?"

He lifted his feet off the ground, tightened his stomach muscles, straightened and held his legs out over the wing-less fire, and began to speak quietly from the memory of a distant childhood.

"You and I have been brought up to endure pain. Always, they told us to endure. But the mind grows tired of such an expectation. And the body, the body has a will all its own anyways."

"Maybe it's time you made your way home."

"Maybe. I think about facing that direction sometimes. I do."

"Not today though, right?"

"You may have been someone's angel once, Mark. But you're not mine."

No, if I had been someone's angel I'd have fallen and gone with her into those weeping waters. I'd have sipped the color of death cradled warm and waxy by a mirrored sun, and lay forever with the tears of my lover.

When Jimmy's legs fell back to earth, he lifted his eyes from the fire and locked his gaze on the mangled crib he'd placed upstream.

"After the death of our child, I would do most anything to — to avoid being left alone in a room with my wife."

"Because you blamed her. Some did, as I remember."

"No. Because it's for each of us to decide how much pain we can bear. I couldn't bear my own and hers too. I couldn't."

"Anyone who knew you would have understood."

"Maybe. I think about it that way sometimes. That it should have been — that it should have been that easily understood. No, I was wrong to do such a thing. There was a kind of betrayal in the way I left her alone with her sadness. Of that, everyone felt."

The dump seemed to moan as the last of a preemptive light darkened her earthen floor. Dusk, green and golden, wishing only to descend upon our camp. Far from the fire, some brown bottles lay off to the side of a frozen tire rut, unbroken for a time, in its swale of settled dust. On the southern horizon, a few stars cajoled with the last of the sunset's fisted line of light. The voice in my head growing louder and speaking of *another's* truth awakened — *that the missing and the dead return to us their fullest and longest hour remembered within that thin black line which holds back night to come from day determined.*

Jimmy lifted his feet over the fire once more, tightening his washboard stomach muscles as he stretched his legs over an eruption of new flame.

"When is she coming back? Where did she go?" His teeth tightening on the requiem of each word.

"Come back with me. We can talk this out. We can find a way, you and me, to somehow live with this."

"Ain't that what we been doing?"

"Christ Jimmy, if I had a white flag I'd wave it."

"You wouldn't. And I wouldn't want you to."

"I loved her so much."

"I know you did."

"You're right to hold me accountable, for all my life."

"I've never once have thought about you that way."

"You ever want out, Jimmy?

"I am out."

The scarcity of human voice on his apocalyptic stage.

"Maybe you are."

I said goodnight to him and crossed over the creek. Disappeared thru a rip in the darkness that would take me back to my boat. Called out to him from beneath the sweep of a tree branch.

"Quit tattooing your body with fire. You're good looks are about all we got left in our bank account."

Work at the *Campground* rolled over us with a discipline and orderliness that made it easy for us to put in ten, sometimes twelve hour days, days of solitude with fewer and fewer interruptions from the street. Her new ribs set and fastened — a poled framework of beautifully knotted, skinless logs stretching their autumn colors upwards to the bell tower — the new *Campground* was becoming "ship-shape on dry land," as Danny liked to put it.

On most days, we ceased all use of power tools by mid-afternoon and concentrated on quieter work. The boys spending the last hours of their work day collecting lumber scraps for Sally's fire pits and raking out the ridges in Ike and Tom's tractor grading, while I worked alone on the *Campground's* weedy slope. I'd begun replanting and terracing sections of her eroding hillside, adding the native plants, which Jackie had dug for me, to the open ground around the older azaleas and umbrella maples that had survived the fire. Danny had scrubbed and washed away the last of the fire's soot from every hillside boulders, and now the small truckload of dwarf conifers that I'd purchased could be planted alongside the outcroppings of hillside rock. Norwegian weeping spruce, bird's nest spruce, tiered hemlocks, golden mops, and stone pine — each of these dwarf trees, strikingly colorful and contorted in form, would provide exclamation to the weave of Japanese blood grass we'd planted, in the hopes that it might one day spread uphill from the courtyard. The *Campground's* garden had come back and people had taken notice. Even the tallest of our oldest trees, the clump birches, which had lost their leaves in the fire's whip-sawing heat, had cheered us on by throwing new buds.

For the boys, the pace at which the *Campground* was being rebuilt was not always an encouraging and satisfying thing to sign off on. Summer was threatening to push its unwanted ending out from under their lucrative routines, stalking their coiling of extension cords, ropes, and red licorice with a little too much mention of the school days that lay ahead. August had long since docked and anchored, and just off shore, September was winking that its turn was coming.

All week long, Danny had been chatting up a storm about ideas he had for the *Campground's* interior, ideas which could only be explored and fully appreciated by one more trip to Seattle.

"When's Ike and the boys coming back to put up the walls? Hey, maybe while you're waiting on them we should make a run back to Seattle and have another look around. There was that salvage company down on the waterfront. Remember. We could buy some of them old oars, cheap I bet. Cut the handle ends down, shorten them up some, and use 'em halfway up on all your new walls. It could look crazy good that way, it could you know. Hey, you turn every other one of them oars upside down on the wall and you know what you got, Mr. J? You got *'wanes-coating.'* That's what old *Ike the mike* says."

"Hey Juan?" From the hillside, I offered both boys my unsolicited opinion. "Ever notice how much *we* there is living inside Danny's head lately?"

Juan looked up from the Washington state driver's manual he'd been studying over lunch break.

"*We* be back in school by the time that job needs doing, Dan?"

"Hey, if the boss ain't going back why should we? I say we follow suit, like Jimmy-boy did."

"Mr. Jacobs didn't take us to Seattle and back to have you go stupid on us, Dan. Besides, both him and me got a feeling this is going to be your year to shine in school."

"You really say that, Mr. J?"

"I might of."

"Hey, just so you know. We ain't giving up on you when school starts up. We got Saturday-Sundays off for the rest of our sorry lives, you know."

"If I had a bell I'd ring it for you, Dan." I said.

Danny shook out his red hair and brushed off the back of his arms. "Is that something I'm supposed to think about all afternoon, Teach?"

"Shovel the gravel first."

"Then what?"

"Get yourself to the bell tower. Get yourself ah-ringing."

"Huh?"

"So when are Ike and Tom coming back?" Juan asked.

"They're not. Their work is done here."

"No way. There's tons of building left to do."

"That's up to Jimmy to decide now. We've brought him as close to home as we could."

"You mean we're just gonna leave her in the middle of the street with no cloths on? That don't seem right."

"*Doesn't.*" I corrected him. "Doesn't seem right."

From the courtyard, Father Jerald's penny loafers careened over the stone in a collection of clicks. An unsolicited wind climbed with him up the slope, and when the priest reached the top of the hill the man stood straight as an arrow up against my backside.

"Mark, we must talk."

"Must we?"

"Please. About the configuration of your tavern's new roof."

"Too late, the architect has left the site."

"My God, man, are you after the wrath of the entire community? Putting a roof on this tavern that intentionally mocks a church steeple!"

"A vision from God, father."

"Bullshit."

"Who's to say? Not you. Not this day."

"So you are out to provoke a battle with the community? A community that had nothing to do with the actions of those men."

"Think of it as a gift. A crown for your precious community."

The priest scoffed. The square foot of hillside between us, quiet but for the slip of my shovel blade in the hole I'd been digging.

"And the bell? Is it true what the boy tells me?"

"Every last word. Purchased by the blood of a boy's body. Shipped in from Seattle by the cross of some other's fallow regret. But don't you fret, father, we're all the better for it."

"You put that bell in that tower, and you will accomplish nothing but a provocation."

"You've got that pointing stick of yours turned wrong way 'round again."

"No, I have not."

The permanence of wounds spoken of, the seed of presumption it plants in each of us. I stuck my shovel hard into the ground and looked up to face the arrogance of my accuser.

"Where was the community's wrath when those stump-fucks set up camp on this island? Crouching in your Sunday pews all year, was it? The wrath of *my* community? I'd like to see such a wrath."

"You are arrogant if you believe you can judge the people of this community in colors absolute, Mark. You know better than to pass such a judgment."

"And you are ignorant to think there is always a space between black and white. Priest."

In the *Campground's* back yard, the sunlight shined on Danny's bell bright as an Easter break. But on the hillside before us, where the priest and I had locked horns, the earth slipped suddenly into a dark fold of shade at my feet.

"No Mark, I am not. I am not ignorant, nor am I naïve of a path so justly chosen, so black or white as you so eloquently have shoved it in my face. But there is not a speck of light, divine or earthly, to be salvaged from the bleaker choice you are making. It is a choice I would expect from a man weaker in spirit than yours. Those criminals may have fallen, rightly so, into your doctrine of black and white. But this community is not deserving of such a judgment. I'm asking only that you reconsider the symbolism of your roof's construction, both physically and spiritually. And I make my request to you with all due respect, and in the spirit of Christ."

"So was the boy's. The bell in the tower? That stays."

A thousand yards away from the mountainside concealing Jimmy's camp, our boat's hull slapped at the icy white spray opening wide the foul mouth of the channel. A sea of iron behind us. Ahead of us, the day's best light about to be swallowed up by the Sound's patrolling, shark-skin skies. Smiling, we motored on.

Twilight, always an atoll far from these preaching waters.

The boys and I had agreed it was better to navigate our own house of cards, sink or swim, than suffer one more lashing from the eyes and lips of shuttled gamblers. No more of their suffocating smoke and chatter for us. No more conspicuous crossings thru its pandering parking lots and candy-cane petunia beds. We would make our own passage, and anchor in the wash of a cove more stimulating than any gambler's wide-eyed anticipation could fathom.

By the time we'd climbed up the mountainside and reached the dump creek, a stew of bullhead stars had emerged from the prowling clouds that raced across the northern skies. A fleecing rain had come and gone and made a paste of the dump floor, and there was still the threat of more rain to come from the low cloud cover battering most of the island.

Danny quickly left my side and ran ahead to investigate everything new he'd spotted about Jimmy's camp. He stopped, first, outside the door of Jimmy's shack, kneeling to inspect a shadowy square of green earth less bleak than the mess around it.

"He-eey! Lookey here." The boy patted the green ground with his palm. "He's got strawberries planted like mad. Over here, see 'em? He's cut the ends off of all these soup cans. See here? That's so he can keep a bunch more of the heat in around the roots. That's smart. But it's too late for growing strawberries. Season's over, mate."

A maze of spidering trenches surrounded Jimmy's strawberry patch. Each trench was filled with water, and the surface water in one of the widest ditches slewed a film of blue oil.

Danny jumped each of the trenches until he stood next to the camp's sputtering fire. The same chainsaw lay on its side, on the same mattress, its open fuel tank too close to the fire's edge. Danny dragged the saw back from the fire and capped the tank, mumbling some obscenity before hurrying to cross over to the other side of the creek.

"God, look at all the tires he's found." The boy fumbled to pull a tire shaped like a slice of melon from the weave of a greater pile of roofing shingles and rotten lumber. "Talk about a guy that lives for changing a flat. Crap, what's this? God, there's some kind of nasty painted all over the outsides of them Juan."

"What is it?"

"It ain't your neighbor's nice cologne, that's for sure." Danny answered with a belch.

Juan pointed at the collection of steel drums across the creek.

"What's with all those empty oil drums?"

Along the grassy edge of the creek, a fence line of steel drums and stacked tires had made its way towards the trunk of the alder tree. Some of the drums had been crudely brushed with several layers of paint. Others looked to have been painted with a mixture of oil and kerosene. A single drum lay on its side, apart from the all the others, and was tagged and surrounded by a scattering of empty paint cans. The barrel of this drum bore the crude image of a human head hovering above the stickman shape of its pink and purple amputated body.

Beneath the alder's split canopy of leaf, a ring of six fifty-five gallon drums had been tied to the tree's ax-scratched trunk; the barrel of every standing drum snared by two tire halves, and the severed ends of each tire-half punctured and strung with twisted remnants of wire so as to connect and hold the two halves around the barrel of the drum. Looped over the sawed off stubs of the alder's lowest branches, coils of rope, garden hose, and barbed wire dangled in an apparent free for all. A tattered tow line collared the bulk of the steel drum collection, and where the reach of the first tow line had petered out, a frayed piece of nylon rope had been joined to swing like a horse's loose lead over the trampled grass and vines before being tied chest-high to the blackberry.

"Night lights!"

Jimmy had stepped out of his shack and made his way unnoticed to the fire, his voice startling us but good as we'd stood spellbound by the bizarre assembly of so many painted drums.

"In case I want to go fishing in the fog."

Jimmy's explanation spoken as if he were calling some serpent out of the darkness. One of his hands wielding a knife, and a piece of rubber tubing, which he waved at us when we turned to face him.

Danny was deep in the math of finger counting the drums when Jimmy's voice had jarred him. The boy shrugged, flashed me a two-handed finger count, and walked back to the fire.

"Why'd you cut all the car tires in half, Jimmy?"

Jimmy flopped onto his truck seat and spoke into the fire. His eyes bug-eyed and the glow of his face rubbed with oil and paint and sweat.

"It's a net I'm making, nosey boy."

"Where you gonna go fishing with it? This little sweetheart of a stream?"

"I've said too much already."

"I see you got your strawberries in. What's that over there you got planted by the creek?" Danny pointed and poked his chin out at a mounded patch of weeds and what looked like a row of young corn stalks.

"Planted me some white daisies. They gonna bloom in the winter and shine like golden cat eyes. See how I arranged them? Planted them in the shape of a child's skull. Best you take that lesson with you now and go off to bed, Rooster."

"What else you got new around here?"

"Planted Iris and Lilly on the other side of the stream. Put 'em in the ground last night. Put 'em in deep, up to their ears."

"What are they?"

"Old girlfriends that tired of my preaching. Walk downstream a ways, sometime. Maybe you'll spot one of 'em crying by all those pretty tombstones I been carving. Thought it was Easter Sunday when I begun digging. Real reason went up in smoke by the time I'd found my way home."

Danny looked perplexed, or frightened.

"It's not Easter. But it was the fourth of July in Seattle a while back. What you doing with the knife and the bicycle tube? Fixing a surprise party for Joe?"

"Planning my parade," Jimmy rubbed at his poached eyes and coughed us up another riddle. "Want to be in it, kid?"

Danny moved back from the fire to take up a stance alongside Juan. The boy's fingers testing the nail point of a spindly trash stick he'd picked up and drawn close to his eyes.

"Like on a holiday or something?" Danny chirped.

"I've already said too much. But if it does float — gonna cast a fish net behind it."

"You'll have to get permission from the tribal counsel to do that here. Won't he, Juan?"

"They'll approve. I pay half their utilities bill. You forgotten?"

"Why'd you put that crib in the creek?" Danny asked. "Personal reasons, I suppose?"

"Orders from the tribe. Came in over the wires when I couldn't sleep."

"Just what we need, huh Jimmy? Another government fish ladder. Know what you could really use way out here? You ought to have a radio, you really should."

"I make the news, I don't listen for it."

"But a decent radio can be real good company. Then for certain you'd be on your way again. Music can do that. It did it for me when I was in Seattle."

"You're uncooked, lad. Get yourself some sleep. Tomorrow we swim the channel."

"No thanks. You know your rug is kind of cock-eyed? Want me help you fix it?" Danny now held the point of his trash stick close to his chest while he spoke, as if considering its use as a weapon.

"Me and this old rug, kid. Helps me remember that I'm a ship-in-a-bottle. Now get yourself inside the shack. Go on now. And put another record on the radio when you get inside. One that's not all scratched up this time."

"Why you want me inside the shack? For being too entertaining on a Saturday night or something?"

"Go in the shack like I told you."

"Alright, but just to see if you done the dishes."

Inside the shack Danny called out, "where's the light switch?"

"Down the hall. Last door on your right if you're a Christian." Jimmy cracked his second smile over the fire since we'd arrived. "Otherwise, there ain't no light at all."

"What am I looking for?"

"Peanuts on the half shell. Bring us out a couple bags."

Danny came back to the fire with two bags of peanuts. He opened one bag and passed it around.

"We're some bunch of hobos, aren't we? Too bad we ain't got any beer and popcorn too."

Fumbling to keep hold of both the knife and tire tube in one hand, Jimmy's free arm reached under the truck seat. He pulled out a box of store bought cat food, shook it a bunch, and tossed the box at Danny's feet.

"Mind feeding that stray for me tonight, Rooster?"

"Okay."

"Oh, and Danny."

"Yeah?"

"Water seeks its own level. Try and remember that when you're pushing a stroller."

"I'll probably forget."

"Touché, Danny." I said with a grim smile.

A lacework of squash vines had twisted one of its monkey tail vines around one of the steel barrels, near the shack door. Up came the head of a black and white Manx to peek out at us from under a squash leaf. The cat's nose cleverly ratcheting its slinky body into a wider opening of leaf. Its round head swaying from side to side, and its eyes settling on us like the slash of a sudden rain about to snuff out a fire's night smoke, Danny's stray pounced free of the squash vines.

"How's your house of cards treating you these days?" I asked.

"Money's water, that's all it is." And repeating his sorrowful mantra, his body rocked with a bout of coughing.

"You gonna run that cough of yours to death, before you go see a doctor?"

"Your good friend — Father Jerald — he stopped by this week. Wanted to know if my life at the dump brought me joy. If it brought joy to others in my life. What a prick in a robe he is. Told him so."

"How'd he take to that?"

"Not well. Took to my scotch well enough, though. What's left of the bottle is inside. Take it with you, if you want."

"No thanks."

"All week long, two-legged animals been stopping by. Old friends, they say. Liars for all I know. I don't know any of them. They don't know me."

"People from town really come all the way out here to see you?" Danny asked, while shaking kernels of cat food onto a piece of cardboard.

"Can't be sure where they were from. Had their backs to me, and mine to theirs, the whole time they were sniffing around."

"They were probably afraid. On account of how you look, I mean."

The nail on the end of Danny's trash-stick, which the boy was using as a brace to hold a wooden towel bar upright in the fire, lost its hold and the towel bar tumbled from the flames.

"See there, Jimmy?" Danny touched his stick to the smoking towel bar. "That's like the fire's agreeing with me or something."

"Some others have been snooping around inside my shack. When I'm gone. And more been banging on my painted drums when they think I'm not watching. You know anything about that, Rooster?"

"I know my dad drank big time and saw things that weren't there sometimes." Danny had left the fire and returned to the pile of cat food on the cardboard, where he'd begun to make the shape of a cat's head with eyes, ears, and long whiskers out of the kernels. "Once he made me keep drinking with him until I threw it all up. That's the lesson he wanted to teach me about boozing, I guess. He probably don't know I forgot it."

"A father's mistake, son. Best you forget all about it and get on with taming that lion now."

Jimmy stood and stuck his knife into the rug which lay over the back of the shoddy truck seat. Over the handle of the stuck knife, he draped what was left of the bicycle tube he'd been cutting into three-foot long strips. Satisfied, he limped to the farthest outside corner of the shack, jumped for his chin-up bar, and grunted out twenty-two perfect chin-ups. When he'd finished his performance he let go of the bar, placed one hand against the shack and the other across his stomach, and prepared to endure another red-faced bout of wretched coughing.

I shelled more peanuts by the fire, watching Jimmy's coughing spell pound and shake the wire and wood of the shack wall, the moths living beneath the shack's flat tin roof scattering to flutter above his chopped head of hair. The winged creatures bumping at his sweat-lined temples and hairline like pollinating bees. His coughing had frightened the cat, too. The animal snarling and showing its tiger teeth at the thrashing, possessed shack, before running the creek bank upstream and crossing into the thorny undergrowth.

"Best you don't smoke around my drums tonight, Chief." Jimmy lifted his head, wiped his mouth of its stickiness with the back of his hand, eyes rushing the fire and jumping the creek to fixate on the empty oil drums Juan was revisiting.

"Christ Jimmy," I said, "all there is up here is smoke."

He scoffed. "Smoke don't bother me none. *Boom* might. Best you keep your boys on this side of the creek. Paint and kerosene on those drums take a long time to dry in this salt air."

Juan and Jimmy walked back to the fire and seated themselves in unison, a tossup as to whose face was pitching more defiance. Reaching for the handle of his knife, Jimmy hesitated, then threw Juan a grin and pulled the blade out of the rug. He saddled the bicycle tube over his knees, his hands inspecting and rubbing whatever good rubber he could find between the tubing's many pink patches. He pressed his knees together over the tubing's stem, stretched out a ruler length of rubber, and began cutting another lashing from the gutted bicycle tube. His knife cuts were slow and precise, and between cuts he used the point of the knife to stab at pieces of petrified strawberry from the jam jar he'd wedged into one of the coiled springs in his truck seat, sometimes quietly cursing at the knuckled stickiness that would not leave his fingers even after he'd licked them and wiped the hand on the rug's filth.

The boys and I ate our peanuts and watched the tip of Jimmy's knife cut away more of the tubing. After each cut, he flung the strips of rubber over his shoulders, where they landed with an uncanny degree of accuracy on the greasy surface water shining from the trenches behind him.

From the black quiet of the canyon, a sapless wind spoke up. The wind barely bottling the needles of pines growing tall by the bridge's poled legs, but shaping easily the lazy smoke in the branches of the pine into images of shiftless, ghostly drifters hoping to make their way down the canyon to our campfire, moving like a great migration over Jimmy's sorrowful camp, and riling his concentration when it gathered to flush curly chips of Styrofoam from a squashed tire rut, wistfully making the scratches and scabs on Jimmy's hands and face look less injurious and more an incurable condition that befalls all animals that take up a hazardous life in a landfill.

The wind slipped out of Jimmy's camp as meekly as it had funneled down upon us, my friend's harlequin grin tracking its path across the rutted dump and thru the gate to the brittleness of broken alder that shielded the dump's entrance from the highway. His eyes corrosive and lost looking — eyes like those of a sick animal hopelessly searching where no hope can be found — before releasing his stare and dipping the blade of his knife into a second glass jar by his side, only to withdraw it quickly and flick a few drops of the jar's waxy blue fuel at the flames. The fire playing its part well, swallowing the liquid fuel and growing green teeth, shape-shifting more colors before hissing and farting dishwater-blue smoke into the night sky.

Jimmy's grin widened, pleased to see how the fresh sting of kerosene fumes blossomed frowns under our noses.

"Leave the fire alone." I snapped. "Christ, the oceans are beginning to boil."

Ignoring me, he sought Danny's attention.

"Don't mind him, Rooster. That's just father grief worn him down. It's you I need to know we can count on. Well, answer me. You with us or not? Because when all you do is chase after that stray and talk about popcorn, I think maybe you don't have the feathers for it. I get to thinking maybe you ain't up to chasing down what's gonna swim up that channel one of these nights. Hey, I'm talking to you. You forgotten what you're a part of boy?"

Danny went pale. His eyes trotted over the ground at his feet like California quail running for cover.

"That's enough, Jimmy."

"I guess maybe I'm with Juan. And Juan's with Mr. J on most things. So I guess I'm with him too."

"Hiding in plain sight. That's what our enemy is doing, gentlemen." He walked his fingers over his thighs and into the air. "Someone ought to slip them a helping hand. Somebody else going to have to pluck them out of the deep blue sea."

Fog was rolling in and beginning to build under the trestle. It folded over itself like a theater curtain, and made the sky high rails appear to float in a sky of black treetops and the occasional, distant headlight.

"You think the Campground fire eased their hunger to inflict pain on us?" Jimmy's voice broke strong thru the cooling night. "Worst kind of terrorist, they are. Think it's their country, not yours."

"I guess I'll head home now, Mr. Jacobs. I'll see you at the Campground on Monday."

Juan had been standing near me the whole time. When he'd spoken my name, I'd playfully pulled at the scruff of denim around his kneecap.

"Alright, Juan. Thanks for all your hard work today. There's no way Danny and I could have done half of it without you."

"Sure thing. Goodnight Jimmy."

The springs in the truck seat cupped out a dry squeak as Jimmy's butt skidded over the seat's torn vinyl to reach for Juan's other pant leg. He patted the boy's leg roughly.

"Goodnight, Juan Rodriguez."

From my pocket, I pulled out two sealed envelopes from my pocket. I handed both envelopes to Juan.

"Would you see that your mothers get these? Their names are on the envelopes."

"Sure. Okay."

"What's inside? Our walking papers?"

"No. Nothing but praise and admiration, I assure you."

Juan was about to step back from the fire, but the fingers on Jimmy's knife hand pinched a bit of the boy's denim more firmly and held the boy's leg in place.

"I'll stop as many as I can, Juan. But even so, a few are likely to come ashore."

"Wait, I'm going too." Danny piped up.

"Hold up, Rooster. What's your hurry?"

"I can't."

"What say you and I walk this little creek down to the ocean and push a few of my drums out to sea?"

"I can't. I'm supposed to be home tonight."

"Let go of Juan's leg, Jimmy. The man needs to get home."

"Sure. Sure, okay."

Danny dug his dump-picking stick deep into the center of the fire's coals, one last time, pulling it out seconds later to wave the smoking stick in the night air like a swishing sword.

"You're good boys," Jimmy sighed. "Go off to bed now."

In the faltering light of the fire, I could not tell if my sick friend was grinning or about to cry.

Monday morning. Enough wind and whistling and chimney smoke come and gone up Main Street to wake the dead. Time we rang Danny's bell. Time we woke the living.

Ike and Tom's timber construction of the *Campground's* three story, open-air, bell tower was impressive. All the more so because it was the only room of the *Campground's* new design any of us considered finished. Galvanized grating, on the tower's first and second floor landings, highlighted four small balconies of Ipe wood and stainless-steel — the steel work Sally's design and fabrication with equal parts installation by Ike and Tom. Each of the four balconies, two waterside and two garden side, would eventually be fitted with a simple bar plank that could accommodate up to six standing patrons. Higher up, the open beams which would support Danny's big brass bell had already been fitted with the tastefully reduced proportions of a copper-paneled church steeple, fabricated and installed by an outfit out of Mount Vernon. With any luck at all, Danny's bell would hang today.

The slight spin of tires on gravel announced Sally's appearance. He popped the clutch, gave the truck engine more gas, and continued up the *Campground's* service driveway in Joey's Christian clunker — the heaping stack of antique pulleys and tangled tackle in the truck's un-gated bed threatening to slide out of the truck bed the whole way up the hill. Joey's rumbling beast came to a jarring halt dead-center in front of the bell tower.

Sally had brought with him enough rope to circle a small island, long thick braids of polished hemp which would soon slump over the shoulders of his long-sleeved white dress shirt like tired exclamation points. Back and forth, from Joe's bottomed out truck bed to the base of the bell tower, Sally sauntered by me in his leather sandals, black jeans, and duck-tailed white dress shirt, regularly pinning camera-flash smiles on his dogs which waited, impatiently, inside the truck's windowless cab.

Ignoring Sally's joshing that they not go near the truck — *"wired with explosives, you know"* — the boys laughed and continued on their path to the truck's cab. Jenny and Brynnie whined and danced in the front seat — at what to them must have felt like the lifting of a curse — over the prospects of seeing both boys reaching for the truck's pitted door handles. Tongue kisses all around for the smiling boys, before both dogs leaped from Joey's once-upon-a-mountain-road pulpit to mark Sally's scented path with their trickles of urine, least their king and savior still be at it after dark and forget his way back to the cab.

For the rest of the morning, Salvador continued to refuse all offers to lend a helping hand but Danny's, except for the one time when Brynnie's back-stepping rope-pulling fangs instinctively dug in to keep the boy from going more than a couple of feet skyward with the bell — a comical feat, which Juan and I clownishly commented on, at the expense of our artists in residence, *Salvador-Danny*, once the boy's feet had touched earth again. At last, all the components required for the great hoist were in place, and we could watch with awe and wonder our benevolent circus master, his faithful dogs, and one wide-eyed boy call the meek and ill at heart to worship the *Campground's* resurrection.

"Chapel Hill, Mr. J!"

The courtyard, the sidewalks, the streets strangely absent of anyone to appreciate Danny's eloquence. Only the sight of the fat Angora cat, sitting atop Jackie's and Hazel's deserted crepe stand, playfully pawing at a loop of loose chain on the women's chalkboard sign. But even without the eyes of the town upon the *Campground's* new voice, Danny's bell made a powerful curtain call — swinging with the sun so high up off the ground.

During lunch break, I ate my soup and sandwich with the boys, and listened to Danny shoot the breeze with Juan and the snoozing dogs.

"Hey Juan, know what I heard just come into my head?"

"School bell?"

"No-ooh — Joey's truck. I think Joey's truck is your ticket out of town."

"That old jalopy? No way."

"Want me warm the boss up for you after lunch?"

"Mind your own business for once, will you."

"You are my business, bro. Hey Mr. J, you got a minute?"

"Got sixty, then I'm closing the doors on this church."

"Juan's looking for a coach."

"What kind of a coach?"

"Someone that don't mind sitting on the bench with him. So as when he goes off the road and drives Joey's limo into the pond."

"Speak English — my ears are still ringing Spanish."

"That's funny, Mr. J. You could of made a living at it somewhere."

"You think?"

"My mom signed off on me getting my driver's license." Juan explained. "But she's working a lot once I'm back in school. I was wondering, would you ever consider, think you'd ever have time to teach me how to drive?"

"Maybe you hadn't noticed, but my candy-apple red Cadillac's been missing since high school."

"Forget it."

"Hold on. No need to go sour on me. Got one friend done that already, don't need another."

"Sorry."

I wiped the bottom of my soup bowl with the last of my cheese sandwich and stuffed the brown bread in my mouth.

"Danny's been talking to me upside down for so long, I guess maybe I might have missed his drift. You need a driving lesson, eh?"

"I'd pay for the gas. And I'd pay you."

"You'd pay me?"

"A dollar a lesson."

I smiled and choked out a bit of laughter.

"A dollar a lesson?"

"Yes, sir."

"How'd you arrive at that lofty figure?"

"'Cause I know if I offered more you'd find it insulting."

"Alright wise guy, tell you what. How 'bout we ask Joe if we can borrow his truck next week. Be better you learn to drive on a clutch anyway."

Juan's cheeks wrinkled out a cuff link of a smile. "Thanks Mr. Jacobs."

"You're welcome." I grabbed hold of my shovel. "Hope I live long enough to spend all that dough you're gonna be paying me."

"With any luck, we both will."

The bald tires on Joey's truck startled the loose gravel on

the side of the road, for what seemed like an angel's life and death, before Juan corrected his steering and safely tucked us back under the humming grit of the road's freshly oiled stone.

One by one the velvet angels surfaced from the weeping shoreline waters. The mirrored sunlight across their broken hearts to wash ashore the reign of terror they had yet to endure. So tiny the colorless death cradled stillborn warm and waxy in their folded arms.

"We ought to find us a big city mall so Juan can practice his parallel parking, eh Mr. J?"

Danny's elbow rested on the missing window of the truck's passenger door. The boy's pithy voice severing the cold weight of fear on Dianna's face, as I watched her take the baby from the baptizing sea and carry its death to the barn.

I managed the meekest of smiles. "I trust him."

The island road, which the boys would have me study to summer's end, would become a wand of wishes for each of us, vanishing and reappearing in the truck's fractured mirrors in smaller and smaller glimpses of what we wished returned to us come each new turn, each sparkling cove re-traced. And that it should be a looping island road, and not the sloshing sea, that would return to me the last forgotten lines of one of Jessie's unfinished poems.

Fly away bleached sail
Penchant of time and title
Command all language go with you
And weave the blue sea quiet once more

Every little wasp of fluttering trash jeered at our unannounced arrival in the dump.

Jimmy opened his bloodshot eyes to the stars, and the words swam from his mouth.

"Can't be helped, son. They've been planning their foul birthday party for almost a year now. Want to throw their big bash in one of our backyard pools. Know what I mean, son? The fire? That was just their way of telling us to bring plenty of candles."

Danny's eyes flashed like the eyes of a helpless fish out of water. The boy had been hanging on Jimmy's every word, until he'd heard the word *fire*, and felt it drop like a bead of fuel over the coals of the campfire where he'd been warming his hands.

"No they're not, not no more." Danny countered with great confidence. "Red says you sent every one of them back to the homeland."

"I suspect no more than a hundred of them will try and board the ferries, Juan. I'll give you all the warning I can. Still, when they come, it's probably best you and the Rooster lock up your pretty mothers in the cellar."

Jimmy's pale ranting had fallen like a cold rain on the camp's fire. And no sooner had he delivered his ominous warning to the boys when a ferry's distant horn sounded from the channel below. It was unsettling how the ship's morose horn blast had traveled up the mountainside, and thru the treetops, to punctuate the man's squalid mutterings, and Jimmy seemed to take great pleasure in having timed his remarks with the ship's passing. He lowered his gaze from the stars, smugly locking his eyes on my own, before casting a magician's smile upon the fire.

"No, they're no longer here Jimmy. Gone. Vanished. Vanquished." I echoed Danny's sentiments. "And if they were to come back, it would be with a police escort home this time. On that, Juan, you have my word."

"I know what I'm talking about. And I know when they're coming."

Jimmy uncrossed his folded legs on his truck seat and went to work massaging his knees.

"White whores, every one of them. Flapping their filth on the flag of this country."

"Jimmy, listen up."

"Why would I? For too long we've allowed them to piss wherever they feel like."

"Jim —"

"Need one more mother of a moon to track them proper. One more leash to untie."

From a garbage bag, which he'd carefully placed on the wooden spool behind his back, Danny pulled out a store bought radio packaged in plastic and held it up over his head for Jimmy to see. In its see-thru package, the new radio displayed its shell of molded ribbings in bars of grey and silver plastic made to resemble metal and chrome.

"Look Jimmy!"

Like a compelling command meant to break the feverish spell Jimmy looked to be under, Danny's words had erupted like the sound of a cowbell in a children's play.

Jimmy looked up from the fire and squinted at the packaged radio. "Got no electricity, Einstein."

Danny dropped his arm, placed the radio in his lap, and reached back in the bag for the two packages of D-cell batteries he'd thought to bring with him.

"No, see? I got you batteries to go with it." Danny's arms shot out to hold the packaged batteries and radio up for Jimmy's inspection. All smiles, the boy waited for Jimmy to show some sign of surprise or appreciation.

"Thanks Santa, but I got me another canal to build."

"No but, but it will help you do your work better. Keep you

going long after the others have stopped. And we can bring you more batteries. Whenever we come back, we'll bring more."

Jimmy jumped to his feet. He reached for the cracked handle of his pickax. In the few seconds that it had taken him to secure his grip on the pickax, he was up to his knees in oil and water and working one of his oily trenches. With one arm, he began to scrape the pickaxe over the murky bottom of the ditch, pausing after just a few strokes of his axe to grab hold of a toy bucket with his free hand, which he used to begin skimming the ditch water of some of its runny-nosed watermelon rinds. Each pail full of foul water and garbage he'd removed, sloppily splashing against his bean hills of soil which coursed the edges of the long narrow trench, and most every bucketful of the toy pail's mealy garbage and brown water trickling right back into his souring trench.

"Jimmy, Danny's talking to you."

"Plug it in over there, if you must."

"You got it, boss. What do you want to hear first? A freakin' Russian ballet or something?"

"Turn it on, but keep the sound off." Jimmy powered on with his mindless, offensive work. Another pail full of dump sludge cresting a bean hill before sliding back into the ditch.

Danny droned a nervous laugh.

"It's not turned on yet, Jimmy. You want to put the batteries in yourself? You want to? That's the best part of getting a new radio, if you ask me."

Jimmy arched his back and rested the pickax on his shoulder. He sniffed the night air, seemed to be listening for something that might be about to announce itself, something that might be prowling behind the blackberry canes or watching from behind the trestles. But all any of us heard was the glob of soil and foiled plastic falling from his pick-axe and plopping back into the ditch water.

"Some of their pups been checking up on me deep into the pee of the night." The high arc of his pickax suddenly swung down fast and ferociously into the water and planted the heavy tool deep into the ditch bottom. "Won't stand for it," with newfound fury both his hands fought to free the axe handle, "can't have leakage when you're trying to resurrect Paradise now can we Rooster?"

"Hang on. I've almost got your radio out."

"Too loud already. Turn it down."

Danny's hands were fumbling with the package, but he forced another nervous smile.

"You gotta wait. I ain't even got the batteries in her yet."

"Too loud, I told you. Turn it down."

In the fire's fanning light, I could see that a bead of pearly pink sweat had erupted on the Danny's upper lip. The radio's packaging was proving difficult to remove. And the more the boy's thumbs struggled to pry apart the hard plastic cover, the more I thought I was seeing a trickle of blood run out from under one of his thumbnails.

"Danny, let me help you with that." I offered my hand.

"Rooster, change the station why don't you."

"It's jammed inside this plastic pretty good. God, I don't want to break it or nothing. What's that? Hold on, I almost got it."

With a loud pop the radio snapped free and fell to the ground, the handle still in the boy's hand. Danny's face froze with alarm.

"Perimeter security, lots of it. That's the secret to sleeping in on Saturday mornings, Rooster."

"No-ooh! Why'd that have to happen. Hey wait, wait. I think I can fix it. I got it! Lookey here, Jimmy. See, the handle slips right back on."

Danny unsnapped the battery box on the back of the radio and pushed in four big batteries, pushed the power button, rotated the tuning knob, and found the music Jimmy's dismal camp had been craving. Some of the natural wonderment in the boy's eyes returning to marvel at how a French-Canadian accent could travel over invisible airwaves to cover up so much of the dump's rubble.

"How's that sound to you, mister?"

A singer's sultry voice surged over the radio waves, climbed the cliffs of its own rapid-firing articulation, then faded beneath an unnatural shrill as the radio's speakers crackled for a few menacing seconds before dismally eking out a jumbled gurgle — the singer's voice at last dying completely corrupted.

Danny checked the radio's batteries. He checked the power switch. Swished the radio's antennae sideways, up and down, backwards and forward again. Nothing. Only the scraping of Jimmy's pickaxe catching the edge of some submerged thing on the bottom of the ditch, a piece of stone or steel whose screech was hardly softened by the splashing water.

Danny's inspection of the broken radio turned vicious. He mauled the radio's bulbous dials and switches with his fingers, trying to recapture a signal, bent the tip of the antennae, and shook the radio by its handle until the box unhinged and fell to the ground.

"Danny, don't sweat it." Juan intervened. "We can take it back and get another one."

"They done gypped us. Stupid sucko radio. I hate it here! I hate everything always breaking. I hate that we ever came back here!"

Danny yelled out the last of his spoken frustration in loud, angry, twisted chunks of anger. He reached for Jimmy's radio, smashing it against a hunk of concrete as he ran off towards the trailhead.

Juan had been standing on the loose earth piled between two irrigation ditches, nearer the one Jimmy was panning for garbage in, eyeballing Jimmy's foolishness and growing justifiably irritated with the disrespect the man had been showing for Danny's gift.

"Go after him, will you Juan." I asked.

Juan turned to face me. His eyes defiant, and one of his hands made into a pulsating fist.

"No. No, I won't. He's got every right to be pissed off."

Juan took a step backwards, and was preparing to jump one of the irrigation ditches when Jimmy dropped the pickaxe and lunged for the boy's ankle with a sweeping, ground-level forearm strike meant to take the boy off his feet. But Juan proved too fast for him, deftly avoiding the unexpected assault by high-stepping Jimmy's sweeping arm and gracefully skip-jumping the adjacent irrigation ditch to drier ground, leaving the momentum of Jimmy's swiping arm to contact only the injurious grid of an unearthed car radiator.

I was on my feet, and positioned on the flat of ground to the side of Jimmy's ditch, by the time his body had righted itself. He stood half-crouched in the chop of the ditch, holding his injured hand, and looking at me with a hyena's grimacing smile muzzling his muddied face. I felt the ball of my boot planted in Jimmy's heaving chest, before my anger rip-sawed the bone of his body back against the bank of the ditch.

"You White fuck!"

Never in my life had I racially slurred him.

In the time it had taken me to put a voice to my anger, his elbows had caught the soft sides of the ditch. He arched his back, his feet kicking beneath the water to find some better footing before the edge of the bank gave way and his body folded into the full narrowness of the ditch. Too quickly, he tried to sit up. Tried to put on a stoic face and appear unscathed. But my insult had been crucifying to him, and some part of it he could no more pull away from than the mud and oil he was attempting to wipe from his face.

"Well, look at you." He spoke almost gleefully. The mud and oil from the ditchwater burning his eyes. His injured hand held high against his chest. "Of all the islands I could have dumped you on, you come ripe for me on this patch of desert."

But I was already on the far side of the creek, making my way to the trailhead with no memory of what he'd just said to me, no memory of the black tunnel of space I'd walked thru to reach the creek, no understanding of how the club of firewood in my hand had got there, or why there was but one color covering the night sky in all its mercurial form.

Juan stood waiting for me on a pecked heap of Styrofoam and bubble-wrap. Danny was poking his trash stick at a half-buried slipper in the blackberry vines, shrugging his shoulders in response to Juan asking him if he was still pissed. Behind us, the sound of a feathering wind swept a patch of sky poking out from between the waving treetops — white to black to a darker skin of quiet.

"You got the same bad feeling I got?" Juan chanced a question.

"Which one?" I placed a comforting hand on the boy's shoulder.

"That Jimmy's gonna do something the rest of us are going to regret?"

"Yeah, it's in there with all the rest of my worries."

Heavy footed and flashing a disturbing grin, Danny stormed by us. When I asked him to hold up, he footstomped a twig in his path and ran into the trail's tunnel of quiet darkness without saying a word.

I looked across the creek at the camp's cave of firelight. The man I'd assaulted now out of the ditch and busy rolling one of his tattooed, rubber-necked steel drums nearer the fire. Juan and I watched him finish the task and cross back inside the cone of his camp's firelight, where he squatted and dipped one hand into the bucket of kerosene and oil he kept near his truck seat. He stirred the contents of the bucket, targeting us with a brief stare, and scooped out a glob of the soupy mixture, which he proceeded to smear onto the drum he'd rolled closer to the fire. More beast than man to me now, Jimmy's oiled arms played like puppets against the banded steel of the upright drum. The man's clumpish shadow dancing with spearing jerks that pulled his conjoined twin in and out of the pallid ring of firelight.

On the trail, Juan and I spoke at length about Jimmy's inexcusable behavior.

"All I know is that my old man got to being alone like this guy, sometimes. Not as bad as Jimmy, but nearly."

"Go on."

"He'd start mixing up the past with the present, that's all I'm saying. Like somehow both places were happening at the same time for him in his head. Talking about people and things that my mom and I knew were dead or gone a long time ago. And always afterwards, always a couple days after his spells, sheriff Bodine would come knocking at our cellar door."

"Jimmy is nothing at all like your old man. Sorry if my saying so hurts."

"I know he's different than other men. Same way you are —"

"I'm no more like Jimmy than he is anything like your father. You ought to know that much about both of us by now."

"That's what you keep saying. But I see similarities sometimes."

"Hey! Who's been watching your back all summer? That would be me, last I checked."

"Yeah but, but that's today." Juan eked out the slightest of bowtie smiles. "Who's to say about tomorrow?"

"You can get that out of you're head too. You'll be the first one to hear of it if I'm fixing to run off."

"Promises, promises."

Danny was hurriedly untying the boat's bow line from the trunk of the madrona, by the time Juan and I reached the cove. He made eye contact with Juan, while looping the rope in his hands, but he would not speak to either of us.

The boat ride back to the marina was mile after mile of chop and salt spray, and Danny's tongue ran still as stone the whole way. His long face generating about as much enthusiasm among the rest of the crew as the drifting stars could shed light on Jimmy's escalating behavior.

It was late by the time we tied up at *Red's*. The marina a refuge exuding the murmurs of shuteye sleeping berths over the amber docks. We headed for the showers, each of us carrying an extra quarter to drop inside the slotted dials of our stalls. The extra coin it would cost each of us, for three extra minutes of hot water, looking like the best deal any of us had made all day.

Walking with the boys up to Sally's house was like coasting into someone else's pleasant dream, and served to narrow the view from the grassy bluff overlooking the marina and the new garland of red and blue neon now draped across Red's storefront window — his store's new sign resembling more a palm reader's invitation to step back in time than an advertisement for cold beer. Ahead of us, the cart-less fairway becoming wet underfoot as we picked up the pace and headed away from the chowder of blue laughter, which would funnel down distant Main Street and move us closer to the lanterns looming in Salvador's elfish woods. Jenny and Brynnie's lapidary greetings soon opening the compound's slouching gate for us. The wonder of watching both dogs trotting across the patio to settle on cushioned chaise lounges. The wonder of seeing Sally's dogs safe at home.

The boys said their goodnights and made their way around the pond to their tents, Danny talking shoulder close to Juan just as each boy reached for the open flap of his tent. Words spoken too softly for me to be certain of all that Danny was sharing with his friend, something about *never going back*, or maybe, *if we was ever to go back...* And Juan's response — to what must have been an oath or a promise made by Danny — all the more thunderous for having traveled over the mirrored pond to reach my ears as clearly as Father Jerald's eyes had, disapprovingly, conveyed his understanding of why the crack in Danny's bell was to be permanently positioned facing Main Street. *But Jimmy ain't gonna have no music to listen to tonight, is he Dan?*

After the boys had quieted, I said goodnight to the dogs and walked back to the marina. Too tired, when I climbed aboard my boat, to hound my thoughts with any more images of Jimmy's profanity.

Hours later, I awoke within the mask of a night dream. In the dream, a page of newsprint, bearing full page photographs of missing children, skidded over the twirling dust of Jimmy's camp. The dump's trestle bridge was gone, burned to the ground, and in its place an enormous dune of ash swirled with incredible speed and was all that supported the sway of train tracks spanning the leafless canyon. The whirling dune expanded, darkened every crevice of space on the lettered walls of the decimated canyon, shriveled, and grew again to form a womb with ribs of orbiting stone and sand. The ribs became thought, thought became voice, and the carom of its torment burrowed deep within my head, until all that I understood was that there was still time for Jimmy to flee. When I thought I could take no more of the dream's anguish, the dream collapsed unto another and gave birth to the canyon wind. The wind held the sharpest of white-washed edges, grew skittish, sometimes fanned the dump's gyrating ground fires, sometimes spun itself into a ball and shot skyward the pages of flaming newsprint targeting the wings of frightened gulls — the arc of a rainbow the wind's form for them to chase for a time. The dream transitioned. *Come the flies, Came the men.* Spiritless, pimply-eyed men gathered around a rose of a fire blue and lichen fed. Hate-mongers whose littering presence oozed spittle over the bristled hairs of our noosed necks. Our injuries sitting us straight and stiff on our wooden spools. Red and Hazel on their knees before the fire. Salvador, Jackie, Juan and Danny, and the robed priest all praying that Jimmy's decrepit body might show some sign of life before the fire and rise from the net of blowflies burrowing beneath his flesh. The dream collapsed, shifted time and space. Filthy and dressed in rags crawling with the paste of dying bluebottles, I found myself clinging to the deck of a torpedoed boat. Over the rails of the boat, Jimmy climbed from a frozen sea carrying the fins of sharks in his arms and dressed in his tuxedo. I reached out for his hand, wanting only to hold him, wishing only to touch some part of him that he might know Jessie was alive in me. But there was such hatred for me in the rage which had taken a father's eyesight that he would have no part of my friendship, his thoughts somehow physically speaking to me... *I don't want you or Jessie coming back here after tonight. Not ever.* Without warning, he had then jumped from the ship's railing and melted into the sea, and my night dream had ended.

I lay in my sleeping berth resisting the bleakest of wagers. Thought of all the tales I could remember ever having survived grief's vengeance — bridges of endearment or madness — and wondered how flesh and spirit could possibly reunite in a man whose resolute worship of grief's treachery seemed destined to prevail. The sea lapping at my boat. The night sky numbered with the patterns we have chosen to construct. The frail and faded window lace of my sleeping berth caressed by some *other's* light born, or extinguished, entirely for our time.

Juan drove with his elbow out the window of the truck, the look of a fisherman on opening day tying his eyes to the horseshoe bend in the road ahead. Danny sat beside him, talking fondly of their afternoon responsibilities to sail Red and his wife, and Salvador and his dogs, over to Jackie's picnic. I rested my hand on the side mirror outside the truck's passenger window, the sun streaming its morning course over the pebbled asphalt left clean and steaming by last night's rain. The truck's new radio, which the boys and I had installed in Joey's truck, jagging some fine jazz out of one of Seattle's midnight, blue-note nightclubs. Our own sunlit morning like no other we'd ever known.

"Why is it you're not going with us anyhow, Mr. J? Saturday you're new Sabbath or something?"

"Would if I could but I can't."

"Last time we went out there the company was okay. But Sally told us this morning he went over and put a hoop up for Jackie and the rest of us. Make for a better game of hoop if you were to come along with us."

"It would, and that's a fact." I looked the boy in the eye and gave him my biggest game smile. "Maybe another time. Say Juan, mind pulling the truck over next sunny spot you see."

"Good idea. I gotta take a leak myself."

Danny put one hand on the dashboard and joked as the truck hugged a leafy shoreline corner. "You boys shouldn't drink so much of my coffee on D-day. You know how I hate stopovers on my island tours."

Juan and I smiled.

"This work for you, Mr. Jacobs?"

"Paradise."

"Or something real close to it, huh?"

"I'm gonna miss going around in circles with you, Dan."

"Mrs. Gilmore my English teacher tells me the same thing. Her name's Carol. I'm not supposed to call her that, but I've been getting away with it."

"Everything okay with you in school? Anyone bothering you?"

"No. No way. It's like the best start I ever had. Mrs. Gilmore, she says I've matured a lot. But I don't feel any different. I feel just as funny as I always do. Know what I mean? Maybe 'cause I seen the world a little bit. Think that's it?"

"You hang on to that feeling. It's yours to take anywhere in the world with you."

"Nobody stays innocent for ever, Juan says. You opened our eyes, Mr. J. I don't want to ever go back to how I was. Not for nothing. It would be disrespectful to you after all you done for us."

"You've a heart big as an island. That's for sure."

"You think? But I don't read enough, do I? And my math is not so great."

"Ah, what's in a number anyhow? Hardly a heart."

"See that boney sailboat out there?"

"I've had my eye on it."

"He put the sail up and the pulpit into the wind and she'd look like something, wouldn't she?"

"She's his last chance."

Danny thumped his backside against the truck's dented rear fender panel. "I bet you made all the girls cry."

"Danny, you are my friend always."

"Thanks Mr. J. I'll put that in the bank for a rainy day."

"You do that. It's about all the math you're ever going to need. That and a bit of geometry for building houses and taverns."

"This the spot you picked for to break the news to Juan?"

"What do you think?"

"It's a real good spot. Nice and romantic."

"Going to be a long walk back to town if he tells us *adios amigos*? Did you chill the wine?"

"I think so. The bottle felt cold enough when I wrapped it up in the towel. Know something?"

"What?"

"I've never had sparkling cider before. I've seen it on the shelves in Red's store at Christmas. But I always thought it was booze."

"Funny, I thought the same thing first time I drank it." I ruffled the boy's hair, and with my thumb and forefinger rubbed the torn button hole in his seasoned vest. "You wearing this ratty old thing to school?"

"Yeah."

"You need a new vest."

"Probably not."

I slapped the truck bed, and walked to the edge of the bank to look for Juan.

"What's taking your brother so long?"

"You know he's gonna practically go all girl on you, right?"

"Probably cry like a baby, huh?"

"Hope you brought plenty of tissue and a clean shirt."

"You need a new vest."

"Probably next year."

Juan high-stepped it up and over the embankment.

"Juan, hold up a minute would you. Dan and I got something we want to say to you. A word or two, before you take us around the speedway one last time."

"Sure."

"Want me fetch the hooch, Mr. J?"

"Absolutely."

"What's going on, Mark?"

"Tailgate party." I put my hand on the boy's shoulder. "Not to worry. It's a bottle of apple juice."

The tailgate popped opened with a monstrous chewing burp of scraping metal and dropped with a rattling excess of bicycle chain and flaking rust, the sounds spilling out over the gate's shotgun blasted lip.

"The truck is yours, Juan. A gift from Danny and I. Joey threw in four new tires. His nickel — be sure to thank him. Tires are being mounted on some sweet chrome rims Danny and I thought you might like. They'll be waiting for you down at Red's tonight. Insurance is paid up for another year, and the truck's title will be sent to your house in a couple weeks. Your mom knows all about it. Place called Jake's, over in Anacortes, has an undamaged door and tailgate they're pulling from their yard. We can take the truck over there, next weekend if you like, and they'll change out the old ones and put on the new. She's gonna look like a scrambled egg when we're done, I know. But if you save your money for a decent paint job, one day she'll look respectable. The rest you know. Danny, how'd I do? You got anything to add?"

"I never heard you talk so much, Mr. J."

"I've always liked a truck that packs a bit of muscle. Excites me."

"What do you think, Juan? Didn't have a clue, did you?"

"I don't know what to say."

"Say you'll take it."

"Thank you, Mr. Jacobs. Thank you so much."

"All I got you was the radio so far, Juan. But I can chip in for gas sometimes."

"Thanks Dan. It wouldn't be the same driving without our music."

Danny centered the cider bottle in a punctured ringlet of the tailgate's beleaguered alphabet. The bottle uncorked, it was handed with gratitude to Juan. He passed it back, flat out insisting that it was I who should take the first sip. A bit of bantering ensued between us, none of it with half the propriety with which we held the other's friendship close to our hearts, and our attention apologetically shifted to Danny, who finally did the honors without another word spoken. Sparkling cider, after all, was a vice he'd never tasted before and therefore naturally superseded all ties to friendship.

Juan was the first to catch sight of the rider in the truck's side-view mirror. A brush stroke of green and orange daring and athleticism painting my side mirror by the time the rider had banked a wall of a corner, whipsawed center-road, and jockeyed bull cock tight up against the road's shoulder stripe.

"It's Joe. I'm going to pull over."

Juan let up on the gas pedal. The truck's uphill climb found second gear, and the steering wheel veered towards the squabble of a pair of pecking crows being shooed from the muddied edges of their off road puddle.

"Mr. Jacobs," Joe's handlebars stopped inches from the

door's mirror, "was hoping you'd see me before this hill took me. Hey Juan — Dan."

Joe dismounted and rolled his bike back to the side of the truck's bed.

"Hold on, gotta catch my breath."

Joe's chest heaved heavy and intrusive to the side of my windowless door. Bending, he placed his hands on his knees, sucked more air, and spit out whatever cold and soreness lay in his throat and beneath his wheezy groans.

"Hardest ride I've ever had to make." His head faced the ground, his knees pumping out weakened squats like the arm of an old hand pump being primed. Even hunched over, the top of his head was higher than the door's mirror. "Sorry to cut in on your lesson, Juan. Got something important to tell you, Mr. Jacobs."

"You want some apple cider to drink, Joe." Danny asked.

"Nope, forgot my inhaler, that's all."

"Don't' talk 'til you get your breath back. We got time."

"Actually, you don't." Joe straightened and stood tall, his head leveling the cab roof, his forearms resting against the roof's gutter line. "Red sent me out hoping to find you. Mrs. Rodriguez called him about an hour ago real concerned. She brought Jimmy out a meal this morning, and I guess when she got there his camp was practically deserted. His, his shack was there but nothing else. She looked around for him awhile but never saw him. She left but came back out to his camp just two hours ago. He's sicker than a dog inside his shack. But he wouldn't let her inside to have a look at him. He's got the dry heaves pretty bad. Mrs. Rodriguez says there was no helping him. He'd put some boards up, over the door in his shack, and he wouldn't come out or let her inside to have a look at him. She called Red, because before she left the dump Jimmy told her anyone but you show up, Mr. Jacobs, and he'd do some killing. She's afraid, was afraid maybe he meant himself."

"Alright, Joe. I'll head back to Red's and go out and have a look myself. I appreciate you finding us so fast."

"Joe," Juan spoke up, "you want a lift back to town."

"No, I'm not far from the farm. Thanks."

"You got a phone at your house, Joe?"

"Yeah."

"Do me a favor. Give Red and Juan's mom a call. Tell 'em both, tell them you got the message to me."

"Sure thing."

"You heading straight out to check on him? Soon as you get back to town, Mr. Jacobs?"

"I am."

"You want me go with you."

"No. I think it's probably best I go alone this time. You sure you don't want a lift back to the farm."

"No. You need the minutes on your end."

"I'm sure grateful to have your truck, Joe. Hey, and thanks for the extra tires."

"He told you already? I wasn't sure you knew yet."

"I'm not sure I even know now. It's kind of overwhelming me. It's a great truck, Joe. I'll take good care of it."

"Two of the tires are studded snow tires, brand new. But I never drove the truck after the accident. So I never got around to finding rims for 'em."

"Joe?"

"Yeah, Dan."

"You didn't stutter even one time."

"Huh, I hadn't noticed."

Joe pushed off from the truck. He slipped his hand over my arm, his eyes locking my own to his heartfelt gaze.

"God's speed, Mr. Jacobs."

At the marina, Red was already fueling my boat.

"Clobber him. Then tie his hands and bring him back in a gunnysack. Anna and I are full up with his requests for more and more room service. You want my gun? I got one."

"Sick as he is, he'd probably still find a way to take it from me."

Red's sternness broke into a broad smile. "Well, anyone but him, I'd say this foolishness couldn't go on forever."

"He's weak, Red. If I have to, I'll finish him off tonight by telling him I've signed my half of the Campground over to the church."

"Good on you. That just might bring him home. You taking the boys with you?"

"No. They're staying at Sally's tonight."

"Their moms been called?"

"Yup."

"Alright. See you when I see you."

The trail from the cove to the dump is strewn with fresh pine needles and a few autumn leaves, a sight making for the scent of a child's playground. A safe place to remember the good times, if I could end my hike here, but not what I find when I reach the plateau of the dump.

"Jimmy?"

"Go wa-aay."

"Come on, sit up. Come on, try and sit up."

"I don't know —"

"Sure you can. Take my hand."

"Where we —"

"Come on, sit up. Jesus, you're burning up. We got to get you to the creek. Jimmy? Come on, sit up. That's it. Let go of the rug. Let go of it. Stand. You've got to stand. Try. Put your arm around my neck. Come on, I've got you — yes I do."

"Where you taking me? Not the canyon."

"We gotta get you cooled down. You're burning up."

"No. Someone's been in the canyon crying all day. For sure someone was up there. I'm so cold."

"I know. Come on, I'll help you walk to the creek. God, you smell? No, nobody's making fun of you. Your big-ass fire is crackling at us that's all."

"Something — someone behind us."

"No, no one."

"Probably your boys."

"No. I came alone this time."

"They safe?"

"Yes, they're safe."

"They're good boys?"

"Yes, they're good boys. Almost men."

"They safe?"

"Yes, my word on it."

"Okay. I'm so cold, Mark."

"We're gonna fix that."

Together we walked his feverish body to the creek. His eyes closing and opening as often as his lips fought to speak half formed utterances, eyes watered and weeping like those of the sickly stray watching us from the shack.

In the breathless cold of the creek, I helped him remove his cut-offs. He was wearing no other clothing, no shoes. His scarred hands touching first my shoulders and then grappling to take hold of my forearms, he let his forehead slump against my chest.

"It's alright, Jim. It's alright. We've both cried here a time or two before, haven't we. Got no secrets between us this time. That's reason enough to hold our heads up."

Together, we folded his shivering body into the knee-high stream. His torso swaying some in the current cresting mid-rib before the reach of his hand could find the creek bottom and he was able to seat himself.

In the folds of a plastic bag tied to a stake on the bank of the creek, I found some broken pieces of soap he'd mashed into a crude ball. Hair, and specks of dirt and gravel, layered the surface of the soap-ball and gave the hardened marbled mass the look of a baseball that's had its stitched leather covering torn away. A bone-handled butcher's knife lay in a sheath of reeds and grass, near the plastic soap bag, its blade sharp and polished and cutting thru the soap like butter.

I reached down to hand Jimmy his half of the soap, but the task proved too difficult for him and the clove slipped thru his fingers to be quickly taken downstream. He moaned and gave into the fatigue the effort had caused him, his body slumping towards the thicket side of the creek, his head falling first upon his outstretched arm and then tucking its despair into the grassy bank. The stems of some oil drenched reeds, which the clutch of his hand had searched for and found, bending like desert flowers under the threat of frost.

While the slump of his body trembled against the panning current, I soaped his neck and backside. He tried often to lift his head from the deep grass and to pull some meaning from the drizzle of his incoherent mutterings. When I asked if he could muster the strength to sit up and turn my way, he managed to do so with an unexpected swiftness to his movements, performing a one-arm pushup while his encrusted eyes struggled to remain open long enough to find my face.

"Rest your backside against my legs. Keep your head down."

"You gonna drown me?"

"Not today. Put your head down. Hold onto to my ankles."

"I gonna be your bitch tonight?"

"Quiet. You'll scare the boys away."

"I knew they were here with you. Hiding, they're hiding?"

"No. No one else is here. I was just messing with you."

"Okay. Okay. Mark?"

"What?"

"You love those boys?"

"I do. You've got to close your eyes. I'm going to wash your hair."

"Mark?"

"What?"

"I miss her."

"I know."

"More than you."

"Yes — more than me."

I washed his hair. Washed his backside. Washed his bruised and blistered legs. Scrubbed his feet with a bottle brush I'd found and dug out from a ring of paint brushes he'd left to harden in the gluey bottom of a coffee can rank with the smell of urine. Blisters the size of button tumors dotted both his legs — the brandishing signatures of cigarettes that had been intentionally set ablaze on his skin — the largest of these blisters blooming heaviest along the tan lines marking each of his thighs, making it difficult for me not to open some of the fleshier ones as I washed him.

I helped him to his feet, bracing his body to one side of me so that he might better steady himself in midstream. Slipping my arm under his armpit, I handed him the last of the soap so that he might wash his ass and genitals. When he'd finished soaping, I took hold of his hand so he might squat and rinse himself and splash water on his spine where the current could not reach. He tossed what was left of the crumbling soap into the bank of grass, when he'd finished, little more than a child's uncoordinated strength behind his shaky toss.

I helped him back across the creek, and together we walked towards his blanket of trampled cardboard which lay between two pillared drums by the fire. Walking with him, holding him so close, it was as if I were carrying a beloved animal's fearful trembling in my arms.

He collapsed onto the cardboard and pulled his legs up tight to his chest, closed his eyes.

"Jimmy? Jim?"

"What is it you want from me?"

"We need to get you out of here, get you to a doctor."

"No."

I put my hand to his forehead. "I'm going back to the island for medicine."

He struggled to sit up. One arm managing to straight arm the cardboard beneath him, his other hand groping to cover his genitals.

"Don't do that. Don't go back to the island."

"I'm certain I could find you penicillin. The pharmacist keeps an emergency number posted on his store window."

"Don't go back."

"Jim, you're so sick."

"Don't go back. I'm begging you. Please."

"What then? What would you have me do?"

"Casino's closer."

"They won't have penicillin."

"They got cough syrup and stuff. They got ice. You could double up some garbage bags — carry back much as much ice as you can — maybe get us some food. Some ginger ale."

He lay back, rolled over on one shoulder, cupped his hands around his genitals, and rocked a little to find some semblance of comfort.

"So nice here, Mark. Just you and me now."

"Here, take this."

"Okay."

On his side, on the wet cardboard, he worked his arms up tightly under his chest.

"Sleep and ice — all I need."

His fingers wormed to scratch the skin covering his protruding ribs. His bony bum white as an oyster shell.

"Alright Jim. We'll try it your way for a couple of hours."

"Safe here," his voice shriveling to an almost inaudibly latch, "long as they know you're around."

He drew his knees up close to the hollow in his stomach and closed his eyes to the last of the sun's warmth.

"Yes, you're safe now. Of course you are."

When I once more put my hand to his forehead, his eyes squinted at some unknown thing he seemed to think he'd heard coming down the creek. Some poisoned claim about to be made on the desolation which had lain with his body, just minutes earlier, on the grassy bank of the creek. Or perhaps, he'd felt some *other's* self-erected refuge of salvation he believed was coming for him, a witnessing force to the shadow of his life which he knew he no longer had the strength or time to prepare for.

"It's nothing, Jimmy. Close your eyes and rest."

But watching his cadaverous body struggle to find comfort on the cardboard, I thought, *this is what happens to men who try to bury their grief, this burn that isolates and divides whatever happiness they once sought.*

"I'm going to the boat for clothes and blankets. A half hour —tops. Then I'll go to the casino."

I returned from the boat with a sweatshirt, a pair of sweatpants, socks, towel, toothbrush and toothpaste, a bottle of aspirin, an unpackaged bar of soap, a stale bottle of water siphoned from the boat's tank. All of these items, I had wrapped and tied in a woolen blanket while aboard the boat, and carried with me on the return hike up the mountainside. Several times, on the trail, I had looked back at the boat, the cove's protective cape, and the channel's darkening waters — never once seeing any other vessel but my own in sight of the channel, nor any prowling boat lights stalking the steep wooded shoreline of the neighboring island.

While I'd been gone, he'd found his old rug and had tried covering himself in its raggedy braids. Under the bridge of his left hand, poking out from under the flaps of some fresh pieces of cardboard he'd positioned under his body, a wire tie secured some twelve inch long flares and three large padlocks which lay beside him. The fire I'd stoked for him, before I gone to the boat, had pulled back much of its warmth from his naked body. But he was asleep now, and softly snoring.

Near the edge of the creek, I kneeled and untied the blanket. I rolled the towel out over the grass and placed the items I'd taken from the boat on each of its four corners. The rug, which partially clothed him, I replaced with the clean Pendleton blanket. Never once did my movements cause his body to stir.

By the time I'd made my way thru the fields of baled hay, and crossed the highway, the sun had dropped its halo behind the treetops and the valley air was cooling. A few cars rolled on down the highway like the boxcars of a slow-moving train. After the noise of the vehicles passed, the road ran long and quiet all the way to the casino's upper parking lot.

Most of the upper parking lot had been sealed off and secured with galvanized fencing. Inside the fencing, construction machinery now filled the blue-lit parking spaces; trailers bearing generators and backhoes, an industrial welder, a mobile office, a small crane with the image of a giraffe painted on its boom. Outside the fenced lot, steel I-beams rested on the tracks of creosol beams. On the hillside beyond the casino's marina, where the shuttered cabin looked to be under siege from the day's construction activity, a barge sized shelf of fresh soil and ancient stone had been cut away from a nearby ravine.

The casino's gift shop carried cold and flu medicines. The deli sold prepackaged sandwiches. An honest explanation, and a five dollar tip, recruited a cocktail waitress willing to bag up ice from a bin behind the mirrored bar.

The hike back to the dump was a constant push to try and keep warm in my wet cloths. A cold spit of rain had been tracking the southwest tip of the island most of the evening, and now the clouds were beginning to drop a beating of hail over the hay fields. A few white-tailed deer had bedded down amongst some of the bales of hay corralling the trunk of a dying oak. The deer watching me pass, some stillness of thought frozen in their eyes, until I had safely distanced myself from their camp. The hail which danced on the hides of the animals now as much a part of the evening's coloring as the skeletal, silver oak.

In camp, Jimmy was awake and watching for me to emerge from the woods and cross over the dump's bulldozed dunes.

Once I was again by his side, he drank viciously from the bottle of ginger ale while I unwrapped some of the ice. He unscrewed the cap from the bottle of cold pills and shook out three of the blue tablets onto the cardboard mats. One by one, he swallowed the pills, chasing down each swallow with a swift swig of cough syrup. He capped the glass bottle of cough syrup, set it aside, pulled the Pendleton blanket over the sweatshirt and cutoffs he'd put on while I was gone, and cinched one corner of the blanket between his knees before drawing his body into a ball on the cardboard mats.

An hour passed, another, and still he slept — time which took me back to the boat for a jacket and sleeping bag. Time which allowed me the small pleasure of rekindling his campfire. I kept his legs covered with my sleeping bag. The towel, which lay across his forehead, I kept wrapped with ice. The road flares and the padlocks, which I'd seen resting under the bridge of his hand before I'd left for the casino, were no where to be found.

Sometime after midnight, he awoke from a dream which still carried a piece of him far away from the fire's warmth, referencing a time not measurable by any coalescence of space to be found in our waking hours.

"Mark, you're supposed to pick up her birthday cake. Mark, Mark?" His hands folding to one side of his body in foiled prayer, he sat up quickly and scratched out a queer laugh.

"Right here. I'm right here, Jim. Here, drink this. It's real cold now."

He took hold of the bottle and gulped.

"Parts of you look better. How do you feel?"

He stood and walked to the creek without answering. On the bank's flattened grass, he sat and crossed his legs.

"Been a nightmare for you, hasn't it Mark?" He spoke with his back to me, and his words were colored with a pale kindness.

"Don't turn sweet on me now."

"After all I've done to you, you keep coming back? You think you can save me, that it."

"No one can save anyone."

"This is not your world. Not any more."

"Whose is it then?"

He tossed the bottle in the creek and watched it bob and float downstream.

"Go find her. If she were mine, I would do no other thing."

"Go with me."

He extended his legs out over the trampled grass, and with hands planted on the ground beneath him, walked his stiffened body a handshake closer to the water's edge, dropped and inched his ankles into the creek.

"Jump from one island to another? Without reason? Without a purpose? No. No."

He made a bridge of his hands and held the cup his fingers had formed close to the water's skin, all the while steadily looking upstream, looking for some unknown conjuring only he might dispel before dipping his hands into the rippling current.

"But what I'll do without you by my side, I don't know."

"Finish the Campground. See that no harm comes to Juan or Danny. See that they get a few extras."

"I could do that. I'm ready to go back."

The strangeness beneath his words prowled over his hallowed piece of ground to reach owl-eyed proportions in my head.

"You could. You could finish what I started."

"What I do best. Finish things. You know that."

"It might be better if we tried to leave now."

The droplets of water ran down his fingers to sooth the back of his neck. He splashed more water on his face and neck, rose to his feet, and walked back to his piece of cardboard.

"Tired, Mark. Sleep awhile."

He made a pillow of the blanket and gathered the sleeping bag around him.

"Sure, Jimmy. We can leave in the morning."

In minutes, he was asleep. The small, almost smokeless fire casting its hypnotic blessing over both of us.

While he slept, I walked the perimeter of the dump and ate my sandwich. Mrs. Rodriguez had not exaggerated.

Except for the two steel drums standing guard by the fire, the yard surrounding his shack had been cleaned of all his hoarding and litter, the irrigation ditches filled in with stone and soil, the ground surrounding his summer trenching leveled and raked smooth. The stacks of rubber tires, once cable-leashed to the trunk of a tree, gone now. The creek cleaned of all metal, and showing no evidence that a squatter had taken refuge along its banks.

Inside the shack, all that suggested that someone may have lived here for the summer was a roll of toilet paper, a jug of water, and a heavily duct-taped toothbrush which served as a paperweight on a torn, and many times opened, paper envelope with my name on it. The envelope displaying the date of Jessie's death, a number spelled out in her own hand above the red ink of my name.

By the light of her father's campfire I read, for the first time, the words which Jessie had put to paper during the final hours of her life. Words meant for my eyes only, but which her father had obviously found first and seen fit to keep hidden from me.

After reading Jessie's words, I walked with her voice to the creek and into the canyon, and from the smothering coldness of the canyon I climbed the trail to the top of the trestle bridge. From the abandoned rails, I watched the wind sifting its own line thru the dark waters separating the tribal island from its thumbing, uninhabited neighbor. The wind shape-shifting the channel's brindled skin, before gathering an arrow's momentum to carve a spine for itself center channel, where it once more shape-shifted and proceeded to carve out the heckles of a poked and prodded animal wishing only to rest.

I returned to camp with nothing to offer Jessie's father but my silence. Sometime later, he awoke in the darkness to ask what time I thought it might be.

"Maybe two. Later, maybe. Not three, I think."

"Did you sleep?"

"No."

"Someone watching you in the dark at the garden gate again?"

"No. Leastwise, no one either of us would recognize."

"Out here, alone, it's always the wind that wakes me at this hour."

"How you feeling?"

"Weak. Got any more of those cold pills?"

"Under the blanket."

"Have I ever thanked you?"

"Just now — inside the shack."

"More pain brought into your life. I'd hardly call that a thank you."

"We should leave now."

"I thought by keeping her letter from you, I might protect you some. It was wrong of me. I'm sorry."

"We should leave. You can sleep some more on the boat."

"Yes, your boat, I almost forgot. Well, we can talk about her letter later. Lots of time left for you and me to get this right between us."

"Anything you want to bring back with you?"

He coughed out a little laughter and lifted his hand to point at the shack, making a trigger of his thumb over the barrel of his forefinger.

"About ten thousand of them. Inside, in a coffee can under the spool, there's ten thousand dollars in black chips. I know you're tired, but would you mind hiking back to the casino for me one last time? Leave me one pretty black chip, though, before you go. If you were to cash out the whole ten thousand we'd have to pay taxes on it."

"Couldn't we take them with us? Cash out another time?"

"I'd like to make a clean break of it. If you've got it in

you to walk back there one more time, I'd feel I was — I'd feel I was finished with what I came here to do."

"Alright."

"If there are any questions, tell the cashier I'm sick and that I sent you. They know I've been saving up those chips awhile."

"Anything else you want while I'm there?"

"No. Just get back here safe."

The hike back to the casino was a godless stick of seeing the suffering on Jessie's face alive again. The trail, the fields, the desolate highway one big trap offering her pleas no way out from each of our betrayals. And the indecency of my anger, washed out, washed away with each of her cries for me to come back to her.

From behind an iron cage, the casino's sole cashier assured me there was no problem in cashing out so many hundred dollar chips... 'So you're the mystery man Jimmy's always telling me about. We haven't seen him in here for awhile, everything okay...Well, there's a lot of that going around... No sir, there's no problem. Anything over five hundred dollars we just have call upstairs, that's all. Just take a minute. *Yes, he's a friend of Mr. Young's...Yes, all of it... Nine thousand nine hundred, all in black chips...*Emma, can you verify my count...Okay, let's count these bills out for you... There you go, Mr. Jacobs. Will there be anything else... Would you like security to walk you to your car...Alright, then. Goodnight to you, sir...'

That I should walk out darkness with the color of its loss in my heart, this night, thru the chill of pasture and awakened memory, and that she will not know even the paleness of another colorless daybreak.

From the rutted edge of the dump, the black outline of the shack stood lifeless against the rim of the canyon. No light from a campfire. No sign or movement of human suffering. The creek but a paler shade of charcoal flayed against the foul line of underbrush. The blanket meticulously folded like a flag and set out with the bottles of cold medicine on the bank of the stream.

No one inside the shack.

Not a scent of his illness roosting on the trestle bridge, or a crag of a whimper cowering in the frost of the canyon floor, where I called out for him. The trail leading down to the cove twisting its oppressive silence all the way to shoreline's ledge, but putting an end to a summer of speculation.

The bow line leashing the boat to the trunk of a madrona had been untied, and the boat set adrift to swing mid-cove from the stern anchor, her bow shunting a light north wind and already drifting dangerously close to the cove's shoreline rock. In the waters off her stern some wake-less, homeless treachery pursed her. Its purpose cloaked by a compassing of steel drums cabled and saddled with the remnants of old car tires, the lecherous peel of its skin discharging the smell of oil and kerosene into the backwaters of the cove. The haunting, disfiguring moan of the idling engine all that distinguished the drifting boat from that of a ghost ship.

It was no longer my boat when the faint cast of Jimmy's head surfaced from the waters of the cove. His long arms treading the water's sting and marking his body's distance from the hull's waterline before the sea took him under once more. The postulate of his form taken from me, until the roll of his shoulder broke from the water's void and he was within arm's reach of the boat's waterline. With one arm swiftly treading water and the other slap-tracking the hull's curvature, he made his way towards the stern rail — a strength of will, which he'd hidden from me in camp, now allowing him to place one fist over the other and lift his body from the sea like an unleashed serpent deaf to the weight of the world it had just breached. The bareness of his chest shimmying over the rub of cable and onto the sway of the deck, the cold wind coveting the pale disjointed flash of handcuffs and a knife's willowy blade dangling from the rope sash of his cutoffs, so that, for the strike of a single breath or something akin to one the man held no place or position aboard the boat.

From the boat's cockpit, he rose to his knees — more apparition than man, one blinded, the other bound by the sound of the boat's idling motor — and tried gathering his breath and balance against the rudder arm. The configuration of drums corralling the waters, off the boat's stern, looking transfixed by his prayerful posture.

When he let go of the rudder arm, he stood holding the handle of an oar which he used to push back one of the drums drawn to a line in the tidal current sloshing the bow. When he'd succeeded in pushing the drum back, he set the oar aside and wrapped his arms tight against some great spasm which had taken hold of his stomach — perhaps the water's cold, or the ache of hunger, or the unyielding thought of some greater sickness anticipated.

The thin paleness of his body searched the dark hollows of the shoreline for the fear he knew would bind me to its stone ledges. His mind gauging any chance — doing so with the same certainty with which he had calculated the amount of time it would take me to return from his house of cards — that I might somehow overcome my fear of water and risk everything to try and reach him.

A fleece of colors red and green fell from the mast and was lost to the night, as the boat's running lights switched off as suddenly as they'd come on. The friend I'd lost, but whom I'd believed had returned to me, ducking shroud lines and breaking for the bow of the boat with the quiet of a leopard's stalking. Movements like those of an animal whose mind has considered the most unlikely of shoreline ambushes, a hundred times over, and walked its way out of each trap a hundred more.

"Jimmy, wait. Hold up, I said!"

The shoreline underbrush ran thick and tangled to the tip of the cove's cape, and much of its top growth had climbed head-high in the branches of pines. In the struggle to push thru its cover to reach cape's end, I knew it was hopeless to think I could stop him. Already he was pulling up anchor with a fierceness of hand that would leave him breathless and knotted with pain, by the time he'd fallen his way back into the cockpit.

"You don't have to go thru with this. There are other ways."

"No. Their kind, they are the savages the law protects."

"Listen to me. Listen to me! This is foolishness."

"They took her from us, Mark. Don't you remember? Like she was no more than a stone on the beach."

"There's other ways. Don't do this."

"Another fight? Another fire? No. Joey's god wants something more of me this time."

"I could go with you."

"You would talk it out of me."

I looked back at the trailhead, searching for the boxed black shadow of the hidden rowboat.

"Oars are onboard with me. Sorry friend."

"You made a promise."

"I did." He lowered his head to some ancient memory of shame or regret. "But never really mine to keep, was it."

"This is silly. This is crazy whatever it is you're planning."

The steady methodical chug of the boat's engine throttled louder and the boat's bow shifted and set its sights on the mouth of the cove. A leader of two steel cables, strung together with a large turnbuckle, a boat length's back, lifted from the waters off the stern, drew taught, and spun once around before the chain of drums which had quietly corralled nearly all of the cove's shoreline gave a jerk and began to plow water.

The boat rocked, its pulpit lifted, settled, rose again to glean some immeasurable light from the wings of night birds before the stern sunk coffin low in the water and set a stronger course for the open channel. One by one, the twelve drums fell into a line of paternal obedience behind the boat. Each drum harnessed with a webbing of barbed wire, cable, and rope — and to this a saddling of burlap matting, tire halves, and the primitive images of marauding faces stretched thick with the paste of white paint over the ribs of each barrel — the lair of drums giving rise to the reek of fuel oil seeking the channel.

The small rowboat rested on a natural headstone, a few scrappy salal vines severed or trapped beneath its bow. The boat's bottom wet to the double knot in a long lead of rope slipped thru the bow's eyelet and tied off to a high pine branch some thirty feet from the waterline. A second line, this one a steel cable, had been looped around the trunk of the same pine and each of its two eyelet ends padlocked to the rowboat's iron eyelet. The oars were not in the rowboat, but had only been carried a few yards up the mountainside before the hand that had carried them there had tossed them into a hollow strewn with scrap tire segments and roofing shingles.

In the openness of the channel, the sea was no more like water than blood is life, and moved beneath the rowboat like a mountain of anguish and terror. The oars of the small boat clattering to shed distance from the caging of the cove's cape, its once prayerful waters. The darkness colder out here and drawing back its deepest furrows from the branches of pines to reveal the suspended silhouette of a large wooden spool — an axle sleeved thru the spool's hub and secured to the roped trunks of two large pines leaning out over the cape's waterline — before the eastern sky will jig-saw its shale gray light thru the branches of cedars running the ridge of the neighboring island. Tags of fog pushing flight along the rocky shorelines of both islands, like the flags of ancient enemies howling at the slaughtering to come. Dawn's blue shadow a sword yet to fall upon the sickness in the hearts of men, heartless to the understanding of such a colorless agony.

The first flames appeared mid-channel — no more than a few thin red lines taking flight from one of the tire-strapped drums — and erupted without noise or commotion or the leprous screams of the fires which were to follow the second and third shots of a flare gun firing from the boat's cockpit. The man behind the gun falling, or reaching for something else on the boat, by the time the fire's sickening waltz had leapfrogged from drum to drum and set the heart of the channel ablaze. Fire which threw daggers of green flame over the mired waters of the channel and choked back the light of dawn with the waffling smoke of burning tires. Fire that wielded song and fury and raced across the channel like the severed tongues of banished prophets.

The sailboat had come up bumper-close to the high banks of the uninhabited island. Its mast caught within the crotches of an uprooted madrona hanging by the roots on the edge of the bank. The steel leaders attached to its stern still joined by two blackened floats, but otherwise, the boat completely severed from the arc of fire blocking all passage thru the channel. The channel's northern entrance, a thousand meters out from the fire's panic, banded with the soundless scream of smoke and the candle-eyed lights of a motionless ferry staring back at us.

His folded body lay like a rag running with blood over the slashed cushions and across the cockpit floor, where much of the blood that had soaked thru his cutoffs now rutted with the spill of oil and kerosene. The wrist of his left arm had been handcuffed to the stern's railing, the fingers of the trapped hand smeared with blood clear to his bare shoulder which lay awkwardly hyper-extended over the vinyl seating. His head resting like the broken neck of a bird on the lap of his pinned shoulder, his injured face clocking side to side and brandishing its grisly theatre at the looming daybreak.

"Oh Jimmy, what you've done."

He tried opening his eyes but thought better of it.

"I touched her face. So scared. She was so scared."

"Where is the knife? What did you do with the knife?"

"Betrayed you both."

"No. No."

"I did." His tongue writhed to say the words and then sought the taste of its body's blood.

"I've got you."

"My angel. My black angel."

"Don't talk."

The blade of the knife had found his face three times, twice opening the flesh of his forehead from temple to temple, and once along the right side of his face where the blade had cut from cheek bone to chin before the knife point had twisted and dug deeper still to leave a bolus of flesh hanging from his jaw. But the blade's savagery had not ended here. It had sought the flesh of a larger palate for its most horrific work. Working its savagery thru tissue and muscle, the blade had made two deep incisions from his chest to his stomach, lifted to answer *another's* command, and twice more cut its way thru the rip of his stomach muscles — each of the four butchering cuts to his torso drawn straight, and deep, and willed there by a mind determined not to surrender to the sickening cries the blade would orchestrate from each new mutilation. Every new inch of flesh the blade had splayed from his body bearing witness to the same measure of desecration it had left behind it, a commandment of human spirit to destroy what God had turned his back on. The folds of physical pain in a father's grief-stricken eyes an aguish beyond words, of words evoked but not spoken, an appendage of grief no scream could ever service.

The fingers on his cuffed hand clutched at air, and then reached to take hold of cable, but there was no escaping the pain.

"Jim?"

"Did good. I did."

He screamed trying to pull himself up onto the seating before giving up and giving way to the pain. Fingers wet with the oil of life and by so much of life taken from him. Fingers that fell from the railing like a black glove tossed over a descending casket. Dauntless pain, breathless and suffocating, and burning his body stiff. And there, in the depths of his most vicious of moans, we held the other's fear in our eyes for a time.

"Our stories, Jim — they got to add up."

He made one more attempt at rolling his shoulder off the deck by bracing himself on one elbow, cursed the sight of the fire so close to the boat and at the cage the handcuffs had put him in. Eyes wide shut and trackless, like the gouged eyes Trump had once screamed out with from the pit of the Campground's fireplace.

"My only ever friend." He took hold of my hand and patted it as if he would make a face of its strange features.

"What we've done here, Jim. We need to get our stories straight."

"For men like them — all the right things been done."

For a few desperate breaths, he struggled to find some corner in his mind the pain had not completely wrapped. A steady drone of some *other's* single-syllable prayer voicing itself within his struggle, before he could make a fist of my hand and speak.

"Details are mine to tell. But they will question you first. This first part — you got to wrap your brain around it good. Tell it exactly as I say. No more."

"Say it. Quickly."

"Gone from the camp when you returned. That's the truth. The channel was chained from shore to shore with fire when you reached the cove — your sailboat gone — the rowboat padlocked to a tree."

"I don't know — the authorities — they will be hounds for details."

"The rowboat. How did you cut the cable? How'd you cut the padlock Trump's men tied it with?"

"I used a rock to break the eyelet from the bow."

"Wouldn't know, wasn't there."

His free hand tethered to mine by a history neither of us wanted between us any longer, he spoke with more urgency.

"Once you freed the rowboat you rowed out to answer my cries for help. You may have heard another boat — maybe a powerboat — but you never saw one. Never saw any boat. Never saw more than how you found me cut up like this."

"The engine's gone. Why?"

"Don't know. Neither do you. It was gone when you came aboard. Trump's men must have taken it."

Except for the rags pressed to the cuts of his forehead and face, the toweling I'd placed to his severest wounds had not helped to stop the flow of blood from his body. The bandage of sopping rags covering him continued to bloom with the life it was taking from him. A life which ran thin and sickly thru my fingers before turning strangely grey and vile in the wash of the sea, where my hands would later find the silk of the ocean's cold, wanting only to wash away the righteousness of my friend's crime from my own story.

When I looked up from his wounds, the running lights of two coast guard vessels had come out of nowhere to color both entrances to the channel.

"Where is the knife? When you were done what did you do with the knife?"

"Overboard."

"Are you sure? Look at me. Are you certain?"

"Yes."

"No chance it might have been tossed ashore?"

"Channel's three hundred feet deep — a grindstone on the bottom." His speech tightened trying to hold back more of the knife's burning. "It's there forever."

"Okay. Okay Jim."

He pulled his knees up into the cast of something primordial and screaming.

"I've got you. I'm here. I'm right here, Jim."

The minutes passed us by and returned to pace themselves thinner against the hull's waterline. Jimmy's moans breaking often into sorrowful muted cries that brought with it spasms of more choking, more blood from the troughs of opened flesh on his body. His eyes sometimes opening to search for the drums burning like funeral pyres and to find my presence and to ask if I was certain there could be no God we might pull from the fire to hold accountable and bear witness to the righteousness of all we'd unleashed in His name and in Jessie's.

"Their kind. They would kill all chance for God in men like us."

More weeping had come with his words and transfixed his gaze upon the cockpit floor black with blood — the blood of our forefathers seeping from withered bone white to grey to merciless cruelty — a butchering as exhaustive and painful to watch as the march of despondent snowbound cattle hoofing the trackless hour to the slaughterhouses, where God explains to no man, intervenes nowhere.

"Secrets — what you and I do best. No one better at it than you."

The sea around us an icy birthing blanket of caroling drums.

The pinging darkness of daylight come to harvest all that we held in our arms.

CHAPTER TWELVE

AT AN OUTPOST OF a train station, halfway between Greymouth and Wellington, the passenger train sloshed to a stop. On the ocean side of the train station an abandoned set of rails set out its unpolished silver alongside a run of calico colored weeds, and between the abandoned tracks a distressed tea tree had grown out of the shale colored cross ties and been allowed to ungraciously wither in solitude. Beyond the cast of the tea tree's slim shadow some flax and a stringy cabbage tree to frame a weathered bench facing the Tasman Sea. From the bench to the isolated rails a ribbon of a path had been cut from the run of colorful weeds, and from the rails to the plank steps which abutted the station's ticket booth, two car lengths away from my window seat, the path now carried a woman teasingly quickening her pace while holding the hand of a struggling young girl close to her waist. Woman and child smiling at one another after they'd hopped the last step up to the ticket booth, and the young girl frequently caressing the woman's arm and shoulder and long braid of sunlit hair which traced the chocolate wave of the woman's sundress.

"That's Faye, Peter and Gwenda's niece." The thin lady with the floppy purple sun hat seated behind me explained, her voice dusky and her breath heavy with the smell of peppermint Schnapps. "Twice a year she travels up from Wellington. Lovely little girl. Absolutely shines for Gwenda."

"And the woman with her?"

"American, like yourself."

Except for two weary looking backpackers up front and the woman seated behind me, the rail car was pleasantly empty. One of the backpackers smiled back at me and moved across the aisle to open more of the train's windows. The sea breeze warm and unhurried and soon passing thru the sleepy railway car like a box of sultry piano notes.

When Faye entered the rail car there was such excitement commanding her spastic body that Dianna playfully wrapped her arms around the child's flailing limbs to protect the young hikers from injury. Then, playfully, Dianna began to penguin-walk the child up the aisle to the empty seats next to mine.

"Aau-ck, Aauck!" Faye uttered what sounded like a high pitched dubbing of bird calls, and wormed her frail body into the leather seat beside me. *Slap, slap-slap*, the girl's contorted hands palm-smacked her right thigh as Dianna took the seat next to the child.

"Gentle, gentle," Dianna whispered into Faye's ear while quietly placing one hand on Faye's wrist and the other against the girl's rocking shoulders. "With the help of Peter's conniving, Faye has convinced herself that all she has to do is ask and the train will take her to Auckland before returning to Wellington. Haven't you, you rascal. Haven't you learned that from Peter the rascal?"

"Aauck, Aau-ck." Faye erupted into another round of piercing, bird-like squawks and twisted free of Dianna's hold. *Slap, slap-slap,* Faye's hand excitedly found the armrest between us. Her head swaying and her mouth opening wide to smile at Dianna. The child's determination to pronounce some fragment of the city she wished to speak of traveling thru the carriage car and out the windows, but not before she gave it another ferocious shot.

"Aau-ck. Aauck!"

"She's an angel, once the train begins to move. Aren't you, Faye? Aren't you an angel? No-ooh, not a rascal, an angel. Yes, you are. You're an angel. Isn't Faye an angel, Mrs. Erickson?"

"Oh yes. An angel with stunning red locks."

"Please excuse my lack of manners, Mrs. Erickson. This is my husband, Mark."

"A pleasure, sir. Evelyn — Evelyn Erickson."

"Mark Jacobs, ma'am. Nice to meet you."

"And this is Faye."

"Hello Faye. I've heard quite a lot about you and Peter the rascal."

The train jerked forward, gave way to a cabling stop which vibrated the glass in the steel-framed windows before moving forward once again to begin its rocking chug thru the seaside hamlet. Dianna pulled an art pad from her shoulder bag and placed it on Faye's lap. Faye's body contortions settled and her speech quieted and she began to draw squiggles on the paper with her coloring pencil, holding the coloring pencil to the pad as if she were holding the handle of a heavy paint brush.

At the railway station in Wellington, Dianna walked Faye into the arms of her parents and said her goodbyes to the child. She kissed Faye on the forehead, tenderly pushed back the red curls from the child's eyes, and promised she would come back to visit after the Christmas holidays.

Twelve days after Christmas, Joey's letter came from the States.

Dear Mr. Jacobs,

There was snow falling on our mountain this Christmas Eve. It was a pretty good snowfall for the islands, maybe as much as four or five inches. Snow as bright and pure as the wings of an angel I would hope to see some day. And you will be pleased to hear, and maybe even quite surprised and amused by it, that Jimmy and I took full advantage of its beauty by hiking the trail up the backside of the mountain, and back down again, by way of that "devil of a road" you now know all about. You may take further comfort hearing that there was not a trace of ice, nor the sound of a runaway truck, nor a lollypop rope of school children whose lives Jimmy and I once thought we held in the palm of our hands up there on that beautiful mountain. Thank the Lord our Savior for nothing more than just a bit of snow coming down up on the mountain, eh Mr. Jacobs?

The hike up was dark as pitch and the snow already sticking to the pines by the time we crossed the creek. Neither of us felt much like spoiling it with too much talk. But the hike back down the mountain, by way of the road, that was another story all together which I will share with you if my cold hands ever warm up!

About all the snow hadn't covered on the road down were the fresh tracks of a rabbit zigzagging across the road ahead of us but never in our sights. You know bunnies, Mr. Jacobs, half hop half cocked. On that sharpest of switchbacks, the one where Jimmy once towed all those children on a rope and where my "Christ our Lord" sign is still holding true to that tree, a rabbit ran right up the middle of the road at us and right between Jimmy's legs. Well, we both must have been a bit snow-crazed because we got to laughing about the thing just happened. And, of course, the possibilities of explanation took a mighty hold on both of us, each in a different way. Jimmy saying that the rabbit must have been temporarily snow blinded. But my take, it was all a very different show I was watching.

It seemed to me that we were both being given a sign by the Holy Spirit right then and there on that same switchback we both knew so well, too well. But Jimmy would have none of it, though I might add he was a complete gentleman about disagreeing. After we got back to walking the snow a ways down again, Jimmy suddenly wanted to hold up a minute. He found a stump near the side of the road, brushed the snow off it, and sat down. That's when he surprised me by having a little crying spell. He has some pain still, especially around the cuts Trump's men put to his stomach, so I figured that's what he was dealing with. But that wasn't it at all. I guess Jessie had a rabbit once that ran away and was never found. And I guess when she was a little girl she loved tying a rope around both their waists so her dad would have to tow her up the mountain, same as he did with that school group. Guess every big and sad thing that ever happened to him on this island just crossed each others path for a moment when God's rabbit ran thru him.

After we finished our hike, we stopped by my brother's house to walk with him and Jackie and the dogs over to the Campground. By the way, Jackie and my brother are seeing quite a lot of each other lately. Maybe you know that already. You probably know this too then already, that your bar has taken on a new name. The locals got to calling your place "Jacob's Church" soon after Danny's bell went up in the Campground's new steeple. The name seems to have stuck, because when Jimmy got wind of it he went off to Anacortes and came back the next day with a new neon sign for the bar. Your own name is capitalized in red letters but the church part is not!

Jimmy and I made a sort of a pilgrimage out to the dump on Skow Island during Christmas week. He wasn't crazy about me going with him, at first. Told me: "suit yourself, kid, but I ain't going there to gamble." Very funny, I told him and tagged along anyways. We took the ferry to Timberlee Harbor and from there he walked the whole way to the dump, never once stopping to catch his breath or to complain about his cuts I know are still bothering him some. He did have pain walking that last cow pasture and up that last steep hill. But he said he wanted to push his body a little, this being only his second real hike since the attack. The cuts to his body have practically all healed and the stitches removed, but the scars the cuts have left behind are real bad. They look like gruesome pieces of red rope glued to his body and they sometimes makes him wince if he moves too quickly or coughs long and hard, which he does sometimes.

Against my advice, he'd carried his knapsack in with him on this venture. One of those big old bulky canvas leather-strapped army surplus packs. Big brass buckles and the canvas all kind of mossy green. Weighs about twice its usual weight when it gets wet, which has been quite a lot this week in the islands. Inside the pack he'd stashed what he calls "a tombstone." Little block of cement with a pair of handcuffs cemented right into the middle of it. The way one handcuff dangles outside the block of stone, the whole contraption looks a little like a big piece of Red's fishing tackle. I told Jimmy so and he cashed in one of his famous smiles all over me and said "my King Author sword." He's got a new hunting knife he keeps in his pack too, but the most bothersome thing to me is the hand gun he feels he must now keep in the knapsack.

There was a lake of winter rain covering most all of the dump floor that we had to get around before we could get up to the canyon, which is where Jimmy wanted to go. The lake will probably be there next June should you get a fancy to come see it for yourself, Mr. Jacobs, I would like it if you did. Jimmy's shack is gone now from the dump. I guess the people investigating the crime finally gave the *tribal counsel permission to bulldoze the thing down. I guess they were satisfied that there was no evidence hiding in the attic that might help them with their case against Trump and his men.*

Soon as we got close to the canyon the wind started blowing down on us like a freight train. Right then and there, I got to experience for myself what I never quite bought into as a kid (the island old-timers used to like to talk-up the wind of Skow Island around my dad's campfire), that the winds out of this canyon carry the voices of lost children laughing and whistling thru the treetops. I won't say it was a frightening event, but I will say that it rather drew my attention, when, just when my eyes were following the legs of the trestle bridge up into the treetops I could have sworn I'd heard something or someone call out my full name! The sound of that wind so shrill, so sudden, and so human that I can now understand why some say they have run for cover out here at night. Then, like a prayer answered, the canyon winds just stopped cold over us.

He built us a fire up by the old railroad bridge, right there alongside the creek where the water winds down between two of the tallest bridge supports and where the creek pans out to a wash of stone and trickles, where the creek "plays a little song" as Jimmy likes to tell it. He says to tell you that you know the spot, and wishes to remind you that it's where the creek winds around that washboard of sand and stone before disappearing into the underbrush and running down the mountainside, but the creek not running quite as fast as you did once upon a time in the night out here. Jimmy had four shoddy-looking lawn chairs stored up in the brush across the creek. He set the lawn chairs out two on each side of the creek's stone wash. He was careful not to get his feet wet when doing so, and when he was done the chairs made a kind of circle around the stone wash. There was a wide plank already set out across a section of the split creek for me to walk across when he asked me to sit and join him in prayer. For a second or two, the world seemed very odd, Jimmy asking me to join him in prayer and all.

It wasn't much of a fire he'd built for us. I guess he was worried some that the fire not be in sight of the dump's main gate. The fire was just a jumbling of little sticks he'd put into a coffee can he'd picked out of the heaps of casino garbage. He was very slow, very gentle about how he went about placing each stick inside the can. When he'd finished, the sticks had been arranged like a picket fence around the inside lip of the coffee can. Inside this arrangement he set up more sticks, and these ones he crossed a bunch so that when he was finished they looked like the stick frame of a toy tepee. I can't say that it was totally childish how much thought he put into making this little fire that turned out to be no more than a five-minute lamp, but it didn't seem like something the Jimmy you and I know would hardly bother messing around with. Except for one thing, which, no sooner had I thought about it this way when I figured it out. I think his little fire in the can was maybe just another one of his exercises helping him to find his way thru his own valley of darkness. He will never be the same for having lost a child, his only child, will he Mr. Jacobs?

After a few minutes, he asked if I would kneel close to the fire and warm my hands. I wasn't convinced he wasn't playing me or luring me into some practical joke of his. But he quickly told me that he wished for me to recite a prayer for you and your wife, and that whatever I decided on would I be sure to include Jessie in the prayer. He said he wanted forgiveness from each of you, you and Jessie. As I spoke in prayer, he touched the holy cross he was holding up to the knife, and then he placed the holy cross like a beautiful necklace over the barrel of the handgun he'd pulled from the pack. When I finished my prayer, I asked him why he'd done those things with the holy cross. "Protection," he said. "From what," I asked. All he said was, "each of them, one protects me from the other."

Later on, he kind of whispered some prayer of his own, but by then the fire was nearly out, and he'd spoken the prayer so fast and in a whisper so that I wasn't able to make any of it out. I pressed him to share it with me but he said he's not ready to share it with anyone unless it's answered. So I told him, rather smartly for my part I think: "You mean, I have to wait and watch for a sign?" His reply was brilliant: "Hunger feeds the soul, Joe."

The authorities do seem to have accepted Jimmy's story of what happened that night. That some of Trump's men had entered his camp on foot thru the dump's gated entrance that night, where four of the men had overtaken him with little or no resistance, hand-cuffed him, and forced him to go with them to the cove. And that once he was put aboard your boat, he was handcuffed to the stern rail. He did see their power boat working the shoreline along Mir-ror Island and he thinks he did hear some of the barrels hitting rock as they were being dumped into the channel. But after that, as you know already, all he remembers is fire everywhere on the channel and the horrific laughter and the cutting Trump's men did to him. That you were making your way back to the casino that night, Mr. Jacobs, does truly seem to have been a godsend. And, for what it's worth, Jimmy does seem to take some pleasure in the telling of that part, how Trump's men were beside themselves with anger not to have found you in camp with him that night.

I guess no charges have been brought against Trump and his men, yet. The authorities, they are calling it an "act of terrorism." I do not like that word, Mr. Jacobs. It is very bothersome to me that a word like that has found its way into our beautiful islands. I will always bear the shame of having allowed some of Trump's men to take up camp for a time on a piece of my family's property, and for listening to some of their sinful beliefs about your race. For that, I am truly sorry. I am different now, and I hope you will find it in your heart to believe so, Mr. Jacobs.

From time to time, some people in town will suggest that Jimmy may have been involved in his own attack. Some say, they say he was never the same after Jessie died and that they wouldn't put it out of "a father's reach" to engage in an act of martyrdom if he thought it might point the finger at Trump's men. But isn't that like calling the world flat, Mr. Jacobs? I don't understand why some would believe a different thing in the face of the facts, Mr. Jacobs.

Every newspaper from here to Seattle has reported and confirmed the same facts. No less than two hundred of Trump's followers were aboard the Tillicum that morning. And every one of them, they all boarded the 4:30 ferry out of Anacortes. The captain said himself that his crew reported that Trump's men made no bones about all of them getting off the ferry at Timberlee Harbor. And the empty oil barrels, which some of the locals reported seeing Jimmy collect over the summer, the authorities found them just where Jimmy said they would find them, farther up the channel made into a raft for fishing which the same locals verified seeing him fishing from. And besides, Mr. Jacobs, the authorities themselves never had no idea until it happened that there were so many of Trump's followers on board that ferry that morning. So how would Jimmy have possibly known? I swear, Mr. Jacobs, what some people will believe.

Father Jerald feels the same as I do. He got wind of some of this gossip too. I guess he about went bug-eyed with anger. It was down at the public docks when it took place. Guess he was fit to be tied when he confronted some of the loud-mouth dock hands that done it. They didn't deny it. So he told every one of them just about four inches from their faces that anyone who believed one man was capable of lifting and securing a forty pound, land-bound leader of cable and turnbuckle onto a two hundred foot long moving chain of steel barrels, while trying to hold a thirty-two foot sailboat dead in the water, has never sailed thru the Skonomish channel, slack tide or otherwise on his side. That's just about word for word what Father Jerald told them. I did a little investigative reporting of my own. Hope you liked it.

A memorial for Jimmy's daughter took place in Jessie's court-yard today. The crowd grew so large that the service spilled all the way out into most of Oyster Street. And may I say that what happened next, after the memorial was over, was just as moving. Juan and Danny were in attendance, and of course, their moms too. Mrs. Rodriguez thanked Jimmy in front of the whole town for what God had asked him to endure, and for waking the whole town up to the danger on our doorsteps. And then Mrs. Rodriquez did the most eloquent speaking I've ever heard. She spoke with tears in her eyes about how you had left instructions with Ike and Tom not to contact her and Lorraine until you had left these islands. She talked in detail about her and Lorraine having real houses built over their cellar holes, and how you had set up a tuition account that would pay all the costs for both boys to attend their first year at your university. She thanked you many times over, Mr. Jacobs, and she finished with a beautiful toast, saying that she wished you and your wife the spiritual union you both deserved. There was not a dry eye in town, I think, when all was said and done. And Danny's bell, it rang loud and clear for you when it was over.

I began writing this letter to you on Christmas Eve. Today, I am finished with it and will walk it down to the marina before dark to personally see the look on Red's face when he takes it from my hand and drops it with a smile into the "Overseas Mail Bin." When I began this letter it was my intention that the letter would be my Christmas gift to you. I'd hoped it would bring you some joy and maybe ease your mind somewhat that Jimmy is not alone in his battles in this troubled world. But now, having seen my thoughts on paper, I think maybe you will find the letter to be an intrusion or that you will simply be made sad by what I've written. I've reread my letter twice, Mr. Jacobs, and now I think maybe it's not so easy to make someone feel the hope and joy that's in one's own heart. But that was my prayer, and I hope some part of it finds its way to your heart and helps you to heal.

P.S. Oh, I almost forgot. The day we were out at the dump, Jimmy trapped a stray cat and brought it back on the ferry kicking and screaming in a trash can. The whole ride back to the island Jimmy and I were hard pressed and wet to the whistle just trying to keep the lid on the poor thing! Jimmy had a big-old-hurkin' cage my brother made all ready and waiting for the poor beast up in

Danny's bell tower. He plans on giving the cat a good home once the vet can wrestle the animal to the ground and look it over good.

Your friend and student, Joe

"It's a good letter, Mark. Joseph means well."

"Yeah, I suppose."

"Walk with me to the bluff. I've something I wish to say."

A rendering of Jessie's voice walked with us, between us, for a time. Beliefs sifted or bent by the jacket of a spoken word so as to preserve the superior moral line of Jessie's life.

"You loved her so much."

"Even now."

A rocking of sadness formed in Dianna's eyes. Her hand reaching out for mine before some severing dropped the heart out of it. That she once loved me as much coloring the tears in her eyes.

"I'll walk ahead, Mark. Come along when you're ready."

The limestone cliffs overlooking the Tasman Sea bore the land's isolation and its iron rails running cold with rain as far as the eye could see. Where a chasm had broken the cliff line and pushed inland to undermine a course of train track, a monolith had arisen to watch over a totem of a beach far below. The beach made all the paler by the dreariness of the rain and by a wash of black stone blanketing the sand and by the surf's sallow froth which had nursed all life from Jessie's vanquished body. The tufted sea beyond the rain's edge mute but for the voice it would give to the ancients who had come ashore for her. Black warriors with white-striped faces and scalded bodies shielded only by the garlands of shells and the shards of bone, and by a warring within their hearts which had long since sacrificed the song of their fathers to every beaming moon and sunrise to feed a withering obsession. Each a vessel to bear witness to the other's dream in the passing of Jessie's body to the one beside him, the one within. Men, or perhaps only the prayers of men, whose tongues roared with a holiness that sent out a fallow flame for Jessie's crowning, and if not this their testament then their cry was for *another's* resurrection, and if not this their bridge of clay and fire then to perish each of us.

My mark, my love

You think that with a few spoken words you can command your heart to stop loving me. That is a shameful thing for you to ask of either of us.

I don't know how to find the place where we might meet and begin again. Without you by my side I don't know where home is. I have only this soundless place you've chosen for us. And I hate it. I hate that you alone have chosen this place for us.

You know me. You know your love for me is my home. You know that. You know that.

Come back. But you won't.

So ashamed of what I've done to you.

The words Jessie had fought for during her final hours were to remain where I would entomb them — in my heart and within a ring of jade that rests inside a mended pocket of her father's canvas knapsack — years after Jimmy would take his own life on the outskirts of the tribal dump. His foddered knapsack now hangs its emptiness from a spike in my sleeping birth, and its one remaining brass buckle is always the first form in the room to surface from dawn's labret of light. And *hers* to follow, from the prayer opening the bedroom door, where she walks in the cast of the hallway's shellacked light seeking the room's fondled bedding — her shadow lost to the buckle's cold line crosses before she would speak my name.

CPSIA information can be obtained at www.ICGtesting.com
Printed in the USA
BVOW03s1600081113

335768BV00001B/8/P